A HUNDRED TINY THREADS

Also by Judith Barrow

Pattern of Shadows
Changing Patterns
Living in the Shadows

A HUNDRED TINY THREADS

by
Judith Barrow

HONNO MODERN FICTION

First published in 2017 by Honno Press, 'Ailsa Craig', Heol y Cawl,
Dinas Powys, South Glamorgan, Wales, CF64 4AH

1 2 3 4 5 6 7 8 9 10

A catalogue record for this book is available from the British Library.

Published with the financial support of the Welsh Books Council.

ISBN 978-1-909983-68-7 (paperback)
ISBN 978-909983-69-4 (ebook)

Cover design: Jenks Design
Cover image: © Shutterstock, Inc
Text design: Elaine Sharples
Printed by Bell and Bain Ltd, Glasgow

For David

Acknowledgements

I would like to express my gratitude to those who helped in the publishing of *A Hundred Tiny Threads*...

To all the staff at Honno for their individual expertise, advice and help. To Caroline Oakley for her thoughtful and empathetic editing.

Special thanks to Sharon Tregenza and Thorne Moore, dear friends and fellow authors, for their encouragement and enthusiasm for *A Hundred Tiny Threads*.

And to Janet Thomas, for her support with all my writing down the years.

Lastly, as ever, to my husband, David; always by my side, always believing in me.

Chains do not hold a marriage together. It is threads, hundreds of tiny threads, which sew people together through the years. *Simone Signoret.*

Prologue

1911

The whistling in his ears faded. He listened to the silence as the seconds passed, measured by the laboured breath from his lungs. Slowly the sounds surrounded him; a hollow drip of water, faint groans, a shifting of props holding up the roof. And then a scream, a yell, echoing along the tunnel.

Despite the pain of the weight on his shoulders, pressing him into the ground, Bill Howarth knew he should stay still. He ran a gritty tongue around his dry mouth and swallowed, trying not to cough.

Instinctively squeezing his eyes tight against the dust, he forced himself to stretch them wide, staring in front of him. Nothing. Blackness.

He could smell the dynamite. Bloody Gibson, bloody know-it-all. He'd hammered the hole in the wrong place, too deep, too wide, used too much charge of explosive, tamped it in with sodding dry coal dust of all things. He'd shown the stupid bugger the cracks on the rock surface, the amount of coal dust on the ground. But oh no, Gibson knew better; he was the Blower.

Bill couldn't remember what happened immediately following the shock of the blast but, feeling around with one hand, touching sharp edges of rock he realised that the wall had splintered and been crushed inwards, releasing methane, firedamp, from the cavity behind the tunnel wall. He could smell, taste, the explosion that had inevitably happened. He closed his eyes again, felt the tightness in his chest growing, the whole of him trembling. Stay still, stay bloody still, he told himself. The whole bloody area around must be broken, scattered; yards of fractured loose rock, ready to fall on him any second now.

He waited, listening to the wailing of other men. He took in a shuddering breath, glad he wasn't alone. Shifting slightly, he paused to see if anything moved, tensed to feel what hurt. Nothing, other than a sharp stab of pain in his leg. Tears scalded the back of his eyes; he screwed up his face, forcing them back. Reaching over his shoulder to push the weight off him, he touched a face. Lukewarm, smooth as candle wax. Smoother than it had ever been in life. Gibson, Unmoving, unresponsive. He shoved the man off him, uncaring whatever else was dislodged.

The groans, the cries for help increased. He wondered whether he should add his voice but what was the point? No bugger would hear them, this tunnel was too far away from the upshaft. And too far away from the downshaft to bring in any air from the top. They were sodding goners.

He let his head rest on the hard floor,

For a moment Bill thought about his family; his dad, a man he'd hated, long gone in another accident like this, his stepmother, his stepsister. And, just for a brief moment, he wished he hadn't quarrelled with them before his shift; had told them, for the first time in his life, that he loved them. Even if he hadn't meant it; it would have made them think about the shit way they'd treated him as a kid. Despite the pain in his leg, he grinned, his mouth moving against the splinters of coal under his face They were a couple of hard bitches, them two, they'd have jeered him out of the house. Better off as it was, he thought, letting the comfort of the dark wash over him.

PART ONE

Chapter 1

February 1911

Winifred stretched her arms above her head, quickly pulling them back under the covers and drawing her feet up from the icy corners of the bed. Through the thin curtains she could see it was still dark outside. She could smell the acrid smoke from the cinders of the kitchen fire drifting up the stairs; yesterday's flames struggling under the slack and dust of coal.

'Get a move on; time to get up.' Her bedroom door was banged open, her mother's hair-netted head haloed by the light from the landing. 'Get up. You know it's stock-taking day.'

'I know, I know. I'm up.' Winifred took a deep breath and flung the covers back. Shivering, she knelt on the bed and pulled her cotton nightdress over her head, tempted to put her clothes on without washing. As every morning over the past weeks, when frost patterns covered the panes of the windows, she'd have to force herself to pour cold water into the bowl and lather up the carbolic soap to rub over her face, under her arms and between her legs.

Hopping around after the hurried wash, she dried herself with the threadbare towel before pulling on her knitted vest and long drawers. The corset her mother had bought in Leeds market, the day Winifred turned sixteen, was draped over the back of the chair. Even though it was lighter boned than the one her mother wore, Winifred hated the way it clung from just below her bust to her thighs, restricting her movements.

3

She sat back on the bed, wrapping the shiny maroon eiderdown around her, and stared towards the window.

She'd heard the knocker-upper man going down the street rattling on the windows with his peashooter ages ago, heard his little Jack Russell's yelping bark. Now the clatter of clogs and iron-heeled boots passed the house; lines of men making their way to Stalyholme mine.

Winifred glared again at the corset. She wanted to look elegant, she knew it made her look slimmer, especially around the waist and she liked looking good in front of the customers. She sensed the blush start on her throat at the memory of the admiring look she'd had the other day from that lad who lived on Harrison Street. Even so, she couldn't face the discomfort of working all day in the thing.

She wouldn't wear it. Instead she put her petticoat on and pushed her arms through the sleeves of her wrap-around house frock, fastened the ties at her side just below her waist. Swinging open the wardrobe door Winifred studied her figure in the mirror. With a bit of luck no one would notice.

Downstairs, her mother was already in the small stockroom of the shop, crashing and banging around. Winifred tried to shut out the shrill tirade.

'Poor Dad.' She grimaced. It was always the same on Mondays; he got the brunt of her mother's discontent.

The grandfather clock in the back parlour sounded out six doleful chimes.

Her mother's voice rose, along with an increasing slam of cupboard doors and Winifred knew her father was suffering her mother's temper for longer because she hadn't gone down yet. Hurriedly fastening up her hair she slipped into the white cotton shop overall and ran downstairs.

'You took your time.' Her mother made a great show of carrying a large tray of tins from the cupboard, brushing aside her husband's attempt to help. 'I'm not the shop girl here, miss, you

4

are and I expect you to be on time. It's not my job to do the stocktaking, it's yours.'

Winifred exchanged a glance with her father. He raised one eyebrow, slightly moving his head. She knew he was asking her not to answer back but she couldn't resist. 'I'm here now.'

'Miss the knocker-upper then?' Ethel Duffy banged the tray onto the counter before lining up tins of beans onto one of the shelves.

'No. I heard him.'

'And that blasted dog of his,' her mother snapped. 'Good mind to complain to Blackhurst about it.'

'You could lose him his job, if you do that. Blackhurst wouldn't care; there are plenty of other old miners he could get to do it.' Winifred's father adjusted his flat cap before wrapping his scarf around his neck.

Even though his tone was mild, Ethel swung around and glared at him. 'When I want your opinion I'll give it to you.' She put her fists on her hips. 'And why're you still here? That bread won't walk from the baker's on its own.'

Without a word he left the shop. On his way, he touched Winifred's hand. She returned the gesture, knowing he'd tried to divert her mother's wrath away from her.

But Ethel hadn't finished. 'You going to stand around all day? Counter needs wiping and everything needs to be tallied.' She tipped her head toward a small book on the counter. 'Looks like we're two tins of evaporated milk missing.'

'I took them to Granny's.'

'Well, you haven't put the money in the till.' Her mother's face tightened. 'And the bacon slicer wants cleaning. I told you that on Saturday night after we shut up.'

'I did it.' Winifred peered at the slicer. 'It's perfectly clean.'

'Well, the cake stand's filthy. I told you about that yesterday but I suppose you were too busy gadding last night to properly clean up.'

'I only went round to Granny's after chapel to see if she was all right.' Winifred saw her mother's hand twitch; Ethel Duffy hated her mother in law. If Mother hits me again, I swear I'll hit back, she thought. The small burst of rebellion made her feel better. 'I'll get the bowl and a cloth for the counter,' she said.

'And go easy on that bicarb, we're not made of money, my girl.'

Winifred pulled a face behind her mother's back. In the kitchen she took the kettle off the range and poured the water into the bowl before adding a tablespoon of bicarbonate of soda. Then, with a grin, she tipped in some more and swished it around with her fingers before hurrying back into the shop. With a bit of luck, once she got going, her mother would leave her alone with the stocktaking.

Chapter 2

Winifred looked over her shoulder at the half-open door to the parlour when she saw Honora O'Reilly crossing the road to the shop. It was only a week since she'd been in with that leaflet; trying to persuade Winifred that there was more to life than working in the shop and going to chapel on Sundays. That there was more to life than waiting for a man to make her his wife. Her mother had overheard and gone mad afterwards.

Winifred secretly admired Honora's lack of care over her appearance. Self-conscious of her overall, she quickly took it off and pushed it under the counter, re-pinning and patting the swirl of hair at the nape of her neck. Silently mocking herself that it mattered, she still didn't want to look dowdy in front of the Irish girl who'd casually told her she earned her money by painting and had the freedom to live as she wanted, wear what she wanted.

When the door opened, the cold air curled around Winifred's ankles.

'Did ya look at the leaflet?' The girl spoke without preamble. She wore her hair loose and now pushed a lock of it away from her face with impatience. There were splashes of blue and red paint on the skin on her hands; her nails were engrained with colour. The smell of the turpentine on her clothes wafted towards Winifred.

'No.' She glanced again behind her.

'Why not?' The girl's Irish lilt held a surprised tone.

'I haven't had time.' Winifred felt her cheeks grow hot; she'd hidden the paper in her room. Her mother would have been furious if she'd seen it. 'And I don't know why you gave the leaflet to me in the first place. Now, what is it you want today?'

'Hmm, a cake I think.'

'Which one?' Winifred looked towards the cake stand. Get the girl served and out of the shop, she thought, before Mother comes through. When Honora had first come into the shop last week, Ethel had looked askance at the carelessness of her hair and the colourful, unrestricting dress she wore. In a sibilant whisper to Winifred she'd pronounced her a loose woman; one that no respectable person would associate with. But Honora's casual attitude had fascinated Winifred. 'Which one?' she repeated, watching the girl stare absently around the shop.

'I'm looking.' Honora glanced at the cakes, then quickly directed her gaze to Winifred again.

'I don't understand why ya haven't read the leaflet. Don't ya want to see what's in the real world,' she challenged. 'What really matters?'

'What does really matter?' It was as though she couldn't help herself. What was it Honora saw that she didn't?

'That it's men that rule us?'

'Rubbish.' Winifred thought about her mother and the way she reigned over the household. 'There's no man rules my life.'

Yet, not for the first time, Winifred wondered fleetingly what was really behind her mother's bitterness... why she had to have so much control over everything. It had always been the same; even as a child she remembered the way her father measured his words. She didn't think she'd ever heard him lose his temper. Only once had she known him defy her mother and that was when he'd insisted on helping Winifred to read and write and do her sums before she even started at the local school at the age of five. He only won his argument by pointing out she would be needed in the shop when she was older.

He'd had no say though when, as an eight year old, her mother put Winifred behind the shop counter each afternoon after she came home from school.

So she said again. 'No man rules my life.'

Honora tossed her hair back, oblivious to Winifred's words. 'As women, we should have a say in who rules the world we live in. We should have a vote.'

'I don't see how that will ever happen.' Winifred slowly shook her head

'When's ya half day?' Honora cocked her head on one side.

The change of subject surprised Winifred. 'Wednesdays. Why?'

'So ya can't get out today then?'

'If could I wanted to.'

'So?' Honora tilted her head.

Winifred took a step backwards and, pretending to be rearranging the tins of baked beans and canned vegetables, peeped through the door to the parlour to see where her mother was. She hoped Honora couldn't hear the apprehension in her voice. 'And go where?' she whispered.

A shrug. Honora didn't bother to lower her voice. 'There's something I want to show ya.'

Winifred took in a long breath, apprehension mingled with unfamiliar excitement; she never went anywhere on her own. Not like this girl was suggesting anyway. 'I don't know if I want to go out today, it's cold.' She knew her mother would try to stop her.

Honora pulled a face. She studied the cakes on the stand. 'I'll have one of those.' She pointed at an iced bun. 'Don't bother wrapping it; I'll eat it here in the shop, while ya go and ask for permission.' She grinned.

Irritated, Winifred snapped open a small white bag and dropped the cake in it. 'I don't need permission.' Even so, after she'd handed it to Honora, she said, 'but you can't eat in here. Go and wait outside.'

'Outside? Bejaysus, Win girl.'

'I'll be five minutes. Tops.'

'No longer,' Honora warned, 'Like ya said it's pure bloody cold out there.'

Winifred winced, hoped her mother wasn't in the kitchen; hadn't heard the swear word.

Her father was cleaning the range in the kitchen, his hands black and grimy from the cinders.

'Dad, can you take over for the next couple of hours? I'm going out.'

'Out?' Her mother appeared from the back yard, bringing the chill in with her. 'Today? Out where? You can't just go gallivanting around as and when you feel like it. And how can he? Just look at the state of him. He's filthy.'

'Just a walk; I need some fresh air.'

'Why? What's wrong with you?' Ethel's frowned, suspicious. 'You had enough fresh air yesterday with chapel and then off to your grandmother's.'

'Dad?' Winifred kept her eyes on her father. She knew if she replied to her mother an argument would start. 'Can you take over for me?'

'I want to know where you think you're going.' Ethel Duffy's voice rose. 'Gallivanting off at a minute's notice.'

Winifred's tongue was thick in her mouth; she hated these confrontations. For a moment she thought of backing down; whatever it was Honora wanted to show her it wasn't worth a row. But she'd never been on an outing with another girl. Ever. She swallowed, the spark of resentment against her mother flaring. 'I only want to go for a walk.'

'A walk? Who with?' Ethel's eyebrows disappeared up behind the elastic line of her hairnet.

'No-one. I just fancy a walk.'

'In this weather?' Ethel tried to peer past Winifred. 'What are you hiding?'

'Nothing.'

'You've never been for a walk on your own. And I can't remember the last time you saw any of the girls you knew in school.' Her mother's eyes narrowed. 'It's not that Irish girl who came into the shop last week, is it? The one you insisted on talking to.'

'Why would you think that, Mother?'

'Because you don't go out on your own.'

'Well, today I am.' Winifred kept herself firmly between her mother and the shop door.

'I bet she was filling your head with all sorts of rubbish,' Ethel persisted. 'We know nothing about her. Chasing the lads is what she wants you to do with her, no doubt.'

'If you know nothing about her, how do you know that's what she wants to do?' Winifred kept her voice even. 'Anyway, it's nothing to do with her. I just need some fresh air; I've been serving in the shop for the last three hours.'

'Poor you.' Ethel's face closed into a sneer 'You don't know the half of it. I could tell you more than anyone about being stuck in this shop; year after year.'

'And me, Mother; I've grown up behind that counter; I've been *stuck in this shop*, as you say, for years.'

'Now, now, you two.' Her father pushed himself up off his knees. 'Don't worry, Mother, I'll get cleaned up and go behind the counter. You sit and have a rest; you've been on the go since first thing. It's only a walk. Let our Winifred have a bit of fun. Anyway, it's almost time to shut the shop for lunch.'

Ethel sniffed. 'A bit of fun can get a girl into bother.' Still, she

10

perched on the edge of the chair by the range. 'But if you want to be her dogsbody, you won't find me arguing.'

Winifred and her father exchanged furtive grins.

'I'll rest my bones a bit. As you say I've not stopped today – unlike some people who had a lie-in.' She glared at Winifred. 'Back by five, mind. Be here to lock up and clear away, you can't leave everything to him.'

'Thanks, Dad.' Winifred gave him a hug and kissed him on his cheek.

She ran upstairs. Sitting on the bed she quickly laced up her black outdoor boots. Pulling her coat out of the wardrobe, she closed the door, looking in the mirror and arranging the blue hat with the satin ribbon and tiny feather that she'd bought with her wages at Christmas. She'd never worn it. 'Too fancy for chapel,' her mother had pronounced. So it had stayed in the box. Until today. Studying herself she arranged the hat a little more towards the front on her head and then pulled on the matching blue gloves.

'Hmm.' She nodded at her image; fashionable.

'I'll only be a couple of hours, anyway,' she called, running down the stairs, buttoning her coat and going through to the shop, a tremor of anticipation in her stomach.

'Wait. Let's see what you've got on—'

The shop bell tinkled as Winifred slammed the door behind her.

Honora stood outside the window, tapping her foot, still munching on the cake; ignoring the disapproving looks of two matronly women walking by.

'Go, go,' Winifred urged.

The two girls ran along the road, only stopping when they turned onto Morrisfield Road.

'I'll be for it, when I get back,' Winifred gasped. She bent over, holding her side, her words making a white mist in front of her face. 'Running out like that.'

11

'Ah, d'ya care?' Honora twirled around, the full skirt of her dark green coat swirling. 'From what I've seen ya work like a slave in that place. Anyhow, what can your ma do?'

'A lot,' Winifred snapped. Too often she'd been on the receiving end of her mother's temper. And the slaps. Too often she'd seen her punch her father, while he stood there, arms down by his sides or trying to catch hold of Ethel's fists to stop her.

'Don't lose your rag,' Honora said. 'Go back if ya want. To be sure, I won't stop ya.' She sauntered off but looked back at Winifred as though testing her.

Winifred noticed and frowned; the girl was so exasperating: 'No point. Too late.' She straightened up. 'So, where are we going?'

'Into town? We can catch the tram, do some shopping. I can show ya places in Morrisfield ya never been.'

'I've come out without money.'

'No problem.' Honora grinned. 'I sold a painting.'

'People buy your paintings?'

'Sure they do.' She frowned, visibly offended. 'They're good. I've sold loads of my work. I get commissions, as well.' She looked along the road and yelped. 'Oh, Jaysus, there's the tram. Run.'

'Wait for me.' Winifred picked up the front of her long, heavy coat, revealing her boots and woollen stockings and ignoring the scandalized look of the two women as they overtook them. 'Wait for me. I'm right behind you.'

Chapter 3

Winifred held on to the rail of the seat in front of her, her knuckles white, when the tram set off with a squeal and a jerk. She didn't look out of the window at the terraced houses, the horse and carts, the people on the pavements; the speed of the tram scared her. But she wasn't about to tell Honora that it was only the second time she'd been on one of these contraptions.

Trams had only appeared in Morrisfield a few months ago. Her father, in great excitement, had dared Winifred to go with him and she'd clung on to him as they'd rattled along, terrified of the noise and the sparks from the iron rails below that guided the vehicle through the streets. Needless to say they hadn't told Ethel.

'So? What are we going to do?' Winifred kept her eyes on Honora.

Honora didn't answer. She was gazing towards two young men on the other side of the aisle. Winifred looked at them at the same time as one touched the neb of his flat cap and grinned at her.

The Irish girl giggled.

'Stop it.' Winifred was horrified; it was one thing exchanging glances with a lad from behind the counter, or taking sly peeps along the pews in chapel when she sat between her parents. But this was in public and they were unaccompanied.

'Ach, to be sure, it's only a bit of fun.' Honora laughed, tossing her head and winding a long lock of her black hair around her finger.

Winifred set her mouth into a tight line. 'If you don't stop it, I'm getting off.' The thought of standing up on the tram while it was moving frightened her, but she meant what she said; she'd take her life in her hands if Honora didn't stop the awful flirting. This was more than she'd bargained for. Perhaps her mother was right after all, and Honora was a bad influence.

What was it her mother said all the time? 'Reputation is all, once it's gone, it's gone. It's been the ruination of a lot of girls.' Her mouth was always set when she said it, her eyes hidden by their heavy lids.

'Ladies.' The voice was deep, confident.

Winifred squinted at the young man from under her hat brim; she was annoyed to see him leaning towards them, his hands on his knees. And irritated with herself for the small flutter of excitement in her stomach. It's nerves, she thought, that's all.

'And how the devil are ya today?' he said.

Irish, like Honora, Winifred thought She was tempted to give him a caustic answer but she could tell it would only encourage him. And when Honora turned to her, the wide-eyed look of innocence and the shrug of the girl's shoulders told her she was being teased by them both.

She pulled at the cuff of her gloves, smoothed the back of them. 'That's it,' she said. 'I'm getting off at the next stop.'

She braced herself to stand up, her stomach knotted. The tram shuddered to a halt, the trolley poles shrieking on the overhead wires. Before she'd raised the courage to move the two young men left their seats.

'Ladies...' The brazen one lifted his cap to them. Winifred ignored him but saw Honora grin and flutter her eyelashes, looking up at him as he followed his friend down the stairs of the tram.

'If that is how you're going to act today, Honora, I'm going straight home and you can find someone else to accompany you on your shenanigans.'

'Away with ya.' Honora laughed and pushed her shoulder at Winifred. 'Ya need taking out of yourself, sure ya do. "There's no need like the lack of a friend,"' Honora said. 'To quote one of my Granny's sayings. And I could tell ya were lonely the minute I saw ya behind that blasted counter. Now shut up and enjoy the afternoon.'

But she must have seen how worried Winifred was, because she shrugged and sighed. 'Fine, I'll be a good girl from now on. Cheer up, it'll be a craic.'

But still, as the tram set off, Honora waved at the two men standing on the pavement looking up at them.

Chapter 4

Getting off the tram on High Street in Morrisfield, Honora tugged at Winifred's arm, impatient. 'Will ya come on now?' she demanded. 'I told ya, there's something I want ya to see.'

'Stop pulling.' Winifred shook the girl's hand from her arm. 'You still haven't told me what it is?'

'You'll see.'

'I'm not going to the theatre,' Winifred said, suspicious of the sudden gleam in the Irish girl's eyes. 'It wouldn't be proper for us to be seen there on our own.'

Honora blew out her cheeks in obvious exasperation. 'No, ya said. It's not the theatre; it's not even open at this time of day. No, it's something important. Something ya should – ya will – be interested in. This way.'

Winifred allowed herself to be tugged along the street, swerving to avoid the people lingering in front of shop windows: a small, scruffy man, slightly unsteady on his feet, a couple of portly women, almost matching in similar brown hats and coats, chatting, a boy sitting on a doorstep.

They passed the few street vendors who, sweeping an arm over the goods on their carts – brightly coloured cloth, saucepans and kitchen utensils, hats and gloves – called out in anticipation when Winifred and Honora hurried towards them, then turned away when the two girls didn't stop.

'Fresh apples, ladies?' A young man appeared from behind a stall of fruit and vegetables. 'Ripe as the two of you.'

Winifred stiffened, glared at him and lifted her chin.

Honora waved him away. 'Not today, Sam. Not today.'

Winifred saw him sniff and wipe his nose with the back of his hand.

Honora pulled her into an alleyway. 'This way.'

Winifred wanted to hold her hand to her nose; the ground was covered in rotting fruit and rubbish. A sour smell made her

15

eyes water. 'Honora!' she protested, lifting up the hem of her coat.

'It's just a shortcut.'

They walked out onto another street at the end of the ginnel.

'This way,' Honora repeated. After a few minutes she stopped at the foot of a row of steps leading up to a large brick building. There was a poster stuck to the wall.

NATIONAL UNION
Women's Suffrage Societies

****

NON-PARTY AND NON-MILITANT

****

MEETING
of the
MORRISFIELD WOMEN'S SUFFRAGE
SOCIETY
Will be held on
WEDNESDAY 15th March 1911
At 2.00pm
Here at the Parish Hall
With Rev. Harold Wood
In the chair

ADDRESSES WILL BE GIVEN

'Well?' Honora looked at Winifred, obviously waiting for a response.

'What do you want me to say?'

'What do ya think?'

'About what?' Winifred moved from one foot to the other, flinching with the pain; besides the ache in her ankles she was now convinced she had blisters on her little toes. Too much walking.

'About this?' Honora squeezed her arm tight with impatience. 'About the meeting?'

'What does it mean?'

'It means we're going to have a say.'

'A say in what?'

'A say in how the country is run, eejit.'

'Who?'

'Us. Women.'

'Ridiculous,' Winifred said. 'How could we do that?' And what would be the point? Everything she'd ever read in the newspapers told her that it was always men who ruled the country. Even overbearing women like her mother had no say outside their own home.

'We'll vote.'

'We can't.'

'We will.' For the first time Winifred saw the sardonic humour disappear in Honora's expression, replaced by a determination. 'We will,' the Irish girl repeated.

A church bell rang four times.

'We have to go. I'm going to be late.' Winifred panicked. Her father would get the worst of it if she wasn't home to shut up the shop.

'I was going to say ya'll want a hot chocolate?'

'No time.'

'Aw, to be sure, there's plenty of time. The tram at half past will get ya home by five.'

'Anyway, I told you, I've no money.'

'My treat.' Honora turned and walked away. Winifred followed her along the street, afraid to be left behind; she hadn't a clue where they were.

Before long, Honora halted at the entrance of a large building.

Winifred gazed up at the set of double doors with the leaded glass decoration of dark pink and silver. She'd passed Willow Tearooms many times but would never have considered going in; the place looked extravagantly expensive.

'You're certain?' she said, when Honora gave her a prod in the back. 'Can you afford it?'

Honora laughed. 'Looks posher than it is. Anyway, I told ya. I sold a painting. Well two, in fact; I was commissioned for portraits of the wife and daughter of a grand man. At least he thought he was grand.' She linked arms with Winifred. 'Come on, *cailín,* I'll not be standing out here like an eejit. I feel like celebrating and blow the cost – let's treat ourselves.'

'Someone told me there's a store called Selfridges opened in London that has a posh café in it. I bet it's not posher than this.' Winifred stirred her spoon around the froth on top of the hot chocolate, whilst looking through the full-width, curved bay window down onto the street below. The room was positioned on the first floor at the front of the building, slightly above the level of the tea gallery. In the background classical music played quietly. 'I feel I shouldn't be here,' she whispered.

'Why?' Honora frowned, as if puzzled. She held a thick lock of hair away from her face as she gulped her drink. 'We're as good as anyone else here.'

'Hmm.' Winifred pursed her lips, concentrating on the embossed menu card on the table. 'I wouldn't be here without you. I wouldn't have the money for these prices. She kept her eyes fixed on the card. 'That poster? The one we looked at.' It had been preying on her mind ever since she'd read it. Getting involved in something like that was asking for trouble. She needed Honora to know she couldn't go to anything like that.

'I knew it.' Honora grinned. 'I knew ya were interested.'

I'm not. Honestly I'm not, Honora. I can't get involved in something like that.'

'But ya're involved, Win. Ya're a woman. I'm a woman. And we have no say in anything. The men have it all their own way. Last year the Liberals called a General Election to put off passing the Suffrage Bill. I believe what the WSPU say—'

The WSPU?'

'The Women's Social and Political Union.' Honora lifted her eyebrows. 'Did ya not know that even? They're fighting for the vote for us all.' Honora leaned across the table, put her hand on Winifred's arm. 'They are, ya know,' she said, dismissing Winifred's doubtful shake of her head. 'The Government said they would try to get the vote for us but the politicians haggled over it. We think Asquith was against us from the start.'

Honora pressed her lips together and drew in a long breath. 'They try to make out it's our own fault, that too many of us have taken action. Been violent, they say,' she said as Winifred opened her mouth to ask what she meant. 'But I ask ya, what choice have we had? They'll all too busy watching their own backs against that other blasted House – the House where all the toffs are. And the trade unions – they're fighting the unions all the time. And they're frightened about what's happening back home; about us wanting Home Rule...' She stopped, having run out of breath.

'Keep your voice down, Honora. Please.' Winifred looked around the room, nervous; even though she understood little of what her friend was saying, it sounded too dangerous to be talking about in public.

But when Honora spoke again her voice was louder, bitter. She glanced around. 'They don't like that we've taken things into our own hand, ya know; they say women are not strong enough. Some of 'em say we're mad. But it's all an excuse; they're frightened of us. And so they should be...'

Winifred blenched. People were watching them. 'Shush,' she said, noticing the frowns from the people seated at the tables nearby, uncomfortably aware of the icy stares of their companions,

the whispers hidden by napkins as women leant towards men who averted their eyes.

Honora seemed satisfied that she'd caused a stir. She smiled brightly. 'So ya see, ya have to come with me to the meeting. It's your duty as a woman.'

'No.' Winifred was determined. 'No, I won't.'

'Ya will.' Honora nodded. 'For sure ya will. Now, finish your drink if you want to catch that tram.'

Chapter 5

Wednesday 15th March 1911

'We want deeds, not words.' The ubiquitous cry of the Suffragette movement rang out to be drowned by the clapping of the women surrounding Winifred.

It hadn't occurred to her before that she had such a small life, lived in such a small world. She'd paid no attention to politics in the past, so despite her protests to Honora, over the last month, she'd read any articles on the Suffragette movement she could find in her father's copy of the *Yorkshire Evening Post*. The violence often meted out to the women aroused an anger in her she didn't think she was capable of. The description of how one group of women, protesting outside Leeds town hall, were dragged by their hair to the local police station and beaten with truncheons sickened her. She'd been unable to get it out of her mind for days afterwards.

She looked across the large hall towards the three tall windows which threw slants of weak sunlight over the women crammed into the room. Dust motes floated erratically above them as they clapped and moved restlessly, standing on tiptoes to see the people on the stage at the end of the room.

Was this something she wanted to be part of? She flapped her handkerchief in front of her face in a vain effort to cool herself.

The three girls they'd met at the door of the hall were on the other side of Honora, cheering and clapping as well, their faces alight with enthusiasm as they exchanged glances with her. Winifred had never been amongst such a crowd; such passion frightened her yet it was also thrilling.

'All right?' Honora put her arm around Winifred's waist, her head close. Even so she had to shout. 'Ya look a wee bit hot.'

The sweat was trickling down Winifred's back. 'I'm fine. I'm listening.' She nodded towards the front of the hall, not meeting Honora's eyes.

'We women must make a clear and positive case.' The woman at the lectern let her eyes travel over the audience. 'We have only one thing to say and I urge the men amongst us to listen.' She paused. 'Women are human beings, the same as you. We are entitled to vote.' The applause rose, then fell as the woman held up her hand. 'We are entitled to vote.'

'Who did you say she was?' Winifred's words were caught by the woman in front of her who turned to give them a withering look.

Honora shrugged, aligning herself with the plump woman and raising her eyebrows in acknowledgement of Winifred's ignorance. 'I told ya,' she shouted, without looking at Winifred. 'It's Ada Wood; she's a friend of Emmeline.'

'Emmeline?'

'Pankhurst. Emmeline Pankhurst. Ye gods girl, did ya not listen to a word I've said,' Honora kept her eyes on the broad back of the woman, before lowering her voice and putting her mouth close to Winifred's ear. 'At least that's what the woman at the door said.'

Honora's words made Winifred smile; less ashamed of her ignorance.

She stood on tiptoe, peering around the array of broad-brimmed black hats at the stage where there was one man, the Reverend, amongst a line of stern looking women. They sat, straight backed in chairs, behind the imposing figure at the podium. She'd certainly held the crowd in thrall, Winifred thought in envy. She couldn't ever think of a time when anyone had really listened to anything she'd said in all her life.

Another woman got up from her seat and stood at the front of the stage. 'We all know what happened in London last year. The cruel and disgraceful way we were treated by the police. We will not let that deter us, Members. We will fight all the way.' She flung her arms wide. 'We will get the vote. However many of us have to suffer—have to die even. We will get the vote.'

There was a roar of approval throughout the hall.

A raft of placards suddenly appeared in front of Winifred, closing off the narrow view she had. They were twisted around so she could read some of them.

Votes for Women
The Bill, the Whole Bill and Nothing but the Bill

Her lips moved as she took in the words before glancing towards Honora. The girl's cheeks were red and she was shouting out the chant with the other three girls, their hands linked and raised above their heads. 'Votes for women.' When she returned Winifred's gaze her dark eyes were glittering with excitement. 'We'll show the beggars,' she mouthed. 'We'll show them.'

We? The chill that crawled over Winifred's scalp accompanied her thoughts; what had she got herself into? And what would her mother say if she knew her daughter was here? The answer came all too quickly. Her parents must never know where she'd been this afternoon.

She wouldn't go to anything like that ever again. Anna, one of the three girls had wanted them to go back to her house but Winifred insisted she needed to go home. She barely listened to the chatter of her friend as they hurried along. The meeting had frightened her; all those women shouting; the unseemly fury.

'I went to London that day.' Honora's words brought Winifred to a halt. She held onto her friend's arm stopping her from walking.

'You went?'

'Yes. I've not told anyone, not even my brother, ' Her face was flushed with defiance. 'I didn't tell Conal because I knew he'd stop me; he said it was asking for trouble.'

'And from the sound of it, it was. What on earth were you thinking?'

Honora clenched her hands together. 'We had to protest. They'd taken the coward's way out; put off the decision on our suffrage?'

'Yes, but to put yourself in danger—'

'We thought if we went in great numbers they would see how wrong they'd been.' Her voice cracked. 'There were hundreds of us but we didn't stand a chance. There were just as many police, on horses, with batons. One of the women in our group was killed. I didn't see it; it was after we'd all been driven away. We never saw her again.' The tears welled and fell.

'Don't. I can't bear to hear.' Winifred brushed her thumb against the wetness on Honora's face. 'You have to stop this.'

'No!'

'Women getting the vote... It'll never happen.'

'One day it will. If we protest long enough. If we show how strong we are—'

'I've read so much in the last few weeks, Honora. The law is on the side of men; they have all the power in government, the police are all men. Women have no control over what happens to them.' Except at home, her home; she couldn't stop the thought flashing through her mind. 'We could never win against all that—'

'We can.' Her friend's words were fierce. 'We should.' The tears had gone as quickly as they'd arrived. 'You can.'

'No, I'm sorry, I couldn't.' Just thinking about all that hostile fervour was more than enough to deter Winifred. 'It's not something I dare get involved in.' She became aware that people were having to walk around them, eyeing them in curiosity, as they stood in the middle of the pavement. 'Now I need to get home. And I think it's going to rain.'

'Just a minute.' Honora fished in to her coat pocket and brought out a handkerchief. She gave her nose a long blow. 'There,' she said, 'that's better. Come on then.' She linked arms with Winifred. 'We'll go through the park, it'll be faster.'

Chapter 6

Winifred kept her eyes on the ground and quickened her steps along the path in Balfour Park. The day had been all too much. The excitement of secretly defying her mother had long since dissipated. She wasn't looking forward to all the earache she was going to get when she got home. How would she explain where she'd been all afternoon? Especially on this cold, damp day. She'd have to find a good lie to cover up. Shopping in Huddersfield perhaps; though she had nothing to show for it.

'Well, it's the gorgeous Honora, so it is.'

Lost in the story she was trying to concoct, Winifred hadn't notice the group of young men lounging around the benches at the side of the path. She almost stumbled when Honora stopped suddenly. Looking up she saw one of them snake his arm around her friend's neck and pull her towards him, lowering his face to kiss her.

The indignation that rose in Winifred boiled over into angry words. 'How dare you…' before she saw that Honora was actually laughing under his kiss. It was one of the youths from the tram.

'Honora!' Winifred couldn't believe what she was seeing. Keeping her head down she pushed her way through them, only to be forced to stop when one of them refused to move. She stood still, looking down, her fists tight to her sides. His brown boots were planted squarely in front of her, the toes coated with dust from the gravel path.

'Well now, Sis, and are ya going to tell me who this is, then?' The voice, deep and thick with the Irish accent, held a hint of laughter.

Honora moved next to Winifred. 'Leave her alone...' She pushed at him, linked arms with Winifred. 'This is my new friend, Win. Isn't she just lovely?' Putting her mouth close to Winifred's ear, she said, 'This is Conal, my brother.'

Winifred let her eyes travel from the boots to his face, with what she hoped was a disdainful expression. And was shocked into recognition when she saw it was the impudent youth from the tram; the one who had so much to say for himself. Except he wasn't a boy, he was a man. And he was the spit of Honora. Coal black hair, strong straight nose, determined chin. And long-lashed dark eyes that seemed to look right into your soul, she thought. They held the same slight mockery in them as her friend's.

Her mouth slackened when the brother and sister laughed.

'Like what ya see?' His voice even held the same rhythm as Honora's.

The anger was quick in Winifred. Everything she'd just been through; that sweltering meeting, listening to Honora talking about those horrible things that had happened in London. And now this; they were laughing at her. She glared at the two of them, and then twisted round to glower at the group of boys.

'Well, now you've had your fun...' The words came out strident with the effort of preventing the tears. 'So, if you'd let me pass...' She adjusted her hat so that the side of her face was hidden.

'Don't do that,' Conal said, reaching towards her and straightening the brim. 'I can't see your gorgeous blue eyes, if ya hide behind yon daft hat.'

She knocked his hand away. Not daring to trust her voice she shook off Honora's grasp and pushed past him.

'Aw, Win...'

Winifred ignored her, looking towards the large iron gates at the far entrance to the park, blurred with the hot tears of humiliation. She wouldn't be here if she hadn't let herself be persuaded to go to that meeting. A sudden chilly breeze made the leaves on the large privet hedges at the side of the path quiver, carrying Honora's voice towards her.

'Aw, Win... I'm sorry, so I am.'

She ignored the apology. A splash of rain hit her hand; glancing up at the sky she saw it was rapidly filling with darkening banks of clouds. Holding the skirt of her coat together with one hand and clamping her other hand on her hat, she quickened her steps.

The first drops were heavy and cold on her skin. There was no chance she'd make it home. Her hat would be ruined. She looked across at the bandstand in the centre of the park. There were already people hurrying towards it. She could hear the cries of surprise, the shrieks of children running in front of their parents, dodging the benches, and leaping up the four wooden tiers of steps. Changing direction she followed the wide paths that were rapidly darkening with patches of rain.

She was out of breath when she joined the crowd under the roof of the bandstand. Good-naturedly they moved to let her in.

'Well, that was a surprise and that's the truth.' The man who spoke to her lifted his trilby. There was no doubting the admiration in his eyes but Winifred had had enough of men. She smiled briefly without looking at him and moved to be amongst a small bunch of women with children clustered in the middle of the stand. A nanny with a navy blue baby carriage was quickly helped up the steps by three men and the women divided to make room for her.

'Goodness me!' The nanny manoeuvred the carriage and laughed. 'What a downpour.'

The shoulders of her dark coat glistened with rain; her white cap had been flattened to her head. She unclipped the wet hood of the pram and bent to check on its occupant. Her presence seemed to relax the group of strangers. One small boy and his mother peeked in to see the baby. There were a few low smiling comments as the baby started to wail. The nanny pressed down on the handle, jiggling the pram. The edge of the carriage dug spasmodically into Winifred's hip so she retreated to lean against one of the posts.

'Win–Winifred? I'm sorry.'

Winifred closed her eyes against threatening tears. Go away, she thought, just leave me alone.

Honora pushed through the crowd and, breathless from running, caught hold of Winifred's arm. Winifred looked over the girl's shoulder. No-one was following. At least she'd had the courtesy of not bringing those louts with her. For the first time since Honora had come into the shop she felt less in awe of the Irish girl and the way she disregarded all the conventions that she, herself, had been forced to live by. The anger she felt for the way she'd been laughed at fuelled her words.

'I don't want to know.' Even though she had to whisper she kept her tone cold. 'I came with you to that horrid meeting. I listened to you telling me about the stupid way you put yourself in danger. This is the final straw, Honora. I care about my reputation even if you don't.'

She wouldn't make eye contact with the Irish girl, preferring to look past the nanny to the park. Water poured off the roof of the stand and bounced onto the path with loud splats. Shining swirls of small puddles formed on the benches. In the distance, across the large area of grass bordered by flowerbeds, now only bare lengths of dark soil, she could see figures sheltering in the long glasshouse.

'It was only a joke,' Honora wheedled. 'Can ya not take a joke?' Winifred knew the girl was trying to push the blame onto her and was determined not to let her. 'No, I can't. Not when it's at my expense.' Winifred's cold wet gloves were stuck to her hands. She wished she had a fur muff like one or two of the women who stood by them. She also wished the rain would stop so she could go home.

'To be sure, I'm sorry. Liam, he's my fella. I should have told ya. It was only meant to be a bit of fun.'

'Not to me.' Winifred was shivering now. 'Oh, this is hopeless. I'm going.' It was more important to get away from Honora, even more important than avoiding the wrath of her mother for being late. At least the weather gave her an excuse.

Holding her hand above her hat in the hopeless task of saving it from getting wet, she splashed her way down the steps and along the path. The rain wasn't as hard now but, when she glanced up, the sky was still a glowering grey. She brushed again a small birch tree, dislodging a shower of water onto her. Blast it; she shocked herself with the thought. Perhaps Honora was a bad influence, swearing hadn't always come so easily to her. But she repeated the words to herself when she heard the Irish girl's voice.

'Hold on, will ya, Winifred. Please...'

Lying sleepless in bed that night Winifred stared out of the window, watching the thin trails of shadowy clouds pass across the bright disc of the full moon. It had been a dreadful day. One she was determined to forget.

She turned over onto her side and pulled her pillow around her head. The last thing she remembered was the way Honora's brother's dark eyes had fixed on hers. The tremor that ran across her skin wasn't fear or annoyance. But Winifred wasn't ready to acknowledge it was excitement or attraction. Not even to herself.

Chapter 7

Of course, as expected, Honora came into the shop the following day.

Winifred turned her back. 'Mother, can you serve this customer, please? 'I need to go to the lavvy. I won't be a minute.'

Going through to the back yard she heard her mother speak. 'And what can I get you?'

Ethel hadn't spoken with her usual 'shop' voice, as Winifred and her father called it. They'd long shared the joke between them about the royal tones Mother adopted just for the times she stood behind the counter. No, this time the broad Yorkshire vowels weren't disguised at all and there was clear satisfaction in her question. She'd obviously cottoned on to the fact that there was something wrong between Winifred and Honora and probably hoped the new friendship had ended.

Of course her mother would be pleased; it would mean Winifred would lose the freedom she'd gained lately, would always be on call to work in the shop.

Listening to the mumbled reply, Winifred almost felt sorry for her new friend. Her ex-friend, she reminded herself, straightening her back and marching out to the yard; determined not to forget what had happened the day before.

The next time, when Honora appeared, Winifred was on her own in the shop. She had no choice but to serve her. Handing over the usual small cake and taking the money she avoided Honora's eyes, looking past her shoulder to the next customer.

'Mrs Cox, what can I do for you today?'

'This cheese bought yesterday is mouldy.' The woman made a show of peering around Honora, jostling her arm with her shopping basket. The girl had no choice but to move to one side.

Winifred took the parcel that Mrs Cox slapped onto the counter and unwrapped it. 'It's Lancashire cheese,' she said.

'Yes, and it's mouldy.' She peered over Winifred's shoulder at the closed parlour door. 'Your mother sold it to me – yesterday.'

'I'm sorry, that's not possible.' Winifred shook her head, keeping her voice calm. It wasn't the first time Mrs Cox had tried to cheat them.

The woman's face flushed. 'I want my money back.'

'I can't do that, Mrs Cox.'

'Why not?'

'Because we haven't had Lancashire cheese in the shop for a week – we're waiting for a delivery from Cumpsty's farm.'

The woman leaned over the counter and poked a fat finger into Winifred's shoulder.

'You calling me a liar?'

'Do you know, Mrs Cox, I rather think I am, because last time it was mouldy bread you brought in. That wasn't even the sort we sell. And I'd thank you to keep your hands to yourself.' Winifred re-wrapped the cheese and held it out. 'Now, I'd like you to leave. And please take your custom elsewhere in future.'

'Well! Well, I've never...' Glaring, the woman grabbed the parcel and pushed her way past Honora, leaving the shop door wide open.

'Ya certainly gave that Mrs Cox her marching orders, Win.' Honora grinned. 'I knew ya had it in ya.'

'And now I'm giving you yours,' Winifred snapped. 'And close the door behind you.'

Honora came into the shop the following day, too, just as Winifred was sweeping the floor.

'Half day, today,' she said. 'Are ya going out?'

'I'm not. And if I was it would be nothing to do with you.' Winifred pushed the brush towards the girl's feet. 'Now, if you don't mind, I'm closing up.'

Honora stopped by every day for the next week. Winifred knew she couldn't keep it up much longer. The following Saturday she leaned on the back wall, her arms crossed. 'I'd thank you not to come into the shop again. There are plenty of shops in Morrisfield where you can buy cakes.' She swung herself away from the doorframe and went through to the parlour. It wasn't until she heard the bell above the door sound that she went back behind the counter.

Winifred was glad the following day was Sunday and the shop would be closed.

She went to morning chapel alone. The service passed almost without her hearing a word of the sermon and only pretending to sing the hymns.

The light outside was glaring after the gloom of the chapel. Anxious to get away from the gossiping groups of women, Winifred debated whether to go and visit her grandmother. She hadn't been since before that awful day in the park. But the old woman would see instantly there was something wrong and, much as she loved Granny Duffy, she couldn't tell her. How could she? The old woman wouldn't understand why she'd gone to that meeting in the first place. Would she even know what Suffragettes were?

So Winifred dismissed the idea and, with a few words of greetings to the women, she left the churchyard and turned onto the lane that led to the moorland. A long walk would give her some time to think.

The blustery wind and cold air made her face tingle and her eyes water. Leaving behind the roads, she turned onto the narrow track at the base of Errox Hill and picked her way through the stones to the stile. Perched on the top wooden bar she stopped to take off her hat. The cries of moorland sheep were carried towards her; thin mournful bleats. She was surprised they hadn't been taken down to the farmer's lower fields; it was way past the time for that. She closed her eyes, tilting back her head, revelling in the quiet. When she opened them she saw rooks swirling overhead like stark black crosses against the pale grey sky.

There was no-one else around. Winifred was comforted by the quality of aloneness that belonged to this place. It was different from the loneliness she'd carried inside her all her life; she was used to that. Even in school. Especially in school, she corrected herself. She'd never been encouraged to bring any friends home and the other girls soon recognised that there was no reciprocation after she'd been to tea at their house. But whenever she stood on the edge of the moors she'd never had that sickening feeling of isolation, of being an outsider, of not fitting in.

She'd hoped she'd found a friend in Honora. Obviously that wasn't going to happen now.

Slapping her hat against her leg she jumped off the stile. Brooding on a friendship that had barely started was a waste of time. Resenting the control her mother determinedly exerted over her was useless. Mourning the fact that she would probably never have the chance to meet any young men; respectable young men, she added to herself, was useless. Looking up at the summit of the hill, she knew things wouldn't change unless she made them change. But how?

The climb to the top was steep and rugged. Many times she was forced to stop to drag in huge gulps of air, and the heels of her boots kept getting tangled in the winter heather. But she was determined.

It took her half an hour. She thought back to her escapes here as a child; then, unhampered by long dresses, daft boots and heavy coats, she'd done it in fifteen minutes.

When she eventually hauled herself over the last patch of rough-heathered ground to where the hill flattened out, she leaned forward, hands on knees, breathless and looking towards the huge, flattened rock that dominated the area. It was where she'd often sat in the past, looking down on the village and the surrounding moorlands. She gazed at the skeletal grid works of the pithead at the mine. The windows of the four straight rows of miners' houses, on the slopes above Stalyholme pit on the edge of Lydcroft, glittered intermittently in the sunshine.

The wind whipped at her clothes, she felt some of the pins in her hair becoming dislodged and she pressed them back before climbing the rock.

There was a hollow in the middle of the rock, still filled with rain. Sitting alongside it she dipped her fingers into the cold water sending ripples across the shimmering reflection of the sky.

Whichever way Winifred twisted her head, she could see for miles; tiny villages huddled in the dips of the moorland, small dark coppices of conifers stood out against paler fields. In the misted distance she could see the tall mill chimneys of Huddersfield, devoid of dark smoke this one day of the week, the stone quarries disfiguring the hillsides.

Below her the roads of the village were empty. She could just make out a few figures outside the Wagon and Horses public house. Children were playing in a field near one of the outlying farms. Wisps of smoke trickled from the chimneys of some of the terraced houses. She could see the roofs of the houses, their shop on Marshall Road.

Winifred sighed, reluctantly allowing her thoughts to yet again linger on a tall figure with thick black hair, beguiling dark eyes and an insolent smile, as they had been over the last fortnight. There, she admitted it to herself; she had been quite smitten with Honora's brother. Pointless feeling like that now, she chided herself; she'd probably never see him again.

Restless, she stood and climbed off the rock, carefully following the same ledges on the stone. It was as difficult going back down the hill. She picked her way between the rough ground and the hidden stones.

When she jumped down off the stile, Honora was sitting on a large stone leaning against the wall.

Winifred sighed. 'What are you doing here?'

'I followed ya from church.'

'Chapel,' Winifred corrected.

'Chapel then.'

Winifred noticed Honora's slight shrug with irritation, before the girl raised her hand to catch hold of Winifred's. 'Come here to me?' She shuffled along the stone to make room.

There would always be these differences between the two of them. Perhaps that's what she liked about Honora; the difference.

33

Maybe she was hoping to find another life besides her own? To see what she was missing?

Winifred sat down next to her. 'No talk about Suffragettes,' she warned.

'Okay. And I am sorry.' Honora raised her hand again to catch hold of Winifred's. 'I shouldn't have teased like that. But all I wanted was for my new friend to meet my favourite brother – my only brother – my only family.' She laughed. It had a strange note in it, Winifred thought, before Honora added, 'I'd like to think ya would be my new friend in this begotten country.'

'You've got friends in the Suffragettes…' Winifred stopped; she'd said no talk about those women and yet she was the one to mention them.

'Aw, yeah.' Honora flapped her hand dismissively. 'Anna, Dorothy and maybe Mildred. But they're not like you.'

'What do you mean, not like me?' Winifred frowned.

The Irish girl shrugged but didn't explain. 'I had true friends back home in Derrymor. Here it's hard. I get lonely; Conal's often away in Leeds.' She turned on a bright smile when she looked at Winifred. 'Ya did like him, didn't ya?'

'He was very forward,' Winifred said, then relented. 'And very handsome but—'

She was interrupted by a delighted laugh.

'I knew it; I knew ya'd be besotted—'

'I'm not,' Winifred protested, 'I just said he was handsome.' She joined in with Honora's laughter. But when they controlled themselves she added, 'But he is forward.'

'Aye, you're right there.' The Irish girl smiled. 'And he likes ya. He asked me when I was seeing ya again. I haven't told him ya won't talk to me.'

'You didn't play fair—' It sounded stupid even as she spoke.

Honora snorted. 'What's fair in this life?' Her mouth turned down, she grimaced. Grabbing Winifred's hands between hers and holding them to her chest, she said, 'Be my friend, huh?'

'I'll think about it.'

Honora pushed her face in front of Winifred's and crossed her eyes. 'Please?'

'No more tricks, mind.' Winifred couldn't help laughing but still said, 'And I don't want to see that brother of yours.'

'Oh, I'll keep Conal away, to be sure.' Honora nodded, solemn for a moment before grinning. 'If that's what ya want...'

Even the sound of his name conjured up his face, his eyes but Winifred refused to be drawn. 'I'd better get home,' she said, standing. She held out her hand and hoisted Honora to her feet.

They walked along the lane arm in arm.

'I need to talk.' Honora pulled Winifred to a stop.

'What about?'

'Now don't ya get cross at me.'

'If it's about the Suffragettes, Honora, I don't—'

'Please—'

'I can't.' Winifred shook her head. 'Did you come to look for me just for this?' She untangled her arm from Honora's. 'I've told you, I don't want to know.' How could she have been such a fool, the girl was trying to manipulate her. 'I'm going home.'

'No, please...' Honora stood in front of her, her hands cupping Winifred's face. 'We – all women – should stand together to get us our vote. I've been talking to Anna and the others; they really want ya to join us. They think someone like ya could help a lot.'

'You said that before. What do you mean; someone like me?'

'I told them about that day in the shop with that woman who tried to cheat you.'

'Mrs Cox?' Winifred was surprised. 'That was nothing.'

'It showed me ya can stand up for yourself – for what's right. And getting the vote is right for us, for all women. I – we – think ya'll be able to speak for us. Ya know what a lot of people say about us – that we're just troublemakers. As for the likes of me... Irish trash is a polite term for what some of them say, so it is.'

Winifred did know what people said, her mother was a prime example. She hesitated.

'Please, Win, join with us. You're a strong woman; like I said, I saw it that day with that woman. And I could see that the first time I was in the shop, with the leaflet. I watched the way you dealt with some of the women then; ya were...'

Honora stopped, as if searching for the word. 'Ya were dignified; ya didn't let them talk down to ya like some of them tried, just because they were older than you.' She let her hands fall from Winifred's face. 'I want ya to be with us; to have a say in what happens to us. Please...'

'You just don't give up, do you?' Winifred began to walk again.

'Is it your ma that's stopping ya?' Honora caught up with her. 'Are ya afraid of her?'

Those last words stung because Winifred knew they were true. 'Of course not.' But she knew she wanted to do something, anything that would get her out of the shop and away from her mother and her sniping. She allowed Honora to link arms with her again. That wasn't reason enough to join the Suffragettes, she thought. But then she remembered what Honora had told her before about those women in London. She pushed away the apprehension she'd felt at that WSPU meeting in Morrisfield.

'All right,' she said, at last. 'I'll go with you to meet your friends.' At least if she met the other girls properly, she could question them; find out exactly what was happening. 'I'm promising nothing other than that. And it's just the once, mind.'

Seeing the excitement instantly return to her friend's face she regretted the words as soon as they were uttered. But there was no taking them back.

Chapter 8

April 1911

'Dorothy lives here? Winifred looked in surprise at the large red brick building. 'In a vicarage?' For some reason she'd assumed all three of the other girls were as unconventional as Honora.

'What?' Honora glanced back at her as she led the way along the wide gravelled driveway. 'Oh, yes. Her father is the vicar there.' She waved her arm vaguely in the direction of the church on the other side of the line of beech trees at the far end of the garden.

Winifred stopped to stare at the building with its tall steeple and arched mullioned windows, so different, so ornate, from the small chapel she'd gone to all her life.

'I don't think I've ever been in a C of E Church,' she said.

'What? Oh, come on with ya.' Honora ran back and grabbed Winifred's arm. 'Come on.'

Honora had wasted no time setting up the meeting for the following Wednesday; half-day closing for the shop.

Surprisingly, Ethel hadn't asked any questions, though when Winifred was leaving she'd tightened her lips and turned away, refusing to say goodbye. The sense of freedom in Winifred, helped by the enthusiastic chatter of Honora, increased with each mile as the tram neared Morrisfield, despite her reservations since she'd read the report of some Suffragettes setting fire to post boxes in Huddersfield in her father's *Morrisfield Observer*.

Sitting in the lounge of the vicarage with the other girls was exhilarating even though their assumption that Winifred was fully committed to joining the Suffragettes made her nervous.

Mildred, at twenty-two, and three years older than Winifred, took on the role of spokeswoman.

'We have to make the Government more aware of us. We're

willing to go to prison; to fight for our right to vote and those men in Parliament need to realise that.' She looked around at the others girls for agreement. They nodded vigorously. 'We've needed someone like you to help us to do that.' She adjusted her wire-rimmed spectacles and looked in earnest at Winifred. 'Although we go to all the meetings and Dorothy here has been on marches in Huddersfield and Manchester…' Dorothy gave Winifred a shy smile. 'None of us feel able to give the kind of speeches that will rouse other women.'

Winifred doubted that; she found Mildred quite imposing, and quite capable of holding the attention of an audience with her fervour. 'I don't really see what I can do that you aren't doing.' She shuffled uncomfortably in the wide leather armchair.

'As I've just said…' Mildred pursed her lips in an impatient gesture. 'We don't feel we can speak at meetings; not from the platforms anyway.' She stared at Honora who shrugged. 'Honora said you were the one woman we've been looking for.' She smiled. 'And she was right, Winifred. I think she was right.'

'I'm sorry.' Winifred glanced out of the large window; daffodils, dotted around the grounds of the vicarage, moved slightly in the air. It was a sunny day and she wished she could be outside. The room was musty and smelt of mildew. There was a patch of damp in the corner, half hidden by the heavy brocade curtains. 'I haven't ever spoken in public. I don't know enough about all this.' She held out her arms and spread her fingers.

'Do you believe that we women are part of society?' Mildred asked.

'Of course,' Winifred clasped her hands together, uncomfortable at being the centre of attention. 'But—'

'But what?' Mildred frowned.

'Well, I don't see how we can make them change.'

'We have to believe we can, Winifred.' Anna clenched her fists on her knees. 'It's all so wrong. Women have every right to say what happens to them. And, until we get the vote, they won't.'

38

'I understand that.' Winifred hesitated. 'And Honora has told me that there are dreadful things done to the women who have protested.'

'Indeed.' Mildred grimaced. 'But we can't let that stop us. We must not let imprisonment – or the torture – deter women from demanding the vote.'

'All you need to know, to understand, is that this government is not a democracy. The richest men are governing, ruling, women. And surely you can see that's not right.' Mildred produced a pile of papers from behind her on her chair. 'Read these, you'll soon see what we mean.'

Winifred was relieved when the lounge door suddenly opened and a small woman with grey hair backed into the room, carrying a tray of teacups and a fruitcake on a plate.

'Thank you, Mother.' Dorothy rose to help her. 'I'll take it.'

The woman smiled. 'Father says to make sure you take Winifred to meet him afterwards.' She turned to her. 'He's very proud of our daughter. He's proud of you all,' she said. 'He also says he hopes you enjoy the cake; he thinks it's one of his best recipes.' She laughed. 'He does love to bake,' she said to Winifred in a confidential tone.

'It does look delicious,' Winifred said. She wavered before asking, 'Are you also in in the Suffragettes, Mrs...' She stopped, realising she didn't know the surname.

'Goodness me, no; my husband's congregation would be horrified.' She gave a low chuckle. 'Now don't forget, pop in to see your father before Winifred leaves.' Dorothy's mother closed the door behind her.

As though they not been interrupted, Mildred continued. 'The Government has passed more and more laws to stop us.' She took off her spectacles and rubbed the bridge of her nose. 'Women's suffrage is inevitable. One day men will understand that. We are determined; nothing on earth or in heaven will make us give up the fight.'

'What we're asking, Winifred,' Anna said, 'Is that you join us in our cause? We've discussed this between us and we're hoping you'll be our spokesperson. When we go to the next meeting in Morrisfield, we'd like to put you forward as the speaker to represent our group.'

An hour later, Winifred was already regretting giving in to the girls' persuasion. Meeting Dorothy's gently benign father, up to his elbows in flour making bread in the vicarage kitchen, and being given what seemed to her to be almost a small sermon on emancipation had reinforced her doubts. But she'd promised to read the papers that Mildred had given her and to prepare ideas for a speech and there was no backing out. The thought terrified her. 'Sure it will only be a small meeting, ya know that,' Honora said, linking arms with Winifred as they stepped off the door step. 'Ya'll be fine.'

Winifred was glad to be in the fresh air. But, when turning off the drive, she saw Conal waiting for them further along the road she pulled away from Honora.

'You told him where we'd be?' she hissed.

'But I didn't know he'd be here, I promise ya.'

There was nothing for it but to be polite as he fell in step with them on the other side of Honora.

'Miss Duffy.' Conal touched the neb of his cap.

Winifred dipped her head in acknowledgement and murmured a greeting.

On the way to the tram stop, on the tram itself, Conal kept up a general chat. As far as she could make out he spoke on nothing in particular; only catching the odd word as, first the traffic passing on the road and then the hum and rattle of the tram, muffled what he was saying.

It seemed to her that he was only actually speaking to Honora. And when they at last alighted from the tram in Lydcroft, and he merely doffed his cap again and walked away, she didn't know whether she was glad of or offended by his lack of attention.

Chapter 9

April 1911

Bill Howarth stopped at the end of the gravel drive, rested his hand against the tall stone pillar, and looked back at the large square building where he had spent the last four months. Towards the end he'd felt as trapped in the hospital as he had that day in the mine after the explosion.

At one of the upper windows two figures watched him. The taller one, Arnold Blakely, lifted his arm in a gesture of farewell. What he was going to do now with only the one arm was a bloody mystery; he'd be no good down the mine. The other slighter figure, stiff in her white apron, her cap flowing across her shoulders, stood motionless besides the man. Bill couldn't see their faces but he waved back; a jaunty gesture, before moving out of sight to lean against the wall that surrounded the cottage hospital.

His legs shook; they felt too weak to hold him up and he didn't trust himself to walk far. Not yet anyway. He closed his eyes against hot tears and cursed himself for being soft. Looking around he was relieved to see there was no-one on the road and allowed himself to take a moment longer to stop the shuddering deep inside his chest.

He didn't know where he would go. From the day he'd arrived at the cottage hospital neither his stepmother nor his stepsister had been to see him. He'd be buggered if he was going to beg them for bed and board now.

It would have been different if it had been his real mam; she would have cared what happened to him, she would have insisted he went home with her. He was sure of that. He only vaguely remembered her; just an elusive smell of lily of the valley and the softness of long dark hair on his face when she kissed him goodnight. Her hushed voice lingered at the back of his memory. But he remembered feeling loved by his mam and how he'd

41

adored her. She'd gone years ago, giving birth to a brother who was hadn't lasted a week before he'd died as well.

Bill hated his father as much as he loved his mam. He remembered the first time he'd retaliated after his father hit him. He was six years old. Wilfred had lifted him by the front of his jumper and slammed him into the scullery wall.

'You'll not raise yer 'and to me ever again, yer young bugger.'

Jessie, Bill's mother, jumped on her husband's back. 'Bastard!' She hung around his neck, pulling at him as he gave one last kick to the small inert figure on the floor. Falling to the side of her son she covered his body with her own.

Without looking at them Wilfred grabbed his jacket and cap from the hook behind the back door and, flinging it back, pushed his way through the small crowd of neighbours who had gathered at the gate of the back yard.

'Get out the way, go on, bugger off.'

The silent crowd let him through. Then the shawled women jostled into Jessie's kitchen.

'Come on, hen.'

'There, there.'

'Rotten sod.'

'Put the kettle on.'

Bill heard them all as they helped the weeping woman to her feet and carried him to the old Chesterfield in the corner of the kitchen. One of the neighbours wrung out the grey dishcloth in the sink and wiped his face.

He knocked it away. 'Hey-up, missus, that stinks.'

The women laughed, the tension lifted and, eventually, they scattered to their own homes, the excitement over for today. Jessie and Bill gazed across the room at each other.

'Don't try that again, son.'

'One day, Mam, one day.' Bill gingerly touched the growing bump on the back of his head and scowled.

The day Jessie died Bill's father disappeared for two weeks, leaving Bill dependent on the good will of the neighbours for his existence. Wilfred returned, stinking of drink and defiance.

It had taken exactly a month before his father had moved Marion into their home, the woman who became Bill's stepmother. He had wanted to like her, for her to love him but he was on a loser from the start. She was a woman completely opposite to his mum, a coarse bitch who resented him from the off and didn't miss a chance to get him into trouble with his father.

The memory of lying injured after the accident in the mine, thinking he should have told them he loved them, made him cringe with embarrassment. He didn't even fuckin' like either of them, never had. So he wasn't bloody sorry his stepmother and sister had kept away.

A few of his work mates had called once or twice but the people who'd looked in on him every week were the bosses. And they only came to let him know he was there by their goodwill; that it was them that'd funded the hospital with their own money. At first he was in too much pain to argue but in the last month he'd made it known to them that he'd paid his dues with his weekly subscription towards his sick pay, taken from his wages. Once he'd started on that tack, he known his time there was limited.

So here he was, almost a fuckin' cripple and out on his ear.

He didn't remember arriving at Rowlands House on the back of the horse and cart but some of the other patients, the ones lucky enough to have a bed by the windows, told him they could hear his screams above the sounds of the horse's hoofs and the general clatter from inside the ward way before they saw him coming along the road. They hadn't thought he'd make it. Neither did he; every rut in the lane from the pit, every jolt as the horse stopped or turned corners onto yet another road along the two mile journey to the mine owner's hospital, tortured him. He'd thought he was going mad with the pain.

43

The lad lying next to him, making just as much row, they said, didn't last a week what with almost every bone in his body broken.

Crushed under the fall of rock, Bill's pelvis and right leg had been broken. Remembering the weight on him that day, he knew he was lucky it hadn't been his back. And he knew he owed the fact that he could walk to the doctors who'd operated on him. But lying flat on his back all those months had been painful and boring. Now he was upright there was no way he'd be going back down that bloody mine. He wasn't daft; he knew the doctors were as controlled by the owners as much as he was. Practicing walking along the narrow corridor one day, he'd heard old Rowlands in the doctors' office accusing one of them that they were keeping him in too long; that he was malingering. They wanted him back working on the seams; they owned him.

Well Bill Howarth was owned by no bugger. And now he needed to get away.

Swinging himself off the wall and with one last glance at the slate roof of the three-storey red-bricked building he limped away, his clogs scraping, uneven on the flagstones. He'd be long gone before management showed their faces. Let some other poor sod do their dirty work.

Chapter 10

April

Winifred turned off Wellyhole Terrace into the entrance that led into the courtyard of the three storey back-to-back houses where her grandmother lived. It was bedlam; children playing a noisy game of tag, a baby crying, a couple at the far end of the yard quarrelling, dogs scampering around and barking.

Two women were washing clothes in old dolly tubs, the muscles in their arms straining as they pounded at the bundles beneath the water. They didn't look up as Winifred passed them. She dodged pools of scummy soapsuds and green-slimed flags, holding her breath when she passed the dustbins outside the communal lavatories.

She pushed at the door of number four. 'Granny?' The smell of the outside lavvies followed her into the scullery and she quickly closed the door and looked around. As usual the sink and the narrow worktops looked spotless but the small room smelt damp and a cockroach scuttled into the far corner. There was a large lidded saucepan on the trivet over grey ashes in the grate. She recognised it as the pan of soup she'd made and given to her dad to bring there the day before. 'Granny?'

'Up here, ducks.'

Winifred trod carefully up the wooden stairs avoiding the silverfish which lined the corners of the treads. Her mouth turned down in disgust; this was no place to live.

The room was dim even though it was bright sunshine outside. Florence Duffy was sitting in her chair by the small window, holding back the net curtain, a large grey shawl around her shoulders.

'Hello, Granny.' She dropped a kiss on top of her grandmother's head. As usual her white hair smelt of lavender and carbolic soap. How she kept so clean in this place Winifred could never fathom.

'Mrs Fisher never stops washing for those ten kiddies of hers,' Florence said. 'She keeps 'em as clean as she can and feeds 'em on a pittance. *He* drinks every night, I tell you. D'you know that's the second black eye she's had this month.'

'It's a disgrace.' Winifred peeped out of the window. 'Why does she have so many children, Granny?'

'It's what happens when you marry, ducks. You'll find out one day. Men will have their way.'

Winifred shuddered.

'But if you love your husband, Winnie, it'll be your way as well.' Her grandmother's eyes were anxious; it was as though she thought she'd said too much. 'It's nothing to be frightened of.'

She closed her lips together firmly before saying, 'Though such as Mrs Fisher doesn't have a lot of say in such things, I reckon.'

They watched the woman in the courtyard struggling to raise dripping washing on a line with a clothes prop, apparently trying to catch the last of the sun before it disappeared behind the roofs of the tall houses around her.

'Nip down and help her will you, ducks.'

At that moment a sturdy looking boy came from one of the doorways and gave the prop an extra shove. In seconds the line of clothes was a v-shape above the two figures.

'Think they've sorted it,' Winifred said. 'You all right, Granny?'

'I'm fine, Winnie.' The old woman let the corner of the curtain drop and lifted her hand to pat Winifred's cheek. 'Yourself?' The lines around her faded blue eyes deepened as she smiled up at her granddaughter.

'Same as usual.' Winifred held Florence's thin fingers closer to her face for a moment before straightening up. 'Your fire's out downstairs.'

'I thought it would be. My knees are playing up a bit today and I haven't been down yet.' She crossed her shawl across her chest and let her folded arms rest on her lap. 'But it's warm so I didn't bother.'

'But you've not eaten?' Winifred checked the clock on the old-fashioned oak sideboard. 'It's nearly three o'clock. Are you telling me you haven't had a drink all day either?'

'Nay, don't fret, the Misses Johnston next door brought me a brew this morning. And when you get to my age food doesn't have the same interest. But I did have some of that soup last night; they warmed it up for me in their place.'

And helped themselves to some of it as well, I bet, Winifred thought.

Florence smoothed the black bombazine skirt over her thin knees and leaned back in the chair. 'Don't fret,' she said again, as though she could read Winifred's mind. 'It doesn't matter.'

'You should have got a message to us, I'd have come earlier,'

Winifred chided. But she knew her gran was too proud; she would never ask for help, she wouldn't give Ethel the satisfaction of refusing. 'You know Dad or me would always come.'

'Aye, well…'

'Right then, I'll get that fire going and make a pot of tea. I shan't be long.'

It took a little time to persuade the flames to catch hold of the few pieces of wood she found in the bucket. Placing small chunks of coal on top she blew on the fire for a few moments before squatting back on her heels, waiting until she was confident it wouldn't go out. Then filling the kettle with water she rested it on the trivet.

On a more careful study of the kitchen she saw the grit on the flag floor that had been trodden from outside and that black mould had formed on the hem of the net curtain where it rested on the windowsill. Despite the closed door the smell of the courtyard still pervaded the room.

And there was something else. Winifred wrinkled her nose, looking around before going to the sink and lifting off the muslin cloth that covered the jug of milk standing in water. There were lumps of sour curdled cream on the surface. Holding her breath, Winifred poured it down the sink and, turning on the tap, flushed it away.

Her gran shouldn't have to live in this hovel, not when there was a perfectly good spare room at their place. There was no reason why she couldn't live with them. Except for her mother, of course; the two women hated one another. Winifred didn't think either one had ever stepped foot in the other's home.

When she'd brewed the tea she replaced the kettle with the saucepan of soup and took the two cups upstairs. Her Granny was dozing despite the rowdiness coming from the back-adjoining wall of the house. Winifred was tempted to knock on it to quieten the family that had recently moved in there but thought better of it; she didn't want to cause trouble for her grandmother.

She knelt by the chair. 'Tea, Granny. It'll have to be black, the milk's off. I should have brought some with me, sorry. Drink it while it's warm. And the soup won't be long.' She waited until Florence had a grip on the handle. The cup trembled as she lifted it to her lips. 'Ah, that's good,' she said after swallowing. She motioned towards the wall with her head. 'New neighbours moved into the front house.'

'So I hear. Are they always this bad?'

'Not always. Five children, though, I believe. Eldest three must have just come home from school. It's all right, I don't mind. Bit of company to hear them, really, ducks.'

Winifred frowned. 'As long as you're sure.' She had to raise her voice above the din.

Florence lifted her head and sniffed. 'Is the soup burning?'

'Oh heck!' Winifred put her cup down and ran. The soup was bubbling. She sniffed it and poked at the bottom of the saucepan with the ladle. 'No, it's okay,' she called. She carried the bowl up on a tin tray and put it on her grandmother's lap. 'Here's a spoon and there's more soup if you want some afterwards.'

'Thank you, Winnie.'

Winifred stood and went to get one of the wooden chairs. She put it next to Florence's. She was nervous; she'd made up her mind to ask her grandmother's opinion about her agreeing to go to the next protest meeting with Honora. Would she react in the same as her mother had to hearing about the Suffragettes? She loved her grandmother and it was important that she at least approved of what she was about to do.

'May I ask you something, Granny?' She'd raised her voice before realizing it had gone quiet next door. There was a babble of faint shouts from the courtyard; the children must have been shooed out to play. 'Something important,' she said, quietly.

'Of course.' Florence Duffy studied Winifred, the spoon halfway to her lips. 'What is it?' She pushed out her lips and blew on the soup. 'Trouble at home?'

'No. Nothing like that. It's something I think – I might – have got myself into.' She swallowed, nervous. 'It's something I want to talk to you about but I'm not sure what you'll think.'

'Listen, Winnie, you can't shock me. I'm too old to be shocked by anything.'

'Okay.' Winifred laced her fingers in front of her, loosening them when she looked down and saw the whiteness of her knuckles. 'Right.' She paused slightly, before saying, 'What do you know about the Suffragettes, Granny? About women trying to get the vote?'

From the look of surprise, the faint smile on Florence's lips, she could tell her Gran was relieved and pleased. Clearly the question wasn't what she'd expected. Winifred wondered what her grandmother thought she was going to say.

'Ah, well now, you'd be amazed by what I know, ducks.'

'Oh?'

'The Misses Johnston next door tell me all about it. They read it to me from their newspaper on Saturdays.' She placed the spoon into the half-finished soup. 'I've had enough.'

Winifred took the tray off her.

Florence pulled her shawl tighter and knotted it over her chest. 'And they have quite strong views about it, them two, you know. And I agree.'

'You do?' Winifred put the tray on the floor and waited.

'I do.' Florence nodded her head vigorously, her lips pulled into a tight narrow line. 'I think it's appalling how those women are treated. I think them police need a good thrashing themselves.'

'You do?'

'I do.'

Winifred gave a low laugh of relief. 'I've been asked to join the Suffragettes, Granny. One of them came into the shop a while back and I talked to her about it. Then I went to meet some of them in Morrisfield. They gave me a lot of stuff to read about it all.' She took in a long breath.

49

'I can't believe I knew nothing that was going on under my nose. Some of the things that happen to these women, just for wanting to have a say in what happens in their lives, is unbelievable.' She studied her grandmother before saying, 'I decided I would join them.' Her next words came out in a rush. 'In fact, they asked me to speak for them at a meeting sometime and I've said yes.'

The reaction came quicker than she thought it would.

Florence threw her head back and laughed. 'Well, ducks, you've never done anything by halves, I'll give you that.' She patted Winifred's cheek. 'Good for you. If I were younger, I'd join too.' She leaned sideway, closer to Winifred. 'I'd give them what for, I can tell you.'

'Mother doesn't agree.'

'She wouldn't.'

'What do you mean?'

Her grandmother pursed her lips. 'Never mind, Winnie. If you think it's right, you must follow your heart.'

Follow her heart? The image of Conal was suddenly there. Winifred's heart thumped, she closed her eyes; what was this feeling? She'd never been in love. She knew nothing about it other than what she'd read in the secrecy of her bedroom, knowing that her mother wouldn't approve of the works of George Eliot. And was it really like that anyway; all the conflicts, the tribulations of class divides that the author wrote about? She wasn't sure she was strong enough to deal with the problems love seemed to bring.

She was brought out of her contemplation by her grandmother's next remark.

'I'll tell you something, shall I, Winifred?'

Winifred? Her grandmother never called her by her full name. She opened her eyes. Florence was looking straight ahead. When she spoke her voice was low but strong.

'It's about your grandfather.' She directed her glance towards Winifred for a moment, as though to assess her reaction, before

50

looking away again. 'Something I've not told you.' She shifted as though uncomfortable in her chair, her mouth working as she swallowed. 'I haven't always lived here, you know. When I first married we lived in a lovely house in the village – on Harrison Street, near the chapel. My parents gave it to us as a wedding present.'

'I didn't know that.'

'No? Your dad's never told you?' Florence smiled. 'He was born there.'

'No!'

Florence nodded. 'Mother and Father were quite well off. They owned the shop as well.'

'Our shop?'

Her grandmother nodded again. 'Rented it out to a chap called Richards, as far as I can remember and, after he died, they gave it to your father when he was twenty-one.'

'I didn't know any of this. I thought you'd always lived here, Granny.'

Now Florence looked directly at her. 'Here?' her voice took on a bitter note. 'How long has your grandfather been dead?'

'I don't know, I don't remember him at all.'

'No? Must be near enough twenty years, then. After your dad and her – your mother – were married.' She rubbed her hands together and then smoothed them on her skirt. The slight rustle of her clothes sounded loud in the silence. 'He left me penniless. Gambled away everything we'd got. I didn't know how much debt we were in until afterwards; until I was turned out of the house by the bailiffs. My house.' Her eyes reddened with the tears she was fighting to hold back. 'That's how long I've been here.'

'Oh, Granny.' Winifred knelt by her side and put her head on Florence's bosom, her arms around the thin figure. 'I'm sorry. Don't cry.' The anger was swift against the unknown man who'd done this to her beloved grandmother. 'But I don't understand. If it was your house, how—'

'When you marry – I think it's still the same, Winnie – when you marry – everything you have then belongs to the man.' She stroked Winifred's hair. 'It's not right and it's not fair. But that's how it is.'

Winifred heard the deep breath her grandmother took.

'It's men that decides what happens with women. Them in the Government don't want to change that, they're sitting pretty, all right. They don't want anything changing. But it has to. We women have rights too.' She lifted Winifred's head and smiled. 'So, you ask what I know about the Suffragettes? I know they're right. And if you think they're right as well you should join them, never mind what your mother says. Like I said, you follow your heart.'

This time Winifred remembered the fervour and determination of the women at the meeting. 'I will, Granny, I will.'

'It won't be in my time, I shouldn't think. But one day, perhaps.' The old woman patted her hand. 'Let's hope women do get a say in what happens to them. Perhaps *you* will, ducks.' She nodded slowly and then leaned closer, two worried lines between her eyebrows. 'But promise you'll be careful, Winifred. Stay safe.'

Chapter 11

May 1911

The alleyway was flagged and dipped in the centre to a guttering. Along it, oily water flowed sluggishly, carrying a faltering clutter of debris with it. Bill hesitated; the houses edged on either side were grim and dark, the afternoon sun didn't reach beyond upstairs windows. It looked as though its warmth had never touched the greasy ground. The glass lantern, displaying the word BEDS, was in the middle of the three-storeyed terrace. Two men lounged outside the door, smoking.

One of the men rolled his cigarette to one corner of his mouth to speak. 'Looking for a bed?' He tipped his head towards Bill as he walked slowly towards them.

'Aye.'

'Poor man's hotel, this. None finer.'

The other man gave a snort of laughter and hunkered down, resting his arms on his thighs. 'Not sure they have such small beds, mind.'

Bill stiffened; no bugger made fun of him. He dropped his bag and squared up to the man. He was bloody sick of the jibes about his size. All his bloody life it had been the same.

'Sorry mate, no offence.' The man rose from his haunches; he was only an inch or two taller than Bill. 'Just summat that I 'ave to tek as well. It's a sod being a titch ain't it?' he held out his hand.

Bill ignored it. 'Your place is it?' he said pushing back his cap and looking the first man up and down. He picked up his bag and adjusted it over his shoulder.

'You must be bloody joking.' The man spat out the tab end of the cigarette. 'Think I'd be 'ere by choice?' He gestured over his shoulder with his thumb. 'Doorkeeper's down there. If you want a bed in this 'ovel yer'd better be quick, most of beds 'as gone for tonight.'

The sour warm smell wafted up from the stairs as Bill stepped through the doorway. He swallowed, cursing himself that he'd left it so late in the day that he'd run out of choices. This place was the tenth he'd seen since getting into Huddersfield; each one worse than the last. His clogs clattered on the stone steps as he descended into a large gloomy cellar.

'It's sixpence if you want a bed. Pay up front.' The woman's voice was rasping, her breathing laboured as she pushed herself up from a small wooden chair to face Bill. Her dress, almost open to the waist, showed large drooping breasts that moved slowly from side to side as she scratched the skin. 'I'm the Doorkeeper. I'm the one you'll answer to if you cause bother. And don't think because I'm a lady you get owt but short shrift from me.' Her small eyes, almost lost in the folds of fat, glared at him. 'Sixpence.' She held out a grimy hand.

Bill dropped the coin into her palm and took the brass check.

'Kitchen's through there if you've owt to cook.'

He looked over her shoulder towards the end of the cellar. He could hear the muffled clunk of pans and low voices but the smell that emanated from there was like nothing he'd ever smelt before. He swallowed the sudden bile that rose in his throat. 'No, I've nowt.'

'Right. Your room's on top floor, third along on the right.'

For such a large woman she moved swiftly to block the way as he made to climb the steps. He turned his face away from the musty smell of sweat and dirt.

'You leave yer bag here.'

'Why?'

'You might pinch summat.'

'I doubt you've got anything I want, missus. Now I've paid my sixpence– you'll let me pass.' Bill shouldered her from him.

'I'll have yer out.'

'You won't.' He passed the front door and climbed the next set of stairs to a large room that held four long tables. Men, sitting on the benches, were eating silently; keeping themselves isolated from the others.

'Stairs? Beds?' Bill asked no-one in particular. The man nearest to him dipped a chunk of dark bread into a large bowl of salt in the middle of the table and shoved it into his mouth, washing it down with tea from a big mug. Without a word he pointed the mug towards one of the corners of the room.

'Thanks.'

He climbed two more set of stairs before he reached the top floor, his leg aching. He passed the first two doorways, one tiny room was empty, the next had an old man sprawled on the narrow bed. His was the next one. He stood looking in. It was slightly better than any he'd been in before; not much but at least the bedding looked a bit cleaner than others he'd slept in since leaving the hospital. Thin walls separated the rooms but, as usual, there was no ceiling to them. Nor a door. He grimaced, listening to the hacking cough from someone along the landing; it wouldn't be peaceful night. Edging along the side of the bedstead he shoved his bag under the thin pillow and sat down. His knees touched the wall. There was a yellowing handwritten notice stuck to it. With difficulty he read *No smoking, No spitting, No pissing in the rooms. Lights out at 10 o'clock.*

Without taking off any of his clothes he lay on the bed, the copper wire mattress creaking under his weight, and folded his arms under his head. The stench from the kitchens had filtered upwards; together with the stink of sweat and farts the air was fetid. One night would be more than enough in this stinking hole. There was a market in the centre of Morrisfield; he hoped to find a bit of work there before he moved on.

Yet, despite the noises and the smell he did sleep and felt better for it. Even so, at first light he threw back the sheets and blankets and rolled off the bed, his knees banging against the wall. He stood up, stretching and yawning.

'Shut your row.' The old man in the next cubicle shouted a curse.

'Piss off,' Bill answered automatically, shouldering his bag and giving the wall a thump with his fist.

To a chorus of angry yells he went down the stairs, his clogs thudding on the wooden treads.

At the front door he stopped and turned the large key to unlock it.

'Eh up.' The woman was already sitting in her chair, both hands scratching at her hair, flattened by sleep. 'Check?'

Bill flicked the brass check in her direction; there was no way he was going near the stinking cow again.

Flinging the door open he stepped out onto the flags and

looked up, taking long breaths of air into his lungs. It wasn't going to be a bad day.

Chapter 12

May 1911

Winifred let the hat rest in her lap, the needle halfway through the material, remembering her grandmother's words. She hadn't been able to stop thinking about her grandfather and what he'd done. For her grandmother to lose her home through his gambling was awful. It was so unfair. That men had such a hold over women, that they could do whatever they wanted in a marriage, wasn't right.

She wondered why her father hadn't ever told her about what had happened. The answer quickly followed the question. He would be ashamed. And he would be ashamed he'd not been able to give his mother a home. John Duffy was one man who had little say in what happened in his life. Winifred had long accepted how it was between her parents even though she didn't understand why he put up with it.

Absently, she smoothed the silk ribbon between her finger and thumb. Next time she saw Granny Duffy she'd ask her why *she* thought he accepted how things were between him and her mother.

Taking up the hat again she focused on her stitching. Over the last few days she'd veered between excitement and apprehension at what she was going to do. Having read all the papers Mildred had given to her and listening to the girls at Dorothy's house last week, she'd begun to believe that she could make a difference. She'd even written down a few ideas; things she could say at a meeting if she was chosen to speak.

What if they were right? What if it did happen? If women did get the vote– get suffrage, and she'd been part of the fight, she'd be so proud. It would be something she would remember all her life; something she could tell her children. That thought startled her; she wasn't sure where it had come from. Or why Conal's face had been instantly conjured up. She put the back of her hand to her burning cheek. Children? She had only a vague idea how *that* worked. It wasn't something she could ever talk to her mother about; the thought of it horrified her. If she couldn't even talk about suffrage to Ethel, she surely couldn't ask her about *that*.

Suffrage, she turned the word around in her mind, firmly pushing aside the image of Conal's face... She would go to the next protest meeting. 'Be careful!' her grandmother had called out to her as she'd made her way down the narrow staircase to the outside door. She shuddered, remembering what Honora had told her about what happened in London. It scared her. Could such things happen? What if it was all exaggerated? Well, if it was, so much the better, she told herself, and anyway, she gave a small shake of her shoulders, the protest was going to be in Morrisfield, not London. Probably no-one would even notice. She ignored the small voice in her head; *you hope, Winifred*.

But she was determined not to stand out as different. Honora had given her the ribbons for her hat; she said all the women would be wearing them.

Winifred tightened the last stitch and bit through the thread. She massaged the ache in her shoulders and sat back. She'd been crouched in the chair for the last two hours, revelling in the quiet of the kitchen. The soft light from the gas mantle on the wall above her was enough for her to see what she was doing and cast the rest of the room in comforting shadow. The crackle of the fire behind the door of the range was muffled. Winifred closed her eyes, eased into drowsiness.

The gate in the yard screeched on the flagstones. Even before the back door opened she could hear her mother's complaining tones. She only had time to push the hat behind her back and to sit up, straight-backed.

'It wasn't the right subject to be discussing in Bible class.' Ethel Duffy swept into the kitchen pulling at the tips of the fingers of her black gloves before flinging them onto the kitchen table and tugging at the fox fur around her neck. 'Totally improper in front of the ladies; especially with the men being there as well.'

Winifred noticed one of the ribbons trailed across her knees. Watching her mother she quickly wound it around her hand and pushed it down the side of the chair.

'But it is one of the seven sins, my dear.' Her father's voice was apologetic. 'As the minister quoted; "lustful appetites can be destructive—"'

'Huh!' Ethel stood in front of the mirror, unpinned her hat and patted her hair into place. 'Just shut up.' Her face and throat were mottled and there was a sharp irritation in her voice. She stopped and turned, her stare settling on Winifred sitting in the chair by the fire. 'What are you doing? What's that you're hiding?'

'Nothing.' The brim of the hat was digging into her. It was bound to be crushed; her careful work ruined. 'It's nothing.'

'I think that's for me to decide, miss.' Ethel grabbed hold of her daughter's shoulder and pulling her forward, dragged the hat out. 'What's this?' She held it out, the purple and green ribbons swayed as she shook it Winifred's face. 'These...these are the colours that those blasted women wear.' She lifted the hat out of Winifred's reach as she tried to take it from her. 'I should throw this...this rubbish in the fire.'

'No.'

'I will, I'll burn the damn thing.'

'Mother!' There was shock in her father's protest. 'There's no need to swear.'

Ethel rounded on him. 'No need to swear? Is that all you can say? You...' She didn't finish, whirling round she threw the hat. It landed in the hearth.

Winifred launched herself at it, but was swung around when

her mother grabbed hold of her arm. 'It's that Irish girl. That trash. She's got you into this.'

'I've done nothing. Let me go.' Anger tightened Winifred's chest. 'You're hurting—'

'I will.' The grip tightened, pinching her skin. 'I will, if you ever think of having anything to do with those women. Troublemakers.' Ethel yanked her towards the stair and shoved her onto the first tread. 'You have no idea what you're getting into. They will ruin you, ruin us, ruin our business.'

'What are you talking about? Ruin us?' Winifred clung to the bannister. 'And what's it got to do with the shop?'

'Reputation – yours – ours. The shop depends on it. I won't have it…' Ethel glared at her.

In the silent struggle, Winifred met her mother's eyes. For a moment she thought she saw an emotion there that she couldn't put her finger on. But then it was quickly replaced by anger.

'Dad!' She appealed to her father.

He watched, helpless against the fury of his wife. 'Sorry, love…'

'You will be.' Ethel glared over her shoulder at him, still pushing at Winifred. 'If you interfere… I'm telling you, you will be.' She was breathless, her words coming out in harsh gasps. 'I'm warning you, madam. You need to watch your step or you'll be out on the streets. Now…' She thumped Winifred's back. 'Get up those stairs. You'll stay in your room until I say you can come out.'

Winifred fell to her knees. 'You can't make me stay in my room. That's ridiculous. I'm nineteen—'

'And you live under our roof. Under our protection—'

'I don't need your protection. I'm a grown woman.' Winifred pulled herself upright by the bannister and held on to her skirt to stop herself tripping on it as she allowed herself to be shoved up the stairs. There was no point in struggling against her mother when she was like this. But still she said, 'And it's nineteen-eleven, Mother, not eighteen-eleven—'

'I don't give a fig what year it is, my girl. You'll do as I say.'

In the darkness, Winifred lay on the bed, her fist clenching the covers. One day, she'd escape from this place for good. One day she'd find a way to live her own life.

Chapter 13

May 1911

'Have you come to your senses?' Ethel stood in the doorway of the bedroom with her hands folded in front of her.

'Are you going to let me out of here?' Winifred said, still angry. She sat with her back to the iron bedframe and looked at her mother.

'You're needed in the shop.' Ethel crossed to the window and pulled open the curtains with an impatient tug of both hands. The dazzling daylight revealed small particles of dust flying from the material and floating around in a haphazard pattern. The sudden brightness made Winifred blink. 'And that's as far as you'll be going, as well.'

'I'm not a child to be ordered around anymore, Mother.'

Ethel sighed, standing with her back to the window, meeting Winifred's stare. In the long silence it was as though her mother wanted to say something. When she did eventually speak it was with hesitancy.

'I know we don't talk; you've always been your father's daughter—'

'I won't be stopped, Mother. You have no idea—'

'And you have no idea, either, miss.' Her voice returned to its usual sharpness. 'Don't you see? Women will never be as free as men. Men can walk away anytime they like. Women are stuck with the lives they are given—' She stopped herself before saying, 'We deal with our lives as best we can.'

And in that moment Winifred thought she understood her

mother at last. 'Is that what you do, Mother? Deal with your life as best you can? By the way you are with Dad and me?'

Ethel took a step forward. Winifred thought she was going to slap her again. She braced herself to move out of the way.

Instead Ethel stood still, her hands linked in front of her. She opened then pressed her lips together in a tight line and lifted her chin. 'Don't you ever listen to what customers say in the shop?'

Still shocked by her mother's previous words, Winifred wasn't prepared for the change of subject. 'The customers? Of course I do.' Some days she was sick of hearing the gossip. But she was surprised by what she said next.

'I mean really listen.' Ethel crossed her arms. 'About what's going on beyond these four walls? My goodness, girl, I wish you would understand what I'm trying to say.' She let her arms drop to her sides. 'It's not just that I think that girl and her tinker friends are ignorant, common trash...' she stopped. 'Which they are, of course.'

So we're back to this, Winifred thought. 'You are such a snob, Mother.'

Ethel shrugged and repeated, 'They're not only trash, they are also dangerous with their marching and fighting. These so-called Suffragettes are mainly the Irish and—'

'They're not!' Winifred remembered the cultures tones of the woman on the stage at that meeting, of the voices of the women around her that day, of Dorothy, the vicar's daughter.

'And, in Ireland, there has always been trouble. Didn't you hear Mr Wright the other day, telling us that there are riots and bombs and murders over there? Do you really want to be part of all that?'

'I'm not. It's not the same thing. Mr Wright doesn't know everything, Mother. Just because he works for a local newspaper—'

'The *Morrisfield Times*—'

'Oh, for heaven's sake; it's a little local newspaper.'

'I'm not arguing, Winifred. That girl, those women—'

'The Suffragettes.'

'Those women are dangerous. The Irish are dangerous...' Her mother was spluttering as though searching for words. 'It's dangerous. You could be... you shouldn't...' She stopped, her chest heaving. 'Your reputation will be ruined.'

'My reputation? *Your* reputation, you mean. Even the shop's reputation. You said that last night. But it's not that, is it Mother? What you said before about men and women—'

'I forbid you to have anything to do with those women.'

'You can't.'

'I can. So it will be better for you if you promise to stay away from those people.'

'Or what, Mother?' Winifred could scarcely believe she was defying the woman who'd ruled her life for so long. She kept her voice even. 'I am sorry, I really am. But I can't, won't, promise. I believe they're right. I believe women – me, you, all – women should be able to vote.'

Her mother gave a scornful laugh. 'And what would I do with a vote, madam? What use is a vote to me?'

There it was again; that resentful note in her voice. 'You could help to make things better for all women.' Winifred met Ethel's stare.

'Why would I want to do that? Especially for that Irish trash and her disgraceful friends?'

'Like me, you mean, Mother?'

They kept eye contact for a while. Then Ethel marched to the door.

'Well, on your own head be it. You and I have nothing else to say to one another on this matter.'

Winifred sank back against the iron bedstead. For the first time in her life she'd caught a glimpse of the real woman inside her mother. The flash of sympathy that followed the unexpected understanding stunned her.

Chapter 14

May 1911

'That'll be ninepence.' Bill placed three apples into a brown paper bag and swung it over and over between his fingers, twisting the corners. He winked at the middle-aged woman who flushed and frowned but couldn't help a small smile turning up the corners of her mouth. Giving him a short nod she turned away.

He noticed the girl behind her in the queue grinning and he raised his cap. 'Yes, miss, and what can I get for you today?' He clapped his hands, rubbing them together, thinking for the umpteenth time how much he enjoyed working on this veg and fruit stall. The pay wasn't so good but he always managed to take home something that was left at the end of the day.

And he loved the outdoor market with the rows of canvas-covered stalls, set on the large cobbled square in the middle of town. He enjoyed wandering around the aisles; looking at the colourful piles of cotton and wool material, touching the soft white net curtains, gently wafting from the poles fastened to the frames of the stalls, buying a bag of broken biscuits from the old baker on the corner stall.

As soon as he became part of it, the market had resurrected an elusive memory; Saturday outings with his mam to some market or other. Of her telling him to hang on to her skirt because she needed her hands to choose and carry the food she bought. He remembered being terrified of losing her among all the other skirts and legs that squashed against him; the relief when the shopping was finished and they'd sit on a bench eating meat and potato pies, so hot they burnt the inside of his mouth even as he relished the taste. Bill smiled; a good memory.

So, yeah, he reckoned he could carry on working on the market; settle in Huddersfield. The small room he had in the house on Archer Street wasn't much, but it was his for as long as he paid the rent and he had his privacy. He shared the kitchen of the house with the five other blokes who lived there as well. But they kept their noses out of his business and he left them alone, other than the odd greeting.

Taking the penny from the girl and dropping two pounds of potatoes into her basket he looked around to check where his boss was. Seeing Ernie Bolton deep in a chat with the man on the hardware stall in the next aisle, he took an apple from the barrel and pushed it into her hand. 'Little present. And what are you doing tonight?' he said, grinning.

'She'll be 'ome wi' me.'

Bill looked up at the burly man who appeared at the girl's side.

'You spoiling for a fight, pal?' The man scowled.

Bill held up his hand. 'No offence, mate,' noticing too late the wedding ring on the girl's finger. 'Only joking.' He picked up a bag of onions and waved them above his head. 'Last of the onions today,' he shouted. 'Only penny ha'penny a pound.'

Relieved when the couple moved off, he dropped the bag onto the stall and took off his cap to wipe his face. It had been a warm day before but that little do hadn't helped; the last thing he needed was any trouble.

'You get off now, lad.' Ernie Bolton rested a hand on Bill's shoulder. 'You've done a grand job today but I'm packing up early.' He handed a couple of bags to Bill. 'Help yourself to owt you want.' He watched as Bill chose some carrot, potatoes and onions. 'Making a stew?' he asked.

'Aye, I reckon.' Bill stopped what he was doing, all at once wary. 'Everythin' all right, Mr Bolton?'

The man looked uncomfortable. 'It's like this, son. My brother's daughter's fifteen now and needs a job…' He twisted his mouth and lifted his shoulders as an apology. 'Family has to come first. You know?'

Bill wiped his hand over his mouth, pushed away the cold sudden panic. 'I know. There's nowt you can do about that, Mr

Bolton.' He gestured to the bags in his hands. 'I can still tek these?'

'Oh aye.' Ernie Bolton put his hand into his money belt and taking out a shilling, shoved it at Bill. 'Just to keep you going like. Reckon that'll help.'

'It will. And thanks.' Ashamed, Bill knew he was near to skriking. Just as he was starting to feel good about everything, shit happened. And what the hell was he going to do for brass now? 'I'll be off then.' Abruptly shaking hands with the man he left before he showed himself up, he weaved his way through the stalls.

'Hey, hang on a minute.'

The shout halted Bill as he waited for the double decker tram to pass on the edge of the market ground. He looked behind him. A woman in a black dress and headscarf waved to him. When she stood by him she pressed her hand against her throat, breathing rapidly. 'By, you walk quick for somebody with a limp,' she said.

He waited, shrugging his bag further on to his shoulder. 'What?' Bells started a peal in the church across the road. A horse, startled by the sudden sound, reared up in front of them almost tipping over the small empty cart it was pulling and causing the man holding the reins to stand, cursing.

The woman looked up at him, rolled her eyes. 'Fine time for them to start their practising,' she yelled. 'Hang on while I get my breath.' She grabbed his arm and pulled herself up straight. 'I just heard what Ernie said. I'm on the crockery stall behind his. My brother, he's a fishmonger, has just lost the lad what helped him in his shop in Morrisfield. He asked me to keep an eye out for someone who was a good worker. I've been watching you. If you're interested...'

65

Chapter 15

June 1911

He missed working outdoors. He missed the noise, the colours, the smells of the market. Sometimes, as Bill swept the blood-swirled scalding water towards the central drain in the floor or gathered up the discarded dead-eyed fish heads, he even missed the mines.

The feeling, the memories of the shared camaraderie between the miners, took him by surprise. He'd thought he'd never want to work underground again. But, as the months passed, he'd realised that it was the mine owner he'd hated and the way he'd been treated by him after the accident that had soured him.

Still, he'd needed to get away from that part of Yorkshire and Morrisfield was new and welcome territory for him.

The first time he saw the girl she was with an older woman, a sour-faced old bitch. The two didn't speak to one another, didn't discuss the fish laid out in neat rows on the white slabs and divided by the lines of parsley. They just stood side by side. And then chose some fish each; a piece of cod for the girl, half a dozen herrings for the woman.

Cleaning the shelves and floors at the back of the fishmongers in Morrisfield he'd watched her, his heart thumping. It was a long time since he'd been so nervous in front of a girl. She was small, pale under that big hat. He couldn't tell what colour her hair was but she was lovely; small mouth and nose, high cheekbones. Her dark blue eyes slanted upwards when she smiled at Bertie Butterworth. He couldn't tell what her figure was like under all those layers of clothes but she looked slim and had lovely ankles and little feet. Being a small chap himself he liked small women; they didn't make him feel daft about his size.

Even though he hated the stink of the place, he stayed on at the fish shop so he could catch a glimpse of her when she came in each Friday. The days she didn't come into the shop he went back to his room in Archer Street in a sour mood. The days she did, he cursed himself for the humiliating heat that rose from his throat to his face, the way his hands shook, his inability to bring himself to look fully at her in the way he would any other woman, with a cheeky wink. And, because it was always bloody Bertie who insisted on serving them, there was no way he was able to speak to her. Even if he could have thought of anything to say.

Then, one day, she noticed him as she'd glanced over Bertie's shoulder while paying him. Holding the white-parcelled Finny Haddock, she called out 'Goodbye' to him. Stupidly he'd grinned, dipped his head and pulled on the neb of his flat cap. Only afterwards did he realise he'd walked backwards into the bucket of fish heads and slopped it all over his clogs. He couldn't get the stench from them and got curses for stinking out the house for days.

But she'd noticed him. That night, on his way home, he couldn't stop grinning.

'How do you fancy a bit of time on the market? Wednesday?' They'd just opened the shop and Bertie was washing his large red hands under the cold-water tap at the sink. 'I'll pay you.'

Bill didn't get paid for the day the shop was closed, when Bertie took his fish to Lydcroft. He resented that. And he did fancy some time on a market again. Still, he weren't going to do it if it wasn't worth his while.

'How much?'

'Tuppence. On top of your wages for what you get here, it's not bad pay. It'll give you more experience.'

'I'm not for doing this forever.' Bill was indignant; he didn't intend to work in a fish shop all his life. 'It's just 'til I sort stuff out.' He saw the look of disappointment on the man's face and knew that the fishmonger, not having family of his own, had been thinking of training him up for the job. So when Bertie answered in a testy voice he wasn't surprised.

'I know that, I'm only asking. There's plenty others on the street who'd jump at the chance.' Bertie slapped a large haddock onto the wooden bench and began gutting it, his veined cheeks flushed as he worked.

'You're right, I'm sorry.' Bill watched the man's bloodied hands pull at the fish's insides and drop them towards the bucket under the bench. It seemed to him that he deliberately missed and the guts splattered on the floor. More shit to clean up, he thought. But then he was diverted by the man's next words.

'And that lass you fancy? Winifred Duffy? She lives in Lydcroft.' Bertie's smile was sly. 'Thought you might like to know that?'

Bill grinned, surprised he'd been found out. But it soon vanished as the man added, 'Mind, she'd never look at the likes of you; her father owns the grocery shop in the village. She's a cut above you.'

It was then that Bill knew he'd stick around. One way or another he'd prove Bertie wrong. He already was wrong, in a way; more than once, Winifred Duffy had smiled and nodded at him. Perhaps, working the market, he'd get the chance to chat with her. So long as the mother wasn't there to glare at him.

He remembered his mam often telling him he was as good as any other boy. 'And better than some,' she'd add, kissing him, when he came home bruised and bloodied; when he'd been jeered at and knocked about by other boys for having only clogs to wear instead of shoes, or the backside hanging out of his short trousers, or frayed cuffs on his jumpers.

One way or another he'd drag himself up by his bootlaces and get Winifred Duffy to take him seriously. No bugger was going to tell him he wasn't good enough.

Chapter 16

July 1911

Honora's dark hair hung wild around her face as though she'd been running. She looked near tears.

Winifred gave her father a sideways glance. He didn't look up from the bacon slicer, concentrating on lowering the thin slices of meat onto the greaseproof paper.

'Where's your ma?' Honora's voice wobbled. She peered over Winifred's head.

'Out.' Winifred shrugged. 'What's wrong?'

'She'll be gone all afternoon.' Her father didn't lift his head when he spoke.

Winifred glanced at him in surprise. 'I didn't know that, Dad?'

'She said I hadn't to tell you.' John looked at both girls. 'You can go in the back for a natter if you like. I'll hold the fort.'

'Can she not come out, Mr Duffy?' Honora wrung her hands. 'I need to show Win something.'

'I don't want her drawn into something that's not right.' He looked doubtfully at Honora.

'No, no, I wouldn't do that, Mr Duffy. Honest.'

'Can I go, Dad?' Winifred was already plucking at the buttons on her overall as she spoke. 'It's driving me mad, being stuck in here in this heat.'

Wiping his hands on the damp cloth kept for the purpose her father studied her and then the Irish girl. Taking a long breath, he pushed his lower lip out. 'Go on then. But mind you're back before six – she'll be no later than that.'

Honora pulled open the shop door, looking back at them. Winifred's father reached up to the coat hook on the wall behind him and handed her the blue blouson jacket and straw hat. 'Stay away from trouble,' he warned.

'I will. I love you, Dad.' She gave him a quick kiss on the cheek, then hesitated. 'Sure you'll be all right?'

'Ya're a grand man, Mr Duffy,' Honora called, already outside the shop door.

'Go on. And be careful, the pair of you.'

Winifred couldn't help feeling the pleasure of being out of the shop without her mother. Above the roofs of the houses on the other side of the road she could see Errox Hill; a dark silhouette against the glare of the sun. The air was warm on her face. She took in a long breath, wondering what her friend was going to get her involved in this time. 'Now, what's wrong?' she asked again.

Linking her arm through Winifred's Honora hurried them along Marshall Road. 'I've been to your place every day, looking for ya.' There were lines of tension around her eyes and mouth.

'I didn't know.'

'No. I was hoping to see your da – get a message to ya, but I never. Your ma saw me off every time.'

She would. The frustration and anger that had boiled inside her recently reared up instantly in Winifred. 'You're upset. What is it?'

Honora didn't answer. She chivvied Winifred around the corner of Cook Street and passed the row of low, stone cottages owned by a few of the shop's customers and her mother's friends. She hoped there were none peeping through the curtains; they'd have a field day gossiping about why the two of them were scurrying along like rabbits.

'Ya have to see this, Win. If your ma has made ya promise not to join us, if you've changed your mind by being locked in your room, ya have to see this.'

'What is it?'

'Some of the women from the march in London are still in prison, Win. But we got one of our own back this week, so we did, and I want ya to meet her.'

'But why are we running? It's far too hot to run.'

'You'll see.' Honora slowed her stride. Without looking at Winifred and in a flat tone, she said, 'They force-feed them – when the women are in prison – when they refuse food. Do you know what that means? The bastards tie them to a table, force their mouths open with metal gags and shove a tube in their mouths or up their noses and push it until it reaches the women's stomachs.'

'Don't.' Winifred stumbled on the uneven pavement, the image her friend's words conjured up made her stomach churn.

'Sorry, but ya need to hear it.' Honora caught hold of Winifred's arm to stop her falling. 'They pour food, not proper food, disgusting stuff they've mashed up, through the tube. It's monstrous, so it is.' She clenched her jaw. 'I've heard that the screams can be heard from outside the prisons.'

She quickened her steps, dragging Winifred with her.

The familiar roads were left behind as Honora led them through side streets and narrow alleyways until, after twenty minutes, they were almost on the edge of the village. A faint disquiet filled Winifred. This was an area her mother had always told her to stay away from; 'Filled with ruffians, ready to whisk you away to slavery,' had been her declaration and, as a child, Winifred had worried that she would be unable to tell who was a 'ruffian' who would kidnap her. Although now she knew her mother's words were rubbish, still the boarded up terraced houses, the silence of the shabby streets, the feeling that there was someone, a shadow, lurking around the corners and just inside the ginnels, prickled her skin with apprehension.

She tried telling herself that this was no worse than where her grandmother lived but it felt different. She'd been going to Wellyhole Yard for years and no harm had come to her. She'd never been frightened of the people there, they were just poor. Here there were strangers and she was afraid.

'Where are we going?'

71

'Gilpin Street. We're nearly there.' Her friend's fingers gripped her elbow harder, steering her towards another alley.

They stopped in front of a door in the middle of the terrace. The doorstep was crumbling and looked as though it had never had a donkey stone rubbed over it. There was hardly anything left of the brown paint on the door and the brass letterbox and handle were badly tarnished.

'Here.' Honora pushed it open. The worn floorboards held remnants of thin oilcloth, the pattern indistinguishable under the grime.

Winifred wrinkled her nose against the damp, greasy smell of the dark hallway. 'This is terrible. Who lives here?'

'I do.' The Irish girl's voice was brusque. 'Up the stairs with ya then.' She waved an arm past Winifred. 'Go on.'

Careful not to let any part of her touch the wall, Winifred climbed the creaking treads. At the top she was faced with three doors.

'That one.' It was partly open. Trying to adjust her eyes after the gloom Winifred struggled to make out some figures sitting in the room beyond. She stopped; Conal and four other men. She sensed the pulse in her throat quiver and the heat rise to her face. It was the first time she'd seen any of them since the meeting in the park.

With a tut of impatience Honora reached round her and gave the door a shove, pressing against Winifred until she was forced to move.

The men barely glanced up. One of them had red, swollen eyes. Conal gave a slight nod to acknowledge her and then leaned towards the man, resting his hand on his shoulder.

Despite the warmth of the sun filtering through the grime of the curtainless windows, Winifred's skin puckered. There was a small tatty rag rug on the wooden floor in front of the fireplace which held old grey ashes and half-burned branches. In the corner a stone sink was piled high with a mix of crockery and jars of paintbrushes. A rusty tap dripped water over everything. On the floor a dolly tub held clothes in water, a film of grey suds around the edges. How could anyone live like this, she thought.

'How is she?' Honora spoke directly to Conal.

'I cleaned her up and put Iodine on the cuts.' He gestured towards a small, ridged bottle with a dropper in the top. 'For all the good it will do.' He ignored Winifred's sharp intake of breath and look of surprise. 'I've given her some of the morphine I had from the hospital; it's made her a comfortable as possible.' He shrugged.

'Grand. Ya did your best, surely, brother.' Honora said, moving towards a door at the far side of the room. 'This way.' She glanced over her shoulder at Winifred who followed, unheeded by Conal and his friends.

The room was stuffy, unbearably hot. Unlike the room she'd first entered there was a fire roaring up the chimney. Yet still the figure, lying in the bed, huddled under blankets and coats, shook violently.

'This is Sophie.' Honora pulled Winifred closer.

The girl's face was pallid, clammy with small beads of sweat across her face. Both eyes were almost closed, the lids swollen and purple. There was a patch of bare torn scalp at her temple; it looked as if her hair had been ripped out. Like the cuts to her face and neck it was surrounded by the yellow of the iodine solution.

'Hello.' It was scarcely a whisper. When she tried to smile Winifred noticed her front teeth were broken, her lips cracked and caked with dried blood.

The three girls that Winifred had met before stood around the bed. Dorothy was holding a damp cloth to Sophie's forehead. Anna and Mildred held her hands. Both glanced up at Honora. Mildred gave a small shake of her head.

'This is what the pigs do.' Honora touched Sophie's cheek. 'Lie still, *a mhuirnín*. Lie still, sweetheart,' she murmured. 'You'll be fine.' When she turned away from the bed tears were welling in her eyes.

73

Winifred caught her lower lip between her teeth, her eyes fixed on the pitiful figure. 'I don't understand—'

'For god's sake.' Honora hissed the words. 'Did ya not hear me? It's them bastards in the jails done this. It took them less than a month to get her in this state. They force-fed her.'

'Why?' Bewildered, Winifred looked from one to the other. 'Why would they do that?'

'Because they can.' Anna spoke quietly. 'Then, when they know they've gone too far...' She stopped on a sob. 'They get a message out to the families to collect whichever woman they've done this to. We were outside the Leeds Borough Gaol, protesting, so, when they just dumped her outside the gates we brought her here for Conal to help her.'

Winifred still didn't understand why it was Conal looking after the injured girl but before she could ask Sophie dragged her hand from under the covers and crooked her finger. Winifred bent low over her.

'They hurt me.'

'I know.' Winifred's voice wavered.

Sophie ran a dry tongue over her lips. 'Honora says you've joined us?' Her next words, lisped through the gaps in her teeth, chilled Winifred. 'Will you take my place; fight for our cause for me? Please?'

'I don't...' Winifred wasn't sure she was brave enough to go through what this girl had endured. But, chiding herself for her cowardliness, she said, 'Yes. Yes, I will.' She stroked the girl's hand. 'Now rest.'

No-one else spoke, but acknowledging what she'd just said, they smiled at her. Winifred's earlier fears of being in a part of the village she was fearful of disappeared; these women had far more to fear than anything she'd ever faced in her life. She was ashamed of her previous unwillingness to get involved. In the stillness there was only the murmur of low voices from the other room and the harsh intake of stuttered breath from Sophie.

And then, from outside, came the noise of metal wheels crunching over the cobbles.

Honora moved to the window, peered out. 'They're here.'

The bedroom door opened. 'They're here.' Conal's eyes swept the room before settling on Sophie. 'I'll carry her down.'

The three girls fussed around the bed, wrapping the girl into the covers like a cocoon while she squeezed her eyes tight and held her breath, tiny whimpers escaping now and then.

'She's ready.' Honora brushed Sophie's hair away from her face and bent to kiss her forehead. She whispered something and was rewarded with a slight smile.

One of the cracks on the girl's upper lip opened and began to bleed. Pulling a handkerchief from her coat pocket Winifred bent over her and dabbed at the blood.

'Thank you.'

Winifred could barely hear the word but when Conal gently lifted Sophie, she pushed the small white square into her hand.

'Keep it,' she said.

And then, as all but Winifred followed Conal out of the room, Honora began to sing.

Shout, shout, up with your song!

Cry with the wind, for the dawn is breaking...

Winifred listened in amazement as they went downstairs and then out of the house. Honora had a beautiful soprano voice.

She wasn't sure what to do and stood staring at the slight damp imprint of the girl's head on the pillow before turning towards the window and looking down on the street where Honora was still singing. The last phrases brought tears to Winifred's eyes.

March, march, many as one,

Shoulder to shoulder and friend to friend.

A small woman was unfolding a grey blanket, letting it billow before settling over the layers of straw that covered the floor of the handcart. Two of the young men who'd been in the first room with Conal lifted the handles of the cart when he appeared on the pavement, holding Sophie in his arms. Unable to take her gaze from them, Winifred gripped the gritty windowsill, pressing her head against the cold pane. She watched as, helped by an older man, Conal lay Sophie on the straw. The youth who'd been crying crawled in and lay next to her cradling her head, his shoulders still shaking with his sobs. The two others straightened their arms to take the weight of the cart. Unable to watch anymore Winifred backed away from the window. She didn't know if she should go down to them. Quick footsteps heralded Honora's return.

'I'll need to go with them, Win,' she said. 'We all will.'

'Where are you taking her? To hospital?'

'It's too late for that.' Honora scowled. 'Her ma and da are taking her home. Look, thank you for coming with me but best if ya go home as well now.' She held up her hand stopping Winifred's protest. 'Ya can't come; ya don't belong—'

'I want to.'

'I know but ya can't,' Honora stopped her next words. 'Not yet. An' I know you'll not find your own way, so our Conal says he'll take ya.' She picked up a tartan shawl that was draped over the bedstead. 'Her ma and da... they'll need us with them over the next few days, so they will.'

'Is she... Will she?' Winifred couldn't get the image of the girl out of her head.

Honora's face tightened. 'To be sure, she'll die. Them pigs made sure of that. They battered her where the bruises couldn't be seen.' She wrapped the shawl around her shoulders. 'Her insides are all mashed up.' At the top of the stairs she turned. 'Conal's waiting for ya downstairs.'

The high-pitched screams started when the cart moved away. Winifred could still hear them long after the footsteps and the scrape of the wheels on the cobbles faded.

Drawing in a long breath she tried to steady herself before leaving the room. But her legs still shook when she went down the stairs.

Chapter 17

Conal was sitting on the doorstep, smoking. He looked up at her, his head on a tilt. 'Are ya ready?'

'I am.' She settled her hat firmer on her head. 'Yes.' She needed to leave as quickly as she could. She had something to do. And she had to do it before she lost the courage.

'Right-oh. Ya'll need to tell me where to go when we get out of this warren.'

They walked in silence for as few minutes. Winifred was conscious of the stares of curiosity, aware of the way Conal quickened his strides when someone spoke to him; so fast sometimes that she struggled to keep up with him.

Once, a man, slouching against a wall outside one of the shabby terraced houses, grabbed Conal's arm as they passed. 'Are you not going to introduce us to your fine lady friend, Conal?'

But Conal shook him off, his hand under her elbow.

Searching around for something to say, Winifred ventured, 'You were very gentle carrying Sophie.'

'There wasn't much else I was after doing for her.' He sounded resigned. 'Sophie's for a wooden overcoat anyhow.'

She didn't know what to say except, 'What did you expect to be able to do?'

'I'm training to be a doctor. There should have been something...' He looked away, waiting for a horse and carriage to pass before he guided her down a short ginnel. A line of scruffy young boys were perched on the top of the wall, swinging their legs. They catcalled and jeered. Winifred kept her head lowered and didn't speak until they'd passed.

'I didn't know that.' She hadn't even wondered what Conal did for a living.

'There's a lot ya don't know.' Though the words were abrupt, when she glanced at him he was smiling down at her. He shrugged. 'It costs money to train, so it does. I'll take any odd job to keep the roof over our heads, clothes on our backs, food in our bellies. And Honora does well with selling her paintings.' There was some pride in his expression but, she thought, some shame as well. 'I'll do anything that comes along. And when some of our friends are kicked out from their rooms and come to stay with us, they help out as well.'

It was a whole different world than the one she lived in. It had never occurred to Winifred how fortunate she was; how lucky that they still had the grocery shop her grandfather had founded all those years ago. She knew, however much she sometimes hated the tedium and long hours behind the counter under her mother's eye, she wasn't trained for anything else. Hadn't had the chance to see what else she could do. But at least she didn't have to worry about money.

She touched Conal's hand, still holding her elbow. 'I'm sorry. I didn't know,' she said again.

'Bejaysus, why should ya?'

He was right; she knew nothing about him. But it didn't stop the strange feelings she had when she was near him.

'Me and Honora came over here two years ago. She was only sixteen then so I brought her with me to keep an eye on her.' He grinned. 'Ya've noticed she can be a bit wild?'

Winifred laughed. 'A little, perhaps.'

'To be sure, a lot.' He joined in with her laughter before becoming sombre again. 'Our ma died when we were little, and Da died three years ago.'

'I'm sorry.'

He lifted his shoulders. 'He was a good man, so he was. A good doctor.'

'So you're following in his footsteps. How wonderful!'

Conal smiled a wry smile. 'Not quite. I could have trained in Dublin, had a practice in the villages surrounding the hamlet where we lived like our da. But things were, are, getting bad in Ireland. You're either with the Nationalists wanting Home Rule or you're against them. At least that's how they look at it…'

78

'Did you mind having to leave?'

'No, like I said, I thought it best we got away. Nationalist politicians think Home Rule will make Ireland into the Promised Land; old wrongs put right and old scores settled. Course it wouldn't be like that.' Conal shook his head.

'Ya'll have noticed neither of us have any religion?' he said, abruptly changing the subject.

'I did know about Honora.'

'Well, to be sure, I have no time for it, either; the Catholics believe they've been denied so much – and who am I to say they haven't?' He raised and dropped his shoulders. 'And the Protestants have always thought there've been plots against them. There'll be more trouble, more riots, sure to be.'

'Do you think there'll be riots here about it?' The thought of it frightened Winifred.

He must have seen her fear because he caught hold of her hand. 'I shouldn't think so, *macushla*. There's been a lot of anger against the English for a long time; ever since the famine, but it hasn't meant the Nationalists have dared to do anything over here.'

Winifred nodded. 'I remember Dad telling me about it once. The Great Potato Famine? I was about nine, I think. I remember I cried at some of the stories he told me.'

'Except they weren't stories; it happened to real people.' Conal's voice was hard.

Winifred flushed. 'I'm sorry.

It was as if he hadn't heard her. 'Our da used to tell us about his father and the bad times. People died. The British landowners didn't care; they exported food while their Irish tenants starved to death. Those who didn't starve, left. It split families; loads went off to America, some came over to Britain. But they didn't fit in here. And we're still not wanted by many folk this side of the Irish Sea. We're seen by some as wanting to cause trouble. I've even heard they think anybody with my accent wants to blow up Parliament.'

The image of her mother came into Winifred's mind. 'I'm sorry,' she said again.

He glanced at her. 'Aw, ya're grand. No worries. Anyhow, after the famine, for a long old time, whole parts of the country were left empty. Those left were poor. Grandad was new with the qualifications then. Da said he worked for free most of the time and they sometimes didn't even have bread on the table. My da was different; he thought his family came first. And I feel the same. I want more for Honora and me than what *Seanathair* had; for a wife and family, if I ever have one.'

Winifred felt unexpected warmth in her throat and face at his last words, and turned her face away in case he noticed. 'Still...' she said. 'Still, you're helping poor people here, like Sophie. And I'm sure you'll be a good doctor.'

'Aw, one day. Anyhow, Da left us a quite a bit of cash when he died. Enough for us to get here after I'd won a place at the Leeds School of Medicine, enough to get me through to be qualified if we don't squander it. We manage. Just.'

'And you don't mind living like...' She stopped, aware of the irritation in his eyes. 'I mean that house, that street...'

'You think we have a choice?'

'I'm sorry.'

'It's free. That street is down for demolition. No-one cares that we're there. Not yet.' His voice was grim.

'I'm sorry,' Winifred said again.

'When we have to move on we'll find another house. We've done it before, we'll do it again. As long as I can save enough, and we can earn enough for me to keep on training – working for a future for Honora and me, I'll keep on fighting...'

'I'm sure you will.' There was nothing else to say.

'I'm sorry, carrying on like that.' He looked at her.

'Aw, you're grand.' Winifred tried to imitate his accent. 'No worries.' She thought for a moment he was offended, was surprised when he grinned. His laughter was infectious. He

80

grabbed her fingers and they walked hand in hand until they left the narrow streets behind and emerged onto Cook Street.

'I know my way from here.' She'd actually known her way for the last ten minutes but was enjoying the feel of his long, slender fingers wrapped around hers. And he made her feel safe.

'I'll go a bit further with ya.'

'No, honestly. Don't you want to get back? Don't you want to find out how Sophie is? If your friend is all right? The one who was so upset?'

'Denny? He's her fella.' Conal stopped so suddenly she stumbled. 'Steady, now.' He held out his other hand to balance her. 'And Sophie? They've done for her. They've killed her.' His tone was vehement. 'And they'll get away with it.' He dipped his head, his dark eyes fixed on hers. 'Cos that's what they do, ya know.'

'I know.' She shivered. 'I saw.'

In the distance the hooter from the mine sounded. She looked in the direction of the noise. She didn't want to get caught up in the crowds of men making their way from the last shift of the day; it wouldn't be seemly to be walking amongst them. 'I should go.'

'Like I said, I'll walk with ya.' He gestured for her to move and his hand brushed hers. Her skin tingled. 'Just a little way,' he added. 'I know your ma and da wouldn't approve, so I'll not be going near the shop.' He smiled. 'I promised Honora I'd get ya home safe, sure I did. And she'd have my guts for garters if anything happened to you.'

'All right.'

He was as good as his word and stopped when they reached Marshall Road. He peered around the corner. 'Ya'll be okay now.' He tilted his head towards the muffled sound of clogs on tarmac a few streets away. 'Ya'll be in before...'

She nodded. 'Thank you.'

Before she could turn away he stopped her, caught hold of her hand. 'So? So, I hear ya joining the fight? Or so ya said to Sophie, I'm told. Honora, she wasn't so sure; she thought ya ma had stopped ya.'

Winifred lifted her head, her face flushed with embarrassment. 'I'm a grown woman. I can do as I please.'

'Well I'm glad to hear that. And you'll put yourself forward as a speaker at one of the meetings?'

'I will.' Winifred spoke without hesitation. 'I've not done anything like that before, but I'll try.' The thought terrified her but, after today, she was determined.

'Will ya with us come to the next protest march?'

'You go?'

'Surprised? It's not just women who think ya should have the vote, ya know. There's some of us men believe we're all equal.' His mouth formed a tight line. 'Believe all men are equal an' all.'

Winifred recognised the frustration in him. Didn't she feel it often enough herself? It must be just as bad, maybe worse to be a man who thought himself seen as lower than other men.

She'd barely acknowledged to herself the way he made her feel by his close presence; her stomach tied in knots. How she stopped herself from gazing at his handsome face, even from touching him, she didn't know. She knew it was wrong to feel like that; it was sinful. But now she surprised herself. She realised that, in seeing a different side to him, as well as all those feelings, she actually liked Honora's brother.

'So?' he said, 'Ya will be there?'

She surprised herself by her forwardness when she squeezed his fingers and smiled at him. 'Yes,' she answered. 'Yes, I will.'

Chapter 18

July 1911

Bertie Butterworth came to the stall much earlier than Bill expected. The previous three times he'd been on his own at the market in Lydcroft it was five o'clock when the fishmonger arrived to help for the last hour, to take the money and close up.

'Anything up?' Bill asked. 'It's only one o'clock.'

'Just thought I'd better bring more ice.' Bertie wiped the sweat off his forehead with a large blue cotton handkerchief. 'You look warm as well, Bill. Here...' He took out tuppence from his waistcoat pocket. 'Have the afternoon off. Go get yourself a pint.'

'Thanks.' Bill took the money and whipped off his blue and white striped apron. 'I could do with a wet I must admit.'

'I'll be leaving here at six on the dot if you want a lift back to Morrisfield,' Bertie warned. 'No later.'

Bill couldn't believe his luck. He'd go for a pint at the Wagon and Horses later; they served a good beer and the people were friendly. But first he was going to look for the shop that Winifred Duffy's father owned. Why would she have told him about it if she wasn't just a little bit interested in him? Even as he mocked himself, he was still hopeful. She'd stopped to chat to him earlier, even though she hadn't bought owt.

He'd been careful how he spoke to her, after all, it had been obvious from the start she was a well brought up young lady...

Bill spooned the crushed ice on top of the pieces of cod and rearranged the wilting parsley. He was worried; it was a boiling hot day and the fish would go off quick if he didn't sell up soon. The ice bucket under the stall was almost empty and it was still only mid-morning. He finished wiping the edges of the white trays.

'Morning.'

He'd know that voice anywhere. When he looked up at her Winifred was smiling, a small, shy movement of her lips.

'Haven't I seen you in Mr Butterworth's shop?' she said.

'You have, miss.' Bill heard the stammer in his voice. What the hell was wrong with him? By, she was pretty.

He'd waited every week for her to come to the stall. When she didn't, his disappointment was almost unbearable. There was nothing he could do about how he felt; he really had fallen for her.

Now here she was and he could do nothing but grin like an idiot.

She looked around at the fish on the stall, her voice casual. 'Do you like working there?'

'It's okay – for the time being.' He knew he was nodding as though his head was on springs but couldn't stop. 'I'd like my own shop, one day.' Why the hell had he said that; he'd no intention.

'My father owns a grocery shop here.' She offered the information with another smile. 'Duffy's.'

'Oh.' Think man, think. 'Do you help in the shop?' was all he could say.

'Sometimes.' She tucked a strand of hair that had escaped from under the broad brim of her straw hat and then adjusted the brooch on the high collar of her blouse. 'In fact, most days.'

Bill noticed how small and pale her hands were; the nails short and oval. He coughed, aware he'd been staring. He glanced down at his apron; it was faintly smeared with blood. He crossed his arms across his chest, covering the marks. 'Do yer like working there?' he said.

She gave a low laugh. 'It's okay – for the time being.' Adding, 'But I'd not like my own shop, one day.'

Was she making fun of him?

But then she smiled again. 'Sorry, I couldn't resist. When you asked me the same question I suddenly knew how silly I must have sounded. It was only something to say.'

So was she as nervous of him as he was of her? Bill lifted his chin and let his chest swell. 'I'm ' ere every week, same day, same time. If there's owt… anything yer fancy…' He stopped when she raised an eyebrow. 'I mean, if there's any particular fish you'd like, I can make sure I can get it for you. Save it like?'

'Well, now you ask—'

Before she could finish, her mother appeared at her side, a fox fur wrapped around her scrawny neck despite the warmth of the day. And a face like a smacked arse.

'No Mr Butterworth today?' She sniffed. 'This fish smells off. No surprise in this weather.' She tugged at her daughter's arm. 'We'll leave it.'

So he'd had no more chance to speak to her. But he remembered every word Winifred Duffy had said, especially about the shop her father owned. He puzzled about that; why had she told him? For a moment his pulse quickened. He hardly dared hope she might be interested in him. That he might have a chance with her.

It didn't take him long to find the place. It was handy that the shop had a gold-painted sign over the window: DUFFY'S. At first he just watched, customers came and went in a steady stream. Once, an older man came outside with a long pole, to pull a cream sunshade over the front of the shop to keep the glare off the goods displayed.

It was then he wondered if he was kidding himself. That, however much she'd smiled at him, whatever she'd said; it was odds on Winifred wouldn't look twice at him as a suitor. 'They must be earning a bloody fortune,' he muttered. Way out of his league, as Bertie had said.

It was warm work, hanging around on the corner of the road. Deliberating whether he should go in to buy something, he jingled the few coins in his trouser pocket and shifted from one foot to the other. The old crow had left the shop a while back. There was a chance that Winifred would be serving. The thought made him feel nervous and excited at the same time.

It had been a long time since he'd felt like that about any girl. He pushed the memory away. He'd been a lad then, he was a man now. And there'd been a fair few women since then.

Taking a last drag on his cigarette he dropped the tab end on the floor and crushed it underfoot. He was partway across the road when a girl, her hair flying around her face, ran towards the shop and went in.

He waited for her to come out; better the shop was empty, he thought. But when she did she was hanging on to Winifred's arm and gabbing.

She was Irish, the mad looking girl; a gobby Irish bitch he didn't like the look of at all. He could hear her voice from where he was standing and caught some of the words.

'Get a message to ya ... Your ma saw me off every time.'

Quite right, Bill thought, hearing the last bit. What was Winifred doing, walking around with someone like that? And she didn't look happy, he could tell. It worried him.

Squinting against the dazzle of the sun, he waited until they'd turned off the road onto a side street before following. There was something odd about the way the Irish girl tugged at Winifred's arm. They were fair running; he was having trouble keeping up with them, his right leg was giving him jip and his clogs kept sliding on the cobbles which didn't bloody help.

He kept them in sight through side streets and narrow alleyways until, after a while, they were almost on the edge of the village. Although he was careful not to be seen, Winifred kept looking round as though she knew he was there.

Turning the corner of another street, he stepped back into the shadows of the ginnel he'd just walked through. The two girls had stopped at a door in the middle of a terrace. He glanced up at the nameplate on the nearest house wall. Gilpin Street. They were a poor row of houses; some of them looked empty, windows and doors boarded up, grass growing from the gutters. The house they'd gone into didn't look much better. Some of the windows had dirty nets, the doorstep was crumbling and there were only patches of paint here and there on the door.

Puzzled, Bill squatted down against the nearest house wall and lit a cigarette. Holding it between his forefinger and thumb, the lit end into his palm, he settled down. He could wait. In fact, he thought, he should wait; this wasn't an area a young woman like Winifred should ever be near.

He'd just finished his third cigarette before anything else happened. He first heard the squeal of metal wheels scraping over the cobbles. A handcart appeared at the other end of the street. Bill pushed against the wall, straightening up and stood on the step of the house, pressed close against the door. He didn't much fancy being seen if Winifred came out.

An elderly couple were pushing the cart. They struggled to hold on to the handles and turn it around when they stopped outside the house across the street.

Someone was singing. Or warbling, Bill thought. A bloody racket anyway.

When the woman unfolded a grey blanket he could see a thin layer of straw in the cart. Two lads came out and grabbed hold of the handles. They talked quietly to one another but their voices carried in the empty street. More fuckin' Irish. Another two men appeared, one holding a girl in his arms. Bill couldn't see her face but he breathed a sigh of relief when he saw the dirty white dress she wore and realised it wasn't Winifred. Then he saw Winifred herself, partially hidden by the net curtain, peering out from an upstairs window.

The girl was laid onto the cart and another lad crawled in next to her. He was blubbering and the first Irish bitch he'd seen clinging on to Winifred earlier was the one making the racket.

When the cart bumped over the cobbles, followed by the lads and four girls, the screams from the girl shocked Bill. He blinked rapidly. The cries were too much like those of the lad in the next bed at the hospital before he died. When he focussed again the group was at the far end of the street. It all happened so quickly that it took a moment to see that the first Irish girl was amongst them. He scrunched his face into a frown; had they left Winifred on her own in that bloody place, in this soddin' awful street?

But then the man who'd carried the girl from the house appeared again and sat on the doorstep, smoking a fag.

'What the hell?' Bill almost stepped out onto the pavement, determined to find out what was going on, when Winifred came out of the house. He watched the man look up at her and say something before she adjusted her hat and pulled it lower over her eyes. He heard her say, 'Yes.'

A surprising resentment burst through Bill. He forced himself to stay in the shadows of the doorway when they passed, waiting until they turned the corner before going after them. He quickened his steps when they did, keeping them just in sight, always trying to make sure they didn't see him.

There were more people around than earlier. He heard some of the men shout coarse remarks, whistling and gesturing, saw the way they stared at Winifred, so obviously out of place in her fine clothes. Bill was glad when the houses became less shabby. He thought it safer for Winifred. But then, just after a horse and carriage passed they turned into a ginnel where a line of grubby kids were sitting on the top of the wall, swinging their legs. Peering round the end of the ginnel Bill saw two of them catch Winifred's shoulder with their feet. They were still jeering when Bill got nearer to them. Without a word he grabbed hold of the feet of the two lads and yanked. The sound of the crack of bone on the hard ground was satisfying.

But then he had to run to catch up with the couple, cursing at the pain in his leg, relieved when they left the narrow cobbled streets.

Once or twice he saw how they moved closer, laughed sometimes; too bloody friendly altogether. The Irish bastard was even holding onto her elbow and then her hand as if he had the right to touch her. The unease merged into jealousy and hatred. He hadn't seen hide nor hair of this chap before, certainly hadn't seen him with Winifred. Now here he was fawning all over her.

They were back to the road her father's shop was on and they'd stopped. Bill glanced across to the Wagon and Horses to see if it was open; he certainly needed a drink after the afternoon he'd had, but the doors were closed. When he looked back at the couple he saw they were talking. Still too close. He was choked up with rage as he watched Winifred, his Winifred, holding the bloke's hand and gazing up at him with a daft look on her face. By, he'd like to punch the sod.

In the distance Bill heard the hooter from the mine, saw the anxious way Winifred looked towards the noise. What was up with her? She seemed upset. The door of the pub was quickly opened and the landlord appeared on the doorstep, pipe clenched between his teeth. He looked up to the sky and then he peered along the road. At the same time Bill heard the thump of footsteps, lots of footsteps. The miners were out.

When he looked back to the two of them Bill saw Winifred walking along the road towards the shop.

The man stood for a few moments watching her. When he passed by he barely gave Bill a glance but Bill could have sworn there was a faint smell of Winifred's perfume lingering between them.

The pulse in his temple throbbed; he thought his head would explode with the rage inside him. He glared at the tall figure until he turned the corner, going back in the direction they'd come from. Bill spat, wiped the back of his hand across his mouth. He wouldn't forget that face. He'd be on the lookout for him in future.

One dark night, Bill promised himself, crossing over the road to the pub to get his pint before the miners. One dark night...

Chapter 19

Winifred glanced inside the shop as she passed the large window. Her mother, still with her coat on, stood behind the counter, arms crossed over her narrow chest. Winifred closed and bolted the door behind her, pausing for a moment, her hand on the lock before she turned. She could hear the sharp huffing and puffing. Straightening her shoulders she faced her mother.

'Well?' Her voice was shrill. 'Well, madam? Just where do you think you've been? What lies are you going to tell us this time?'

'Now, Mother.' Winifred's father was carrying the last of the empty wooden vegetable crates to stack on top of the others in front of the counter. With a stab of remorse Winifred noticed how weary he sounded. She glanced at the shop clock above the bread shelves and saw it was turned seven; he must have taken the brunt of her mother's rage for at least an hour.

'I'm sorry, Dad.' Unpinning her hat, she took it off, unfastening the buttons of her coat with the other hand. Looking down she noticed a smear of dark blood on the cuff of her sleeve. Sophie's blood. She closed her eyes, picturing the girl lying in the bed, trying to smile. She steadied her gaze on her mother. 'I'll not tell you any lies, Mother. I've been with Honora. I went with her to see a girl, a slip of a girl, younger than me, that the police and the wardens in the prison have beaten so savagely she'll die—'

'You! I told you…' Ethel Duffy moved swiftly to the end of the counter and rushed towards Winifred, her arm held upwards.

Winifred caught hold of it before her mother could strike her. She was astonished at her own strength. Stiffening her arm, she forced the woman backwards.

'No,' she said. There was determination and a sense of calm inside her. 'I can't let you do that, Mother. I can't let you hit me again. Ever.'

'Win…' Her father's voice trembled. She saw him put the crate down, run his hands through his hair, take a step forward.

'I'm sorry, Dad. I'm nineteen and I can't, won't, be treated like a child anymore.' She let go of her mother's arm and faced her, seeing the red-blotched anger on her skin. 'I've seen and heard things today you can't even begin to imagine, Mother.' She carried on talking over the derisory laugh that the older woman spat out. 'And I've decided I can't stand by and do nothing.'

'Now love, you're only making things worse for yourself.' Through the dark shadow of his whiskers Winifred saw a set of pale pink fingerprints across her father's cheek. Her mother had obviously vented her vindictiveness on him earlier. Despite the guilt, she spoke again, though she knew this would only make things worse for him.

'There are a lot of things wrong with this country, Dad. And, even worse, things that half the people have no say in. The Government refuses to even listen. Dreadful things are being done to women just because they ask to be heard. Because they see that it's unfair that only men have the say in what happens to us – to women.' She breathed in deeply. The shop smelled unfamiliar to her tonight, as though she'd never been in the place before. The thought struck her that somehow, there was a change inside her, a strange sense of freedom, of being separate from the home she'd known all her life. Of being aware that the last look Conal had given her wasn't only because she was his sister's friend and therefore should be his friend as well. And not because he thought she should stand alongside them and fight for justice. But because he'd seen her as an equal.

The two people in front of her seemed frozen. Waiting.

Into the silence she said, 'I'm going to join the Suffragettes.'

Chapter 20

'I don't know, love.' John Duffy leaned back on the wooden chair next to Winifred's, his hands on his thighs. 'I honestly don't know.'

They were sitting, enjoying the last rays of the sun before it dropped down below the roof of the house and disappeared off the back yard. The gramophone was playing in the kitchen and he was absently tapping his fingers to the tune of '*Alexander's Ragtime Band*'.

Her mother was in the shop counting the day's takings, but still they kept their voices low.

'If I don't get what that lot in Parliament are going on about, how can women?'

'Granny understands. She thinks we should try to make things better for us, for women.'

Her father smiled. 'Aye, well, she's always been feisty, my mother. She ran rings around my father for years.'

'For all the right reasons from what she told me about Granddad?'

'She told you?'

'About how he lost all their money? Yes. Why have you never talked about it? Why didn't you tell me about where you lived as a child?'

He raised his shoulders.

Winifred thought she saw something in his eyes. Shame? Embarrassment? 'It isn't anything to be ashamed of, Dad.' She leaned forward to touch his hand. He covered her fingers with his.

'I hate that your granny lives in that place.'

'Then ask her to come here, to live with us.'

'It wouldn't work.' He slumped in his chair, rubbed his palms over the rough cloth of his trousers on his thighs. 'Between the two of them my – our – lives would be made a misery.'

And then Winifred understood. Underneath, her father was a man who could only deal with so much trouble in his life. She knew he was a kind man, she knew he loved her, that he often defended her and came between her and her mother. He'd had the stuffing knocked out of him years ago, she thought. Marriage to her mother would do that to any man. And to ask him to also stand between his mother and his wife was something he couldn't face.

'I understand,' she said. 'But I hate the idea of her getting older and still living there.'

'She's a strong woman.'

Winifred didn't agree but she decided to revert back to their earlier conversation. 'Anyway, she thinks I'm right to join the movement.'

He cocked his head and closed his eyes. 'But you know she doesn't get out much these days. She really has no idea about what's going on in the world.'

'She knows more than you think. And her neighbours read the papers to her.'

'Hmmm.' He looked at her, bit his lip. 'But like I say, if I don't get what that lot in Parliament are going on about, how can any woman?'

'Oh, Dad!' Winifred stifled the irritation. 'Don't you and her…' she gestured towards the house, keeping her voice low. 'Don't you and Mother ever talk about things like that?'

He gave a short laugh. 'Give over. She's no interest in anything like that. She says she's enough to do running this place and keeping us in order without worrying what's going on with the country.'

Winifred pursed her lips. She remembered the things her mother had said about women being ruled by men, about women having no say in their lives But she'd also said what she thought about the Suffragettes, about her new friends, about Ireland. And she'd heard her mother laying down the law in the shop often enough; telling folk what the Government should do about this, that and the other. Her father didn't know the half of it. 'Don't you believe it, Dad. She grouses over everything. What she wouldn't do if she ran the country isn't worth talking about.'

'Now, love.' He moved his head slowly from side to side. 'What you don't understand about your mother is she doesn't like change; a place for everything and everything in its place, that's her. And that goes for how these women are behaving. It frightens her.'

'Oh Dad, nothing frightens Mother.' Winifred scowled.

'Winifred, that's enough. I know her better than you. I've known her a long time.' He paused. 'Okay, I'll tell you something about Mother, shall I? She feels safe here; she feels this is her place, values her position in this village.'

He didn't know his wife at all, Winifred thought. He hasn't a clue how trapped she feels. But all she said was, 'Dad, we're shopkeepers.'

'We're respectable.' He spoke tersely. 'We don't talk much about it – except for the other night with you. But I know she thinks that those women are trying to change what she sees as natural; the place where women should be.' He waved his hand in the air. 'I know I'm not explaining it well but, you know…'

Winifred clamped her lips together to stop the angry, frustrated words bursting out.

John reached over and patted her hand. 'It's what she calls the natural order of things, Winifred.'

'You're so wrong. She's wrong!'

'She's frightened.'

That was something Winifred definitely didn't believe. Except that her mother was scared other women would escape the lives set out for them, when it was too late for her. 'Well, whatever the reason she doesn't want me to join them, she won't stop me.'

'I know.' He sighed. 'Just try not to talk about it when she'd around, eh, love? For me?'

'I won't.' Winifred stood up. 'I'll see if she wants me to finish clearing away in the shop.' She looked down at him and smiled, her hand resting briefly on his shoulder, feeling guilty that she'd probably upset him. 'You stop here and have a rest; you look tired.'

'I am a bit. But I'm off to see your granny soon.'

'Give her my love. Tell her I'll be round to see her in a couple of days.'

Pausing on the back doorstep, Winifred glanced at him. He'd

leaned back again in the chair, face up to the sky as though trying to get the last of the day's warmth. He looked old, had he lost weight? It worried her. The crash of the shop's till drawer and her mother's rapid footsteps through the parlour and across the flagged kitchen floor stopped her thoughts.

The two women stood face to face without speaking. Winifred knew she'd been right. What ate away inside her mother was the feeling of being trapped in her life. And she certainly didn't want other women to have more freedom than she had.

And, even more than that, she didn't want Winifred to have the power to go out and fight for that freedom. To have that freedom.

Chapter 21

August 1911

'We'll have to keep an eye out for that lot.' Bertie pointed with the long knife he was using to gut the cod on the wooden slab towards the street. The crowds had been building steadily all morning and now streamed past in large numbers. Most of them were women but there were quite a few blokes as well, Bill noticed.

'There'll be trouble, mark my words. *Votes for men under twenty-one,*' Bertie Butterworth scoffed, reading one of the posters held aloft. 'What do kids know about 'ow to vote?' He slapped another cod onto the slab and brought the knife down with a loud thud. The decapitated head fell into the large bucket underneath, already full to the brim with the slime of bloodied fish guts.

They could learn, Bill thought. If somebody took the trouble to show them what's what. He knew nowt about voting because he'd had no-one to explain stuff to him but he knew what was fair and what wasn't. And it wasn't fair that only toffs had a say in running the country. He sniffed. And it wasn't fair his mam had died when he was only a kid. She would have told him what's what, he was sure.

'There'll be trouble I've no doubt.' Bertie shook his head. 'Here, empty this bucket, lad. And then clean the trays.'

'Okay.'

The men and women in the crowd looked around his age, Bill thought, turning to watch them pass while automatically wiping the white trays in the shop window. He envied them. He wouldn't tell Bertie, but he really wished he could be with them. He knew nowt about what them in Government did, but he didn't see why all men shouldn't get to vote. If men under twenty-one did get the vote, he'd be one of them; he'd get to say who gets to be in charge of the country. He didn't believe women should have a say, though. He thought back to his stepmother and sister; thick as two short planks, them two. There's too many of their sort around and not enough of... He let his thoughts trail away before he said her name to himself... Of Winifred's kind; well brought up and knowing what's right – knowing how to listen to what their men had to say.

By dinnertime the street had become even more crowded; a sea of white, purple and green.

And then Bill caught a glimpse of his Winifred in the middle of a line of people. She was pale, her mouth set. The others were laughing and talking but she wasn't joining in. And next to her was that bloke.

He closed his eyes against the sudden flash of temper. His hands trembled. He leant forward into the shop window, trying to see her again, but she was lost amongst the masses.

Soon the crowds dwindled until there was no-one walking past. When Bill finished sluicing down the floor he swept the water out of the shop and across the pavement, into the gutter. He stood in the doorway listening to the chants and singing in the distance. It was as though the air vibrated with the sound. The loneliness that filled every part of him was a shock; he didn't think he'd ever been a part of anything as much as that lot obviously were. No, he corrected himself, being down the mines were near enough; he'd been in a team there, where most blokes looked out for one another.

He crossed his arms, tucked his hands under his armpits, overwhelmed by the sudden sense of loss.

And then there was something else; a low growl. He looked upwards. Iron-grey clouds slid sluggish high in the sky, the air heavy and claggy. He shivered, the feeling of foreboding starting deep inside. It was an old habitual sensation, one he used to get down the mines when there was trouble; a sudden shift in the props, a faint hiss of methane telling them all to get out. And the last time he was below, that instant of deadly silence just before the explosion. Trouble.

Chapter 22

At first there was a hush over the lines of people crushed together in the High Street in Morrisfield. The only sounds were the shuffling of feet on the cobbles, the rustling of clothes, the crack of the material of the banner, waved high by the line of women in front of Winifred.

Winifred's head was too hot under her black, wide-brimmed hat. In the distance there was a low growl of thunder. The air was heavy. Damp tendrils of her hair stuck to her neck, sweat trickled down her back. Over the roofs of the buildings at the end of the street she saw steel-grey clouds slowly rolling towards them, covering the pale blue of the sky.

'I think it's going to rain.' She brushed the green and purple ribbons away from her face, looking anxiously at Honora, wishing she hadn't had to wear her new best hat; now her only one since the ribbon incident when her other was scorched.

'Don't be getting worried about that.' Her friend's dark eyes were narrowed when she turned towards her. 'We've more to worry about than the rain.' She gestured with her hand. 'The eejit bobbies have arrived.'

Policemen on horseback filed out of a side street at the front of the crowd, stopping the forward movement. Winifred could see the straight line break up, a banner drop momentarily before being raised again. Around her there were angry voices, murmurs at first and then, in seconds, shouts.

'Shame. Shame. Let us through.'

'No support for women *from* King George, no support *for* King George.'

She could see the tall square building of the town hall, the long porch fronted by columns, which was the object of the protest; where the local Liberal councillor was holding a meeting to organise a celebration for the coronation of the new king, George.

'Hold tight.' Conal moved between the two women and put his arms around them. The press of bodies increased, and the momentary thrill of feeling his body on Winifred's dissipated in an instant, as panic took over.

'We'll be crushed. We should go.'

'No.' Honora's tone was sharp. 'We need to show our support to the WSPU.'

'Honora – please.'

'No. They tried to show the Suffragettes' patriotism and support for the King when they publicly celebrated his procession in London.' She glared at Winifred. 'The WSPU had been told he'd support the Conciliation Bill. He won't. So we won't let there be any celebrations. He's the same as the rest of them in Parliament.'

'But if we can't get near the town hall—'

'We move forward.'

'I can't. I can't breathe.' She looked up, the canopy of clouds was now a strange mix of leaden yellow and dark grey.

98

And then Conal's mouth was close to Winifred's ear. 'I'll be after looking out for ya. Stay close to me.'

She had no choice. As they were pushed one way and then another, his grip on her pulled her closer to him than she'd ever been before. The thought struck her that, other than her father, she'd actually never been held by a man before. Despite the fear, a quiver of laughter rose inside her. The first time she'd had a man's strong arms around her and she was surrounded by shouting, angry women. If only her mother could see her now.

A sharp pain. Winifred cried out. Something had struck her on her forehead. She staggered. At the same time she was aware that Liam had appeared at Honora's side and heard him say, 'Get her away from here, Conal, I'll look after my girl.'

She saw him bend to kiss her friend. The sounds around came and went in waves, the purple and green colours merged. She was being lifted up and held. Without thinking she put her arms around Conal's neck and rested her head against his chest, giving in to the swirling dizziness.

Chapter 23

'Storm coming in.' Bertie appeared behind Bill. 'Might as well shut up shop anyway.'

The fishmonger stood with his fists on his thick waistline in the shop doorway. 'Listen to that.' He cocked his head to one side. 'Sounds to me there's trouble, like I said there would be.' Even from three streets away Bill heard the smashing of glass and the screams and shouts. 'That lot'll be back this way, and no decent woman'll come out to be stuck among them.' He turned back into the shop. 'Put the boards up, lad.'

Bill had only just slotted the last board over the window when the first few people ran past. Some of the women were screaming, eyes and mouths wide with distress. One or two of them had blood splattered on their clothes, one held her hand to her cheek, blood pouring down her neck.

Bill started towards her. ''Ere, let me help.'

He was stopped by Bertie's shout. 'Get in the shop and shut the door. Now!'

Bill clenched his jaw but let his arm drop to his side. By heck, if he was his own boss, no bugger would tell him what to do. The woman, who had faltered and moved towards him, staggered into a run again. For a moment Bill thought to go after her but knowing he'd get the sack turned on his heel to go back into the shop.

It was then he saw the Irishman. Running and holding *his* Winifred to him. She had her arms around his neck, her face hidden but Bill would have recognised her anywhere. She didn't have the hat on anymore and her hair hung onto her shoulders in long loose locks.

'What the bloody 'ell?' He moved towards them.

'Bill!' Bertie warned from the doorway.

Rage stuck in Bill's throat; he wanted to tell the man to stick his job. More than that he wanted to run after the Irish bastard and tear Winifred away from him.

He watched the man hold up one arm. A tram clattering along the main road at the end of the street, screeched to a halt, sparks flying from the rods.

They disappeared inside the tram.

Chapter 24

'I should go home.'

The air was thick and heavy, and the black clouds were solid by the time they'd arrived at Gilpin Street. Winifred gasped as white light flashed in the distance over Morrisfield, followed shortly by a loud crack of thunder.

'Not in this.' Conal backed up to the front door of the house, manoeuvring it open and carried her into the dim hallway, taking the stairs two at a time.

'And not until I've cleaned ya up.' He settled her on Honora's bed and straightened up, lighting the gas mantle on the wall above her head. 'By yer a right weight.' He mimicked a Yorkshire accent, obviously trying to make her smile.

She did, remembering the time not long ago when she'd imitated his, but the movement caused a sharp pain near her eye and she winced.

He gestured towards the window. 'It's lashing rain out there.' He unfolded the blankets from the foot of the bed and covered her.

He was right, as soon as he'd kicked the front door shut behind them the rain had started, first in slow, heavy drops, then as a downpour. The reflection of sudden lightning shimmered against the rippling water on the panes, lit up the walls of the room.

Winifred closed her eyes, snuggling down under the blankets. 'I'm cold,' she murmured. How could she be so cold when only a short while ago she'd been so stifling hot?

'It'll be the shock.' Conal perched on the edge of the bed, holding a basin of water and a piece of cloth. 'To be sure, you'll have a shiner tomorrow.' His touch was gentle. Even so, she flinched each time he dabbed at the cut. The water in the bowl turned pink. She could tell he was worried from the slight frown and the pulling in of the corners of his mouth. 'I'd like to get hold of the bastard who threw that stone,' he muttered. Winifred lay still, aware of his closeness, their shared breath. Lifting the cloth away after a few moments he peered underneath at the gash over her eyes. His mouth was so close to hers. She closed her eyes. His lips were on her cheek. And then on her lips. No pressure, just a slight brushing, a warmth. And then gone. She realised she was holding her breath and felt the treacherous disappointment of her body.

'Sorry, Win.'

'No.' She couldn't believe what she was saying. 'It's all right.' Her first kiss. Here of all places. Here, unchaperoned, alone with a man. With this man, of all men. But she didn't care; she didn't care that she knew it was wrong, that she hardly knew Honora's brother. She didn't care, she told herself. She raised her face, ignoring the throbbing from the cut as she moved, half closed her eyes, watched as he moved closer.

'My *mhuirnín*. My sweetheart.'

The kiss was the most exquisite sensation she'd ever known. This was what she'd been waiting for, wanted from the moment she'd set eyes on him.

And then it was over.

Disappointed she opened her eyes; saw her regret in his, even as he spoke.

'Try to rest for a while.'

And then he was gone.

Chapter 25

When she woke she was still alone. How long had she slept? The storm seemed to have passed. There was light through the thin curtains but it felt late. Winifred's stomach lurched; had she really allowed Conal to kiss her? She remembered how her body had reacted and wondered if he'd noticed and been shocked, even though he was the one who'd kissed her first. Was that why he'd apologised? She pushed at the blankets covering her at the same time as she pushed away the thought. The only thing she wanted to do was to go home; she should have been there now.

There were voices coming from the other room. When she sat up her head swam, and she took a few deep breaths until she steadied. Putting her feet to the floor she waited, feeling the throb of the cut on her forehead. She touched it cautiously; there was no blood.

The door opened slightly and Honora peeped in.

'You're awake.' She came into the room. She was wearing a long red gown, different from the one she'd worn earlier. Her black hair hung around her shoulders. 'We got wet through,' she said, pulling her lips into a grimace. 'It didn't need all those police to break us up after all.'

Winifred didn't acknowledge her words. 'What time is it?'

'Just gone eight.'

'It feels later. I should go home.'

Honora sat next to Winifred and grasped her hand. 'I feel a bit bad, Win. Ya wouldn't have been there if I hadn't persuaded ya—'

'It was…is my choice I'm involved.'

'How are you feeling?'

'Groggy.' Winifred squeezed her eyes closed, thankful it didn't send the sharp pain through her head as it had earlier. 'Better. I need to go home.' Her mother never missed a chance to snipe about the Suffragettes and the way Winifred was in danger of losing her reputation; there was no point in giving her extra opportunity to nag. Besides, she knew her father would be worried by now.

'Conal's told me.' Honora grinned, tucking a strand of her hair behind her ear. 'About ya – and him.'

'We didn't do anything.' The warmth rose on Winifred's throat.

'I know.' The Irish girl looked affronted. 'My brother would never take advantage.' Then she laughed. 'But I can't say I'm surprised, I knew ya were taken with him the first time ya met.'

'I was not. I hardly know him.' Winifred stopped, startled by the memory of the feel of his lips on hers. 'I hardly know him,' she repeated.

'But ya will. And when ya do, ya'll fall madly in love with him. I promise.' Honora laughed. 'He has the charm of the Irish.' She stood. 'I'll get dressed and then we'll walk ya home; make sure ya get there safe.' Looking down at Winifred she said, 'Conal really likes ya, Win. You could do worse.'

Winifred doubted her mother would agree.

They said little, walking back to Marshall Road. Despite her initial protests, Winifred was glad of their support when they linked their arms through hers.

Conscious of the warmth of his body, she kept herself stiff and upright, trying to keep as little contact as possible with Conal.

Reaching the end of Cook Street Winifred disengaged herself from them both. 'I'll be fine now,' she said.

'And I'll be off. 'Honora walked away with a wave of her hand and no explanation. 'See ya soon, Win.'

Dismayed at being left alone with Conal, Winifred was at a loss for words. Her only wish was to escape; mortified that she'd behaved in such an immoral way earlier.

'Will ya not look at me, my *mhuirnín*?'

Winifred shook her head, refusing to meet his gaze.

'I've offended ya.'

'Oh, no.' Dismayed, she looked at the ground. 'It's me. I shouldn't have let you kiss me.' She mumbled the words. 'I shouldn't have let you take me back to your house. It wasn't proper.'

'Ya were in no fit state to go to yours.' Conal lifted her chin with his forefinger so she had to look at him. 'I don't kiss girls lightly, Win.' He gave a soft chuckle. 'In fact you're the first girl I've kissed in a long time, sure ya are.'

'I don't... I haven't...' She closed her eyes and drew in a shuddering breath.

'I know. I guessed.' He held onto her shoulders. 'I respect ya, I promise. I always will. It'll be hard.' He chuckled again. 'But I surely won't take advantage of you, Winifred, I never would. Do ya believe me?'

She moved her head slightly. 'Yes.'

'So, will ya walk out with me?' He whispered the words as though he hardly dare say them.

'I don't know. I need to think.' She sensed his disappointment.

'It's your ma and da? They'll be against us. Me?'

'Yes.'

'Then I'll wait.'

Winifred knew it wouldn't matter how long he waited, her mother would never allow it. Rebellion flashed through her. She looked up into his eyes, saw the determination and love in them 'Kiss me again,' she said.

Chapter 26

Bill sat in the corner by the empty fireplace in the Wagon and Horses, the misery a cold lump inside him. He couldn't get Winifred out of his head but he knew he had no chance with her. She was too good for him, too posh, too nice, a different class. What had he to offer? He was nowt.

It was a long time since he'd had this overwhelming feeling of helplessness: the lurching in his stomach each time he got a glimpse of her, the yearning to talk to her, to touch with love. It was a very long time since he'd touched a woman with love and not just because he needed sex. He pushed that memory away; that first love. It still hurt.

His hands shook as he lifted the pint pot to his mouth, gulping down his second pint of beer. He couldn't afford another pint and he shouldn't be getting drunk. But feeling like this made him weak and he hated feeling weak.

And anyway, except for being taller...and better looking... what had that Irish bastard got to offer her any different from what he could? From what Bill could tell the bloke had nowt either. But what did he know.

He thumped his pint pot onto the table and looked across to

the bar. He found it impossible to stop thinking about that Irish bastard mauling *his* Winifred. He was going to have to do something about it. But first he'd have another pint and sod the expense.

The storm had gone through hours ago; it had fair rained and the lightning had lit up the sky in great jagged lines for ages. But now the air was fresh, and most of the locals were sitting on the benches outside, which was a good thing because he didn't feel like talking. Not right at the minute, not while he was trying to sort out in his mind what to do. What he wanted to do.

He was unsteady on his feet when he at last stood up and made for the door. He saw the three of them walk along the street and stop on the corner. He saw the Irish girl leave. He saw Winifred talking to the Irish bastard. He saw her lift her face to the man's so he could kiss her.

Bill's despair quickly turned to anger and the anger cleared his head. Why was she acting like a trollop? That wasn't what she was.

The last gulp of beer came back up his throat and he gagged. Had he been kidding himself? Was she was no better than the harlots that paraded the streets at night in Morrisfield? Little better than a threepenny-upright? No, he wouldn't believe that of her. At least he wouldn't have believed it if he hadn't seen it with his own eyes. Taking in a long breath he wiped his hand over his face, feeling the weakness of scalding tears. Well, at least he'd found out before it was too late. Before he made a complete bloody fool of himself.

Perhaps it was best he moved on; forgot all his fanciful hopes. It looked as if she'd made her choice and he wouldn't hang around hankering after her. But he'd miss having a regular wage. And he hadn't saved all that much since he got work. If he was going to get right away from this dump, he'd need more money in his pocket.

Chapter 27

Winifred knew she'd have a fight on her hands with her mother the minute she walked into the shop. With her hat lost there was no way she could hide the cut on her forehead.

But as chance would have it she was in luck, only her father was there, packing slabs of butter for the following day.

'You're late, love. She's been going mad this last hour,' he said, turning to put the butter away. His eyes showed his worry and his smile seemed forced when he looked at her. 'Good grief, child, what happened?' He came round the counter, wiping his hands on a cloth and tilted her head towards the lit gas mantle. 'That's nasty, are you all right?'

'I am. It's nothing, honestly. I fell. Honora tidied me up.' She wouldn't tell him how the protest march had disintegrated into chaos. And she certainly wouldn't tell him where she went afterwards.

'I've been waiting for you. I told Mother I needed to sort the butter out. And then I wanted to do the window display.'

Keeping out of her mother's way, more like it, Winifred thought. 'I'll help.'

'No, you get off upstairs. Get some rest, you look worn out.'

'You're certain? You look tired yourself.'

'I'm fine. Off you go.'

'Where's Mother now?'

He lowered his eyelids and nodded towards the parlour. 'Go quiet; I think she's having forty winks. I'll tell her you've been in ages if she comes in here.'

She gave him a quick kiss on the cheek. 'Thanks, Dad.'

After a moment of hesitation she escaped to her room. Watching herself undressing in the wardrobe mirror she didn't look any different. She believed she was in love with Conal and had always imagined that being in love would make you look different. But no, she was the same. Except, as she looked closer, she saw the way her eyes shone, the way her lips quivered into a slight smile without her being aware of it. Then she touched the cut above her eyebrow. If he was right and she did have a bruise around her eye in the morning she'd need to have an excuse ready.

But her last thoughts as she got into bed were how she would tell her parents about her growing feelings for Conal. He said he was willing to wait until they accepted him, so it was only fair she gave them a chance to. It would probably mean a fight with her mother. She'd made no bones about the fact she despised Honora, so it would be worse for Conal. As a man her mother would be convinced he was an Irish Nationalist in England to plot against the Government. Or after getting his hands on the shop by courting her.

It had always upset Winifred that Ethel had no qualms in claiming that she came from a family "with connections" and by marrying John she had married beneath her. Before her talk with her granny, two months ago, Winifred had known no different. Now she knew it was actually her father's parents who were the ones who had money, who were probably better socially connected than Ethel's. With that knowledge she could use her mother's snobbery against her; make her face the truth, that it was her father who had married beneath him. She could have no argument against her daughter doing the so-called same. She would have to accept Conal. Winifred smiled and snuggled lower under the covers.

Besides, her father would be on her side. She could always rely on that.

Chapter 28

Bill hadn't reckoned on the shopkeeper coming back into the shop.

The gas mantles had been turned off for ten minutes. He'd

watched the man mess about in the window for ages. He'd seen him counting out the money from the till and taking the canvas bag through a door behind the counter. But he hadn't gone near the shop door as far as Bill could tell. Looked like he'd forgotten to lock up; Bill couldn't believe his luck.

He held the bell in his palm as he slid through the door, stopping the clang. He listened. Nothing.

Waiting until his eyes adjusted to the darkness the rasp of his shallow breathing sounded loud but when he held it back the only noise he heard was the creaking of floorboards above.

With a grunt of satisfaction he crept around the wooden boxes of bundled firewood in the corner by the counter and to the back of the shop. Opening the door where he'd watched the shop owner take the bag, he lit a match and held it in front of him. It wasn't a room, it was a cupboard. On the floor were small sacks. He pulled at the top of each, peering inside: flour, sugar, tea. His heart thumped in his chest. The walls were full of shelves stacked high with tins of food and packs of what looked like butter. But no bag of money.

The flame burned along the wood of the match and grew hot against his fingers. 'Blast.' Bill blew it out and lit another, studying the shelves. One line of canned meat looked jumbled in the middle of the shelf. Bill reached up and lifted one off. The canvas bag was behind. Grinning, he lifted it down. It was heavy and rustled. When he shook it coins inside jingled softly. He swiftly tucked the bag under his coat.

He was halfway between the counter and the shop door when the man came through the back door holding a candle.

'What the…'

The two men stared at each other.

Bill's legs began to shake. He could feel cold sweat trickling down his spine. 'Stay there or you'll be bloody sorry!' The words of warning came out thin and reedy. He backed away.

'Get out of here.' John Duffy spoke quietly. 'Go on, clear off.'

109

He looked at the open door of the cupboard and then back at Bill, raising his voice. 'Give that bag to me.' Carrying the candle he walked towards Bill. 'Just drop the bag and go.'

'Keep back.' Bill pointed at the man, fingers trembling. 'Don't come any closer, yer daft bugger. I don't want to hurt you. Keep back.' He looked around, saw the empty wooden crates stacked by the door and, dropping the bag, picked up one of them up and flung it towards John Duffy. The candle seemed to hang in the air before the flame flickered, went out. In the darkness Bill knew the crate had made contact from the groan and sickening thud as the man fell.

Oh God. 'Stupid old fool,' he whispered, unable to make his feet move. 'Stupid old fool.' What the hell had he done? The man moaned again. He was alive. Thankful, Bill forced himself to move. He scrabbled around on the floor for the bag. When he found it he struggled to his feet and limped from the shop. Outside he looked around. The street was empty. He ran as fast as his bad leg would let him.

Chapter 29

The yelling woke Winifred. Without thinking she swung her legs over the edge of the bed. And stopped. Nothing. Had it been a nightmare? The house was silent. And dark. She crept across the room and opened to listen. Nothing. Her parents' bedroom door was open; there was a stub of a candle on the tallboy. Their bed looked strange and then she understood why; on one side the covers were smooth, unused. Only her mother's side had the eiderdown thrown back.

The next yell made her skin tighten. 'Winifred! Get down here. Now!'

Winifred ran. 'What is it?' She peered into the gloom of the shop, lit only by the candle her mother was holding.

110

'We've been robbed. The bolts aren't on the door.' Her mother stood behind the counter by the cash register. 'The old fool hasn't locked up. We're wide open to the elements – and thieves. Go, pull the shade down over the window and lock the door.'

'Where's Dad?'

'*I* don't know. Probably out in the back yard, in the lavatory, the stupid man.'

Winifred pushed passed her mother to go to close the shop door. She had only taken two steps when, with a sharp cry, she stumbled over the still figure of her father lying, face down in front of the counter. She dropped to her knees next to him. 'Dad!' With shaking fingers Winifred put her hand on his back. She wasn't sure if she could sense any movement. 'Dad? Mother, bring the candle.' Panic skittered through her.

'Has he had a heart attack?' Ethel stared down at him. She put the candle on the top of the counter, pulling the sash of her dressing gown tighter and wrapping the ends around her fingers. She sounded calm.

'I don't know.' Winifred glared up at her, her voice harsh. 'I can't tell. For God's sake, Mother. Help me to turn him onto his back.'

Her mother didn't move.

'Well, if you won't help at least you could go for the doctor.' Winifred shouted. She gently straightened her father's outstretched arms down by his side and tried to roll him over cradling his head in the crook of her arm.

'And meet the robbers outside? They're probably watching the shop still.'

'Why? The till's empty. They've got what they wanted. Oh my god...'

There was a huge deep wound at the front of her father's head, the blood already congealing. His eyes were blank, staring upwards. Winifred fell backwards, her hand to her mouth, a wave of dizziness making her want to vomit. Her father, her Dad, must have been lying there on his own for some hours; probably while she slept upstairs.

'He's dead.' She stared up at her mother.

There was a strange expression on Ethel's face. When Winifred remembered it, later that day, she thought it might actually have been relief.

Chapter 30

'Cold he was…'

Bill froze. He held the fish cleaver in mid-air and lifted his head quickly to look into the mirrored wall above the bench. The woman who'd spoken wore the melodramatic expression of someone delivering a line in a play. She jerked her folded arms under her ample bosom. It jiggled under the thin coat she wore.

'Stiff as a board,' she added, looking around to the women queued behind her.

There were a few horrified gasps. Bertie continued to wrap the plaice, his mouth set in a grim line. Putting the fish into the woman's basket on the counter top he said, 'It's a bad do all right. That'll be tuppence, Mrs Kelly.'

Bill swallowed; it couldn't be…?

'Been there all night, apparently.' Another woman, the brim of her hat bobbing in rhythm with her head, peered around from the back of the queue.

The muttering between the customers increased.

'How awful.'

'What is the world coming to?'

'Dreadful!'

'In his own shop…'

Everything began to spin. Bill lowered the cleaver and held on to the edge of the bench. He closed his eyes.

The first woman's voice rose, obviously upset that someone was taking centre stage. 'Thief's run off with the week's takings according to Mrs Duffy.'

There was a murmur of sympathy and understanding before Bill heard another voice.

'Can't see her leaving a week's takings lying around. Not Mrs Duffy. A day's perhaps…'

There was a shocked hush.

'There's your change, Mrs Kelly.' There was impatience in Bertie's voice. 'Next please.'

Bill opened his eyes to watch the woman leave.

At the door she turned. 'Not nice to think there's a murderer running around the streets. I'd make sure my door was locked, if I were you, Mr Butterworth. The same goes for you ladies, as well.'

Bill brought the cleaver down hard on the haddock, just missing his thumb. Trembling he leaned against the bench staring down at the bloodied fish. What the hell had he done? He wiped the back of his hand over his mouth, bile burning his throat. Heaving, he ran out to the back yard of the shop. Pressing the flat of his hands on the wall he retched until there was nothing left in his stomach. When he finally was able to lift his head and look back towards the shop Bertie was standing in the doorway.

'You all right, lad?'

'Aye, must have eaten summat rotten.'

'Aye, well… We best be careful. Take the rest of the day off.'

'I will if you don't mind. I've griping bellyache.'

Bill didn't remember getting to Lydcroft: the tram ride was a blur, the walk along Marshall Road automatic. It was only when he stood in front of a house on the corner across from the shop that the horror of what he'd done hit him again.

The blinds of the window were pulled down, the upstairs curtains drawn, the door closed. Despite the warmth of the July day he shook. When he rubbed his hand across his face his skin was damp and chilly.

A black car drew up in front of the shop and two black-suited men got out and banged on the door. Bill thought his legs were going to give way under him; he slid down the wall of the house and sprawled. Fumbling with the packet he tugged a cigarette out but crumpled it in his fist when he couldn't get the match to light, and threw it to one side.

He was conscious of people passing him, looking down at him with curiosity. A woman sniffed as though disgusted and pulled her skirt to one side, away from him as though he would contaminate her.

'Stupid cow,' Bill muttered, taking his eyes off the shop to glower at her. When he looked back the door was open and the two men were standing on the pavement. Winifred was with them. Bill struggled to his feet. The movement caught her attention and she glanced across at him. He saw the way she took a second look at him, a confused frown creasing her forehead. His stomach lurched, his skin prickled with fear. Any moment now, he thought and she'd remember where she'd seen him, wonder why he was standing there. He couldn't get it out of his head that it wouldn't take long for her to put two and two together. He spun on his heels, walking towards the Wagon and Horses as fast as he could. He didn't dare look back.

In the pub he collapsed onto the nearest chair, rested his elbows on the small round table and held his head in the palms of his hands. Whatever happened next, whatever he did, would affect the rest of his life. And he hadn't a bloody clue what that would be.

Chapter 31

The horse-drawn carriage carrying John Duffy's coffin creaked slowly along the wet street. Turning to look behind her, Winifred saw the long line of people all in black huddled under umbrellas as they followed the hearse through the terraced streets towards the chapel.

Under her own umbrella Ethel walked next to her, keeping her head lowered, the thick veil covering her face. The new full-length serge coat, braided with silk facings and cuffs had cost a pretty penny, Winifred thought resentfully. Yet, unable to bring herself to pay for one of those new motorised hearses, John's widow had declared the carriage '…fuss enough for a man who lived a simple life.'

All week, it hadn't been the image of her father inert on the floor of the shop that had haunted Winifred; it was the worried expression on his face when she'd rushed into the shop the evening before he died. She'd known he was troubled, she'd known he deserved the respect of an explanation, the truth; what had made her so late, the cut on her forehead, what she'd been doing. She'd told him she was going to the protest. It must have been on his mind all day. So he'd probably been fretting for hours.

She couldn't forgive herself for that.

At the gate of the chapel six men waited to carry the coffin in.

She walked around to the front of the carriage and placed her hand on the soft muzzle of the black horse. It nudged her arm and blew down its nostrils. She saw her reflection in the large dark eyes; it didn't look like her.

Her mother's tone was sharp, coming from somewhere behind the hearse. 'Winifred.'

She became aware that the line of mourners had stopped, the drumming of the rain on the large black umbrellas the only sound as they waited for the procession to continue into the chapel. The six men had hoisted her father's coffin onto their shoulders from the back of the carriage and were shifting from side to side under the hard weight. And, grim and holding his Bible close to his chest, the minister was watching her, his cassock streaked with the downpour.

'Sorry,' she muttered, stepping away from the horse and to one side. The black veil of her hat trembled with the breath expelled, but her voice didn't; she'd saved her mourning, her sobbing, for the privacy of her room. She and her mother had hardly spoken to one another since her father's death. Their words had been saved for the police after the robbery and the meetings with the minister and the funeral director.

Not that either Winifred or Florence Duffy had been allowed much say in anything to do with the arrangements for her father's final resting place. She'd understood from the start that her mother was determined to arrange everything as cheaply and as quickly as possible.

'A small, simple affair,' had been Ethel's stock phrase over the last week, even when her mother-in-law had sent a message by Winifred offering to pay towards expenses.

A small, simple affair. Both of them knew that meant over and done with as soon as possible, so Florence had refused to attend the funeral, claiming she would mourn in her own way. And Ethel had refused the offer from neighbours to provide for a gathering in the chapel hall afterwards. Winifred was convinced that, if she hadn't been so conscious of opinion, her mother would have opened the shop as soon as they got back home.

Home. It struck Winifred that 'home' would have a totally different meaning now. Without her father to stand between them, it would be an uneasy existence.

In the chapel Winifred was only aware of the soft scuff of feet on the stone floor, the hushed whispers, the muffled sobs, the theatrical lifting of the veil when her mother dabbed at her eyes. Putting on a show for everyone, Winifred thought, indignantly, when the woman who truly loved her father was sitting alone in that awful house in Wellyhole Yard, grieving the loss of her only son.

The minister's eulogy was impersonal and short. The organ began to wheeze and groan and then, each note held just a fraction too long, rumbled out the hymn *The Day Thou Gavest,*

116

Lord, Is Ended and everyone stood to sing. She didn't, despite the sharp jab into her side from her mother.

The rain had stopped by the time the service was over. The burial took only minutes; everything that needed to be said about John Duffy had been said. Winifred was comforted by the silent presence of his friends behind her as she stared down at the cheap coffin nestled in the rectangular square of soil. She couldn't help the thought that he was at peace now, despite the violent end to his life. She needed to think that, otherwise the unfairness of her father being taken from her would be too much to bear.

Turning away, Ethel rested her hand on Winifred's arm. The distaste that instinctively rose caused Winifred to take a step away from her mother. She didn't care if anyone saw.

Taking a last look at her father's coffin Winifred went to the two men waiting to fill in the grave and pressed a shilling in each of their hands. It crossed her mind that it was as though she was asking them to be gentle. Senseless, but they nodded as though they understood.

Leaving her mother to make her own way, Winifred followed the minister back to the chapel and waited in the porch with him as the mourners filed past, returning the slight pressures on her fingers as some gave her reassuring touches of their hands, dipping her head to the murmured phrases of condolence. She could feel her mother's impatience at her side, and knew she'd been annoyed at the numbers of people who'd attended the funeral; the unknown amount of friends her husband had gathered during his life. Winifred got a certain satisfaction from hearing her mother's sighs of irritation.

'Right, that's that.' Ethel followed the last mourners, wending her way through the groups gathered on the path exchanging memories of her husband and ignoring them.

Winifred watched her mother go through the gate and along the road shaking her head in disbelief at Ethel's last words. Patting Winifred on the shoulder, the minister turned into the chapel with a few murmured sounds of sympathy.

Then she was alone.

'I'm pure sorry, Win. We've been thinking about ya.'

Startled, she turned, to be enveloped in a tight hug from Honora. The familiar smell of paint and white spirit that clung to her friend comforted Winifred. It made her remember that she had a life with friends away from the shop. 'Don't be so long to come to see us.'

'I'll wait for you,' was all Conal said. But the light touch of his fingers on her cheek under the veil made her skin tingle.

Chapter 32

Bill hunched his shoulders against the steady rain and pulled his cap lower over his eyes when the funeral procession passed him. He doubted she'd notice, let alone recognise him, but it didn't hurt to be careful. Once this was over he'd be gone. The thought of not seeing Winifred ever again made his throat tight. But the idea of staying around and possibly being found out was terrifying; he wasn't going to be fodder for the hangman.

He couldn't see her face because of the thick black veil, but he noticed she had a white handkerchief clenched in her hand. He needn't have worried about her seeing him; she looked only into the horse-drawn carriage carrying John Duffy's coffin in front of her.

The guilt flooded through Bill. It was the same overwhelming remorse that had kept him turning in his bed the last few nights. The same shame that brought the nightmares when he did manage an hour's sleep. He gnawed at the inside of his mouth, tasting the blood. If he could go back in time he wouldn't have drunk so much. He hadn't been thinking straight when he went to the shop. He'd needed revenge. To take something from her in the same way she'd taken all hope from him. Even if she didn't know it. All he wanted was to hurt her somehow, in the same way she'd hurt him by giving herself to that Irish bastard. In the way she'd stopped being *his* Winifred.

If only the stupid old bastard had locked the door.

What a bloody mess.

He stared at the coffin in the hearse. The heavy drops of rain smeared the glass so that the white wreath inside shimmered into irregular shapes. Except for the occasional sob and stifled cough, the creaking of the carriage, the gushing of water running in the gutters near his feet, and the clang of metal hooves on the road were the only sounds. The line of people, hidden under umbrellas, moved in the funeral procession without a word.

When the procession stopped outside the small chapel he watched Winifred walk to the front of the carriage and stroke the muzzle of the black horse, heard her mother speak sharply to her. Saw the way the girl stiffened and, with her head held high, follow the coffin.

Waiting until the last people had filed into the chapel, Bill followed, stuffing his cap into his jacket pocket and slipping into the back row. Despite the rain it wasn't cold outside but now, hunched in the far corner of the pew, Bill shivered in the cool air of the small chapel.

He shut out the drone of the minister's voice. Deprived of sleep for so many nights he almost dozed, but was startled by the rumble and whistle of the organ. Coming from a family that had never seen the inside of a church he didn't know the hymn but he stood anyway, craning his neck to see Winifred when everyone rose to sing.

It was a quick service; even he could sense that. As soon as he noticed the restless movement of the congregation; the standing, adjusting of hats and gloves by the women, the men giving release to long-suppressed coughs, Bill left. From behind he heard the scuff of the bearers' footsteps on the stone floor, as they went to take the weight of the coffin again.

The rain had cleared. He ran through the puddles on the

gravelled path to hide behind a large oak that towered over the wall of the cemetery. Heavy drops of water fell off the leaves and down his neck but he couldn't move; the mourners were making their way to the freshly dug grave. Scowling, he jammed his cap on and turned up his collar.

The burial was as short as the service. When the minister led the way back to the porch of the chapel, followed by Winifred, Bill took the opportunity to climb over the wall and down onto the narrow lane. He scurried along to watch from the safety of the sycamore trees that lined Harrison Street.

He saw people stop in front of the chapel to say a few words to Winifred and her mother; gathering in quiet groups before eventually drifting away from the cemetery. At first he wondered where they would go for the wake. But everyone seemed to be going in different directions.

The crowd dwindled, and the mother walked off on her own. Bill moved back so he was partially hidden by the trunk of the sycamore. The old cow didn't even glance back to look for her daughter. And it certainly didn't appear to bother her that Winifred greeted the last of the mourners alone. Bill couldn't take his eyes off her. She looked so small, so lonely. He wouldn't have left her on her own; he would have been proud to stand alongside her, to put his arm around her. Given the chance, he would make up for what he'd done, even if it took a lifetime. He was so consumed with the guilt and the urge, the need to comfort her he took a couple of steps forward.

But there were still two mourners left. Bill squinted to see them better, took in a short harsh breath. It was the Irish girl, and the Irish bastard.

When he saw the way the man put his hand on Winifred the resentment boiled over, swamping the guilt, and Bill clamped his teeth together as the Irish pair walked past him. They didn't even realise he was there. He felt so useless he could have wept.

He waited for Winifred's next move. It was obvious there was to be no wake, no gathering to mourn the man outside the chapel.

Pitiful excuse for a funeral.

Chapter 33

Winifred couldn't stand the thought of following her mother home, of being alone with her. Keeping the thick black veil over her face and averting her head when she passed anyone, she turned onto Wellyhole Terrace and made her way slowly to her grandmother's house, hot in the heavy mourning clothes, the hem of her skirt soaking up the now steaming wet from the pavements.

The smells in the yard were particularly obnoxious today. An unsmiling woman, iron-grey hair falling untidily from a knotted turban, the front of her pinny splattered with greasy stains, was brushing foul water and garbage towards a central grid. She looked towards Winifred without speaking. Behind her, one of the dustbins was overturned and two mangy dogs were scavenging amongst the waste.

Holding her breath until she could open Florence's door, Winifred willed herself to be strong for her grandmother.

Florence's eyelids were swollen, the tears sliding slowly down the creases of her cheek. Winifred perched on the arm of the armchair and they held hands, sitting in silence for a long time.

Eventually Florence spoke. 'She never loved him, you know.' She dabbed an already-wet handkerchief across her face, took in a breath. It was as though she was going to say more but merely sighed.

'But a lot of people did, Granny, the chapel was packed. And, afterwards, there were so many who had nothing but good things to say about him.'

'She got her way, though, I suppose; it was a paltry affair.'

There was a question in her tone that Winifred had to acknowledge. 'She did. I'm sorry, Granny.'

121

'Not your fault, ducks, not your fault.'

'It didn't do Dad justice, Granny. But, like I said, there were such a lot there. It showed how respected he was, how many friends he had.' She studied her grandmother's hand, held in her palm. The knuckles along each finger were enlarged with arthritis, large blue veins pushed up against the thin skin. She ran her thumb over them. 'You should have been there, Granny, you would have seen for yourself.'

'No. It's enough that you've told me, ducks. That's my comfort.' Florence closed her eyes. 'I'm tired, Winnie. I think I'll have a lie down. It's this heat, it gets to me; makes it difficult to breath.'

'I know. Even the rain was warm this morning.' Winifred helped her grandmother to her feet. 'Come on, let's get you settled down.'

They climbed the ten steps to the landing, which led to Florence's small bedroom under the eaves of the house. Winifred noticed that the thin wooden edges of the treads were splintered, sharp. She caught her lower lip between her teeth; the whole place was so dangerous. There had to be a way to get her grandmother somewhere else to live.

'You'll stay for a bit?' Florence eased herself onto the bed and, with a few stifled groans settled back onto the mattress.

'I will, Granny.' Winifred covered her with just the sheet, folding the eiderdown to the end of the bed. 'I'm in no rush to get back.'

She didn't for a minute think that her grandmother would be able to sleep amidst the cacophony of noise coming from the front house and the shouts of women in the yard, drifting from the open window of the parlour below. But, in no time at all, listening at the bedroom door, she heard the soft whistle and snore.

'Goodness me, out like a light,' she murmured.

She pottered for a while, clearing away a cup and a plate of bread and dripping from the table, rinsing a pair of her grandmother's pink bloomers in the stone sink and hanging them on the rack in the kitchen. When she could find nothing else to do she went back up to the parlour and, closing the window against the stench and noise outside, settled into Florence's chair.

She'd always hated the thought of her grandmother living here. Now matters were worse; without her father calling in each day, the responsibility rested with her. She didn't resent that. In fact, at one point in the days since his death, Winifred had debated if she should move in with Florence. But, even if there'd been a second bedroom, she knew she couldn't live with the chaos that was Wellyhole Yard.

The only answer was that her grandmother should live with them at the shop. But with that decision came a lot of difficulties: the main one being her mother.

Winifred knew just how much she was going to miss her dad. There was no-one now to talk to, to advise her. Except her grandmother. And this was one problem she couldn't discuss with her; Florence Duffy would never be beholden to her daughter-in-law.

Winifred closed her eyes and rested her head against the back of the chair. In no time at all she too slept, oblivious to the noise around her.

Chapter 34

She hadn't lifted the thick black veil over her face and she'd turned away when she passed him but he heard her quiet sobs and the guilt rose in him again.

She obviously wasn't going home. He followed her, curious to see where she went. When she turned into some sort of yard he stopped, surprised. Even standing at the entrance he could smell the obnoxious stench of the place. What the hell was she doing here?

He lingered for a few minutes to see if she came back out. Some kids came out of one of the houses, yelling and kicking a tightly rolled up ball of string. Once it came near him and he kicked it back. But they just stared at him, wary of a stranger in their midst. A fat woman, scratching her armpits, came to the door to watch him.

Bill returned her stare, oddly reluctant to leave without seeing Winifred come out of that yard; to make sure she was safe.

What did he care? But he did. He also needed to leave. The longer he stayed around Lydcroft, the more dangerous it was for him. What if he'd been seen that night? What if that person saw him now?

He leant against the nearest wall, trying to look casual, and lit a cigarette. But his heart was thudding. Sometimes, in the dark early hours of the day, he imagined himself explaining to Winifred about that night. Imagined she would understand that he hadn't meant to kill her father.

But then he'd have to tell her why, that all he'd wanted to do was to get some money so he could leave Morrisfield because he'd seen her with another man. And there it stopped, the story he'd concocted. Because how could she understand when she didn't know how he felt about her. Hardly knew he even existed.

It was her fault he was in this mess. If he told himself that often enough he would believe it. Perhaps.

Well, he'd got the money now. Enough to get him right away. And that's what he'd do.

Bill spun on his heel and walked away. He'd leave. Leave Morrisfield. Leave his job. Leave Winifred behind. But inside he knew he wouldn't leave the memory of her behind. Not now. Not ever.

Chapter 35

In the end, it was the reading of John Duffy's will that sorted out Florence's housing issue.

After the solicitor left, Ethel went to her bedroom without a word, lips tight, her face and throat scarlet with anger. She'd listened in glowering silence as Mr Winterbottom ponderously laid out the conditions of the bequests. When he tried to hand her a folded copy she ignored him and didn't look his way when Winifred took him through the shop to the front door.

Winifred picked up her copy of the will and took it into the yard to read. The heat of the day had soaked into the stone of the house and the bricks of the yard's walls. Even though the fierce August sun was no longer on the back it was still stifling hot, and within minutes she could feel the dampness of perspiration between her breasts. Even so she was reluctant to go back into the kitchen where the air seemed rancid with her mother's hostility. She read the document again; there was no doubt what her father had wanted. Her eyes pricked with tears, even as she smiled; he'd made sure she would be all right. She wanted to laugh and cry at the same time as the realization of what she was about to do filled her with relief.

Leaving the shop she hurried along Marshall Road, dodging around whoever got in her way on the pavement, her hand clutching the folded will in the skirt pocket of her dress. She forced herself to slow down before she got to the Wagon and Horses. There were groups of men sitting at the wooden benches, holding large glasses of ale and sucking on pipes, their shirt collars undone and sleeves rolled up to combat the heat of the evening. Head lowered, she ignored their whistles and catcalls and turned onto Wagon Street where she began to run, aware only of the thud of her heels on the ground and the tightness in her chest. Yet still she couldn't stop, she needed to see her grandmother.

At Wellyhole Yard a group of screaming children were chasing one another around the street. One older boy had fastened a rope to the gas-lamp and was swinging on it. A large woman sat on the doorstep of the house that backed onto her grandmother's nursing a small baby in her lap, her legs so far apart Winifred could see her grubby grey bloomers. When she looked up at Winifred her wary scowl changed to a toothless smile.

'You come to see yer gran then, lovely?' She turned her head to bellow down the hallway. 'Shurrup, you lot.' Looking back at Winifred she smiled again. 'I do try to keep 'em quiet but they're such a bloody rowdy lot. I were round at yer gran's again this morning to tell her I were sorry.' She wiped the back of her hand across her nose. 'I stopped fer a bit cos I could tell she were upset. She told me her son had passed over.' She sniffed, raising her voice to be heard above the sound of the children inside the house. 'Yer da were it?'

Winifred nodded.

'Well, I'm sorry. I often saw 'im on his way to see her since we moved in 'ere; he always 'ad a word. I've seen you too. She gestured with her thumb over her shoulder. 'She thinks the world of you, you know, lovely.' Without turning her head she yelled again. 'I'm warnin' yer, keep the bloody noise down.'

'I need to go,' Winifred said. 'I need to see Granny.'

'Course you do, lovely. Well good to chat wi' yer.' The woman opened her blouse and pushed the baby's head to her large breast. 'See yer again. Oh, and I'm Bertha, by the way.'

Winifred smiled. 'My name's Winifred.' She avoided staring at the baby, sucking noisily on Bertha's breast, looking over the woman's shoulder at the peeling wallpaper in the hall.

'I know.' Bertha rocked slightly, not in the least self-conscious.

'Bye then.' Relieved, Winifred turned into the yard, slightly guilty that she'd resented her granny's new neighbours; had even judged them to be common. But moments later she'd forgotten about them when she burst through the door of the house.

'Granny? Granny?'

'Up here, ducks.' Florence's voice sounded hoarse with tears. 'I'm in bed.'

'Granny, I have something to tell you. '

126

Chapter 36

'I've told you, I won't have it.'

'This place belongs to me and Granny just as much as it does you, Mother. Dad left us all equal shares and you know it. I'm not having her live in that hovel any longer.'

'No!' Her mother crossed her arms, her face puce with fury. 'It's not going to happen.'

'It is, Mother.' Winifred was weary of the argument; it had gone on for days. 'It's happening and there's nothing you can do about it.'

She'd seen the way her grandmother had aged rapidly since her father had died. Tears, and a quiver in her voice, were never far away, so Winifred was convinced more than ever that Granny moving in with them was the only answer. The evident relief when she'd told her about her son's will had shown how fearful she'd been about the future. The following doubt emerged almost as quickly.

Winifred had had her work cut out persuading the old woman that it would be all right.

'I need you to, Granny. Please.' Kneeling at Florence's side, Winifred struggled in the heat of the room. It could only be worse for her grandmother. Even though the sash window was down as far as it would go and the net curtain shivered in whatever breeze there was, the place was stifling, and the stink from outside infiltrated the whole house. She had to speak loudly to be heard above Bertha's children behind them and the noise from the yard.

'She'll not like it one bit.'

'She'll have to put up with it. And I'll be there.' Winifred knew she'd be torn between staying home to protect her grandmother from mother's vicious tongue and wanting to escape; to live her life. To fight for the cause. But there was time enough to worry about that. 'Please, Granny.'

She looked around the crowded room; saw the old mahogany furniture so dark and cumbersome, the damp patches on the outer wall, the worn carpet that barely reached the corners. How could they have let her stay in this awful place for so long? Winifred was determined to persuade her this time.

'It's your right. It's what Dad would have wanted.' She could feel the sweat trickling down the back of her neck. 'It's what he always wanted—'

'But was too scared of her.' The words could have sounded bitter but Florence's tone was sad. 'She always had him right where she wanted. And she knew he had no choice…'

Winifred frowned. 'What do you mean…?'

The closed expression on her grandmother's face, the pressed lips told her not to pursue the question.

'Please say you'll come to live at the shop. You have every right to be there.' Winifred played her last card. 'I miss Dad so much, Granny. It doesn't feel like home without him there. And I could do with an ally.'

Florence's eye twinkled. She gave a soft chuckle. Straightening her shoulders she dipped her head in acquiescence. 'All right, ducks, I give in. But only as long you realise I'll be leaving my share to you when I go.'

'Don't talk like that, Granny, I can't bear it.'

'All right, just as long as you know. I'll be making a will with Winterbottom the solicitor to show that's what I want. And I'm warning you, there'll be some right argy-bargy when you tell her I'll be moving in with you.'

'She already knows.' Winifred grinned. 'And there's not a damn thing she can do about it.'

Florence's eyebrows rose so high it gave her face a comical expression. Then she smiled and said, 'Not a damn thing.'

'I will not have that woman in my home.'

'That woman, as you call her is my grandmother, my father's

mother. She will be moving in next week.' Winifred continued to clean the windows in the spare room. 'And that's an end to it, Mother.'

She glanced over her shoulder to see Ethel open her mouth to speak and then snap it shut.

She'd barely spoken to Winifred since.

And she hadn't lasted a week before she'd cleared her husband's clothes out of the large wardrobe in their bedroom.

Chapter 37

September 1911

'I'm sorry.' The young policeman held his helmet close to his chest and fidgeted from foot to foot, keeping an eye on his bicycle which was propped uo outside the shop window. 'It looks as if the perpetrator has fled the county.' He glanced from Winifred to Ethel. Her mother had her back to them, rearranging the shelves in the stockroom. 'Of course we'll pass on any details of the murder we have to the forces in the other counties around.'

Winifred flinched at the word, the awful instant image of her father lying on the same spot that the man now stood. She forced back the tears that came so easily and blew her nose, nodding her acknowledgement to him. 'Thank you.'

He raised his voice. 'But I'm sorry, Mrs Duffy, we have very little to go on—'

'I understand, Constable.' Ethel still didn't turn and, for a moment, Winifred wondered if her mother was crying. But her next words were final and decisive. 'I suppose you'll never find out who did it.' She became still, her hands resting on the tins of soup on the shelf. 'Or who took the money.'

'The same person, Mother.' Winifred couldn't stop herself. 'Whoever took the money, whoever the coward is, he killed Dad for it.'

'Yes.' Now her mother did turn around. She walked to the shop door and held it open. 'No doubt you'll tell us if you have more news, Constable.'

After he'd left Winifred glared at Ethel, her rage making her tremble. 'How could you be so cold? Your husband was murdered in a vile way...just for money.' She pointed to the floor. 'We found him lying there, Mother. We slept while he lay there dying.'

Ethel said nothing.

Winifred straightened up and clasped her hands in front of her. 'Your husband, my father, is dead. Everything has changed. Just for once show you have a heart.' She waited for a response but Ethel's face was impassive.

'I don't understand you...I just don't.' Winifred walked out of the shop and upstairs to her room.

Gradually, all signs that John Duffy had lived above the shop vanished. But Winifred managed to rescue and hide the old sepia photograph of his parents that had been in pride of place above the small table at his bedside.

The unsmiling couple were standing, her grandmother holding on to a hard-backed wooden chair. They weren't touching.

The deep bonnet her grandmother wore was decorated with a line of flowers at the brim, almost hiding the centre parting of her hair. However hard she tried, Winifred couldn't see if, beneath the large bow and frill, Granny's hair was swept into a bun or side coils.

Carrying the picture with her to her bed, she climbed in under the covers, pushed the pillows behind her and drew up her knees, studying the man who'd gambled away all the family's money.

Her grandfather was handsome. The mutton-chop side-burns extended almost to his jaw. The moustache didn't hide the confident smile on his lips, which wasn't echoed in his eyes. Winifred thought he looked cold, uncaring of the woman by his side who was clinging to the chair. He stood stiffly, shoulders pulled back, chin raised over the high starched collar, fastened at the neck with a large tie. His dark single-breasted and semi-fitted coat was slightly pulled back by the way he had one hand to his waist. His other arm, loose by his side, followed the line of the mid-thigh coat. Winifred peered closer; she couldn't tell if he had a waistcoat on, or what his trousers were like. except they appeared to have a narrow checked pattern.

She stretched out her legs and settled back on the pillows. She took a long breath and stared across at herself in the mirror on the wardrobe door. However hard she tried she could see no resemblance to either of her grandparents. Why had she not noticed before? Why now? She bit hard on her lower lip, blotting out that horrible morning. 'Oh, Dad,' she murmured, squeezing her eyes tightly closed. 'Oh, Dad.'

In the next bedroom she heard her mother moving around, the rattle of the curtains being drawn, the closing of drawers and, finally, the squeaking of the bedsprings. Winifred suddenly had an unwelcome picture of Ethel in voluminous nightgown and unbecoming nightcap, and wondered how her father had ever been attracted to the woman he'd married. There'd been no more children after herself, no brothers or sisters. As a child she'd desperately wanted a sister, someone to lie next to in bed and share secrets with.

Lying on her side she curled her hand under her wet cheek. The loneliness hovered, waiting to return, to bring dreams that made her cry even in sleep. How long it would be before she'd be able to see Conal? He'd understand. She'd be able to talk to him, to tell him how she felt.

Chapter 38

Two of Bertha's sons were loading some of Florence's bits and pieces on to a handcart when Winifred arrived at Wellyhole Yard.

They grinned at her and touched their foreheads before heaving an old trunk on top of two wooden crates.

Winifred smiled at them. 'It's good of you to help, boys,' she said.

The taller of the two shook his head. 'S'no problem.'

The youngest blushed, didn't speak.

Winifred hurried up the stairs, avoiding the sticky flypaper pinned to the low landing ceiling that twisted and turned as she passed. There was a slight niggle of worry inside her. Unless they were going to make more than one journey, she'd expected more of her granny's things to be already loaded.

Florence was sitting in her chair in her usual place by the window. The plain black blouse and voluminous skirt made her look even tinier than she was.

'I'll miss here you know, ducks. They're a friendly lot.'

'You're not having second thoughts?' Winifred asked. Not one stick of furniture had been moved. 'I thought you were bringing more than what's on the cart?'

Her grandmother smoothed the silvery roll of her hair above her forehead and settled a black broad-brimmed hat firmly on her head.

'I'm having a fresh start, Winnie. I'm leaving this lot for the next tenant. Bertha's sister's moving here. She's got nothing to her name, no man; her husband got run over by one of them new-fangled trams in Huddersfield. And her with four bairns to look after.' Florence pressed down on the arms of the chair and stood. 'I came here all those years ago, a lot poorer than I am now. The least I can do is tó help someone who's in the same boat as I was then.' She looked around. 'Funny job. I'll miss this house as well.' Shé laughed as Winifred wrinkled her nose. 'Go on with you; I'm only joking.' She held out her hand. 'Come on, ducks, help me on with my coat and let's go. I can't wait to see your mother's face when I walk in the shop.'

Both Misses Johnston were fussing around the cart when the

two of them made their way out of the house. The elderly spinsters spoke in unison in curiously refined voices that belied the shabby, old-fashioned dresses and metal curlers under white cotton turbans.

'Come back and see us sometimes, Mrs Duffy.' And, 'We'll miss popping in to see you,' they said. One of them gave a long sniff that pinched in her nostrils before they pronounced, 'We're not sure how we feel about the new woman who will live here.'

Florence gave them a warning look, indicating the two boys with a slight tilt of her head. 'I know you'll be as kind to her as you've been to me.' She hugged each of them in turn, despite their looks of alarm and flushed faces as she approached them. 'I have no doubt of that.'

There was quite a crowd to wave them off. Winifred noticed there wasn't one door that wasn't bursting with people and she swallowed against the lump in her throat.

'You sure you'll manage the walk, Granny?' She linked arms with Florence.

'I'm positive. I never expected to leave here except in a coffin.' There was a catch in her voice. 'That won't happen now, thanks to John and you, Winnie.' There were tears threatening. She laughed and wiped them away with her handkerchief. 'Come on, best foot forward.'

Followed by cheers, and shouts of good will and an excited group of three barking dogs leaping around them, they left the yard. Stopping only to hug a weeping Bertha, they walked slowly behind the rattling handcart.

'Your mother's face'll be a picture when these two turn up at the door.' Florence gave a low chortle, indicating the boys in their ill-fitting brown hobnail boots and ragged clothes, who were shouting with laughter and pushing the cart in lurching fits and starts along the road.

Winifred pressed her grandmother's arm to her side and smiled. But she knew life was going to be more difficult than ever before.

Chapter 39

'Why don't you come downstairs, Granny?' Winifred leaned on the doorframe of Florence's room.

'I'm all right here, ducks.' Her grandmother, sitting by the window in her new armchair, turned to smile at her. 'I'm watching all the comings and goings in the ginnel. I wouldn't mind a brew though.'

Winifred crossed the room and peered over Florence's shoulder. The baker's son was opening the back gate to bring in the bread for the shop. Something her father used to do. The flood of sadness in Winifred was unexpected. She dropped a kiss on her grandmother's hair. 'How about I cut you a slice or two of that?' she said.

'I'd like that, Winnie.' Florence patted her hand.

Ethel was paying the boy when she went down to the kitchen. Without speaking Winifred took one of the loaves and sliced and buttered it.

'I take it you'll be paying for that.' Ethel closed the back door and stood, fists on her hips.

'Don't be ridiculous.' Winifred didn't look up. 'And there's something you need to know. I'm going to try to persuade Granny to come downstairs today. Except for going to the lavvy she's been stuck in that room for the last week because of you.'

'I've done nothing.'

'Only been nasty every time she set foot in the kitchen.' Winifred poured water into the teapot. 'It's got to stop, Mother. Just remember we own two thirds of this place between us, Granny and me. If we wanted to sell the shop…' The implication might not be true, but she let the words sink in.

Ethel bristled, set her mouth but said nothing.

Winifred sighed. 'Could you not just try? We talked about this before she came. It didn't need that scene when she arrived, and it doesn't need to carry on.'

She'd thought she'd won the battle; that there was no more to be said. That her mother had accepted the fact that Granny Duffy was entitled to live with them, *would* be living with them. She hadn't realised that the resentment boiling in Ethel was so bitter that it would erupt at the sight of the old woman on the day she moved in. And she hadn't cared who saw it.

'I want none of that stuff anywhere I can see it.' Ethel's eyes narrowed at the sight of the handcart in front of the shop. She barred the way at the door, watched by a few interested customers inside. 'Go round the back and then get it all up to her room.'

'I haven't come here to cause trouble.' Winifred saw that Florence's earlier excitement and willingness to confront her daughter-in-law had evaporated. 'We'll come in the back way.' She made to move. 'I'll go round—'

'No, Granny.' Winifred stopped her. 'Mother, do we have to do this now? Here, in front of customers? Remember your reputation, the reputation of the shop?' Winifred had no qualms in throwing out the words her mother once quoted at her.

Ethel flushed but still said, 'Why not let the world see what my husband reduced me to. Having to share a home with a woman from Wellyhole Yard. A dirty—'

'Enough!' The quick anger in Winifred made her voice rise. If her mother didn't care who was listening well neither did she. 'I asked Granny to come and live here because she's entitled to; this is her home now, she owns part of it.'

There was a buzz of excitement from the customers.

Ethel's face grew scarlet. 'This is my home. Mine. Nobody else's.' She hissed the words. 'When I think what I put up with—'

'What? What did you put up with, Mother?'

Ethel ignored her. 'That no good son of hers made sure I had no choice.' She spat the words out. 'After all the years of you and him. All the years I slaved for him. He did this for spite—'

'Rubbish,' Winifred interrupted. 'Dad made sure that Granny has what she's entitled to, that she's safe and looked after.'

'I'll be doing no looking after.'

'Nobody asked you to. Now, please move so we can bring her things inside.'

The two boys hurriedly unloaded the cart, and between them took everything to the back bedroom that Winifred had made as comfortable as possible for Florence.

Ethel stood in tight-lipped silence as they passed her.

Winifred knew the old woman was shaken but her voice was strong when, upstairs, Florence made a wry face at Winifred. 'I didn't think she'd be pleased, but I thought she'd have got used to the idea by now. It's not going to work, Winnie, I think I should find somewhere else.'

'Nonsense.' Winifred made her voice firm but she knew how strong-willed her grandmother was; she needed to convince her to live at the shop all over again. 'Anyway, you can't go back to the yard, Bertha's sister probably moved in as soon as we left. You're going nowhere, Granny. I'll make Mother see sense.' One way or another her mother would have to accept the situation. And what did she mean, what she'd put up with, and having no choice? And *after all the years of you and him*. What was that about?

Outside, the sky became dark as though it was evening. A storm was coming, she thought absently. All at once she was tired. Perhaps she should have found somewhere else for her and her grandmother. The thought was dismissed in the next second; they had no money between them and most of this place rightfully belonged to them. She helped Florence out of her hat and coat.

'See, I've made your bed up. Everything's new. It's a fresh start for you and it will all be fine, I'm telling you. Now, have a lie down for an hour. I'll let you know when it's supper time.'

But when she called up to her later, Florence refused to go downstairs. 'I want no more trouble, ducks, so, if it's all right with you, I'll eat up here, in the peace and quiet.'

And, however much Winifred tried to persuade her, there was

no moving her. Which, Winifred knew, suited her mother down to the ground.

'So, today, I'm going to try to get her to come downstairs properly – here with us.' Winifred stopped at the bottom of the stairs, balancing the tray carrying the cup of tea and the bread and butter. 'And you will be civil to her, Mother.'

Chapter 40

October

It was over a month before Winifred felt able to leave Florence and Ethel alone without worrying about it. There was an uneasy silence between them, but she thought that was at least better than the snide comments from her mother. And, though she knew her grandmother was still grieving, she only spoke of her son to Winifred.

As the days passed the sour atmosphere took its toll. Winifred was desperate to get out of the house. She wanted some normality back in her life, to find out what was happening with the WSPU group, to talk to Honora about the next meeting. At least that was what she told herself; the thought of also being close to Conal made her breath quicken.

She knocked on her grandmother's door.

'Granny, I've brought you some tea.'

'Just as I like it?'

Winifred smiled. 'Strong enough to stand the spoon up in and two sugars.'

'You're a good girl, thanks.'

'I thought I'd go out for a while.' She hesitated. 'Do you mind?' Last night they'd talked for a long time about her father. Both avoided talking of his death. 'Will you be all right?'

'Course I will, ducks.' Florence turned her head and smiled. 'Your mother in the shop?' To Winifred's nod of confirmation her smile grew though the puffiness under her eyes showed she'd been crying. 'Then I'll have a lie in and sup me tea, and when I get up I think I'll make some porridge.'

'Already done. I made it earlier, nice and thick like you like it. It's on the range when you're ready.'

Her grandmother snuggled further down in the bed. 'Thanks, Winnie. And wrap up warm, it smells cold.'

Winifred laughed. 'I think you're right. I'll see you later.'

Downstairs Ethel fumed when she saw Winifred in her hat and coat. 'I can't run this place on my own, you know.' She flung back the locks on the shop door. The keys on her belt jangled when she spun around to face Winifred. 'I suppose you're going to meet up with those people, those women. And I suppose it was on one of their disgraceful protests when you got that scar?' she said. Don't think I hadn't noticed it, madam.'

But she showed no concern like any normal mother would. Winifred couldn't help the thought but all she said was, 'I won't be long.'

'I'm not looking after her.' Ethel raised her eyes to the ceiling.

'I've seen to Granny. There's nothing she wants you to do for her. And I've been behind the counter for the last five days running it on my own because you said you had toothache.' Winifred fastened the buttons on her black coat. She adjusted her hat; the scar on her forehead was now only a pale line but she was still conscious of it. 'In fact, I've almost been running it for the last three months on my own, the amount of time you've come through from the back.'

'I *am* still supposed to be in mourning.' Her mother pushed past her, knocking her against the shelves. 'How would it look if I just carried on here, day after day as normal?'

She'd put weight on since her husband's death. It occurred to Winifred that if her mother carried on eating the way she was there'd be no room for the two of them, behind the counter anyway. The sudden humour twisted Winifred's lips into a slight smile.

'And what's the sneer for, might I ask?'

'I'm not sneering.' Winifred crossed the shop floor and turned the sign to 'OPEN' before pulling at the door. She glanced back at her mother, lowering her voice; she didn't want her grandmother to hear her next words. 'But do you honestly believe that people think you're mourning for Dad? If you want to see what real grief is, Mother, I suggest you look at Granny.'

Chapter 41

The wind flapped open the fluted hem of Winifred's coat, and grit whipped up from the unflagged paths stung her ankles every time she turned the corner of a narrow neglected street or an alleyway. She was grateful that the rain, threatened by the unremitting grey solidness of the sky, had held off. The deciduous trees on Errox hill held branches only recently bare of leaves but there were no trees in the roads she now hurried through, no gardens to show the time of year. She was glad of the cold dampness; it meant there were fewer people around. The noise coming from behind the doors of some of the terraced houses was bad enough: the shouts of men, screams of women, quarrels, crying children, all made her shudder and quicken her steps.

Yet the nearer she got to Gilpin Street the more apprehensive she became. What if the attraction between her and Conal was all in her mind? Or, worse, what if he'd become tired of waiting for her and found someone else? After all, it was over two months since she'd last seen him. Honora had called round quite a few times since her father died, but there had been little chance to talk with her mother hovering in the background. She'd managed to secrete the Suffragette newsletters, given to her by her friend, into her overall pocket and sometimes, in the early days, even a short note from Conal saying how much he was missing her.

Winifred groped for memories of the way Conal had looked at her, the things he'd said, grasping for any reassurance that what she'd held on to since they were last together was true. She touched her cheek where his fingers had briefly rested the day of the funeral. She remembered his words *I'll wait for you*. But had he? The doubt roiled around in her stomach, made her feel queasy.

She needed to know. But she had her pride.

So, when Conal clattered down the stairs in answer to her tentative call, she pushed the front door open with a bright smile. 'Hello.'

She needn't have worried.

'At last!' He grabbed her hands, held them to his chest. 'To be sure, I thought ya would never come.' Still holding on to her fingers he led the way up the stairs.

'It's been difficult.' She didn't explain. 'How are you both?'

'Fine, fine.' His grin as he turned and walked backwards up the last couple of stairs was infectious. She smiled, following him into the first room that was usually teeming with people. For once it was tidy; there were no pots in the sink, none of Honora's painting equipment scattered around. A pile of canvases were neatly propped up against the wall.

'Honora?'

He came to stand by her. 'She's off to Huddersfield. Some important Jackeen wants his portrait painting for on the wall of his big office in some factory there. Been there a week or two. I thought she'd been to tell ya?'

'No – no, she didn't. I – we shouldn't be here on our own.' Anxiety rose in Winifred.

'We could go out. A walk?' Conal offered.

'I don't know. Perhaps that's a good idea.' Struggling with her feelings, Winifred tried to keep her tone casual, but she heard the tremor in her voice. 'It's bitter cold though. Perhaps I should just leave. You know as well as I do that I shouldn't be here on my own with you. It's not respectable—'

'I'd do nothing to hurt you, a *mhuirnín*.'

'I know,' she faltered. 'I think I know that, but...'

'We could just sit and talk?' He moved towards a shabby armchair. 'I'll sit here. You sit there.' He pointed to another chair nearby, making a great point of scrunching his legs up so they were under his chin, as though to make himself look even more distant from her.

She laughed. 'Now you're making me feel ridiculous. Like some silly schoolgirl.'

'Am I not doing my best to look harmless to ya?' He put a mock scowl on his face. 'Is it pulling a man down that ya're after?'

Winifred laughed again, feeling easier. 'I'm sorry; it's just how I've been brought up to think.' She waggled her head and copied her mother, "A girl is never alone with a man. Not if she wants to keep her reputation." My mother, you know,' she said.

'And your mother is right,' Conal replied, seriously. 'We could go out?' He repeated.

Winifred glanced through the window at the steel-grey sky, already darkened with threatened rain. 'No, it's just...' She looked down at her hands, twisting her fingers together. Knowing what she was about to say would change her life, change her forever. 'I want to...' She faltered. 'I want to ask you something, Conal. Do you love me?' There, it was said.

He was at her side in a second, kneeling by her. 'I have loved ya from that first moment I saw you on the tram, Win. Did ya not know that?'

'No. Yes... I think so. Oh,' she closed her eyes. 'I don't know. Because I don't really know how I'm supposed to know.'

'What do ya feel for me, *acushla?*'

'I like you. I think, maybe, I love you too.' She looked into his eyes, remembering the first time she'd seen them, remembering how she'd thought them so dark, so intense it was as though they looked right into her soul, read her mind. Looking at his hands she remembered the feeling when he'd held hers; so comforted, so safe. She caught her lip between her teeth. He was watching her with a serious expression.

'Are ya okay there?' His voice soft, patient. 'I'll walk ya home.'

'No.' She wouldn't go home. She wanted this man in a way she didn't understand, wasn't sure what it meant; what *it* was. But there was a need inside her she had to answer. She stood, unbuttoned her coat and slid it down her arms, throwing it over the back of one of the chairs. Her smile, returning his, was shaky.

'I don't know what to do. I haven't...'

'I know.' He silenced her with a gentle kiss on the lips. 'But ya're sure?'

'Yes.' He'd said he loved her. And she'd never felt like this about anyone. If she let it happen – whatever *it* was, then they'd be bound to one another forever. There was nothing her mother could do about it. Conal would make sure of that; he'd look after her, protect her. They'd marry and – a smile tugged at the corners of her mouth – they'd have a family together.

He took off her hat, his hands lingering on the hairpin at the back of her head. Answering his silent question, she nodded, standing very still when he removed it, letting her hair fall through his fingers to her shoulders.

I should stop him right now, she thought. She didn't.

The ivory tulle lace inner bodice of her black dress was fastened by hook closures. One by one, Conal undid them, his eyes fixed on hers. Winifred was trembling, her breath shallow. He eased the sleeves from her arms and let the dress drop over her hips and to the floor, kissing her forehead, her cheek, her chin, her throat. She closed her eyes, responding to the urge inside her. When his tongue fluttered against hers, she took in a shocked breath before relaxing with the warm sensation that filled her whole body.

She stepped out of the dress, pushing it away from her with

her feet. She was lost. There was no going back. She loved this man.

She became aware that he'd stopped kissing her and she made a small murmur of protest. When he said nothing, she opened her eyes. Hands on her upper arms he leant back, looking from her neck to her feet, amazement in his face.

'My god, Win, how many layers do you have on?

She blushed under his scrutiny. 'You live with your sister, Conal, you must know about women's clothes? Adding quickly. 'The washing? Honora's... things?'

'As far as I know...' it was his turn to look embarrassed. 'My sister owns only drawers and petticoats.'

His discomfort gave her confidence. She leant towards him, pressed her lips to his and stretched up her arms.

He eased the fine-wool petticoat over her head and let it drop to the floor on top of her dress, his fingers following the scooped-neck of her corset cover. She watched his face as he pulled on the drawstrings, first there, and then at her waist. When the garment fell past her knees to her feet to show the ugly corset she was wearing, she was sorry she hadn't just worn her lovely new lace bust bodice with the petticoat over the top.

But she hadn't. Because she didn't know that Honora wouldn't be home. And she didn't know this moment would happen. Not today. Not here.

His fingers fumbled with the laces, pulling at them one by one. She placed her hand over his, stilling it for a moment. 'Kiss me,' she whispered.

He held her closely, his kiss light at first before he took in a deep breath and lowered his mouth again to hers, the kiss more urgent.

She felt him quiver, his hands moving quickly, until the corset dropped away from her and she was standing in front of him covered only in her white combination chemise and drawers.

'Tis beautiful you are,' he breathed, running his hands over the

143

closely fitted cotton material. She could feel the warmth of his hands when he held her waist before moving them slowly down over her buttocks.

'I'm frightened.' Would he stop now?

He did.

She searched his face. There was only anxiousness in his eyes. 'I'm sorry,' she said.

He shook his head, let his hands drop to his sides. 'To be sure, I'm sorry too, Win. But I don't want ya thinking I was after taking advantage of ya.' His voice low he cupped her face between his palms, carefully holding himself away from her.

She knew the next move had to be her decision. The sound of their breathing filled the room.

She undid the buttons at her waist, held onto the flared mid-calf drawers for a second then let them drop. She looked down; the fine lace flounces covered her feet. She didn't move when Conal unbuttoned the chemise, slid it down her arms.

At first neither of them moved. Winifred let out the breath she'd held and then drew in another when Conal, his eyes fixed on hers, prised off his boots, slowly removed his clothes. The low flames of the fire cast shadows on his face. She lifted one hand, traced the line of his beautiful high cheekbones, his mouth.

'Ya sure?'

'I am.'

He lifted her into his arms, the contact of his skin on hers made her stomach clench. When he lowered her onto his bed he followed, lying closely at her side, one leg over her thighs, one hand on her breast.

And then he was kissing her again, stroking her throat, her shoulders, her breasts, her waist. She tilted her hips against his. She was ready for him

He slipped inside her. She gasped against the sharp brief pain, closed her eyes tight. After the first thrust he held still.

'Are ya all right?' His voice quiet.

She opened her eyes, nodded, one hand on his shoulder, the other slowly stroking his back, from the nape of his neck to the base of his spine. Then she pressed him hard against her.

They lay, spent, Conal's head between her small breasts. He shifted slightly, licked at her nipple before taking it into his mouth and sucking on her. Her back arched, her body betraying her, defying the kernel of shame buried within her mind.

He caressed her stomach, lifted his head to gaze up at her, his eyes moist. 'My god, Win, you're glorious, so ya are,' he murmured. 'Thank ya, my darlin'. I love you, always will. I'll be the best man I can for ya. I'll never let you down.'

The rush of relief was instant in Winifred; he didn't despise her for giving in to him, he knew how much she had to lose. Had lost. And he still respected her.

Conal slid out of the covers and stood looking down at her. He held out his hand and she took it. Feeling shy she let her eyes travel from his face to his chest, his waist, his hips. And, for the first time, she saw what a man was. Her heart quickened, realising that only minutes ago he had been inside her and the thought brought heat to her face. She moved her gaze back to his face, saw he was smiling.

And then he said, 'I love ya, Miss Duffy.'

And everything seemed right. She'd given the most precious thing she'd had to the man who loved her.

He squeezed her hand and turned to pick up his trousers; his thighs and buttocks were muscular, taut. Winifred studied him, felt almost possessive about him. He was hers as much as she now belonged to him.

Winifred knew that she was a fallen woman. There was no going back. For a moment she acknowledged the shame, the fear, the fact that she would be seen as spoiled goods if it was ever discovered what they'd just done. But she didn't care. She loved him and was loved in return.

Chapter 42

November 1911

Bill wrapped his arms around his knees and hunched up in the doorway of the barn watching the rain slant across the fields for as far as he could see. Which wasn't far; the Pennines in the distance were shrouded in misty cloud. Sheep, brought down from those hills for the winter, now huddled in the shelter of the meandering stone walls that divided the land closer to the farm. They made no sound. Probably as bloody miserable as he was. God, he was sick to death of being wet through.

He rested his head on his knees, wishing he could just go to sleep, knowing there was no chance; his whole body was shuddering with the cold. Besides, when he did sleep the nightmare returned. He was running, always running, and behind him were hordes of people baying and shouting for his blood. And standing watching, always, the figure of Winifred Duffy, dressed from head to toe in black.

Looking up, he pushed the image of John Duffy's coffin out of his mind, and tried to work out what he was going to do. It was too late in the afternoon to move on. He wasn't even clear where he was moving on to. For the past three months he'd zigzagged aimlessly across the country, dossing down where and when he could, sometimes in a penny flea-pit, mostly sleeping rough. He tried to avoid towns, sticking to remote villages and hamlets; picking up the odd job here and there, stealing food when he had no money to pay for it. The money he'd taken from Duffy's place had long gone; sometimes he had nightmares about what he'd done for just a few quid.

Suddenly remembering the potatoes filched from outside the grocer's shop in the last village, he fumbled, frozen-fingered, in his jacket pocket for the last one. God knows when he'd next eat but before that he hadn't eaten for three days and his belly still thought his throat was cut.

He took a large bite. The sourness made his eyes water. He turned his head and spit out the half-chewed lump. It was rotten, black.

'Shit.' Flinging the potato as far as he could, he shouted again. 'Shit, shit, shit.' A faint echo of his voice floated above him. At the back of the large building straw rustled, there was a murmuring of soft clucking and three hens strutted into sight, feet held high, heads bobbing.

Eyes narrowed, Bill watched them. He held his breath, waited for them to get closer, trying to judge which one to go for. The nearest stopped, it's beady, dark yellow eyes fixed on him.

'Come on, come on,' Bill whispered. He'd eat the bugger raw if he had to.

It moved closer, slowly.

Bill dived, missed. The bird rose high in the air squawking in panic. The others joined in, and then the straw was scattered as dozens of other hens flung themselves from underneath with harsh cackles.

'Bastard!' Bill yelled and rolled onto his back, holding his elbow which had twisted under him.

'Stay…where you are.'

The outline of the man almost filled the barn door, his figure black against the light of the day outside.

Bill heard the quiet click of a safety catch, saw the jerk of the shotgun.

'Sit…up. Do it slowly…slowly.' There was a slight hesitancy in his voice.

Bill did as he was told; there was nothing else he could do. He wouldn't argue with a bloke who was pointing a shotgun.

'I haven't eaten in—'

'Shut…it. On your…knees.'

Struggling, Bill attempted to do as he was told but the stiffness of his bad knee was worse in wet weather and he groaned with the pain. 'I can't…'

'This is…my farm.' The man reached sideway and pushed the door wider. 'Who… who are you?'

'Just a chap down on his luck.' Bill tried a smile but, not being able to see the man, wasn't sure if he'd pacified him.

'Sid, what was it.' A woman appeared, her silhouette small and round. She didn't sound young. At her side were two black and white sheepdogs. Growls rumbled in their throats.

'Thief,' was the short reply.

'I only wanted—'

'To…to kill one of my fowl.' The farmer stuttered. He jerked the gun again. 'Stand…stand up.'

It took Bill a few minutes to stagger to his feet. 'Injured working in the mines,' he explained in the direction the woman, hoping she'd be more sympathetic.

She didn't answer. The rain increased, pounding loud onto the concrete yard then splashing up into the air. Water gurgled in a drain.

'Can I…?' Bill pointed to his cap on the ground nearby.

The farmer grunted assent.

Stiff-legged, Bill bent down and gathered up the sodden cap. Straightening, he wrung it out and slapped it against his thigh, flattening it out. He couldn't stop shivering; he'd walked miles in the constant rain over the last week and his clothes were wet through. In fact, he couldn't remember the last time he'd been dry. It had been a bloody awful winter.

'And he can come into the house and get warmed up.'

It was the woman. The leap of gratitude inside him made him swallow; he'd seen little kindness since he'd left Morrisfield, especially over the last few weeks. He didn't suppose his accent had helped since he'd got into Lancashire.

'What?' The farmer glanced down at the woman. 'Ma—'

'Look at him. Scrap of a lad. You're twice his size.'

She sounded irritated which was nothing to how Bill felt. He'd lived his life being goaded about his height; from the boys in school, from his father. He'd heard all the jokes and nicknames; midget, dwarf, and worse; short-arse being his father's favourite. The familiar resentment of any perceived slight brought instant fury that he'd normally act on. But this time he managed to hold himself in check. He waited until, without a word, the man moved to one side to let him pass. A wary, grumbling dog on each side of him, he followed the woman into the small stone farmhouse, conscious of the heavy sighs and footsteps of the man behind him.

The heat of the low-ceilinged kitchen when she opened the door was stifling. Flames reached high in a large fireplace and licked around the base of an iron pot hanging by chains from a large hook. The smell of cooking meat and vegetables and fresh bread was overwhelming. Bill tried to walk further into the room but his legs gave way.

Without any effort, the man picked him up and, with his foot, pulled a chair away from a large wooden table in the centre of the room and shoved Bill onto it.

The humiliation and the hunger combined and tears scalded Bill's eyes. He roughly brushed the back of his hand across his face as the man pushed the chair nearer to the fire. Steam started to rise from Bill's clothes.

The woman tutted. 'Get those clothes off, young man. Sid, find clothes for him. There's some of your father's still in the wardrobe.'

The man didn't argue.

'He's a good boy,' the woman said, picking up a ladle and stirring the food in the pot. She kept her back to him while he peeled off his jacket. 'A bit slow but a good lad – until you cross him.' She glanced up toward a large sepia photograph of a glowering man hung above the fireplace. 'His father,' she said, nodding at it. 'Not with us now. But Sid looks after me.' The warning was implicit.

Bill didn't know what to say so he kept quiet, feeling foolish in his grubby long johns and vest.

149

When Sid returned he was holding a full set of clean clothes. With an exaggerated frown, he made a great show of holding them out and looking up to the ceiling while Bill stripped his underwear off as quickly as he could. Putting on clean dry clothes was wonderful, even though both the shirtsleeves and trousers were too long and needed turning up a few times.

'Thanks,' he said, 'Thanks a lot.' And meant it.

The change in the man was instant. Sid returned his smile. 'S'all right,' he said.

'You're down on your luck,' the woman announced once he was dressed. 'I'm Bessie Appleby. This here is Sid, my son...' She waited while Sid shook Bill's hand with enthusiasm. 'We need an extra hand on the farm.' Head tilted to one side she studied him before giving an almost imperceptible nod. 'You'll stay with us for a while,' she said, taking his clogs and putting them next to a large pair of boots by the back door where the sheepdogs lay. 'Move: Ben, Flora.' She ushered them out of the way before saying to Bill, 'there's a spare room out back. You can earn your keep by helping Sid.'

Chapter 43

November 1911

Winifred shivered, her feet cold on the thin carpet, and glanced through the window at the afternoon sky. The nights had drawn in, she'd have more difficulty being with Conal; it wasn't respectable for a woman to be out on her own after dark.

She'd see him tomorrow. The thought brought an unexpected heat between her thighs and she groaned softly; she ached for his touch. She tried to ignore the guilt and shame she felt whenever she thought of the times in his bedroom; the times Honora made excuses that she needed to go on an errand for more paint, or canvas, The look of grinning conspiracy when she left, carefully closing the bedroom door.

Sometimes Winifred thought of her craving for him must be an illness, an addiction. And perhaps it was. But she welcomed it even as she feared what would happened if they were discovered; even as she tried to find ways to get out of the shop in the daytime. The images she kept of him, of the times they were together helped, but they weren't enough.

Hopefully they would have time after the protest march in Morrisfield to be alone. She would talk again to him then, plan something; he must be as desperate to be with her. Mustn't he?

The fear of losing him was always with her, just as much as the fear what she, they, were doing would be discovered. The image that most frightened her was of when he walked away from her, each time he'd seen her to the end of the street. He never looked back; his head down, his hands shoved into his trouser pockets. She imagined that was how he might look were he to walk away from her for good. The anxiety was with her each moment of those empty days; that some prettier girl would entice him into her bed. Missing him was a painful physical sensation.

And though, when they lay together naked under the blankets of his bed, legs entwined, her head on his chest, he insisted they could marry, he still thought it wasn't the right time to approach her mother. Winifred thought back to a week ago; the last time they'd spoken about it.

'I don't care who judges us, sweetheart.' Winifred stroked his chest. 'I want to be with you for the rest of my life.'

'An' I want to be with ya, Win. I'm gutted that we need to wait til I'm qualified. I want to prove I amn't a Culchie.'

'What?' She rose up on one elbow, frowning. 'I don't understand. What do you mean?'

'I want to show your ma – an' all the ones ya know – that I'm not a country bumpkin.'

'You're not. We'll tell her your father was a doctor, that you're training to be a doctor as well. We'll tell everyone if necessary. You're better than them. And I'll be the doctor's wife, wherever we live.' She gave a quiet chuckle. 'Mother will be put in her place then, that's for sure.'

'Let me be qualified first and then they can give out all they like.'

'I really don't care, Conal. If anyone won't accept you, we'll cut them out of our lives. Move somewhere else; have a fresh start.'

He kissed her. 'When I'm a doctor, *achusla*, when I'm qualified, we can do whatever we want.' He ran his finger along her jaw and down her throat. When he reached her breast and circled her nipple with his palm she offered her mouth to him and arched her back. 'When I'm qualified,' he murmured.

She'd have to be content with that. But she wouldn't ever give him up, he was her soul mate.

Would her father have understood? Would he have helped her? Winifred believed he would. He had only ever wanted her to be happy and it wouldn't have mattered to him that Conal was Irish, only that she loved him and wanted to marry him.

Had he ever loved her mother in the way she loved Conal? Now she knew what real love meant, it made Winifred sad to remember what her father had endured at his wife's hands. The constant nagging, the scorn, must have been so hard to accept. Yet that was what he'd let happen. Had it only ever been just to keep the peace? Or were there other reasons? Winifred remembered her mother's words the day Granny moved in; 'When I think what I put up with.'

Just what did that mean?

Chapter 44

Winifred studied her reflection in the wardrobe mirror. She'd had to alter the waistband of her long narrow grey skirt; she'd not worn it this winter and had filled out since last year but the stitching wouldn't be seen once she put her coat on. She gave a small sound of satisfaction. It looked perfect; the draped skirt just covered her ankles, showing off her new grey boots. She glanced at her black gaiters, debating whether she should wear them; they would keep out the cold. But they were old, shabby. Today she wanted to feel that everything was right, smart. Today, even more than before, she was making a stand like all the others; today she would show Conal how strong she could be. If she showed her courage in this kind of adversity, she thought, he'd realize how serious she was about becoming his wife despite all the hardship and prejudice they would face.

She took the gaiters off and put them back in the wardrobe, taking her coat from its hanger at the same time.

Fastening her white woollen hat onto her hair with the large hatpin she wondered for a moment if the long swathe of green and purple ribbons as well as the sash over her white coat was too much. But it was too late to worry about such a little thing. She pressed her lips together and took a few breaths, bracing herself to go down and through the shop.

She went first into her grandmother's bedroom. Florence looked around when Winifred opened the door. 'I'm off, Granny.' The fire in the grate had settled into a warm glow. Winifred picked up the fire tongs and placed a few more pieces of coal on top. Waiting until flames flickered and took hold she said, 'Anything you need before I go?'

'No, thanks, ducks. That meat and potato pie you made set me up for the day.' Her grandmother smiled. 'And probably until tomorrow.' Florence was sitting in what had become her favourite place, the armchair by the window.

Winifred crossed the room and kissed the top of her head. 'You will go down and get yourself a brew or something, later, won't you, though?'

'Of course I will.'

'Hmm.' Winifred patted her shoulder. At the door she stopped, walked back to her grandmother and crouched down at her side. 'You are all right, aren't you Granny. You're not lonely?'

'Lonely?' Florence's expression was unreadable. 'With you here, Winnie? Of course not.'

'But I haven't been here much, lately.'

'You have your own life to get on with and your own friends to see. Here...' she gripped the arm of the chair and stood, balancing for a moment before she reached over and opened the top drawer of her dressing table. She took out a small box. 'I've been meaning to give you this.' She held it out.

'What is it?'

A small oval amethyst brooch, surrounded by pearls was pinned to a velvet cushion.

'It was my mother's. The only thing I managed to hide from your grandfather. Wear it today. Something else purple, eh?'

'Oh, Granny, I couldn't.' Winifred touched the stone with the tip of her finger.

'Course you can.' Florence's arthritic fingers struggled to unpin the brooch. 'Oh, you do it.' She gave an exasperated sigh.

Winifred fastened the brooch onto her blouse. 'If you're sure?'

'Yes. Good luck, Winnie. Look after yourself. Now, you get off. Give them what for, for me.'

'I will.'

Straightening her shoulders, Winifred walked downstairs and stood behind the inner shop door. There was a loud buzz of conversation. Drawing in a deep breath she opened it. Might as well face whoever was there.

The shop was packed and there was instant silence.

Without looking round, and folding a small parcel of bacon into a square, her mother spoke in a loud voice. 'Off gadding again, then?'

She's playing to the gallery, Winifred reminded herself, noting the black cotton apron over the equally dense-black woollen dress. She manoeuvred past Ethel.

154

'Leaving me here to manage on my own.' Her mother's voice held a martyred tone.

There were mutterings of agreement.

'You should be helping your poor mother in the shop.' The large-bosomed woman at the front of the queue took the bacon that her mother held out across the counter, and dropped it into her basket. 'Widowed barely a few months ago.'

Winifred didn't answer. 'Excuse me,' she said, weaving through the small crowd of customers.

'I admire you; I wish I could come with you.' A young girl touched Winifred's arm as she passed and gave her a shy smile.

'Why don't you then?' Winifred stopped, returned the smile.

'I can't—'

'Because she's a respectable young woman.' An older woman pulled the girl away.

'That's right.' The only man in the shop, stick-thin and bowler-hatted placed his hand on the shoulder of an equally thin small woman. 'She's not running around the streets causing trouble. She's respectable.'

'And so am I.' Winifred glared at him. The heat rose in her throat. 'I'm… we're… fighting to get the vote for the likes of you.' Her stare took in all the women.

'And never will.'

'Waste of time.'

'Be content to be a true woman.'

The mutterings mixed together in disapproval.

'And what is a true woman?' At the door, Winifred turned to face them. 'Someone who does what men tell them to do? A doormat? Only fit to cook and clean?' Her stare took them all in, one by one. 'No. I'll tell you what a true woman should be, shall I? A true woman should be in charge of her own life. That's what.' She lifted her chin.

Slamming the door and marching along the street she grinned, rather pleased with herself. Her mother wouldn't be surprised now when she was late home. Rather a good exit, she congratulated herself. Swinging her arms she hurried along the road.

Conal was waiting for her on Cook Street. His glance that took in her whole body made her blush and him laugh. He lowered his mouth to hers. Helpless against the urge, she responded.

When he finally held her away from him he said, 'I love ya, Miss Duffy.'

'I love you too, Mr O'Reilly.' Winifred thought she'd never been happier.

'God, I'm after wanting ya all the time, Win.'

She tapped his hand lightly as he reached for her again. 'We'd better get a move on.'

'You're a hard case, Miss Duffy. Can ya not take pity on a poor man?'

'I'll think about that. Later.' She laughed.

He tucked her arm through his. It was strange to Winifred that she was now more at ease in the back streets she was so nervous of such a short while ago than she was among the familiar streets around the shop.

Honora and the two women she'd met before were waiting for them.

'We're meeting the others in town,' Honora said, barely containing her excitement. But even she grew quiet as the tram neared Morrisfield, becoming more crowded with other women.

Conal held Winifred's hand loosely in his lap. Across the aisle, Liam had his arm over Honora's shoulders. Remembering the first time they were all together on a tram, when she'd been appalled by Honora's behaviour, she smiled. How far they'd come.

They tumbled off on High Street and straight into the crowds. The whole area was a sea of white dresses and coats.

She thought back to what the principle speaker had said at the last meeting in Morrisfield. To her own small contribution.

She'd been glad it wasn't the same large parish hall as the first meeting she'd attended. Staring out at the three rows of people she'd swallowed down dry gulps of air, forcing herself to listen to the first speaker.

Winifred studied the way the woman stood, moved her arms, her head; taking in the room of twenty people as she spoke, giving emphasis to her words as she finished her speech.

'The natural characteristics of womanhood are stifled by her dependence on man. She is expected to please a man and, to be accepted into society, woman must agree with her father, brother, husband. To believe and trust, at least in public, his opinions, merits, his reasoning, his bigotries, his depravities.'

Winifred saw Conal shift in discomfort next to Honora, a scowl on his face and muttering. She sucked in her lips to stop herself from smiling when she also saw her friend laugh and whisper something back to him.

'Women know their own needs; have their own problems and concerns for the situations they are in. They, we, are entitled to have our say in how we deal with our lives. We are entitled to a vote.' These last words were shouted, her arm raised. 'Votes for women.'

When the cheering ceased, the woman half-turned and held out her hand to Winifred. 'And now I'd like to introduce to you our newest recruit to the Morrisfield WSPU, Winifred Duffy. A young woman only with us this year, but I'm sure she has much to say that will encourage you to continue in our fight.' She smiled, her voice louder. 'Ladies...' she gestured to where Conal and four of his friends were sitting. 'And gentlemen – Winifred Duffy.'

Winifred wasn't sure her legs would allow her to get up. She pressed her hands on the seat of the bench and rose awkwardly. When she stood in front of the podium she clung to the edges, unable to think of the words she'd prepared.

Panicking she searched out Conal and Honora. They both smiled and inclined their heads.

The silence was beginning to feel palpable. Those seated in front of her began to shift and mutter. When Winifred did speak her words came out in a rush.

'Women are the same as man in this country. Whatever class society chooses to put us into, we are all free in the moment in which we are born. So, whether a man or a woman, we should have the same rights. We should have the same feeling of self-worth because women have integrity the same as men, women have good judgement the same as men, the same intelligence as men.' She paused to suck in air. 'All we women want is that the men in Government, the men who refuse to see us as people, should recognise that.'

The shaking in her arms and legs had stopped but the unexpected awareness of her body's stillness took away her next memorised sentence. Dismayed she met Honora's eyes.

'Are you okay?' Honora mouthed.

Winifred gave a small shake of her head. She'd dried up, nothing came into her mind. Then, as she later triumphantly related to Conal, she had inspiration; a memory rose to the surface of the time she was at the vicarage, of what Dorothy had said that day and what had then happened. 'To vote is to have power,' she blurted. 'We are as entitled to that power as any man.' She gestured to Honora to join her on stage. 'Everyone, I'd like you to welcome someone, the woman who first, not so long ago, brought our wonderful movement to my attention, who became a dear friend very quickly.' She waved at Honora again, watched Conal, with a puzzled grin, shove his sister to her feet and accompany her to the steps of the stage.

'This is desperate of ya,' hissed Honora.

'Well I am,' Winifred muttered, deliberately misunderstanding her friend. She cast a look around the room; saw the bewilderment on the faces. 'Everyone – there is something I thought you'd like to hear. I believe, as I think you also believe that there should be no difference between men and women in

158

law or politics – or art. Honora O'Reilly is an artist, a wonderful artist. And she also has a wonderful voice. I'd like to thank you for listening to me today and to ask her to finish off my time with you here by singing our new anthem; 'March of the Women', by Ethel Smyth and Cicely Hamilton.'

She stepped back, leaving Honora at the front of the stage. There was a soft rustle as a woman from the front row hurried to the piano at the side of the hall. She played the opening notes and then looked expectantly up at Honora before starting again.

Shout, shout, up with your song!
Cry with the wind, for the dawn is breaking…

Honora's mellifluous voice flowed around the hall. Someone from the back of the hall joined in, then another and another. Soon everyone was standing.

March, march—many as one,
Shoulder to shoulder and friend to friend.

As the last words were sung the place erupted with clapping and stamping.

Winifred rushed forward to hug her friend. They wept and laughed at the same time.

The tall imposing woman who was trying to organise the crowd into some semblance of order was shouting above the noise. She was repeating the words with which, as principle speaker, she'd closed that last meeting.

'Remember these words of Mrs Pethick-Lawrence, Ladies: "Wear white for purity in public as well as private life, green for hope and purple for dignity, for that self-reverence and self-respect which renders acquiescence to political subjection impossible."'

They'd cheered at the time, Winifred along with them. It was impossible not to feel excited. The men in Government would see they were acting as respectably as they could. That, as women, all they wanted was equality in voting; to be able to have as much a say as their husbands, their brothers, their fathers.

But as they joined the crowds she sensed the atmosphere was different from other marches. There was a tension, a pent-up anger amongst the women that resulted in a lack of order. There were no organized ranks, people milled around as if unsure which way to go. Standing on tiptoe, Winifred could just see the heads of the police on horseback, two large black police vans and, in the distance, on the steps of the Courthouse in the town square, the destination the parade would be making for. She fingered the buttons on her coat, touched the brim of her hat, reassuring herself by the gesture and stared around, hoping to see the organizers of the march, the women who had rallied them all at the meeting, but she saw none of them. Maybe they were at the front, she thought, looking past the makeshift flags and wooden boards, with crudely written slogans, which were being waved alongside the large WSPU official banners.

The crush was getting worse. Shopkeepers on both sides of the road, previously watching with nervous curiosity, turned their backs and, chivvying their assistants in front of them, went back into their shops, closing the doors.

The new anthem, 'The March of the Women', rose and fell beneath the shouts and cries of those already being jostled and buffeted.

'Stay up close,' Conal bellowed.

Linking arms in an effort to stay together the seven of them formed a line. To Winifred's right Honora was already singing, the exhilaration flushing her cheeks.

Shout, shout, up with your song!
Cry with the wind for the dawn is breaking...

Her voice broke every now and then as they were erratically pressed forward by the people behind them and the breath was knocked out of her.

Jolted each time, Winifred began to panic. Despite the cold, the air was filled with a mixture of cloying perfumes and sweat. Some of the women's faces around her reflected her fear as the throng grew tighter.

Suddenly there were louder screams, the clatter of horses hooves, loud bells rang from somewhere and people were turning, running, scattering in all directions, pursued by the police randomly hitting out with their batons. Horrified, Winifred heard her own scream rising from her lungs.

'Move onto the pavement.' Conal's yell was almost lost in the cacophony of sounds

The splintering of glass and the loud shout of 'votes for women', from someone was the first indication of the stones being thrown through the shop windows. Their group battled to get to the pavement. It was a mistake. People were hitting at the windows with hammers, splintering the glass. Winifred cried out in pain when a fragment struck her ankle.

'This way.' Conal dragged her backwards.

She tried to hold on to Honora's hand, clutching as tightly as she could but her grasp was loosened and there was a sudden pull on the fingers of her glove. 'Hold on, Honora, hold on.' The glove was torn from Winifred's hand. 'Honora!' The last she heard from her friend was the shrill scream, the last she saw was the fear on the Irish girl's face as she disappeared beneath the surrounding mêlée.

A horse thundered towards them, ploughing a furrow through falling women collapsing under blows and hooves. Winifred caught a glimpse of a woman clinging to one of the street lamps, thrashing a riding-switch at the policeman's legs. Then the horse faltered, blood streaming from its neck, a broken shard of slate in a long cut.

Winifred looked up through the protective arms of Conal. Two women were on the roof of one of the shops. Leaning over the edge they threw broken slates down at the police.

'Stop it, ya bloody eejits, stop it,' he yelled, bending his back further over Winifred to shielding her.

She heard his gasp of pain. 'Conal?'

'I'm fine.' He was holding his ear, blood seeped through his fingers. 'We need to get away,' he bellowed above the uproar.

But suddenly the hooves of a horse were looming over her head. The animal reared up, its eyes rolling, mouth pulled wide in the bit. Winifred saw the angry face of a policeman, whip held high above his head.

Then all she felt was the weight of Conal pinning her to the ground.

Chapter 45

There was a rushing of air in her ears; her face cold, pressed against something hard. One arm lay underneath her and her back hurt. Winifred groaned, tried to pull her legs up to her chest. Too painful. She was so cold. 'Conal?' She listened. Through the pounding of her pulse she heard the groans. Where was she?

'Conal?'

'There's no-one called Conal here as far as I can see.' A hand grasped her shoulder. 'Come on, girl, get up.' It was a woman's voice, low, modulated.

Winifred rolled painfully onto her back; the ground was lumpy under her. She was lying on cobbles in a narrow alleyway, dark stone buildings crowding in, showing only a rectangle of dark starless sky. Her arm, at first numb, began to tingle.

The woman, kneeling at her side, was drenched, her hair flattened to her scalp. She wore a white jacket, dirty and wet, the remnants of her long skirt showing ripped stockings, bloodied knee. 'You need to get up. The police could come back.'

'What happened?'

'The police turned the hoses on us.' The statement was matter of fact. 'Can you stand?'

'I–I'm not sure.' Winifred turned onto her stomach and raised herself on hands and knees. 'Where's Conal?' she looked along the alleyway towards the street. The ground was covered in leaflets, torn and trampled underfoot. 'Honora?'

'I don't know.' The woman pushed her hair behind her ears. 'I don't know where anyone is. Except us,' she added. 'And we shouldn't be here. Come on. You can come back with me, tidy yourself up. There's nothing more we can do here. They've beaten us.' She hauled Winifred to her feet. 'For now.'

At the house the woman helped Winifred to clean herself up in the kitchen and found some clothes for her to change into.

'You needn't bring them back,' she whispered, looking nervously towards the door which led through to a large hall. 'These are old and I have too many clothes anyway.'

Winifred stood, letting the woman fasten the tie on the navy skirt and the last of the buttons on a fine cotton blouse on her. 'Just leave now. As quickly and quietly as you can.' She walked round the back of Winifred, helping her to slide her arms into the matching navy three-quarter jacket.

'Thank you.' Winifred turned on the top step of three at the back door. The stone glistened in the dim light of the kitchen. 'Thank you. I'm sorry, I didn't ask your name.'

A church bell rang out in the distance; four doleful clangs. Winifred shivered.

'You don't need to know my name.' Holding on to Winifred's elbow she ushered her carefully down the steps. 'Be careful, it's icy underfoot.' She pointed into the darkness. 'Turn left at the top of the lane and walk towards the road you'll see in front of you. That's Tollmoor Road and the gas lamps should still be on. Carry straight on and you'll see where the tram stops. If you hurry you'll catch the first one.'

And that was it; the woman went up the steps and closed the door before Winifred, holding onto the wall, inched towards the road to make her way home.

Chapter 46

January 1912

They'd gone, Conal and Honora; both of them.

It was two months since the protest march. Christmas had passed with no celebration. Winifred had attended the services at the chapel without thought, had sat across the table from her mother and grandmother in silence as they ate the mean Christmas dinner of stew and dumplings. She'd served in the shop without uttering a word to anyone, aware of the barely hidden contempt of some of the women customers, the curiosity and outrage of the men. Let the malicious words that poured from Ethel's lips wash over her. Bore the brunt of the pointed silence on the days her mother refused to speak to her. In reality, she preferred those days.

'She'll come round.' Florence held Winifred's hand. They were sitting side by side as they often did these days. Winifred had dragged the chair out of her bedroom and put it next to her grandmother's. She gently rubbed the slice of onion over Florence's red swollen fingers, her eyes watering against the sting of the pungent smell.

'I don't really care if she doesn't.' The silence that followed was a comfortable one. 'There,' Winifred said, 'that should help.' She wrung out a cloth from the bowl of warm water and, taking her grandmother's hand between hers, smoothed it over the skin.

'Thanks, Winnie.' Florence smiled. 'I can't remember a winter when I didn't have chilblains. Or a winter when the house didn't stink all the time of onions.'

The laughed quietly.

'I know.' Winifred dried her hands. 'When I was a child I thought you were always making onion soup and never understood why you didn't offer some to me.' She stood and stretched, fidgety against the trapped sensation that overcame her so often lately.

It had been a raw day. When Winifred had made a dash across the yard to the lavvy earlier her breath hung in front of her face like lace and the latch on the door burned the skin on her thumb with the icy cold. She'd shivered when she pulled her drawers down, the wooden seat chilly and damp under her buttocks. And, in the deadening quiet that the snow caused, she swore she heard the faint crackle of broken ice as her pee hit the frozen water.

Now, a few flakes still shuddered down past the windows but the snow, already banked up in the corners of the panes, began to slide away with the warmth of the room. Winifred had made sure they'd enough coal and slack to keep the fire going all night. At six o'clock in the evening it was black outside, the white lines of snow on top of the yard walls in stark contrast.

'Are you—'

'I'm fine, Granny.' Winifred stopped the question. She swallowed, her whole throat working in one long gulp.

'Because, if there is something, ducks, you know you can tell me.'

But Winifred couldn't, even though she knew her grandmother cared so much for her.

She smiled, picking up the bowl of water. 'I'll take this downstairs and make us both some Horlicks.'

On the landing she stood leaning on the wall, sadness seeping through her like a dark wave.

She'd searched for Conal and Honora. Wandering the streets on the outskirts of Lydcroft, she'd looked everywhere she'd ever been with her friend or Conal. Only once, though, did she go back to Gilpin Street, to number fifty. New people were in there; rough tinkers she was afraid of. The women jeered at her and pulled their men inside, slamming the door in her face. The people who lurked in the doorways of empty houses, or peered suspiciously at her as she passed them in the ginnels and lanes, were strangers to her.

It was no use, they'd gone. And so, it seemed, had all their friends. One of the first places she went for help was to the vicarage. But when Dorothy opened the door, the bleakness in her face destroyed Winifred's hope.

'I'm sorry, Winifred, no-one has seen either Honora or her brother.'

'I don't understand it. Where would they go?' Winifred followed her into the room where they'd first met. 'What about Mildred or Anne? Have they seen them?'

'Apparently not; I saw them yesterday and they had no news. I'm meeting them again later in Morrisfield; there's a group get-together to discuss what happened and to organise our next protest. You're welcome to come along.'

Winifred shuddered, remembering the horrific ending of the last.

Dorothy caught hold of her hands, her face sympathetic. 'We didn't really know Honora, you see; just through the WSPU. We really only found out where they were living last year, and that time with Sophie was the first time we'd been. Honora was, is, very much a free spirit. Her painting took up a lot of her time when she wasn't involved in our fight. You saw her paintings?'

'One or two.' Winifred was trembling with impatience. Honora's painting was the last thing she wanted to discuss.

'They are exquisite. Self-taught, she told us once. Mostly

portraits of people from families her brother knew from the university he was at in Leeds; doctors, specialists, the like, you know.' Dorothy hesitated. 'Perhaps some of them might know what's happened to her?'

'Do you know any of them? Her customers?'

'Sorry, no. I suppose you could ask at the university, though. Her brother should be there, surely?'

After Winifred had adamantly refused to go with her to the meeting with Mildred and Anne, there seemed to be little else that Dorothy could, or was willing, to say.

Winifred couldn't even get past the doors of the university. After the best part of a day travelling to Leeds, the porter had viewed her with suspicion. His only concession had been to send a messenger to find Conal. The boy returned with the news that Mr O'Reilly hadn't been to lectures for weeks. And was about to be sent down.

Each night she sobbed, hiding her face in her pillow to smother the sound. She was surprised that neither of the women she lived with heard her. Or noticed her swollen eyes some mornings. Or perhaps her grandmother had, maybe that was why she often studied her with a steady gaze. As though she was willing Winifred to talk.

But Winifred couldn't. Although she ached for Conal, she didn't sleep. The guilt lay like a stone in her stomach whenever she thought of how far she'd fallen. How could she tell her grandmother?

None of them mentioned that time Winifred hadn't got home until five o'clock. And she hadn't seen the woman who'd helped her in the alleyway after the march again. Even though she'd told Winifred not to go back to the house, she had, in the hopes the woman might have seen something after Winifred lost consciousness. But no-one answered the door, even though Winifred could have sworn she saw the curtains move at one of the upstairs windows.

Chapter 47

March 1912

The days had little purpose. When she wasn't silently serving in the shop Winifred was lying on her bed. Some days she cried, the tears slipping down the sides of her face into her hair. At night she stared into the darkness reliving that last day; that last time she'd seen Conal.

Those were the worst times. At least that was what she'd thought.

Through the thin curtains the fuzzy pale glow of the full moon was splintered by the frost patterns on the windows. She didn't need to see the faint plume of breath coming from her mouth to know how cold it was; when she touched her nose with the back of her hand it was freezing. The sharp bark of the Jack Russell had been followed by a rattle of peas on her mother's bedroom window. She heard the irritable shout intended both for her and for the knocker-upper man.

Unwilling to leave the warmth of her bed, Winifred fumbled around for her drawers off the rail-stand and dragged them under the bedclothes. She wriggled out of her thick cotton nightdress and into her underclothes and lay back summoning up the courage to get up to face the Monday morning stock-taking.

Flinging the covers back she swung her legs over the edge of the bed and, grabbing her corset, stood up. Wrapping the corset around her she pulled at the laces.

The cold prickle that crept over her skin stopped her fingers. Slowly she lifted her eyes to the mirror. The dark shadows underneath them were a stark contrast to the white of her face. She swallowed against the thickness that rose in her throat, letting her gaze travel down her body.

The weight that had fallen from her in the months after Conal had gone was now replaced by a fullness in her breasts and waist, a roundness of her stomach.

Her legs gave way under her and she dropped onto the bed, her mind flickering back over the last weeks, trying to place when she'd started to heave at the smell of the cheese as she cut it into blocks to wrap in brown greaseproof paper. And how long ago, when putting on her bust bodice, had her nipples become tender against the material. Or the strange feelings in her body she'd ignored in her misery.

She hadn't had her monthlies. Conal had explained to her why there were certain times that they couldn't fully make love, and she'd soon learned to keep a note of her monthlies' dates. But something must have gone wrong.

The cold sweat made her shake. She bent forward and retched the watery contents of her stomach onto the rug by the side of the bed. Wiping her mouth with the back of her hand she straightened up, gritting her teeth to stop the wail of fear that threatened, trying to work out when she'd last... Rocking, she closed her eyes. It had been months.

Chapter 48

'You don't look a bit well, Winnie.' Florence sat back in her armchair by the bedroom window. 'Proper peaky, in fact.'

Winifred knew that her grandmother had seen her running to the outside lavvy to be sick. 'I don't feel so good, Granny, I think it must be the smell of the gas in the mantle.' The vomiting had become worse. 'Haven't you noticed the gas seems stronger?' Smiling, what she hoped was a bright smile she patted her cheeks in the hope to get colour into them. 'I think I might go out and get some fresh air.'

She lived in dread of telling her mother and grandmother what was happening to her. It was Granny's disappointment that she hated the thought of most.

Florence heaved herself out of her chair and held out her hand. 'Here, give me your overall and I'll put it to soak. Looks like you've got butter grease all down it.

Winifred clutched it to her. 'No, don't bother, I'll take it downstairs myself on my way out.' She gave a short laugh. 'Can't think how I've been so careless.'

In her own bedroom she untied the overall and dropping it on the floor, studied herself in the long mirror. Even her navy woollen dress didn't hide the thickening of her waist, despite having pulled the ties of her corset as tight as she could.

She glanced at her bed, wishing she could lie down; desperately tired. Most nights she lay sleepless, praying to a God she didn't believe in anymore. Or staring into the darkness of the room and pressing down on her stomach, thinking she could bring her monthlies on. The thought that there might be a baby growing inside her horrified her. She knew little about childbirth other than what she had seen, or rather heard, one time when she was visiting her grandmother's. The woman's screams had echoed around Wellyhole Yard. Her grandmother had been reluctant to tell her what was happening, but Winifred was so frightened that Florence gave in. Even then she'd given only sketchy details, leaving the rest to Winifred's imagination. Now that memory both haunted and terrified her.

I should tell Granny, she thought, half-turning to the door, she'll tell me what to do. But the lurch of despair that followed stopped her. 'You can't,' she murmured. 'Not yet.' But when? Both her grandmother and mother would have to know soon. She was being a coward.

She dragged a cardigan over her dress and picked up the overall.

Before going downstairs she tapped on Florence's door. 'Won't be long, Granny.'

'Just a minute.'

Winifred heard the scrape of the chair leg on the linoleum.

'Can't stop. Sorry.' She ran down to the kitchen.

Her mother was standing in front of the fire, her skirt lifted up at the back to let the heat from the flames warm her. She turned her back on Winifred. Her legs were mottled with dark maroon patches from too many hours standing like that by the fireplace.

Winifred grabbed her coat from the stand and shoved her arms through the sleeves hoping to hide her figure. She crossed to the sink and dropped the overall into the bowl, filling it with warm water from the kettle.

'Off again, then? Got a fancy man?'

Winifred ignored the sneer. 'There are no customers waiting, are there?' Winifred swished the overall around, glancing at her mother over her shoulder.

'And why's that then?' Ethel snapped, rubbing her buttocks. 'They're taking their custom somewhere else, because of you and those damn women. That's why.'

'I haven't been to the Suffragettes for ages.' Not since that awful day. Winifred blinked away the tears. She had no fight left in her for that; she had a bigger struggle to face. 'And just in case you haven't noticed, Honora hasn't been near the shop in months.'

Honora. If she hadn't met the girl, if she hadn't allowed herself to get involved with the Suffragettes, she wouldn't be terrified of what was facing her now. Most days she veered from resenting Conal for deserting her, to the fear that he'd been killed by the police during the struggle at the protest march. Sometimes she had to stop herself from imagining that. The thought of him being beaten to death or trampled by a horse was horrific. But, somehow, she felt she would know, that word would get to her or she would have read it in the newspapers. She'd scoured every paper she could get hold of in those following weeks. There'd been nothing. And no letter from either brother or sister.

They'd left her. She didn't understand; Honora was dedicated to the Suffragettes, she'd seen that for herself. And Conal had said he loved her. Bitterness and grief gathered in her throat.

She swallowed. 'I won't be long.'

171

'Leaving me with her.' Ethel jerked her head upwards.

'Granny's having her afternoon nap.' Winifred pulled her gloves over her wrists and adjusted her sleeves. She needed to get out, get away from her mother. 'It's only for an hour, Mother. It's only ever for an hour.'

The park was busy, couples strolling arm in arm, nannies pushing perambulators, children running on the grass. Winifred stood on the bandstand steps and watched. In her heart she knew she had to accept that Conal and Honora had gone for good. But there was always hope that she would see one of their friends, get a message to them somehow.

A vague hope.

'Is it Winifred? Conal O'Reilly's girl?'

Winifred whirled round. She didn't recognise the man.

He tipped his hat. 'Denny. Denny Logan.' He waited for her to respond but when she didn't he offered, 'Conal and Honora's friend. We met once or twice. I'm…was Sophie's fiancé?'

'Oh, yes, I remember. Has she–did she…?'

'She died.'

'I'm sorry.'

He lowered his head, accepting her condolence with a slight movement of his lips.

Winifred pulled her handkerchief from her packet and dabbed at her eyes. 'I'm sorry, I don't…' She gulped. 'I'm looking for them. For Conal and Honora. Do you know where he– they are? Please…'

His forehead furrowed. 'No. I'm sorry.'

'Please, it's important.'

'I haven't seen them since that day.' He held out his hands. 'That day knocked the wind out of everybody's sails; the old crowd just scattered. The house on Gilpin Street was empty last time I went around, which was ages ago.' He gave her a sad smile. 'I'm sorry. Anything I can do?'

'No. Thanks. I just need to find him.' Winifred started to turn away, then stopped. Should she say why? On impulse she rushed on. 'I, we, were going to get married.' It was a lie but there was no other way she would tell this man. 'I'm having his baby.' She saw the instant dismay on his face. 'I need him to know. There's no way he would have left me if he'd known...'

'I'm sorry but I really don't know what happened to them. I asked around for weeks afterwards but nothing. If there *is* anything else I can do?'

'No. Thank you, but no.' There was nothing else to say.

'Well then...' He flushed, looked around and then back at her. 'Take care of yourself. Er, good luck...'

She watched him walked away. So that was it; she was on her own.

And then, for the first time she felt a movement inside her, a rippling inside her womb.

Chapter 49

March 1912

'It'll be dark before long.' Bill rested on the handle of the spade and studied the pale mauve sky scudded over by dark clouds. It had been a good day's work, and he was looking forward to one of Mrs Appleby's stews.

It was a long time since he'd felt so well. Even slept well, except for the reoccurring nightmare: seeing John Duffy slump to the floor and waking, sweating, in the middle of the night knowing he'd actually killed a man. Bill was content, and his waistline was showing the evidence. In fact, every morning when he woke up in the tiny back room he now called his own, he became more used to the idea of staying in this backwater. He and Sid only left Blossom Farm to go to Hebbing Bridge, the nearest village seven miles away, twice a week to sell eggs, and sometimes a chicken or two that had stopped laying. Bill knew he was safer here than wandering the country. And if he ever wanted a woman he could go to the one that Sid used occasionally in Hebbing Bridge. Other times he ignored the image of Winifred Duffy, pushed away the ache her memory brought, and settled himself down to some hard task on the small farm.

'Aye…that'll do for the day.' Sid threw his shovel into the wheelbarrow and lifted the handles.

Lost in his thoughts, the rattle of the spade made Bill jump.

'Right! Let's get rid of this lot.' Sid's strange way of halting in his sentences had become less when he was with Bill. And he smiled more often.

Bill followed him across the yard towards the large pile of hen dung that made their eyes water. Even with their kerchiefs over the noses the smell reeked.

'Never think of selling this lot, Sid, once it's rotted down?' he asked.

Sid frowned, but before he could answer they heard the clank of hooves approaching on the lane.

'Mr…Buckley,' Sid muttered, lowering his kerchief. 'Landlord.'

The horse was a large bay with black mane and tail that swished at the flies when the man pulled on the reins a few feet away.

He lifted his chin above the high shirt collar, his face wrinkled in disgust. 'Over here, Appleby,' he ordered, trying to keep the restless horse from turning in circles. 'And get your father.'

Bill looked in surprise at Sid. From what he'd gathered over the last two months the father had been dead quite a while. Sid glared at him.

'Father's… gone…to Liverpool for…a few days,' he stuttered. 'Get…some lads off the…ferry from Ireland…to collect.' He ran both palms on the outside of his trousers, rubbing them up and down. 'Ready…for next month.'

'Yes, well, that's what I wanted to speak to him about.' Mr Buckley exhaled impatiently.

Looking at him from the corner of his eye, Bill thought he looked furious. But he kept his head averted; he didn't want to come to the attention of this bloke.

'I need to know he's got everything in hand for moving the sheep back up in April.'

'It's all…sorted, Mr Buckley. Got…some lads coming from up North to…to help. Everything…here…' Sid swept his arm around in a clumsy gesture. The horse tossed its head, clattered backwards. 'Everything's in order.'

The landlord ignored him, pulling on the reins. He nodded towards Bill who'd tried to keep his kerchief partly over his mouth. 'Who's this? I didn't know you'd taken on anyone. Your father didn't inform me.'

'Cousin…Mr Buckley.' Sid shot Bill a warning glance. 'Cousin…from a farm near Harrogate. Helping…us out…' His large Adam's apple moved rapidly up and down his throat. 'For a while. He'll be…he'll be…here to help to…help…with the sheep.'

'Hmm.' Buckley yanked on the reins, pulling the horse around. 'Well, it's not good enough. Tell your father to come to the house. Tell him I need to talk to him. He should report to me each month.' He dug his heels into its flanks. 'He hasn't been since November,' he shouted over his shoulder. 'And it's not good enough. There are plenty others looking for tenancies.'

Both Bill and Sid stared into the shadowing darkness of the lane long after he'd gone.

Sid was the first to move. Going back to the wheelbarrow he dug the shovel into it and violently threw the fresh hen manure onto the rotting pile, his face dark with the rage Bill had seen the first day he'd arrived at the farm. 'Getting bloody late now.'

'Sid, I thought your father was dead.' He scraped the muck off the top of the stone wall where the man had missed the heap. 'Passed away?'

For a minute or two the only sound was Sid's heavy breathing. When the barrow was empty he lifted the handles and stood still. 'No, still here.'

They were close enough for Bill to see his face. There was an odd look about him, Bill thought. And then he knew. There hadn't been much in his life that had made him fearful; his father's temper when he was a child, the accident in the mine, once facing a gang of drunks, mocking the size of him, when he was on the streets. But that fear ran through him now.

'Where?' he said.

Sid looked at the pile of hen manure. The top of it was on a level with Bill's head. He looked from it to Sid. He didn't know whether to believe the man.

'Course it'll be hot under there.' Sid grinned abruptly. 'Might not be much left of the old bastard by now.' There was no faltering in his voice.

'I don't understand...'

'Hit Ma. Shouldn't have hit Ma. Won't have Ma upset.' He spoke as a matter of fact. 'Come on, food'll be ready. Don't like to keep Ma waiting. Yon bugger's made us late.'

By the time Bill had washed and changed his clothes ready to sit at the table for supper, Sid had relayed what had happened in his own way.

Mrs Appleby ladled the stew into his dish, her voice quiet when she spoke. 'So now you know.'

'Yeah.' He stared into the food, knew they were both studying him. How could he judge Sid? Hadn't he done worse, killed for greed? At least Sid had done it to save his mother.

'He was a brutal man. I should never have married him. Didn't want to but my father made me. I was one of twelve and the eldest girl still at home. Four of my sisters had gone into service and Sally, my sister younger than me, was better around the house than I was, he said. Jim, Sid's father, my husband, was a bad man.' The words came out smoothly as though rehearsed. She poured

176

stew into her own dish and sat down. 'You do understand, Bill?' She put her hand over his where it lay flat on the table.

'I do.' And he did, there'd been many a time he'd wanted to kill his own father for being too handy with his fists.

'What you don't know, Bill, is that Mr Buckley could evict us if he finds out Jim's... gone.'

'Sid could be hung, an all.' As soon as Bill said it, it brought the fear back; if he was caught the same thing would happen to him.

Bessie gave a low moan. When Bill glanced at her, she was holding her hand to her mouth, her face drained of colour.

Sid rose from his chair with a roar, his huge fist clenched. Only his mother's hand on his arm stopped him from reaching across the table to Bill.

'Go and lock the hens in, Sid, there's a good lad.' She waited until, with another glare, the man slammed out of the house. 'I know he could hang. I won't let that happen to my son.' Facing Bill and looking straight at him she continued, 'But *you* don't know how awful the years were with his dad.'

Bessie wiped her face and blew her nose on the edge of her apron. 'We have what's called an hereditary tenancy, a right to stay here for life. As a father Jim could have passed the farm on to Sid. But he hated Sid – hated what he is – slow, bit backward like. So, one day, just before Christmas, he came home – he'd been drinking in a neighbour's house. He said he'd met Mr Buckley on the lane. He said he'd told him that after his death he didn't care what happened, Mr Buckley could have the tenancy back; he'd sign anything to that fact so, as landlord, he could chuck us out, even though it should be Sid's right to take over the farm.

'We had a row, he hit me. Sid saw it and went for him. Jim didn't stand a chance. I couldn't stop it.'

Bill kept his eyes on the stew; an oily film was covering the surface. The thought of a corpse rotting under all that hen shit made him feel a bit sick. He picked up his spoon and stirred the grease in before choosing a large lump of beef. Chewing slowly he relished the tenderness of the meat; Mrs Appleby certainly knew how to make a good stew.

'I won't say owt,' he said. He knew which side his bread was buttered on. And what had happened before he landed at the farm had nowt to do with him. Just as much as what had happened in Lydford was nothing to do with Mrs Appleby or Sid.

The latch on the door rattled.

'Just one thing,' Bessie whispered. 'Before Sid comes in. Don't talk about it again, especially in front of him. It scared him when you talked about, you know and he won't forgive you for upsetting me.'

'I know.' Bill pushed another spoonful of food into his mouth. 'I'll watch my back.'

Chapter 50

The landlord threw the eviction notice at Bessie's feet. 'I warned your son four days ago, Mrs Appleby. I've been waiting for Appleby to come and report to me on this farm for the last five months. Five months! He's had more than enough leeway.' He stood up in the stirrups, slapping his whip against his boot and glaring around the yard. 'And still no sign of him. Well, that's it. I want you off my land in a week's time.'

'Please, Mr Buckley, I can explain.' Bessie looked back towards Sid who was standing in the doorway, his mouth set in stubborn silence, his arms folded across his chest. 'Jim's not been well—'

'For five months?' he exploded. 'Five months? And I wasn't told?' He swung himself off his horse and walked towards the farmhouse. 'If the man isn't well enough to look after my land he's no use to me. Those sheep should be rounded up and moved by now. And where are the men he was supposed to be hiring?'

Bill watched from inside the barn; he had no intention of

facing Buckley again. He saw Sid plant his feet more firmly on the step; he was obviously not going to move.

'Out of the way, man.' The landlord looked up at Sid who stared past him into the distance. 'I said move, you dolt.'

'Mr Buckley.' Bessie held her hand to her throat. 'Please—'

'This is the sixth time I've been here in as many weeks, Mrs Appleby. I've been far more lenient with you than any of the other tenants, mainly because your family has worked for mine for generations. But I can't, won't, put up with this any longer.' He raised his whip. 'Now get your son to move or I will use this on him.'

Sid uncrossed his arms, his fists bunched. Bill stepped back into the gloom of the barn; he wasn't getting bloody involved in what was going to happen next if the fool didn't come to his senses. He'd be no match for Sid.

Buckley obviously realised that. He lowered the whip. His voice cold, he turned to Bessie. 'Mrs Appleby?'

'I'm sorry, sir…'

Bill could hear the panic in her voice.

'Sid's only trying to protect you.' Speaking fast, Bessie added, 'Jim's infectious and the doctor says it's best if no-one goes near him… Well no-one but us. Of course we need to see to him… but no-one else.'

That frightened the bugger, Bill thought with satisfaction, moving to watch again. The man was visibly shaken as he spun on his heels and almost ran towards his horse.

'I've better things to do than waste my time talking to a lunatic, anyway.' Halting, his foot in the stirrup he said, 'This makes no difference whatsoever. I want you off my land by next week. If you're not gone by then I'll bring in the police.' He wheeled the horse around. 'You've got your eviction papers. I want you out.'

When it was definite Buckley had gone, Bill came to stand with Bessie.

'What will you do?'

'What can we do?' She looked helpless, tears slid silently and dripped onto her apron front. 'We're finished. He'll come back with the Bobbies and they'll find *him*.' She gazed towards the pile of hen manure and then towards her son. 'They'll hang Sid.' Her voice rose into a wail. 'And what will happen to me then?'

'Ma!' Sid stumbled towards her. 'Ma?'

Bill followed them into the kitchen, not sure what to do. He waited until they'd gone upstairs, listened to the low sound of Sid's voice and Bessie's crying. His stomach rumbled, reminding him how hungry he was. Opening the door of the range he scooped out some of the potatoes roasting on the griddle and took out the leg of lamb to cut a few slices off it. Slowly chewing and gazing out of the window at the thickening dusk he pondered on the problem. What next? He'd be leaving, of course. But how soon? And going where? Liverpool?

'Ma...she says you have to... help...help move... him.' Sid stood over Bill as he shoved the bread and dripping he'd had to find for himself for breakfast into his mouth. Bessie hadn't left her bed for two days. Her crying in the room above his had kept him awake and he was torn between feeling sorry for her and being irritated. Sid had made himself scarce most of the time as well, hardly speaking when he did appear. But Bill had got used to that; they'd not had much to say to one another since the day he'd found out about the murder.

He kept his head down. 'I've fed the hens. The eggs are on the side.' He nodded towards the large kitchen table.

'I said...Ma says...you have to...help me move...Father. Mr Buckley is...evicting us. He'll bring in new tenants. They could find...him. They will take...me... to prison.' His voice quavered. 'Ma won't manage without...me. You...have to help me.'

'Why should I?' Bill took a gulp of tea and swallowed the lump of stale bread.

'Because I'll say you killed him if you don't.'

'You bastard.' Bill shoved the chair back and stood up. He didn't care that the sod was at least two foot taller than him and built like a brick shithouse. He'd take him on anytime. 'You're not fitting me up for that.'

'I…won't…if you'll help.' There was fear in Sid's eyes. But there was also a stubborn determination.

'You're mad, man. You can't move him after all this time.'

'Need…to. Can't leave…him.'

Bill flung the chair away from him; it clattered to the floor. 'No.'

'Please…' Sid fixed him with his gaze. 'You owe us. Ma helped you…'

Bill licked his lips, nervous. But he did owe them. 'It'll have to wait 'til after dark.'

'Can't…chance—'

'I'm shiftin' no soddin' body in bloody daylight.' Bill crossed to the door. 'And that's an end to it.'

Sid silently handed Bill a pair of rubber gloves. Neither man looked at the other. Bill wrapped his woollen scarf around the lower part of his face; this was going to be one stinking bloody job.

The evening sky still had a hint of scarlet and gold on top of the Pennine hills, but the lingering light contrasted with the dark shadows around the farmyard. In the kitchen one of the dogs barked, a single sharp yelp. In Bessie's bedroom a candle lit shapes onto the curtains.

The leaden air around the muckheap buzzed with flies when Sid dug into it.

For the next hour they worked without speaking, swatting at the swarms of insects that gathered on the Tilley lamp on the wall and around their heads, cursing to themselves. Bill's woollen scarf was wet through with the moisture of his breath but there was no way he was going to take it off. Surreptitiously watching Sid he saw the flies around the man's face each time he lit a cigarette. Once, offered a fag, he refused even though he was gagging for a smoke. All he wanted was to get this over and done with.

And then the pile of shit was cleared and he saw the hessian sack. It moved and, with a startled yell he staggered back. 'What the fuck…'

Sid took the lamp off the wall and held it up. Fat maggots curled and wriggled in the light, shifting and huddling together in the sudden cool air on the sack. Furrows of liquid made tracks in the last scrapings of the hen manure and spread towards Bill's feet.

'S'only blasted maggots,' Sid grunted. 'Get the bigger shovels and the barrow with the other sack.'

The foul stench was thick in the air as the two men positioned themselves at one side of the sack, and slowly rolled it onto the new one using the two shovels. Both gagged and retched when the material folded and glutinous fluid poured onto the ground. They staggered sideways to the wheelbarrow and threw the heaving mess in. It landed with a dull wet slap on the wood and another release of foul gasses and flies.

Bill stumbled away, tearing his scarf off, and vomited; his eyes and nose streaming. From the far corner of the yard he could hear, Sid chucking his guts up as well. Serve the bastard right he thought, standing upright and wiping his mouth with his shirt sleeve. God, that had to be one of the worst soddin' jobs he'd ever done. Although he was sweating he shook with cold and revulsion. He went to the water pump in the yard and yanked on the handle until water gushed over his head and shoulders. Ripping at the buttons he threw the shirt away.

When he finally stopped, he stood swaying. 'That's my lot,' he said. 'You're on your bloody own now.' He made to go towards the house.

'No…I need…you.' Sid came nearer to Bill, holding the Tilly lamp down by his side. Flies followed the arc of light.

'Don't fuckin' get any closer.' Bill backed away, watching the bluebottles bat against the glass.

'Need…to get rid…' The big man was sobbing. 'Please…'

Water still dripped off Bill. He wiped his hand over his hair and face. 'Where?' What a bloody mess. 'Where, man?'

Sid's cries were noisy blubbers.

In the house both dogs started barking.

Bill looked up to Bessie's bedroom window. He saw her shadow. 'Right, I'll 'elp. Stop bloody skriking, yer mard arse, and tell me where.'

'Quarry…the old quarry.' Sid's Adam's apple worked in his throat as he calmed down. He hawked and spat out a great globule of snot.

'Well, you can bloody push the barrow.' Bill waited by the gate, moved to the middle of the lane to let Sid pass before going after him. To his relief the mass of flies thinned out the further away from the yard they went but he wasn't taking any chances and kept his distance.

The rumble of the iron wheel and the thud of their boots were loud in the night.

I want nowt to do with this, Bill thought again, rubbing his bare arms and shoulders to warm himself. That bastard Buckley'll be back again. And next time he will have the Bobbies with him, that's for sure. First thing in the morning, I'm off.

Without him noticing, Sid had turned off onto the grass verge. Bill peered into the darkness and caught sight of the dimmed Tilley lamp through the tall shrubs at the side of the lane. Ducking under them and brushing aside branches he took his time. With any luck the bloke would manage on his own.

'Bill?' Sid's voice was tremulous. 'Bill? You…there? I don't like the dark…this place…ghosts.'

'Well, you chose it.' Bill made himself sound scornful but the man was right; it was bloody creepy. He pushed through long grass, was stung by nettles. 'Damn.' he said, moving forward faster, almost bumping into Sid.

'Steady.' Sid held out his arm. 'We're right on the edge.'

'Bugger!' Bill stepped back, shaken. The darkness in front of him seemed even blacker when he looked past the grass and ferns

'Help me…tip it.'

Averting his face and covering his nose with his cupped hand, Bill grabbed the nearest handle.

'When I say now…tip.' In the small pool of light from the lamp, Sid's eyes were set in dark hollows as he too turned away from the wheelbarrow and its contents and kept his stare on Bill. He took a deep breath through his nose, his mouth set. Then he shouted, 'Tip.'

His voice echoed in the void underneath them. Bill let go of the handle as the putrid weight left the barrow.

'Grab it. Don't let go,' Sid shouted.

Lurching forward, Bill grabbed the side of it, touched the nauseating stickiness.

'Can't let it…they'll know it was ours. Need to wash it…out,' Sid panted as they hauled it back onto the flatter ground.

'Sod that for a soldier,' Bill muttered bending down and wiping his palms on the grass. He strode away.

Lying in bed, waiting for the house to settle into its usual night time sounds, Bill knew, if it hadn't all gone wrong, he would have stayed in this place for life given the chance. The routine comforted him. The nightmares would have eventually stopped.

Even before the cockerel in the yard began his morning call, Bill shouldered his bag and let himself out of the farmhouse. At the gate he hesitated, looking up and down in the darkness. What did it matter which way? West, not north, he decided; he'd head for Liverpool. He'd heard once that it was easy to get work on the docks there.

A fox screeched somewhere. There was a collective low bleating from the sheep in the near field.

Bill left the farm behind. The only noise before sunrise was the quiet scrape of his clogs on the lane and the occasional clink of stones kicked up in front of him.

Chapter 51

April 1912

With her back to the customers, Winifred rearranged the bottled onions and canned meat on the shelves, trying to shut off their voices.

'Hundreds, it says in the newspapers. Drowned in minutes.'

Ethel handed the packets of tea and sugar to the customer. 'That'll be one shilling and nine pence, please Mrs Collier.'

'Women and children alike. Clutching on to one another.'

There was a collective sigh and muttering in the queue.

'Shocking.'

'On their way to a new life in America as well. Dreadful thing to happen.'

'Awful!'

'Awful,' Ethel repeated. 'Who's next, please?'

'That'll be me, Mrs Duffy.'

Winifred recognised the voice. Edie Wood, a thin-faced elderly woman, was a vicious gossip. She'd have a field day when it was impossible to hide the fact she was having a baby. The thought caused Winifred to gasp and lean forward, her forehead against the shelf. What was going to happen to her? She swallowed, took a long breath.

'Yes, Miss Duffy, doesn't bear thinking about, does it?' Edie Wood called over Ethel's shoulder. 'Sinking down into freezing cold water.'

Shut up, shut up, shut up. Winifred wanted to scream the words aloud. She could imagine the same self-satisfied smug tones when Edie Wood imparted the knowledge of her baby. Her

185

illegitimate baby. The fear ran alongside the contempt for Conal, who'd deserted her.

Edie Wood didn't give her order in. Instead she said loudly, 'I hear the firm that built the ship will be sued by the law. It was supposed to be unsinkable.'

'Impossible.' A man, near the shop door, spoke with authority, his tone derisive. 'No such thing. Any ship that hits an iceberg will go down in minutes and that's what this *Titanic* ship did.'

'Well, you should know, Mr Wright.' Winifred recognised his wife's voice. 'After all, you work for the *Morrisfield Times*.' She sounded proud. 'He's well up on world events.'

Here we go again, Winifred thought, irritated and remembering her mother's belief in Mr Wright's opinion on Ireland and all Irish people. He's just the payroll clerk there; hardly an expert on world affairs. She knew it was an unkind thought but the man was always the same whenever he came into the shop. Pompous.

'Huh.' Annoyed that she'd lost the limelight, Mrs Wood raised her voice. 'Well, I haven't got all day. I'll have a bottle of those pickled eggs.'

'Winifred?'

Winifred handed a jar over to her mother without turning around.

'And we need more tea packeting,' Ethel said.

Winifred went into the store cupboard and pulled the door to. But the man's voice was loud; she couldn't shut him out, even by rustling the small brown bags and scooping the tea from the sack into them.

'Yes, Mrs Wright and I were only talking about it last night. The Atlantic is a cold sea.' There was a collective sound of melodramatic shivering noises. He continued, a pleased tone to his voice, having got the attention of all in the shop. Winifred sensed that even her mother had stopped to listen. 'The ship went down quickly and no-one stood a chance. Their lungs would fill

186

and down they'd go. At least fifteen hundred of them. Gone, just like that. Drowned – floating around amongst all that was left of the ship.'

Without a word, Winifred left the packets of tea unfastened and left the shop. The obvious thrilled reaction of them all disgusted her. She and her grandmother had cried when they'd first read about it. For nights she couldn't sleep, her own worries pushed aside by the images of those hundreds of drowning people. Their desperation and terror must have been dreadful.

She looked at the clock on the bedside table. Her mother would be closing for the lunch hour soon. Would she be able to have a lie down or would her mother nag her to finish putting the tea in the packets?

Making the decision, Winifred began to undress, grateful that the chilly weather meant she could wear more layers of clothes to hide her expanded waistline and stomach. Her corset was a different matter. She tugged at the stays, felt the relief when the uncomfortable garment loosened, freeing her body.

Standing in front of the mirror in only her bust bodice and bloomers, she studied her figure. There was no disguising what was happening to her.

'I heard you come upstairs, ducks. Could you help me with my shoes? I thought I'd go for...' her grandmother opened the bedroom door.

Winifred spun around towards the window, grabbing her dress off the chair.

'Winnie,' Florence whispered. 'Oh, ducks.'

Winifred dropped the dress and faced her. 'Granny...' her voice cracked. 'Oh, Granny...'

Florence opened her arms.

'I was waiting for you to tell me, Winnie.' They'd been sitting on Winifred's bed for the last hour while she wept. Once they heard Ethel come upstairs and go into her room; both giving a relieved sigh when they heard her go back down. Now Florence said, 'I've been that worried.'

'I'm sorry. I'm so ashamed. And I tried to tell you. Really I did.'

'Why didn't yer?'

'I didn't want to worry you.'

'Well that plan didn't work, ducks.' Her grandmother gave a wry chuckle. 'Trouble shared and all that…'

'I know. I'm sorry.' Winifred wiped her eyes and blew her nose. 'I knew I would have to. I thought I'd have time.' A sob caught in her throat. 'I thought Mother would throw me out. And I've seen the beggars waiting outside the workhouse in Morrisfield, Granny. It's pitiful. And what would happen to you?'

The bed creaked when Florence shifted sideways and took hold of Winifred's arms. 'Now look at me, ducks. She can't throw either of us out. This place is ours as well as hers, isn't it?' There was a determination in the way she faced her. 'She wouldn't dare. I'll say no more but she wouldn't dare, believe me.'

Winifred didn't know what she meant, but for the first time in months she was comforted; perhaps it would be all right. She should have confided in her granny long ago.

'Now, have a lie down.' Florence stood up and fussed around with the bed covers. 'Just look at those ankles; far too much standing about. I don't know how you've carried on like you have.'

'It's way past lunchtime. She'll have opened the shop again. She'll want me down there.'

'Then she'll just have to want. Things need to change.'

'Don't tell her, Granny, please. Not yet. Please.'

Florence pursed her lips but she hugged Winifred. 'I'll leave it to you, then, ducks. But the sooner the better, you know. Promise?'

'Promise.' Winifred managed a quivering smile as her grandmother left her bedroom. But then the baby wriggled inside her and she put her hand on her stomach. Florence's reassurances were swept away to be replaced by the terror Winifred had carried around since the day she knew she was pregnant.

She also knew she hadn't the courage to tell her mother. Not yet. Not as long she could hide it.

Chapter 52

April 1912

Bill groaned and rolled onto his back to look up through the twisted branches of the blackthorn to the sky, milky with a covering of thin clouds. The ground underneath him, so soft after a day trudging along the narrow lanes of the hills, now felt knobbly and hard. A stone dug into his left hip and as he shifted the dried heather crackled and dug its spikes through his shirt.

Sitting, he picked up his billycan and shook it. Empty. He'd drunk the last of the water last night, gulping it down; his throat dry from the day's dust and lack of food and drink. Two weeks after leaving Blossom Farm his snap bag was empty. Twisting around to look behind him he saw the land rose steeply, dotted with gorse and clumps of last year's heather. Here and there large rocks jutted out from the hillside, and stunted trees leaned slanted away from the prevailing wind. It was a bleak sight.

Bill sniffed, wiping his nose on his sleeve. By god he was frozen through. If he didn't get moving soon he'd be in trouble. When he stood, stretched and yawned loudly, a scattering of sheep bounded from a dip just behind the Blackthorn, startling him.

'Stupid buggers,' he yelled, his heart leaping. Unrolling his coat that he'd used as a pillow he put it on, thankful for the sudden warmth of the wool and, shielding his eyes, he scanned the area. A small cottage stood on its own about a mile away, a trail of light smoke spiralled from the chimney. If he'd known that was there last night he would have made for it; there were a couple of outbuildings nearby that would have been a damn sight more comfortable than the hard ground.

Gathering his things together and shoving them into his bag he peed against the tree. It steamed in the coolness of the morning. Buttoning his trousers and fastening his coat he wrapped his scarf around his neck; it still carried that foul smell.

For the first time in days he wondered what had happened to Sid and his mother. Not that he was bothered; he was well out of it. And, to make certain he couldn't be found, he'd taken small tracks and sheep trails away from Blossom Farm. One thing he knew how to do was to look after himself. Nobody was going to fit him up for owt he hadn't done.

But then an image came to him; Sid eating one of the sugar butties he relished at least twice a day, his large jaw working around the thick slices of bread, butter and layers of white sugar. Watching, hearing Sid eat them had always made Bill gag but suddenly an earlier nebulous memory returned, of someone cupping his face and pressing something similar into his hand. His grandma, Mam's mother, a small round woman with rosy cheeks and white hair, who always smelled of warm bread. And a smile and a broad-vowelled accent so alive to him at that moment that he marvelled at his ever forgetting her.

But she'd died long before his mam, so he could only have been four or five. Bill wiped his hand over his face, squeezed his eyes shut. Then he grinned, another picture coming to him, him shoving the butty through the bars of a street grid. He hadn't wanted to hurt his grandma's feelings, so he always took the proffered food but got rid of it as soon as he could. What he couldn't free himself of now was the feeling of the love that flooded over him. He cleared his throat, rubbed at his cheeks, surprisingly wet.

'Bloody soft arse,' he muttered, heaving his bag onto his shoulder.

He was glad to be walking again, even though his clogs had rubbed a soddin' great blister on his right heel. He'd be glad to get to that cottage; with a bit of luck he might be able to scrounge summat to eat. Stumbling down the hill, over the uneven clumps of thick grass, the thought made him feel almost cheerful.

Despite limping with the pain of the raw skin he moved quite fast, keeping the roof of the cottage in sight as best he could. Every now and then, over the hedgerows, he could see the misty outlines of Manchester on the horizon. Perhaps he'd make for there instead of Liverpool.

Two small brown terriers raced towards him on the lane, barking furiously when he approached the cottage. Bill stopped, bent to pick up a couple of stones and tossed them in his hand. He dropped his bag. And waited for them to get closer.

'Spit! Spot! Here!' It was a woman's voice coming from behind the line of tall shrubs that surrounded the buildings. 'What have you found now?'

When she appeared through a wide gate she stopped. 'Oh, sorry, I didn't hear anyone.' Her voice was low and pleasant but cautious. She was tall. It was the first thing Bill noticed about her, conscious of his own short stature. He stretched his back, shoulders straight and clenched his fingers over the stones.

'Sorry, they're not used to people coming along the lane.'

'Good guard dogs, though.'

'Yes.' She smiled. 'Can I help you?'

The dogs sniffed round his legs. He halted a few yards away, aware of his appearance and that he must stink to high heaven, no wonder the dogs wouldn't leave him alone. 'Wondered if I could fill my can with water?' He held it up and rattled it.

She clicked her fingers, the two terriers scampered to her and she reached down to stroke their heads.

When she looked at him again he saw the slight frown as though she was considering what to do, yet still she smiled.

'I can do better than that,' she said, 'You look as if a good meal wouldn't come amiss.' She motioned to the dogs to go through the gate and turned, her hand on the gatepost. 'Come on.'

Bill couldn't believe his luck. He threw the stones onto the grass verge where they wouldn't make a noise, and followed her.

Her hair was long and auburn, tied back with a dark blue ribbon. Her hips swayed as she walked. He forced himself to look away.

The ground on either side of the stony path was ridged, ready for planting. But the soil looked dry and untouched; a crust of chickweed covered it. Nearer to the cottage there were rows of short green shoots. Remembering Bessie Appleby's vegetable patch, he knew they were onion plants, but, unlike there, weeds sprouted in between the shoots and when he looked at the front of the building he saw the paintwork on the window frames and the door was patchy, revealing bare wood. The place was shabby, neglected. It didn't fit with the smart way the woman dressed and carried herself. Odd.

He stopped, his head cocked to one side. Except for the far cry of crows in the fields around, the even fainter bleats of sheep on the hill and the rustle of the breeze moving the leaves of the hedges there were few other sounds. Certainly no sounds of voices.

But there was something in the air. Bill drew breath in through his nose. Definitely something.

Pigs. It was pigs. This place was a pig farm. He nodded; satisfied he'd worked it out.

'Come in.' The woman appeared at the door. She left it wide open for him. The kitchen was large, dominated by an oak table. 'Sit down.' She pointed to the chair on the opposite side of the table. He noticed she kept it between them; he wasn't surprised or offended, after all he was a stranger. In a way he admired her reservation. So he would make sure he was on his best behaviour.

'I've made soup. And there's bread I made this morning. And some cold pork.'

He noticed the table was set with just the one place. 'Aren't you and your husband eating, Mrs...?' He'd noticed her wedding ring as soon as she appeared at the gate.

'Winters. Moira,' she said. 'Please call me Moira.'

'I will then, Moira,' Bill said, grinning. 'And I'm Bill. Bill…
Harrison.' Better safe than sorry, he thought. No point in taking
chances, however far away from that place.

She smiled but it seemed a little strained. 'Oh, where are my
manners? Would you like to wash your hands first?' She indicated
the large stone sink under the window.

'Thank you.' He made a great show of using the carbolic soap,
tempted to wash his face but thought she'd see that as a liberty.
When he turned round she was holding a towel out to him.

'Thank you,' he said again. The cloth was coarse and caught
on his broken nails and rough skin. But at least his hands were
clean. 'Your husband coming in for dinner?' he asked again.

'No,' she said, looking at the range where the contents of a large
saucepan was simmering. 'He's not here; he's away at the market
in Bradlow until tomorrow selling our pork.'

'Oh.' The name of the town meant nothing to him. The most
important thing was that the man wasn't at home. He felt there
was something, some tension between him and this woman.

'I'll be eating though.'

Struggling not to gobble his food, even though he was
ravenous, Bill recounted his travels. Well, a version of his treks
across the countryside. He regaled Moira with imagined and
humorous anecdotes; he had no intention of telling her the truth.

She spoke little, seeming happy to listen, make appreciative
noises and, sometimes, to laugh. Bill thought he'd never heard
such a deep throaty chuckle from a woman. He was enjoying
himself. He watched each time she laughed. Saw what amused
her. Exaggerated his tales.

The more she chuckled the more outrageous his stories.

They stayed long at the table after they finished eating. The
dogs moved restlessly around the kitchen.

'I need to feed the pigs.' She took a large hessian apron off a
hook on the back of the door, wrapping the ties twice around her
waist. It didn't look as if it were hers. He guessed the husband's.

'I'll help.' Bill made to stand.

'No, that's fine.' Moira glanced over at the range. 'There's a pan of hot water ready if you want to have a wash.'

'I'll help first,' he said. 'There must be summat I can do to pay for my grub?'

'Well,' she paused, 'There's some fencing around them that needs mending. My husband didn't – hasn't got round to it.'

'Rightyho.'

'I'll find you some wellington boots.'

He felt a bit ridiculous. The boots were obviously hers; they weren't the heavy thick rubber kind that he'd worn at Blossom Farm, men's Wellingtons. He strode a few feet behind her, stretching as tall as he could, breathing in the sweet smell of her auburn hair falling over her shoulder.

The pigsty was a mess. How the creatures hadn't escaped by now was a wonder. He kept quiet, noticing the sharp look she gave him when he stopped to study it. Either her husband was a lazy bastard or he'd been away more than a day or two.

'There's been some strong winds lately,' he said, instead.

'Yes.' The tone was grateful. 'Indeed. We do get some fierce weather here. My husband intended to fix it but the market only comes to Bradlow once a month. He couldn't miss it, so he had to go, but he meant to mend the fences and sty when he got– gets back.'

She was over-explaining; it was a trait of lying. Bill knew that, being a liar himself. Still, it was nowt to do with him.

He found tools and wood in one of the small outhouses. The hammer and saw were rusty and looked as if they hadn't been used in a while, and the wooden planks had mildew on them.

When she'd finished feeding the pigs Moira left him to it. Besides having to jump out of the way when they rushed towards him the pigs were no trouble; he was pretty nifty on his pins.

It took him longer than he expected but he thought he'd made a fair job of it. He was standing back admiring his handiwork when she came down the path again, carrying two buckets and wearing the hessian apron.

There was no disguising her admiration. She put the buckets down and clasped her hands in front of her, smiling at him. 'Wonderful!'

It was enough. His chest puffed out.

'Look, it's getting late.' They both surveyed the sky. The sun had gone down behind the roof of the cottage, leaving the place in gloom. 'I can't let you just walk off at this time of the day. I'll get some bedding together and you can sleep in one of the outhouses.'

'Thanks.' It might not be what he'd hoped for but it was certainly better than sleeping rough.

'I'll give the pigs their food first.' She picked up the buckets.

'I'll do it.' He took them from her and pushed open the gate that he'd just mended.

It was as though the four pigs knew he was a novice at layering the stinking pig slop in the trough. They chased him around the sty trying to get at the food. He managed to chuck one lot in before the biggest sow knocked him off his feet.

He lay, winded, for a few seconds before he realised Moira was trying to get him to his feet, helpless with laughter.

Instantly offended he scowled, but her mirth was infectious and, as soon as he was out of the sty, he found himself laughing alongside her.

Eventually she gathered up the empty buckets and, with one last look at the pigs, said, 'Come on, let's get you cleaned up. I think you need a bath.'

Uncomfortably aware of their difference in height Bill tried to keep in step with her when they walked towards the house and then, between them, they hauled the tin bath in the kitchen in front of the fire.

'There are two lots of hot water on the range.' She looked doubtful. 'Will that be enough?'

After washes in ice-cold streams it would be a luxury.

'Aye, it'll be fine, thanks.'

'I'll go to settle the pigs down for the night.' Moira held onto the latch of the back door. 'I think there's a storm coming, as well.' The evening sky was a mixture of grey and deep purple. 'I'll knock before I come back in.'

As soon as she left he stripped off and poured the water into the bath and added some cold. By, he didn't half stink. Worse than that night with …. He let the thought trail off.

He would have liked to soak for a while but she'd be finished with the pigs in no time. The first splatters of rain hit the windowpane just as he stepped out of the bath and wrapped the towel around him. But when he picked up his clothes he saw with dismay there was no way he could put them back on; they were covered in pig shit and slops.

He was dragging his spare pair of trousers and the last fairly clean shirt from his bag when she banged on the door and burst through followed by driving rain which instantly flooded onto the tiles.

They stared at one another, speaking at the same time.

'Sorry.' She wafted a hand at the closed door. 'Pouring down.'

'Finding clean stuff,' Bill said, lifting the clothes to show her. 'Would have had them on…'

The rain had plastered her dress to her, outlining her breasts and her long slender legs.

'Oh!' She turned away, her cheeks scarlet.

Bill looked down at the towel. Blast it.

Moira slowly turned back to look at him. There was a question in her eyes.

Bill held out his hand, let the towel drop. He might not be as tall as he'd liked to be but he knew he had muscles in all the right places and his skin was bronzed by so many days in the sun.

They both knew he wouldn't be sleeping in one of the outhouse.

It didn't matter she was taller than him; in bed he was the master.

Chapter 53

Bill luxuriated in the softness of the feather mattress and the sensation of release in his body. It was a long time since he'd been with a woman who hadn't been paid for. He listened to Moira's soft regular breathing and smiled. He turned onto his side, his hand on the firm softness of her breast, and went back to sleep.

When he woke again it was just starting to get light, and the shadows in the room were taking shape. The large wardrobe, the set of drawers, the chair in the corner, draped with Moira's clothes, the small window with the curtains half drawn. He could make out the dark line of the hilltop above the cottage and the pearlised pale sky of dawn.

Rising on his elbow he looked down on the woman who had responded to his lovemaking with such a desperation and need, and he wondered about her husband. She'd said the bloke was at a market in a town somewhere and he wondered how far away it was.

And how soon he'd have to leave.

As though she sensed his gaze she opened her eyes and smiled, lifting her arm to pull him towards her. They kissed. Her lips opened under his and she slowly spread her thighs.

When Bill next woke he was alone in the bed and the room was startlingly bright with the fullness of the sun. His belly grumbled and he realised how hungry he was. He flung the covers back and stood, scratching under his arms and yawning. His mucky clothes were still downstairs. Happen he'd have a look at the husband's stuff in that wardrobe; see if anything fitted him before he was off. His bag was downstairs but he could always sneak summat in when she wasn't looking.

Carefully he turned the key in the lock and opened the door. It took a few minutes of staring before he grasped what he was seeing. There were no man's clothes hung up, only women's dresses. Puzzled, he looked around the room. He went to the set of drawers and opened each one. No men's things, just nightdresses and women's underwear like he remembered his sisters used to wear. What the hell was going on?

Downstairs he heard a door slam, the rattle of pots. And singing. She was singing. He listened.

It was a long time since he'd heard a woman sing like that. In fact it was only the once; he was fifteen and he'd made love to a girl for the first time. It was her first time as well. Annie. Annie Heap.

He knew he was smitten the first time he saw her. Small, with warm brown eyes and with a lock of dark hair peeping out from the shawl she had over her head, she reminded him of his mother.

Shy, aware he was black from the coal dust after a long day shift underground, he only glanced and nodded at her. The movement of her head was almost imperceptible but he flushed, quickening his step in his haste not to let her see the self-consciousness he was sure showed on his face.

The second time he saw her again, Harry Wilshaw was chatting to her. She had her head lowered so Bill couldn't tell if she was smiling but, as he passed them, Harry fell into line with him, matching Bill's steps even though he was at least a foot taller.

'She's a snotty cow,' Harry muttered.

'Who is she?' Bill tried to sound nonchalant.

'That new Overman, Bob Heap? His daughter. Come over from Leeds way, so Alf Turnbull says. Says they're renting that cottage on Green's Tenement.'

Bill waited to see if Harry volunteered any more information but after muttering, 'She wouldn't even tell me her name,' the lad lapsed into sullen silence. Bill was glad when he trudged away to join the group of men in front of them.

Over the next week, Bill made a point of chatting with Bob Heap. The chap seemed happy to talk and, before long, Bill discovered he'd been widowed for only six months and he'd had to get away from the place he'd lived with his wife and daughter.

'Start fresh, like,' Bob said, nodding towards where the slight figure of the girl waited by the gates of the mine. 'Our Annie took it bad and she's not so strong anyway. It mithers me sometimes, she's so quiet.' Ignoring the push of the miners around them they stopped by the manager's office. 'Look,' Bob said, 'I've got to go in there and give my weekly shift report in. Do you mind telling her I won't be long?' He studied the crowd of men passing his daughter.

Bill saw the stares, heard the coarse sounds and remarks and tightened his mouth. If he'd been Bob he'd have clobbered the lot of them. 'Sure,' he said, 'If that's okay with you?'

'I wouldn't have asked, lad, if I wasn't sure you'd be respectful.' The look in the man's eyes was a warning. But then he smiled. 'She could do with meeting people her own age. What are you? Fifteen, sixteen?'

'I'll be sixteen soon.' Bill drew himself up, embarrassed.

'Aye, well, go on then. Tell her.'

The mass of men had thinned out and Bill walked self-consciously across the yard towards her, knowing her eyes were on him.

'Your father asked me to tell you he won't be a minute.' Bill spoke carefully, toning down his accent. When she acknowledged him in a soft voice he was relieved to notice her broad Yorkshire twang. 'I'm Bill Howarth. I work with your dad.'

'I can see you do.' There was a hint of laughter in the words and Bill stiffened. But then she said, 'I'm Annie and I'm pleased to meet you.' She started to hold out her hand and then stopped.

'Best not.' Bill grinned, looking at his own hands, grimed with coal dust.

'No.' Her laughter turned into a bout of breathless coughing. 'Sorry,' she said eventually, her palm flat to her chest.

Bill had turned away, not wanting to embarrass her. 'That's okay, get a cough myself sometimes. Coal dust you know.'

'Don't think mine's anything to do with coal dust. Or if it is I'll have to blame Dad for bringing it home with him after a shift.' She smiled. She had perfect teeth and the smile reached her brown eyes with the lovely long dark lashes.

As Bill later told himself, that was when he fell hook, line and sinker for her.

So that, when her father joined them and asked if he was going their way and would he like to join them, Bill said yes, even though he lived in the opposite direction. Although she said little, Annie would often smile at something he said. When she did speak it was only to her father. Bill began to think he would never get to know her properly.

Weeks later, after having to pretend to turn into a street and wait until they were out of sight before he retraced his steps to his house, he plucked up courage to ask Bob's permission to walk out with Annie.

The man stopped, forcing Bill and Annie to stand still at the side of him. The rest of the shift streamed past them, one or two of the men staring with curiosity. 'I don't know, lad, Annie's not too strong and her cough's been worse lately. And you're both a bit young.' He paused, looked from Bill to his daughter. 'Still, I suppose it really depends on Annie.'

Bill's guts twisted in the pause that followed. He heard the scrape of his clogs on the cobbles as he moved from one foot to the other. He sensed the air, tainted by the smell of cigarettes, being drawn in and out of his nostrils, the pulsing of blood in his neck.

Until she said, 'If you agree, Da, I'd like that.'

Bill forced himself not to do the jig he wanted to. And he bit his top lip to prevent the grin. 'We could walk in the park? Take it slowly, like? Or along the canal–feed the ducks there? Sunday?' He waved a hand over his face. 'You'd see me then without all this.'

'I'm used to Da being black as the ace of spades when he comes home from work.' Annie threaded her hand through her father's arm and laughed.

A lovely sound, Bill thought.

'What do you think, Da?' A crinkle of worry marred her smooth forehead.

'As long as there would be other people around and you'd look after her...' There was clear warning in Bob's expression when he glanced at Bill before he looked at Annie. 'And it would have to be in the afternoon; we've chapel in the morning.'

'Bill could join us?' Annie peeped past her father. 'Unless he needs to go to his own chapel?'

She was assuming he went to a chapel rather than a church. For the first time Bill was ashamed for his lack of belief.

'I don't go anywhere.' He heard the intake of breath and hurried on. 'My mam was C of E and Dad was a Roman Catholic. When Mam were alive the priest used to come on Fridays to tell them they weren't really married. Mam wouldn't convert, yer see? I remember how upset she got. So I was never sent to church. Or chapel.'

Neither of them answered. Bill's scalp prickled in panic, he needed to make them understand, it wasn't his fault. 'Then Dad got married again and I think the priest gave up.'

Bob sighed, lifted his head and gazed around. The sun was dipping behind the roofs of the houses, leaving one side of the street in gloom and reflecting a crimson and gold light in the upstairs windows on the other side. They were alone, the collective thump of footsteps had faded.

'Are you up for coming to our chapel, lad?'

Bill answered without thinking. 'Aye. Sure.' Adding quickly, 'I'd like that.' He'd no best clothes, he'd have to go to the pawnshop, see what he could afford. But he wasn't going to mess this up; one way or another he'd get to go out with Annie.

Bill lay down on Moira's bed, his legs shaking. It had been a long time since he'd thought of Annie; he'd buried her memory deep inside him. He closed his eyes, scrunched them tight against the scald of the tears that threatened.

He heard the door downstairs open and close and the yapping of the two dogs in the front garden. A rattling of a poker in the fireplace. Moira was singing again, this time a different song. He listened as her voice rose up to him '...*a beautiful sight to see...*' She was singing '*A Bird in a Gilded Cage*'. Bill folded his arms across his wet face, shutting out the light in the room. Annie's song; something she sang all the time. He'd forgotten. Groaning Bill turned onto his stomach and pulled the pillow around his head but he could still hear the song, and the images of his long lost girl wouldn't leave him.

Eventually the juddering breaths settled and he sat up, pushing his fingers through his hair. He stayed still, listening. No singing now, just the muffled clink of crockery and a sweet sugary smell drifting through the floorboards. As if in answer his belly rumbled again. What the hell was wrong with him? Bloody soft arse, shift yourself. He stood, stretched, forced away the old memories. Then he stood, pondering again on the lack of any men's stuff in the bedroom.

On the landing he opened the two other doors. The beds in there had bare mattresses. There was no sign of a man's stuff; nothing that showed Moira shared a home with a husband. Not that it bothered him but he'd have to go downstairs buck-naked.

Moira turned to smile at him when he stepped off the last stair and then laughed. 'Your clothes are clean and dried there.' She pointed to the fender around the fire.

He crossed the kitchen to get them. The two dogs gently wagged their tails but, warmed by the sun, didn't move from their places on the doormat.

She lifted the saucepan in her hand. 'Porridge?'

He nodded without speaking, fastening his trousers and tucking in his shirt.

Her forehead crinkled but she said nothing, just busied herself spooning the porridge into two dishes, before sitting at the table.

'Where's yer husband?'

'I told you, he's away at the market in Bradlow.'

She was lying; she didn't want him to know she lived alone. She'd opened her legs to him but still didn't trust him with the truth.

Bill sat opposite her. 'Taken all 'is stuff with 'im then,'as e?' His voice sounded rough, coarse even to himself but, for some reason, he was angry. Hadn't he tried to be a gent? Hadn't he watched his manners, the way he spoke, to reassure the woman he was okay, and not some raging bloody axe-murderer on the loose to rape an' pillage?

She put her spoon into the dish. He saw her hands were trembling.

Pushing his chair away from him, he stood. She had her head down, her hands folded in her lap. But he could tell from the quick way she was breathing she was scared.

It was as though the terriers could tell as well. They came to stand on each side of her, the hackles on their back disturbed.

To make himself less intimidating he shoved his hands in his trouser pockets.

'I have my pride, Moira. I'm down on my luck now.' The last time he'd said it was at Blossom Farm and he frowned at the immediate recollection. Look what happened there. If this woman had done her husband in as well and disposed of the body in the bloody pigsty, he wanted none of it.

'But I've always had my pride, and I've always worked for a living.' He sighed. 'An' I've never been in trouble with the Bobbies.' Because he'd never been caught, the sentence ran on in his mind. 'So, I'll thank you for your food, yesterday. And I hope you don't think I took advantage of you, last night. I'll be on my way.'

He waited but she said nothing. 'I can see you don't trust me. After all you don't know me, I just turned up on your doorstep. And your business is your business. I didn't ask where your husband was, you told me he'd gone to a market. You wanted me to think you had a husband because you didn't want me to think I could stay. Well I don't stay where I'm not wanted. I paid for my food by mending yon pigsty. I'd say we're straight.'

He reached the door and was pretending to struggle with the handle before he heard her speak. It was a relief when she did.

'No, please.' Moira rose from her chair and came to stand in front of him. 'I'm sorry. I'm a widow. Jake, my husband…' First time she'd mentioned his name. It made him real somehow to Bill. 'Jake died last year, he was older than me. His heart failed him digging in the garden. I'm on my own. I need to be careful. Please, Bill?'

Now he felt a bit bad for upsetting her but, if he was going to stay, he couldn't afford to show any weakness. He held his hand to her face, slowly moving his thumb across her cheek. 'It's okay, love. I do understand. But I still have to go.'

'No! Please. Stay. I'm lonely.' She'd closed her eyes at his touch but now opened them wide. 'It's awful. Nobody comes here. Nobody has since the funeral…'

Nobody? For the first time in weeks the tension Bill had been carrying slipped away. Was it possible he could live here and feel easy?

'No. Except for the farmer who calls on his way to the market once a month to take one of the pigs or bring provisions for me. I'm lonely, Bill.' She took his hand and held it to her breast. 'Please stay.'

Bill wasn't a religious man. He was the first to acknowledge that. But there was many a time over the next two years that he thanked God he'd stood that day under the blackthorn tree and spotted Moira's cottage.

Chapter 54

June 1912

Winifred opened her eyes wide; something was wrong. What was it? She waited. The grinding pain began as a low ache deep inside her pelvis, rolling in waves down her inner thighs and around her stomach. The agony was pounding in her blood, filling every inch of her.

She took in a sobbing breath. So this was how it happened.

But it was too soon, she wasn't ready, she hadn't told her mother. She needed her grandmother. Opening her mouth Winifred shouted, 'Granny?' But the word was only a rasping croak that ending in a low gasp when the next roll of torture began and the only thing she could do was to clutch the sides of the mattress and grit her teeth.

And then it was over. Kicking the bedclothes onto the floor, she dragged in a long breath, wiping her arm across her forehead. Her hair was wet, her skin slimy with sweat. The room was already stifling with the heat of the early morning filtering through the half-drawn curtain. Particles of dust floated, settling on the dark wood of the tallboy.

The agony began again. Drawing up her knees she wrapped her arms around them and groaned. It was happening, the baby was going to be born whatever she did. How long did it last? Her body didn't belong to her anymore. It was unbearable.

A knife was stabbing her belly time after time and she was helpless to stop it. She could taste the blood as she bit down on her lip to stop herself screaming at each overwhelming surge of pain.

'Granny…' She clenched and unclenched her fists. All she wanted was for it to stop.

And then the torture increased; one long unbearable contraction that filled her whole body.

Winifred yelled, let her legs flop open and arched her back.

With a last agonizing drawn-out push the baby suddenly left her body. The surge of relief was rapidly followed by terror. Pushing herself up on her elbow she looked down on the bed, sobbing. Her thighs were covered in blood; the sheet underneath her was the same. Between her knees the baby lay still, a grey wet cord tying her to it.

She manoeuvred her feet and pulled it towards her until she could reach to lift its slippery body into her arms. It was a boy. A tiny boy. Leaning sideways, she felt around on the floor until she found the top cotton sheet and pulled it over the two of them. Instinctively she opened the front of her nightdress and placed him next to her. He lay still, his quick breaths moved in time with her own trembling.

The bedroom door crashed open. 'What the hell is going on in here?' Ethel shouted. 'All this racket…' Her face slackened in shock. 'What…?' She gasped, swayed in the doorway, her knuckles white with her grip on the handle. 'What. Is. That?' Winifred stared back at her and then down at the baby, still bloodied and attached to her by the umbilical cord.

'I knew it.' Her mother spat the words out, her face distorted with disgust. 'I knew there was something.' She flew across the room her hand raised and slapped Winifred across the face. 'Trollop! Trash.'

The blow jerked Winifred's head back against the iron rail of the headboard. A burst of sharp pain shot through her. Her mother was still hitting her, a torrent of vile recriminations pouring out.

'Mother, stop it. Stop it.' She bent over the baby, protecting him from her mother's fury, wincing against each blow. Raising one arm she hit out, trying to catch hold of her mother's hands. She felt her knuckles against her mother's lips; she heard the sudden gasp, the increase of the force of the blows.

But all at once, the shock of another pain starting, swept over her, the urge to push again was irresistible; something else was happening. She screamed. 'Get off me!' She crouched lower in the bed, unable to ward off the blows; only able to clench her teeth as the rush of pain peaked and ended in a warmth of blood between her thighs. 'Granny!'

Ethel dropped to the floor next to the bed, gasping for breath.

'Please. I need help, Mother. Get Granny. The doctor—'

'I'm paying for no doctor.' Her face was inches away from Winifred's. The hatred was frightening. 'Whose is it? Who've you been given your favours to?' Her voice now was strangely flat.

'No-one you know,' Winifred whispered. 'Please, Mother, get the doctor... I'll pay, I have my own money. Something's wrong.'

'I'm having no doctor here. Spreading your shame all over the village.' Her mother clung onto the bed and hauled herself to her feet, pushing her face even closer to Winifred. The baby's whimpers rose into a wail. 'You asked for it.' Spittle hit Winifred's cheek. 'You deal with it.' She staggered to the door.

'I'm here.' Florence pushed past her daughter-in-law, her voluminous nightgown swirling around her in her haste.

'Granny. Help me. Please.' Tears of shame and relief flooded through Winifred, her sobs mingled with those of her baby's.

'Oh, good Lord.' She bent over Winifred, her hand over her heart. 'I didn't realise how close to your time you were.'

'You knew?' Ethel hissed the accusation.

Neither answered her.

Her grandmother stroked Winifred's sweat-soaked hair from her forehead, her face tight with anxiety. There was a cut above Winifred's eye where her mother's wedding ring had caught her. Florence pulled a handkerchief from the sleeve of her nightdress and wiped at the blood trickling down the side of Winifred's face. She glanced around to glare at Ethel.

'What the hell do you think you're doing? She needs help, not this. Look at the state of her.'

Ethel returned her gaze, unflinching.

Florence shook her head in disgust and looked back at

Winifred. 'I'm sorry, I tried to get here sooner; I couldn't get out of bed, my legs wouldn't work.'

'You're here now.' Winifred couldn't stop crying. 'I'm sorry, Granny.'

They were talking as though Ethel wasn't in the room but Winifred heard the snort of disgust.

'It'll be all right,' Florence said. 'Now, lie still, we'll get the doctor.'

'Thank you, Granny.' Winifred held the baby closer. 'I'm frightened, Granny. Something else happened, after the baby was born.' She couldn't stop the tears. 'I think something's wrong.'

Florence lifted the sheet. 'Don't worry, ducks, it's normal. It's what the baby fed on when he was inside you. It's called the placenta. He, and you, don't need it anymore. Ethel, get the doctor.'

'I'm going for no doctor.' Ethel leaned against the doorframe, arms crossed, her mouth twisted.

Florence stood straight, put her back to Winifred, as if, by doing that she could protect her. 'You'll go for the doctor, Ethel.' Her voice sounded strange, almost threatening to Winifred. 'You'll go for the doctor because I did the same for you, once. Remember?'

Except for the snuffling of the baby there was no sound in the room. Outside, the sparrows in the guttering above the bedroom window squabbled and chirruped. A horse slowly clomped past, metal wheels grated on the road. A man shouted. A whip cracked.

Winifred reached over her head and grasped the rail of the bed-head to pull herself upright, ignoring the stabs of pain between her legs and the hot blood that still trickled out of her. 'Please, Mother.'

'Ethel.' Her grandmother's tone warned. 'The doctor.'

Craning around her grandmother, Winifred saw the rage on her mother's face before she left the bedroom.

She looked down at the baby. Conal's baby. And felt nothing.

Chapter 55

November 1912

'I'm telling you I can't manage in the shop by myself. I'm not your slave.' Ethel lowered the flame on the gas mantle. The kitchen descended into the gloom of the winter's afternoon but Winifred, still ironing, said nothing. She shifted around the table to make the most of the light and placed the cooling flat iron onto the range. Picking up the other iron she touched it lightly with her forefinger and blew on the surface to get rid of the specks of soot.

'And I'm telling you. If you want me to carry on helping in the shop, I need help myself with the baby.' Winifred wiped her forehead with the back of her hand. 'Granny does what she can but she's an old lady—'

'Lady? Some lady.' Ethel scoffed. 'And, anyway, why do you need help? I've hardly ever seen you pick the brat up.' She glanced towards the child lying on the blankets in the wooden apple box that Florence had fashioned into a crib. 'She looks after it more than you do. There's nothing to stop you being in the shop.'

'Stop being so nasty, Mother.'

Winifred was tired. Tired of fighting with her mother. Tired of the outraged looks, the sly gossip every time she was serving in the shop, the sideways glances, the scorn. And yet she knew her mother was right; she only touched Tom when she needed to. Tom; she hadn't even named him, leaving it to her grandmother to decide what to call the boy. There was something that stopped her feeling anything for the child. Conal's child.

She folded the nightgown and put it on top of the pile of clothes already ironed and picked up another. 'Why do you never have anything good to say?'

'Perhaps it's because I have a daughter who's been acting like a woman of the streets.' Ethel's voice was cold. 'You've brought disgrace on the family.'

Winifred banged the iron down onto the table. 'What family, Mother?' She was so far from everything she'd had only months ago, the first taste of freedom and the love of her father. 'We're not a family. If we were truly a family you wouldn't care what anyone would think. I'm your daughter; you'd love me whatever happened. Whatever I'd done.'

Even as she spoke a stab of guilt jolted her, knowing how she was rejecting her son. Yet still she said again, 'Whatever I've done, because I'm your daughter—'

'But you're not.' It was as though the words had been waiting to burst out.

Winifred's hand stilled on the iron. The flame in the mantle popped softly, the coal shifted in the grate, the baby in the cradle next to her sighed in his sleep.

Behind her the stair tread creaked. The rustle of clothes, the vague smell of mothballs, told Winifred her grandmother was with them, but she didn't take her eyes off her mother.

'Ethel.' Florence's voice was a whisper. Yet, in the quiet of the room, it was a harsh sound. 'Enough.'

'Why? What's the point of her not knowing the truth? Especially now. Blood will out, isn't that what they say?'

'Who?' Winifred was barely aware of the smell of the scorched cotton. Yet she automatically lifted the iron from the small nightgown. 'Who says that? And what do you mean?' She was aware that her grandmother was close to her, of the slow ticking of the clock echoed by the steady breathing of her mother.

Ethel's face was impassive. When she spoke again there was no emotion. 'I'm not your mother. You were a foundling; left on the doorstep like a piece of trash. Like the trash that probably gave birth to it.' The poison spilled from Ethel's lips as the angry tears fell from her eyes. 'Well, the apple didn't fall far from the tree, did it?' She stabbed the air with her finger.

210

'I said that's enough.' Florence spoke in a loud sharp voice. But it didn't stop the woman.

Ethel swung round to face her. 'You. And him, your precious son. You both foisted her on me. I didn't want the girl.'

'I don't understand. What are you saying?' The question hung between them. After a moment Winifred moved her head slightly in Florence's direction. They stood together in a group yet were so far apart. Winifred repeated, 'What are you saying?'

This time so loud that the baby, startled in his sleep, jumped, his arms and legs stiffened instinctively. He whimpered. Winifred looked at him. The flames from the range sputtered, casting pale orange light and shadow over him. He was frowning, his mouth puckered. She didn't move towards him. Instead she stared back at each of the two women who knew something about her she had never been aware of.

'Granny?'

She might well as not been in the room.

'You knew what you were doing, Ethel. You agreed—'

'Because I was a fool. Because I loved him.' Her mother's arms were stiff by her side. 'How was I to know I would never be able to have a child of my own?'

'You knew.'

Ethel stared at them for a long moment, her lips pulled tight. Turning on her heel, she walked back into the shop.

Her knees buckling, Winifred dragged the nearest chair towards her and fell onto it. Everything she'd ever known was spiralling away from her. Leaning on the table, she covered her face with both hands.

'Winnie?'

Her grandmother's fingers were on her arm; hot, almost burning, on her cold skin.

The anger that rose shocked her. 'You knew.' She shook Florence's hand off with a flick of her elbow, still covering her eyes. The darkness her palms made was a small comfort. She needed to think but her mind was in turmoil. The flashes of thoughts made no sense, the questions incoherent. Panic overwhelmed the anger, swilled around in her stomach. What would she do? What could she do? Who was she?

'Winnie, listen to me. I know we – I – should have told you about this a long time ago. But as the years went on it didn't seem to matter. I've loved you as my own flesh and blood. Your father loved you as his daughter.'

Winifred strained to hear her grandmother's words. She felt she was at the far end of a tunnel.

'It didn't, doesn't matter where you came from—'

'But it does.' Winifred slapped her palms on the table, her head lowered. 'It does. It's cruel to have lied to me all my life. I trusted you and you were lying. So, tell me. Tell me the truth of who I am. Now!' Her whole body vibrated with the strain of staying calm. She twisted in the chair to stare at Florence. '*She's* not going to, so *you* do it.'

Her grandmother held her gaze, the love visible in her eyes. 'Winnie…' She coughed, cleared her throat. It was as though her face had altered in a few short moments; pallid skin folding around her mouth, changing the shape. Becoming someone other than Granny Duffy. Which was quite right; the thought drummed persistently through Winifred's head, because she was. The old woman was someone she didn't know anymore.

'Winnie, I'm sorry, we never found out.'

Pain coursed through Winifred but she gave a short angry laugh. 'Really?' She should believe it, yet it was wrong just to accept without more questions. 'Did you even try? Did you go to the police?'

Outside the wind rose to rattle the back door. Glancing towards the window she saw it was fully dark now. Making a sudden decision she stood and turned up both gas mantles. Better to see the old woman's expression; she would be able to see if she was being honest in her answers. Before spinning on her heels to confront her grandmother again she held her fingers over her eyes, holding back the tears.

'Well? Is that it? Is that all you can say.'

'That's all there is.' Florence's words were measured, quiet. 'Your father found you. You were on the doorstep of the shop.' Her shoulders half lifted as though to shrug but stopped. 'He said you were only in a thin blanket and blue with cold.' She stopped, her face softened. 'Too tiny, too underfed, even to cry. He wrapped you in a thicker blanket and brought you to me.' She looked away towards the door that led into the shop. 'They'd given up hope for a child – at least he had. Ethel hadn't, even though she'd had two miscarriages since...'

'Since?' Winifred demanded, her voice fierce, struggling to bring a memory back. 'Since when?' Comprehension widened her eyes. 'I remember. I remember something you said, the day Tom was born. It was when you told Mother to get the doctor. I'd been pleading with her but she'd refused. Then you said something.' Her forehead wrinkled in concentration. 'Something about you doing the same for her once.' Winifred moved forward, put her hands flat on the table and leaned towards Florence. 'What did you mean?'

Florence pushed her chair back, the legs scraped on the linoleum. Slowly, stiffly she crossed the kitchen and closed the door to the shop.

'Your mother was pregnant. Before they were wed.'

'Dad's?'

'No.' She stopped. 'He didn't know about it.' She stood still, her hand to her chest, her breath rattled in her throat.

Alarmed, Winifred went to her. Whatever had been said she couldn't stop loving the old woman. Her arm around her grandmother's waist, she led her back to the chair and lowered her into it. 'All right now?'

Florence gave a glimmer of a smile, acknowledging the gentleness in Winifred's voice.

'Just tell me, Granny.'

'Ethel had gone to a woman; someone who dealt with those kind of things'

'I don't understand.'

'Girls who got into trouble. Women who helped put things… right for them.'

'You mean she had an—'

'Yes.' Florence put up her hand to stop Winifred uttering the words. 'It was a bodged job, the woman made a right mess of Ethel's insides. I had a bit of money put to one side, so I paid for a doctor to sort her out as best he could. But there was no chance of her ever having a child of her own after that. I was the only one who knew about it. That's why your mother resents me. That's why she didn't want me here. It was our secret. A secret she's always wished we didn't have between us. What she has never understood is that I would have kept it to my grave; I would never have told your father. I wouldn't have hurt him like that. He never found out she'd been with someone else while they were engaged. I did once tell him she wasn't good enough for him. I couldn't tell him why, though it caused the one and only quarrel we ever had.' A shadow flitted across her face. 'I lied to him.'

'As you've lied to me,' Winifred whispered. 'You lied to protect him, didn't you?' It wasn't so much a question as an understanding. 'And that's why you lied to me.'

'And why it was so easy to persuade her to keep you.' Florence closed her eyes, shook her head. 'Was I so wrong, Winnie?' She let her hand rest on the table.

Winifred covered it with her own. 'No, Granny.'

'Good. I'm glad, ducks.' A short breath quivered her lips. 'I think I'll go for a lie down if you don't mind. I'm tired.'

Left alone, Winifred was filled with a strange feeling of not knowing herself, who she was. The truth that had emerged over the last few hours meant that she had no blood relative that she knew of.

The soft sound startled her. She looked down at the crib. Her son was chuckling, his dark eyes fixed on her. Winifred put the iron on the stand and stared at him. It was the first time she'd heard him laugh. It made his whole body shake. Then he reached out with his arms to her.

She picked him up and held him close to her. He patted her cheek. The sensation that grew and engulfed her stunned her. This baby had been her shame, the burden she'd had to carry for her sins. Now she realised he would be the one light in her life. She held on to the small kernel of happiness, and hope. Her son. Her family.

PART TWO

Chapter 56

4th August 1914

Winifred's voice shook as she read from the paper. "The following statement was issued from the Foreign Office last night: Owing to the summary rejection by the German Government of the request made by His Majesty's Government for assurances that the neutrality of Belgium would be respected, His Majesty's Ambassador in Berlin has received his passport, and His Majesty's Government has declared to the German Government that a state of war exists between Great Britain and Germany as of 11p.m. on August 4.'"

Florence rocked Tom, his head nestled into her neck. He was wrapped into a towel after his bath. 'Well, we've seen it coming since June, Winnie. There's been trouble since that chap, Franz Ferdinand, and his wife were murdered. It's been nothing else in the papers. What a world we live in.' She absently rubbed the toddler's back. When she looked up towards Winifred her eyes were bleak. 'It's all a mess.'

'There's a note at the end of it,' Winifred said, peering closer. 'It says, "British Foreign Secretary Sir Edward Grey tried to organise an international peace conference to prevent further escalation. France accepted his proposals but Germany refused and on the 29th July, Germany requested British neutrality in the event of a European war. Britain refused because German victory in Western Europe would mean they would be close to the Channel coast and pose a threat to Britain's security and trade. So at the beginning of August, the British mobilised the Navy to protect the French coast from German aggression through the Channel. On 2 August, the Cabinet agreed to support Belgium if there was a substantial violation of its neutrality."'

'So, is it because the German's did invade Belgium and wouldn't leave?'

'I suppose so. When I was helping in the shop the other day—'

Ethel grunted. 'Help, she says…' her tone acerbic. 'Fat lot of use – getting in the way, more like it.'

Neither woman looked in her direction.

'When I was in the shop the other day,' Florence continued, 'Mr Watson was in with his wife. He said it was because Germany wouldn't leave Belgium so Britain had no choice. Germany was getting too big for its boots. He said it was up to Britain to show Germany they can't bully and get away with it. He said it was the moral right for Britain to stick up for little countries.'

'So, it's going to be a big war…' All at once Winifred was afraid of the unknown. 'What will it mean, Granny?'

'Lots of changes, ducks. Lots of awful things happening. Lots of young men losing their lives, I should think.' She sighed. 'Word is, many of them want to fight, that'll it be over by Christmas and they want to get over there and kill a few Germans.'

Winifred shivered at the thought of killing another human being. 'Not all, surely?' For the first time in many months, she thought about Conal. Usually she tried to dismiss the image of his face; his eyes, soft and loving, locked onto hers as they made love. His hands on her body. It was too painful to remember when she'd been so happy. Her time with Conal had been so brief. And yet it was a lifetime.

Where was he? She smoothed the paper on her knee to cover up her thoughts before saying, 'But they can't be made to fight, can they?' If she knew anything about Conal he wasn't violent. He wouldn't, couldn't kill another person. But he could hurt people in other ways. He'd left her.

'Well, no…' Florence lifted Tom to her shoulder. 'They can't, they can't make the lads join up, I don't think. But you know as well as me there's enough of them out there that can't wait to be enlisted.' She leaned Tom away from her. 'I think he's gone off?'

Winifred peered round at her son's face. 'He has.' She smiled. He looked so content. She couldn't prevent her next thoughts: so much like Conal sometimes with his thick black hair, little straight nose and determined chin.

But when he was awake his long-lashed dark eyes fixed on hers for constant approval. It was the one thing that worried her, his timidity. Living with her mother it was understandable. The wad of anger in Winifred was always there, ready to defend her son against Ethel's tongue.

'Isn't it time he went to bed?' Ethel's face showed no emotion. The news of the start of a war that was going to alter the lives of so many had obviously not registered with her mother. Ethel folded her arms under her loose bosom; she'd long stopped wearing a corset when she wasn't in the shop. 'Did you hear me?'

'I did.' Winifred didn't look at her mother. She folded the paper and dropped it onto the arm of the chair. 'I'll empty the bath.'

She opened the back door and dragging the tin bath across the kitchen, tipped it up. The water flowed across the yard to the grid. When the bath was empty she heaved it up to the long nail on the wall and hooked it over. It swung rhythmically from side to side, the metal edges catching the stone of the wall in decreasing soft notes. Winifred put her hands to the small of her back and arched, her eyes searching the clear sky. It was warm, the sun only just a little lower than an hour ago. Over the roof of the house, she could hear children still playing on the street. Their shouts and laughter made her feel sad, somehow. What was facing them? What faced Tom in the future? The thought made her heart tighten and she turned back into the kitchen.

She left the door open. Somehow she didn't feel as trapped in her life when the windows and doors let the outside world into the house. Unrolling her sleeves and buttoning the cuffs she saw Ethel watching her, eyes narrowed.

'Mother?' She didn't pause but continued towards her grandmother to take her son from her. 'I'll take him up, Granny, thanks for your help.'

'No trouble.' Florence shuffled to the front of her chair and settled her feet firmly on the ground in readiness to stand, still holding Tom. 'I'll go up an' all.' She handed the baby to Winifred.

'What's up with you?' Ethel's voice was strident. Her hands on her hips.

'What?' Winifred wasn't going to let her mother upset her. Not when she was holding Tom. All she wanted was to go upstairs. 'Nothing,' she said. 'Nothing's wrong.'

'Scared that his father will have to go and fight,' Ethel sneered. 'Not that we know who he is of course. I wonder if you even do.'

Winifred and Florence exchanged glances. The slight shake of the head and warning look reminded Winifred of her father but it didn't prevent her anger.

'Shut up, Mother. I don't want to hear anything you have to say. You're vicious – nasty.' Ethel's jaw loosened. She opened her mouth to retort but Winifred held up her hand keeping her voice steady. 'Tom's father was a good man—'

'But he ran off, didn't he?' Ethel pointed her finger at Winifred, triumphant. 'He sussed what you were. Easy. A strumpet.'

'Something has stopped him coming back for me. For us.' Winifred walked towards the stairs. 'I don't know where Tom's father is. But he will come back…' Did she believe that? Had she been a fool to be taken in by him? She stopped, lifted her son closer to her and waited for Florence to go past her to the stairs.

'And another thing. Unless I really have to, I won't be speaking to you again. If you ask me something I'll answer. That's all. I blame you for the miserable life my father had. I blame you for the miserable childhood I had.' Winifred knew she was being unfair but couldn't stop. 'In fact, I blame you for all that has gone wrong in my life. So, from now on, leave me alone. We may have to live in the same house but I'm telling you, I want nothing more to do with you. You're on your own, as far as I'm concerned.'

Chapter 57

August 1914

Bill liked Ashford better than Bradlow; it was smaller, more friendly than the larger town. And he liked the little pub he'd found on Newroyd Street, just off the tram route. On his trips to Ashford, he often finished off with a quiet pint or two, sitting in the corner, minding his own business and pretending to read the newspapers.

For weeks the chatter in The Crown had been that Britain would soon be at war with Germany. It made him restless; his life had become monotonous, boring.

So that morning, on impulse, instead of going back home with Giles, the neighbouring farmer, he'd offloaded the goods he'd bought onto the wagon and had gone to the railway station to catch a train to Manchester.

He knew he'd made a mistake as soon as he walked into the soddin' recruiting office. He frowned, taking a gulp of his beer. He wouldn't forget the sniggers of the other blokes in the queue when he was turned down because of his height. Lately he'd become more conscious than ever about his lack of inches wherever he went. Even at home. Moira had even been stupid enough to say she was glad he couldn't go into the army and had started to call him "her little man". He soon put a stop to that. She was lucky he hadn't clouted her.

Going to the bar he ordered a third pint, tapping the tuppence on the counter.

'Bad day?' The landlord placed the glass in front of Bill, slopping the beer on the counter.

'No worse than usual.' Bill grunted the reply.

'Just that you're looking like you lost a shilling and found a penny.'

'Mind your own fuckin' business.'

'Now, now,' the landlord said, mildly, wiping a grey dishcloth across the pool of ale. 'Don't want to have to bar you. I'm losing enough customers as it is to this bloody war. Still…' he had the last word, moving to serve an old woman who was peering through the hatch of the snug. 'Don't suppose you'll be going anywhere. Little chap like you.'

'You bastard.' Bill yelled, ignoring the threat of being barred. He rolled his shirtsleeves up, balanced on the brass rail that ran along the front of the bar and pressed his hands on the top, ready to leap over. 'I'll bloody kill you.'

The landlord laughed. 'I wouldn't advise you trying, pal.' He didn't look back.

A hand pressed on Bill's shoulder.

'Steady on, mate.'

He whirled with a roar, fists raised.

The two men standing in front of him where even smaller than he was. They were smiling at him. He weighed them up; the grins weren't mocking. One of them had bright ginger hair and freckles, the other was blond with pale blue eyes. He shrugged and dropped his hands to pick up his pint.

'Aye, well…'

'We know,' the bloke with the ginger hair said. 'And we have something to tell you we think you'll be interested in.'

'What?' Bill glowered, suspicious. He downed his beer in one long swallow. His hand was unsteady when he banged the glass on the counter.

'Another?' It was the blond bloke this time.

'Why not.' Bill blinked, nodded towards his table. 'My things are there. There's a couple of chairs free.' Might as well listen to them. They didn't look like poofters but if they were he'd soon see them off.

'I'm Reilly, he's Boardman.' The one with the ginger hair sat opposite Bill.

'Bill Howarth.' The name he hadn't used for two years came out automatically.

'We're off to Bury to sign up.'

It was Bill's turn to smirk. 'Well, good luck with that.' Stupid sods. He looked down at the glass in front of him. He didn't want any more to drink.

'No, listen. There's some battalions being formed for men like us.'

'Us?' They were, they were soddin' poofters. 'Think you've got hold of the wrong bloke, mate. I'm married.' Well, near enough. Moira had been nagging him for months to get wed. He was bloody sick of her whining, tell the truth. An' she'd let herself go. Fact was, she smelled more like the pigs every day.

The two men were roaring with laughter. Heads back they slapped the table with both hands.

Bill glared, waited for the bloody racket to stop. Most of the pub and the landlord were staring at the three of them. He stood, adjusted his braces and took his jacket and bag off the back of the chair.

'Hang on. Don't go 'til you hear what we have to tell you.' Reilly spluttered, wiping his eyes with the pads of his fingers. 'We're not nancies. Sit down, man.' He looked up at Bill. 'I meant shorter chaps like us. Some bigwig in Parliament has persuaded Kitchener to let him form battalions in the army for men under the regulation size.'

Bill was baffled but he sat down. 'Why?' He'd never heard anything so daft; a load of only small blokes in a battalion. And the memories returned from when he was a kid; the times his father told him he would never amount to much because of his size; would always be good for nothing. What was that bloody phrase he used? 'Cuthbert, Harry, Dai... (whatever name his father could conjure up in any moment) makes ten of you, you

223

soddin' little runt.' Only short blokes? All in one battalion? Bill mentally scoffed at the idea.

'Are you fit?' It was Boardman this time.

'Course I bloody am. I work… I own a pig farm.' Bill held his arms out and flexed his muscles.

'Well then, you can sign up. We've just heard that the War Office says we can. Why don't you come with us?' Boardman lifted his chin in a gesture of a challenge. 'There'll be eight of us including you, if you do.'

They waited, watching him while they finished their pints.

Bill pressed his lips together. He was fed up with his life, lately. He'd cottoned on to the fact that he irritated Moira more and more for some reason and she barely spoke to him. And the stink of pig shit clung to his clothes; he hadn't missed the way folk sniffed and looked at one another when he went near them. A bit of excitement was tempting. The Army. If ever he came across them buggers that had laughed at him in the Recruiting Office in Manchester again, he'd show them what for.

'Aye, okay. Count me in.' He shook hands with each of them.

He was off to a new life.

Chapter 58

Shit. Bill burrowed his head under the covers. Given chance he'd shove that bloody bugle right up that one's arse.

From all around him there were curses and groaning. Bill listened to the sounds of stumbling footsteps on the wooden floor and the rustling of clothes.

'Come on, you lot. Up and at it.' Bill's blankets were pulled off him. 'Get up, Howarth. Now. Unless you want to be cleaning the latrines all day.'

God, he hated the bastard. 'Yes, Sarge, I'm up.' He stood swaying, his eyes still closed.

'Sergeant Bell, to you Howarth. Who am I?'

'Sergeant Bell, Sergeant.' And a right bastard to boot, Bill added to himself.

The sergeant walked away from him, bellowing at any other man reluctant to rise. 'Get this place clean and tidy and I might, just might, let you have a brew after.'

He stopped by the door. 'And you'll be pleased to know you'll be getting your uniforms today.' He grinned. 'After all these months you'll look like proper soldiers.'

A small cheer went around the barracks.

'About bloody time, too,' Boardman, standing by the bed next to Bill, muttered, 'I'm sick of looking like a bloody postman in this lot.'

Bill laughed quietly. The blue get-up hung in their lockers, nicknamed 'Kitchener Blue', what with the cardboard cap badge, did make them look like postmen.

'Will we get a proper rifle as well, Sergeant Bell?' someone asked.

'You will. You can donate your wooden weapon, as well as these uniforms, to the next lot of poor specimens I'll have to knock into shape,' he said, cheerfully. 'Because…' he raised his voice. 'Because today I get rid of you. You're leaving the sunny climes of Bury and you're off to the even sunnier Ashford.'

'What?' Boardman's mouth dropped open.

'Yes, you an' all, Boardman. We all know about your shenanigans with a local lass. Well, you'll be leaving her behind today. Let's hope you haven't left her with a little present an' all.' He shouted above the ribald laughter. 'Just remember you're Infantry, you're Lancashire Fusiliers. You might be called a Bantam Battalion; you might all be little squirts but you're my little squirts, medically fit…fit in any way the War Office requires. I've taught you proper military discipline…' He was interrupted by a few groans. 'And how to fight with your rifle and bayonet.' He stopped speaking, lowered his voice. 'You're soldiers, my soldiers, and I'm proud of you.'

He laughed at the cheers that echoed around the metal building before shouting above the noise. 'You've all sworn your oath of allegiance to King and country. And you've promised to obey any and all orders of the generals and officers who will lead you.' He glowered at them. 'And you bloody well will do. Right?'

'Right, Sergeant Bell,' they shouted in unison, following a ritual that had built up over the months.

'Right.' He grinned again. 'I've done my best with you. If I ever hear that any one of you has let me down, I'll personally come and cut your balls off.'

'Like to see him try.' Bill grinned at Boardman.

'What's that, Howarth?'

'Nothing Sarge– Sergeant Bell.'

'Right!' Okay, clean this shit-tip up and I'll see you on the parade ground 06.30 on the dot. It's our last day together, you lot, so let's make it a good one.'

Chapter 59

January 1916

There'd been rumours for months that they were being sent to Egypt but that morning they'd been told they were being sent to France the following day.

Bill was calm about it in front of the other men. After all he had to keep up the reputation he'd earned over the last sixteen months of being the hardest bastard of the battalion. But inside he was sick with excitement. At last he'd get chance to do what he'd been waiting for; what they'd all been promised. To beat the shit out of the Krauts. It was the carrot that had been dangled before them when they'd slogged for miles in the rain, with blisters on their feet and nowt in their bellies.

Spitting on his boots and rubbing the polish into the leather,

Bill was convinced this was what he'd been waiting for all his life. He was a soldier now, trained to kill.

Bill buffed his boots until he could almost see his face in the toecaps and then put them on the floor by the side of his bed. He took out the folded piece of old newspaper from bottom of the case he kept his polish, brush and cloth in and wiped the inside clean. Intrigued he unfolded the paper. As soon as he started reading he remembered why he'd kept it. It was some bloke called Bottomley who'd set himself up recruiting, He and some of the lads had been to see him in Manchester last year, just to see what he had to say. And then Boardman had found this article on him. And Bill had made Boardman read them out again and again until he memorised them; "...we shall have the Huns on the run. We shall drive them out of France, out of Flanders, out of Belgium, across the Rhine, and back into their own territory." But it had caused an uproar of vulgar hilarity in the barracks when Len had read out the last bit where the MP had said everyone should, *"keep your peckers up."* because Boardman had just received a letter telling him his girlfriend was pregnant.

Boardman was married and a dad now, to a baby boy, and Bill had heard him crying in the latrines when they'd got the news about France. He'd confided to Bill that he didn't want to leave them; he'd lost the taste for a fight.

Bill didn't understand that, he couldn't wait. He lay back on his bunk, pulling the pillow under his neck and relaxed. The place was quiet; everyone had been given a twelve-hour pass to go home and say goodbye to their families. He wondered if Boardman would actually come back. He hoped so, he wouldn't want to see him in trouble, he'd become a good mate, same as Reilly. Besides, he needed both of them to watch his back, just like he'd keep an eye out for them, wherever they were.

He must have fallen asleep because the next thing he knew most of the men had returned and were getting ready to settle down for the night. Nobody was talking. When he looked around he could see a lot of them looked upset, all red-eyed and pale. Why weren't they as excited as him that at last they were going to do what they'd signed up for?

He looked around for Reilly and Boardman. Reilly was across the barracks from him sitting up in bed, reading.

'What's that you've got, Dennis?' Bill lifted his head and looked between his feet at his friend.

'Letter and a parcel from my mum,' Reilly answered. 'She wouldn't come to the station to see me off, she was too upset. But she gave this to Dad for me to read.' He grinned at Bill. 'She's a soppy old cow; she's worried I'll get cold.' He picked a pair of thick woollen socks and waved them in the air. 'And listen to this, "…and don't forget to wear your scarf all the time, you know how soon you get chesty." Can you see Major Allen letting that happen?'

They chuckled, both seeing the ridiculousness of it.

'Aw, she means well,' Bill said. He'd met Reilly's mother a few times over the past months. She'd found out he had no-one to go to when on leave, and had insisted Dennis took him back to their place. 'She's all right, your mum.'

'She is…'

There was something about his friend's voice that made Bill sit up. The man was crying, his shoulders heaving with silent sobs.

'You okay?'

Dennis lifted his head and looked around the barracks at the same time as Bill. Nobody was watching them. Or were pretending not to more like, Bill thought, embarrassed for Reilly.

'Aren't you a bit scared?'

'Good God, no.' Bill settled back on the hard mattress, uneasy for a moment; he hoped Reilly wasn't going to turn out to be a coward. Don't be bloody daft, he told himself, the man had matched him side by side in training. There was no way he was a quitter.

He couldn't get a song out of his head. Him and Reilly had

been to see Marie Lloyd in Manchester and it was the first and last one she'd sung. By, she was a bit of all right, she was. They'd all joined in with her and the words had stuck. Bill folded his arms behind his head and let rip: *"I didn't like you much before you joined the army, John, but I do like you, cockie, now you've got yer khaki on."*

He couldn't remember the rest of the lines but it didn't matter. He repeated the words a couple more times, grinning as he looked around the barracks.

'Shut it, Howarth.' Smith, two beds away, glared at him.

'Too bloody cheerful for your own good, you,' added another voice. 'You're not normal.'

He let it go. He didn't feel like tackling both of them. And Smith might be even shorter than him, but he was a nasty little sod with a dirty way of scrapping. Save his energy for the adventure they were all going to face tomorrow, he thought. Travelling between Yorkshire and Lancashire was the most he'd ever done. To be going to another country, to be on the sea, let alone seeing it for the first time in his life was the most thrilling thing he could think of. He was too stirred up to sleep.

But he fell asleep before he saw whether Boardman was back. The creaking of the bunk next to him woke him. It was pitch black.

'Where the hell have you been?'

'Didn't want to leave Flora and the kid.' Len's voice was muted. 'God, he's grown.'

'Aye, they do.' Bill wasn't that interested in kids. 'How did you get in?'

'Sykes and O'Mallory are on the gate. They let me sneak in.'

'You're bloody lucky, you daft bugger. The major would've had your guts for garters.' Bill turned over on his side. 'Get some kip. Big day tomorrow.'

He couldn't wait.

Chapter 60

October 1917

Bill was shivering but it wasn't only the cold that was making his limbs shake; he was sick with fear and exhaustion. The artillery bombardment from both sides was ceaseless, had been for the last forty-eight hours. The thunderous noise had long since deafened him to other sounds. He saw the mouths of the men around him moving, knew they were shouting sometimes. But he heard nothing only the booms of shells and crack of rifles. He'd thought the fiasco the bloody officers had called the Big Push was bad enough but this was a nightmare.

Six times they'd been stood to. Shoulder to shoulder with Reilly and Boardman, he felt their terror shudder through him, listened to Len's rapid heavy breathing between the massive explosions. None of them spoke; there was nothing to say. Once, further along the trench, he heard a soldier praying and cursing obscenely at the same time until the officer barked at him to 'shut the fuck up'. Bill was both relieved and angry. He realised he'd been repeating the man's words. They'd been strangely comforting.

The shells were still dropping but they'd been stood down for an hour. No false alarms of German advancement. No real threat of one of them standing with bayonet at the ready on the broken parapet above.

A brown haze vibrated oddly over the battlefield, blending with the steady drizzle. At least the downpour that drenched them in the night had stopped but it was little comfort, his feet, sloshing around in muddy water, were wet through and hurting.

'I'm going for a shit,' he shouted. Bugger asking permission from whichever officer was supposed to be in charge. The two friends nodded, too worn out to speak.

Bill sat on his backside and, not trusting his painful feet, inched his way along the trench through the slime of mud, cursing that the makeshift latrines were so far from their position.

Around one corner he disturbed a clutch of rats feeding on something. He kicked out at them, his boot touching a gnawed human hand. Blackened bone stuck out where three of the fingers should have been. Elliot's hand. He knew it was Elliot's hand from the silver wedding ring, grotesque on the one whole finger. He'd copped it two days ago, in the first assault. They'd been ordered to drag what was left of him to the pit at the far end of the trench and shovel lime on top.

Icy sweat ran into Bill's eyes. He rubbed his face against his shoulder, gulping. He hadn't eaten in over a day yet still heaved as though his stomach was overfull. The hysteria built up inside him and he began to swear, at first silently, then out loud. Muttering the words he pushed himself to his feet and slid past the gruesome object, eyes averted. Keeping low, he stumbled a few more yards before turning into the short side trench dug into the ground. Leaving his rifle propped against the wooden boards outside the latrines and holding his breath against the stink he squatted to shit.

Hastily pulling up his trousers and fastening the buttons, he collected his rifle and, ducking down to make sure he was below the parapet, hurried back to the main trench.

The pack of rats was once more gnawing on Elliot's hand.

Reluctant to go past them, Bill stopped, absentmindedly scratching the constant itch from the lice in the seams of his uniform.

'Get back in line.'

The voice was high-pitched.

He ignored the order.

'I said, get back in line or I shoot.'

Still scratching, Bill moved, not even looking to see who the command came from. He couldn't tell who the damn officers were anymore, anyway. They'd lost Major Allen in the first month at

Le Havre; silly sod had managed to get himself run down by a truck driven by a French farmer. Since then him, Boardman and Reilly had lost count of the men promoted to officer rank and then killed.

Out of sight of the man who'd yelled at him, Bill stopped again, closing his eyes.

The shelling stopped. It seemed eerily quiet. All he could hear was the low murmur of voices further along the line, someone coughing, a rattling of the corrugated sheets, fashioned into a shelter for the officers, the whining of the wind above him. Somewhere, in No Man's Land, or was it in the Jerry's ranks, there were pitiful screams every now and then.

Some poor sod dying alone.

'You okay, mate?' One of the men lined up glanced over his shoulder at Bill. He frowned, studied him.

Bill nodded. The thought struck him that the bloke might have been wondering if he'd lost his bottle.

Sometimes he wondered that himself.

'Come on, yer bloody soft arse,' he told himself, moving away from the man. 'What the 'ell's wrong with you?' But he couldn't prevent the huge sob that filled his throat.

The barrage of the British artillery started again and, just a suddenly, ceased.

Bill hobbled back to stand between Boardman and Reilly.

'Bloody feet are killing me,' he moaned.

'When was the last time you changed your socks?' Boardman said, his eyes fixed on the box periscope which jutted above the parapet. 'Can't see any sign of movement.' He glanced sideways at Bill with a look of concern. 'Did you grease your feet this morning.'

'Can't bloody well even remember when it was morning, let alone the last time I used that stinking stuff.'

'Whale oil,' Boardman said. 'It's whale oil.'

'Don't give a fuck. It bloody stinks.'

232

'How can you tell?' This time Reilly spoke. 'We all stink worse than any whale. I pity the poor fish in the sea. I bet whales are the equivalent to Evans.'

Despite the fear, they laughed quietly at the thought of the soldier who hadn't washed from the first week they'd arrived at Ashford until the day, six months later, Major Allen had dragged him to the canal and thrown him in, fully clothed.

'Christ, I'm scared.' Boardman spoke out of the corner of his mouth, back to position in front of the periscope.

'We'll look after you, won't we, Dennis?' Bill gave Reilly a nudge. 'You've got a wife and kid waiting for you in Blighty, Mr Boardman.'

'Yeah, we're the Three Musketeers, aren't we?'

Bill hadn't a clue what Reilly was talking about but it sounded okay so he answered, 'Yeah, course we are.'

The cry went along the trenches. 'Stand to.' Somewhere, further along the trenches, the thin wail of bagpipes started up.

'Fuckin' 'ell,' Bill muttered.

'I'm going to shit myself,' Boardman said.

'Well, let us go first then,' Reilly grinned, glancing at him. 'We smell bad enough without a shower of shit falling on us.'

Bill chuckled, even though his own insides felt as though they were turning to water. 'Stick with us, Len.'

'Ready?' Bill gripped the sandbags on the parapet, trying to get a hold on them. But they were slimy with rain and rotten with age and fell apart. 'Blast!' he grabbed hold of one of the wooden struts. 'Ready?' he asked again, hauling himself to the top.

Bayonets at the ready, the long line of men stumbled over the uneven ground behind the creeping barrage of artillery. Squinting into the smoke and dirt clouds thrown up by the bombardment, Bill tried not to look at the rotting corpses hanging on the barbed wire, the torn limbs all around them.

Crouched low, he was comforted by the closeness of his two mates.

Bullets flew all around them. Bill could hear Boardman screaming. 'Oh God, oh God.'

'Get down,' he shouted, tugging on his mate's arm.

'Move forward.' Bill couldn't tell who was shouting the order but guessed it was a soddin' toff given the posh voice. 'Keep going.'

'Sod off,' Bill muttered. Bill tugged again. 'Keep with me, lad, stay close to me.'

Len staggered. For a second he was in front of Bill. When he fell to his knees Bill stopped, unable to work out what had happened. His face was wet. Lowering his rifle he bent down to help Len to his feet. 'S'okay, mate. Come on, get up,' he shouted above the racket of shouts and screams and rat-tat of the Vickers in front of him. But something was wrong; he found Len's shoulder but moving his hand along there was no head. Something warm dripped down the side of his head into his collar. Knowing, yet not wanting to know, he touched his face. His fingers moved over his skin, moved over lumps and splinters of bone. Of skull. Len Boardman had moved in front of him at the wrong time. Bill shut out the next thought: *at the right time.* The bullet should have hit him but his friend had taken it.

'Reilly!'

But Reilly had moved forward with the rest of them. In the faint light of dawn he saw them; small, ghostly, silent figures stumbling away from him, falling to the ground. Men walking over the bodies of the blokes they'd lived alongside for the last two years. Friends they made, shared laughs and stories with, sworn together with at the fools of officers who set the rules and the punishments.

Mindlessly walking to their deaths.

The hysteria was fighting to get out in one long scream.

'Move forward.' Bill felt the prod of a pistol in his back. 'Move forward or I shoot.'

'Fuck off!' He swung around and stabbed.

234

For a moment he was face to face to the officer. With the boy. It went through his mind, a fleeting recognition that the lad was probably no older than seventeen. Shouldn't have even been there, should have been home with his family. But it was too late. His bayonet had sliced through the officer's throat.

Bill stared at the crumpled figure sprawled at his feet. So this was how the nightmare would end, in front of a firing squad. He looked around. Someone must have seen.

But the soldiers moved past him, faces set, intent on getting to the Jerries before they got them.

Bill turned and walked with them. He didn't feel the crunch of bone under his boot when he stood on what was left of Len's head.

Chapter 61

Crouched in the trench, Bill wrapped his arms around himself and rocked. Back and forth, back and forth. He kept the rhythm going trying to blank out his mind. The shaking deep inside him wouldn't stop. He could hear his teeth coming together in one continuous tapping. And he was so bloody cold. As soon as he closed his eyes the images came back: of the lines of shadowy men, half-hidden by the smoke and dirt, the flashes of explosions, Boardman's wide-eyed terror just before they climbed out of the trench. The face of the lad, the officer, he'd killed. It was the shock he tried to tell himself. But he knew it was really in anger. Anger because the officer didn't bloody care that his mate had fallen, anger because he didn't know anymore why they were fighting over a bit of land. Anger at the faceless sods that had sent them to this god-forsaken place as artillery fodder.

He rocked faster, needing to block out the rage, the frustration. The fear.

For the last two days, since they'd been on the support line, he'd tried not to sleep. And yet he wanted oblivion. It hadn't been the first time they'd marched, unthinking, into No Man's Land. But it was the first time he'd lost a mate. The moment of Boardman's death, those seconds of realisation of what had happened, of what he'd then done, terrified him. Someone must have seen what happened.

He stopped rocking. Listened. Someone was sobbing. No-one told him to shut up. Bill looked along the trench. Most of the men were too weary to even raise their heads. Some stared back at him with empty eyes. Perhaps his were just the same. All were leaning against the sandbags, arms dangling by their side, rifles propped next to them.

Past them he could see the signaller in the telephone dugout. He seemed to be asleep, helmet over his eyes. If the NCO or the captain came through the bloke would be in trouble.

Bill held his head in his hands. With a bit of luck they would be in the support line for another two days. Four days was what they were supposed to have in support. So far it had never been a full four days before they were called to the front line again.

A rat pushed an empty tin along the wooden duckboard. Bill straightened his leg in a half-hearted attempt to kick out at it. It studied him with black bead eyes until it resumed its task and moved past him.

Further along on a man stamped on the rodent. Bill watched with blank eyes. The disgusting mess was added to the mire.

Bill fumbled in his jacket chest pocket and brought out the now tattered piece of paper he'd carried so proudly in his pay book, when he left Ashford to cheering and the brass band playing *Tipperary*. And then again in Manchester, when the old blokes clapped and waved pint pots outside the pubs as the battalion marched past. They must have fought their own wars. But nothing like this.

His reading wasn't up to much but he could read this.

Kitchener's message was a joke. Telling each soldier to be 'courteous, considerate and kind' to local people and allied soldiers, and to avoid 'the temptations both in wine and women' was stupid.

What chance had they had of wine and women? And they'd been ignored by the French, chivvied from pillar to post over the months. None of them knew where the hell they were anymore. Every trench, every road they were forced to march along, every piece of ground they defended against the Germans, looked the same. It took them all their time to make sure they weren't all bloody killed. Courteous, considerate and kind my arse, he thought, fighting back angry tears. Fuckin' manners went out the fuckin' window. And the only kindness any of them could afford was to watch the backs of the men they were stood next to.

And a fine bloody job he'd just done of that. He thumped the side of his head. It didn't make him feel any better. He did it again. 'Shit, shit, shit.'

He chucked the paper onto the ground. A rat pounced, carrying it away.

'Here.' Reilly aimed a kick at the rodent as it scampered past him. He held out a packet in his hand. 'Biscuits. And don't break your teeth on them.'

'Naw.' Bill flapped him away. 'Can't bloody eat.'

'Baccy then?'

'Thanks.' Bill took the tin from him and opened it. He rolled the tobacco between his thumb and his palm, concentrating on the action. Pushing away the images. Although he much preferred a cigarette he liked the feel of the pipe. There was comfort in the way he could clench it between his teeth.

'It wasn't your fault, you know.' Reilly sat at the side of him. 'Boardman getting it wasn't your fault.'

'It was.' Bill packed the bowl of the pipe. It was something he'd have to live with. That and killing the young lad. He'd stopped thinking of him as an officer days ago. It was that last look of surprise in the lad's eyes that he wouldn't forget. But he couldn't tell Reilly about that. He couldn't tell anyone.

Reilly rested his head against the sandbags, helmet tilted over his eyes, the rifle between his thighs. He tapped a rhythm on the barrel, a definite sign of his impatience. 'Bloody hell, Howarth, we all knew what we were getting into.'

'Did we 'ell.' He fought against blurting everything out. He couldn't trust, wouldn't trust anyone with what had happened after Len copped it. But he blamed himself.

Reilly leaned forward, pushed his helmet up. 'Okay,' he conceded. 'But we knew we were going to war.'

'And so 'ere we are.' Bill sucked on the pipe, taking the comforting warmth of the tobacco smoke into his lungs. 'Here we fuckin' are.'

Chapter 62

It was their last day in the support line. By rights they should have been going back to the nearest village for four days' rest in the bombed out buildings. Looking forward to some warm grub and decent sleep in the makeshift quarters. But they'd been told they'd be needed on the front line again in the morning, until the next battalion could be mustered.

Bill slept fitfully waiting for the call. He jumped when Reilly's boot nudged him. 'What the hell...'

'Come on, I've volunteered us to go and have a squint at the Jerries,' Reilly said, his tone grim. 'All this hanging around is getting to me.'

'What?'

'Come on, shift yourself.' He scrambled over the parapet on his belly, looking over his shoulder at Bill. 'Let's see if we can bag a couple of the bastards. Revenge for Len.'

'Shit, Reilly, wait on.' Still trying to clear his head, Bill followed. They crawled through the zigzag path of barbed wire entanglements, avoiding the bodies, slowly navigating around the water-filled shell craters. Every now and then clouds masked a half moon. The intermittent glimmer made crossing No Man's Land easier. Staying still in the light, moving on in the darkness.

Reilly passed the listening post without acknowledging the two infantrymen crouched down in the small trench. Bill grunted a low greeting.

'Okay, lads?'

'Bloody freezing,' was the whispered reply. 'And wet through.'

Bill didn't envy them; he'd done a few stints in the 'saps' and it was bloody scary, perched out in No Man's Land with no protection but bayonetted rifles.

He soon realised he had no choice but to crawl over the corpses covered in flies and maggots. The foul smell brought back the night he and Sid had moved Sid's father's body at Blossom Farm. Christ, he'd hoped never to smell that stench again and here he was knee deep in it day after day.

The moon was hidden for a moment. Reaching out to go on he put his hand down into the middle of a stomach. Slimy guts spilled out between his fingers in a flurry of flies. He gagged, hearing Reilly quietly cursing as he too retched and heaved.

'You okay, Reilly?' Bill gulped. He used his elbows to drag himself towards his friend. 'This is bloody awful. We could go back? Say we saw nothing?'

'No.' Reilly's voice was strange; dogged. 'Come on, let's see what those bloody Krauts are doing.' He lifted up on hands and knees and scuttled forward.

'Get down, yer daft bugger. They'll see you.' And me, Bill added to himself. What the hell was Reilly thinking? At this rate he'd get them both killed. Fear mingled with irritation. 'And slow down as well. D'yer want us both to finish up like these poor sods?'

Reilly didn't answer. It was as though he was determined to go right up to the Jerry trenches. Terror took hold of Bill and he halted. When the moon slid from behind the gauzy clouds Reilly's bayonet glittered in the light.

'Good God, man,' Bill moaned. There was nothing he could do but follow.

But then a distant boom of guns startled him and he dropped, peering through the uneven mounds of grass and bodies.

There was a muted shout. A flare blazed from the enemy trenches and a mortar rose high into the air and hovered, suspended from a small parachute, at the peak of its flight. The time it stayed there seemed endless to Bill.

'Come on!' he whispered to Reilly, shuffling backwards and rolling over bodies, hoping their shapes would hide him from the Germans looking for any sign of movement. 'Shift, yer daft bastard.'

But Reilly didn't.

The rocket fell, dropping like an old boot, in the pool of white light.

It was too close. Bill didn't wait. Holding his nose he burrowed under a pile of the putrid corpses.

The ground shuddered violently when it landed and burst. Through the whistling in his ears Bill heard the cheers from the German trenches intermingled with the heavy thuds that followed. He squeezed his eyes tight, trying to shut out the image of the bodies being torn and scattered around him.

Then silence.

After counting to twenty Bill wriggled free, gasping. The mud and the cadavers gave him up with wet sucking reluctance. Rolling onto his side he sobbed, vomited until his stomach hurt, frantically rubbing his sleeves through his hair, over his face to rid himself of the gore. He was in hell. When he stopped snivelling he rose up on one elbow and looked around. The moon was covered again by a thin veil of cloud but he swore he could see the silhouettes of figures stealthily moving yards away. A smell of explosives hung in the air, fragments floated all around, landed on him. Bill gulped back sobs.

Whispers floated towards him. Foreign voices. Fuck! German voices, coming towards him.

Where the hell was Reilly? Panicking, Bill slowly crawled backwards, stopping when the clouds cleared away from the moon, allowing a contrast of dark and light shadows on the horror around him.

He saw what was left of Reilly; a mess of splintered bones and flesh and blood surrounded the hole in the earth that the shell had made.

Bill bit down on the scream that wanted to burst from his mouth.

How long he stayed with his back pressed against the wall of boards and mud Bill didn't know, but dawn was gradually lighting up the trench. Shit…shit…shit…shit. Looking up at the underbelly of the dark clouds being buffeted in the steel-grey sky by the wind, he couldn't stop the word.

He remembered he was supposed to report back to the officer. An officer. Which officer? Reilly hadn't said.

Placing his foot flat on the ground he tried to stand. His legs gave way and he slid down on his backside.

Fuck it. Fuckin' officer could fuckin' wait. It hadn't been his idea to volunteer. He wished he'd refused Reilly when he'd appeared next to him. It had been a quiet night up to then. What he'd give to have kept it that way. Reilly wouldn't have gone without him. Would he?

'You all right, mate?' The soldier who spoke slid alongside Bill in the mud.

Wilson. Red-rimmed eyes, unshaven, skin grey under the dirt and grime. A poofter. When they'd first joined up he'd got a load of flak from the other blokes for the way he spoke. There was no way he could disguise what he was, even if the recruitment officer hadn't seen it. Or perhaps he had and thought it a good way to get the bugger off the streets of Lancashire.

'You all right?' Wilson spoke again. He put his hand on Bill's.

For a moment anger flashed through Bill, his instinct to draw away from the bloody nancy. But then he saw the genuine concern in the man's eyes and was ashamed of his first reaction. He shook his head. He stared down at their hands.

'Where's your mate? Reilly, isn't it?'

Bill moved his head. 'Gone.'

'Oh God. I hate this fucking war.' The words sounded strange in Wilson's soft, girlish pitch.

They sat in silence. Bill had the sudden urge to rest his head on the man's shoulder and weep. For Reilly. For Boardman. He resisted. Instead he removed his fingers from beneath Wilson's and rubbed at his sore eyes. 'And me,' he said. 'What the hell is it all for?'

The silent shrug was all Wilson could muster, apparently. And what answer was there to this madness anyway, Bill reflected.

From down the line he heard the clang of the gas gong, the rattle of the empty shell casing echoed along the trench. The urgent cry was passed on. 'Gas!'

A slow wave of greenish, yellow cloud was twisting towards them, low to the ground. Watching it, Bill's scalp tightened but he couldn't move. Didn't want to. 'Appen this was the best way to get out of this torment.

'Put your bloody mask on, man.' Wilson dragged the gas mask from its bag and fitted it over Bill's face before putting his own on.

Breathing in the vile smell of rubber Bill began to laugh. Struggling to his feet he pulled the mask off and shoved Wilson. Stumbling to the nearest ladder he climbed, the wood slimy under his fingers.

'Come on then, you bastards,' he yelled, standing well clear of the parapet. 'Come and get us. Finish us off.' The thump of the bullet in his shoulder knocked him back to the floor of the trench. He couldn't see through the thick swirl of gas. His skin began to burn. He couldn't breathe, he couldn't see.

So this was it; this was the fuckin' end to it all. He smiled.

And then there was only pain.

PART THREE

Chapter 63

December 1919

Winifred looked up as the doorbell pinged.

The corners of the window were now covered in white triangles of snow glistening in the reflection of the shop's light. She hadn't expected customers this late in the day. Her image in the dark glass rippled when she moved back behind the counter. She was tired; it had been a long chilly day.

'Can I help you?' She forced a smile towards the lad who hovered from one foot to the other in front of her. He must have been around her age but looked younger, vulnerable. His ginger hair was cut high above his ears which were bright red with the cold, despite the turned-up collar. The left sleeve of his thin jacket was inches above his wrist; the other, empty right sleeve was pinned to the front of his jacket. 'I wondered if I could speak to Mrs Duffy?'

He had a slight stammer and didn't look directly at her, his gaze fixed just above Winifred's head. His forehead, shiny with sweat despite the cold, creased. 'Please.'

There was a tremor in his left hand and, as though suddenly aware of it, he shoved it into his pocket. She noticed the shiver that ran through him.

'Mrs Duffy?' Her stomach clenched in sympathy for him. 'Which one?' If it was her mother he wanted to talk to he would be no match for her these days. 'I'm afraid we have no rooms to let.'

'No, it's not that.' He looked around the shop. 'Florence,' he finally said, 'it's Florence I want to talk to. I'm 'Orace. 'Orace Corbett. I live – we live near where she lived in Wellyhole Yard. I've been away a long time; I was in the army even before the war. And I've been in hospital. I was only discharged last week. Ma says Mrs Duffy was always good with the family when she was next door.' He shuffled forward. Winifred noticed the front of his sole on his shoe flapped open. 'The war, you know…?' This time he looked straight at her. 'It's all changed, and yet it's no different.' There was an expression in his eyes she couldn't fathom yet she knew what he meant.

'I know.' Her memory of the years before the war might be different from his, yet her life had changed too.

'She, Mrs Duffy, knitted me a balaclava. Ma sent it to me.'

'Yes, I remember. Didn't she write letters to you as well?'

'Yeah.' He had a way of lifting half of his mouth in a nervous smile. He raised his shoulders. 'I wanted to thank 'er, to let 'er know I was glad of it and I'm back…home.' He hesitated over the last word.

Winifred pushed herself away from the counter and glanced at the clock on the wall. Outside the flakes were getting heavier, more and were sticking to the glass. No-one else would be making their way to the shop now.

'Turn the sign over, will you, please?'

The pale thinness of the back of his neck seemed to add to his strange vulnerability.

'She's in bed. I'll let her know you're here.'

Her grandmother had stayed in bed, protected from the cold. When Winifred had refilled Florence's hot water bottle and piled yet another blanket from her own bed on top of the tiny figure, she noticed her Granny's breath clouded in front of her face. It worried her. However many times she piled coal on the fire in the bedroom grate barely cast out any warmth. Perhaps she could persuade her to come down into the kitchen to see this lad.

She smiled when he protested.

'She'll want to see you, see you've got back safe.' She didn't add, 'in one piece,' because he wasn't; he was like so many of the other young men who'd returned. She'd seen them around Morrisfield, the maimed, the broken. The ones with only one leg, or worse, no legs. The ones with faces half covered by muslin cloth, hiding dreadful injuries; deformed, with holes where their eyes, noses should be. Winifred swallowed at the remembered images.

'Sit down.' She pointed at the shop chair, more used to the ample backsides of the local gossips who came in to stare and whisper about her. 'Wait.'

Going up the stairs she ignored her mother's irritable call from the kitchen that she'd shut the shop five minutes too early.

'Think we're made of money?'

She only acknowledged her son's, 'Mam?'

'Just a minute, love. I'll be back down in a minute.' Lifting her skirts she ran up each creaking tread and stopped for a moment outside Florence's bedroom door to catch her breath and prepare her words.

'Granny? You awake?' She pushed open the door a fraction.

'I am, ducks.' There was a movement under the huddle of bedclothes. 'By heck, it's gone bloody freezing tonight.'

Winifred glanced towards the windows; the curtains weren't drawn although she asked her mother to make sure they were over an hour ago. She tightened her lips together against the irritation and worry.

Pulling the curtains closed, she said, 'You've got a visitor.'

Florence poked her large nose above the covers. 'Visitor? Me? Who?' Her fingers clutching the covers were white-knuckled.

'Don't look so worried.' Winifred smiled. 'He says he's called Horace. A lad back from the war?'

'Horace? Bertha's lad? Dear God. He's back? Well, bless me and thank God.'

Florence moved faster than Winifred had ever seen her granny move. She threw back the bedclothes and struggled to sit up, pushing against the mattress. 'Here, Winnie, help me.' She stopped, a look of disbelief on her face. 'Don't say you've left him to the mercy of her downstairs?'

'No, he's in the shop. She doesn't know he's there.' Winifred helped her Granny into the beige candlewick dressing gown. 'Granny…' Winifred stopped helping Florence push her arms into the sleeves. 'Granny… he's lost an arm. And I think there's something wrong with his mouth. I thought I should warn you.'

'Oh, dear God. Poor lamb.' Florence's lip quivered. 'I saw a photo of him once in his mother's house. Such a handsome lad he was.' She straightened her back. 'Bloody war!' Shaking her head she bent down feeling for her slippers with her feet. 'Here, love, help me with these.'

She shuffled across the linoleum, tripping slightly on the rug.

'Steady, Granny, take your time.' Winifred pulled the back of Florence's slippers over her heels. 'He's going nowhere 'til he's seen you, I'm sure.'

'I don't want your mother getting at him.'

'She'll have me to deal with if she does. Let me go first down the stairs, you know how lethal they are.'

She walked backwards on the treads holding the old woman's hands.

Ethel Duffy was waiting for them at the bottom, her neck craned, watching Horace in the shop. 'What do you think you're doing,' she hissed. 'Leaving a stranger in there. He could have stolen anything.'

Her grandmother's fingers tightened on Winifred. Before she could speak Florence glared past her. 'He wants nowt of yours, you nasty woman. He's like the rest of his family; as honest as the day is long. His mother brought him up right. Now bugger off back in the kitchen and mind your own.'

Winifred bit inside her cheek to stop the surprised giggle. Nobody else spoke to her mother like that, only her Granny seemed to get away with it.

Horace was standing in the middle of the shop, a strained expression on his face as he looked towards them.

'Take no notice of her,' Florence said. 'Ee, lad, you're home. It's good to meet you at last.' She reached up and put her arms around him, kissing his cheek, before leaning back to look him up and down. 'Oh,' she sniffled, fishing for her handkerchief in her dressing gown pocket with one hand as though reluctant to let go of him with the other. 'Oh, lad.'

The tears were washing down his thin face. 'Looking a bit different from when I joined up, Mrs Duffy.' The youth spoke quietly, scuffling his feet from side to side self-consciously.

She gave a gusty sigh. 'Aye, well, there's a lot come back the same as you and some not come back at all.' She laid her head on his chest. 'So proud you all were – all pals together. Oh dear, oh dear.'

Winifred saw her wobble. 'Let's get you sat down, Granny. Jumping out of bed like that.'

'Hardly jumping, lass.'

'Yes, well. Sit down and I'll get you some water.'

Between the two of them, they led the old woman to the shop chair and lowered her on to it. Horace crouched down so he was level with her.

'You don't look well, lad.' Florence stroked his hair.

'Bit of a cold, that's all.'

'I'll go for that drink.' Winifred left them.

In the kitchen Tom was sitting by the fire, holding his hands out to the flames. 'Who is it, Mam?' Curious he stood to peer over her shoulder. 'Who's the man? He looks odd.'

'He's the son of a friend of your Granny's. From Wellyhole Yard. Back from the war.'

She ignored her mother's harsh scoff.

'Can I go to see him?' Tom jumped up and down. 'Can I ask him what he did? If he killed anyone?'

'No.' Winifred spoke sharper than she meant to. He sat down

with a thump. She saw how he pulled his lips in, how he blinked. 'Sorry, love, I'm not cross. Leave it for now, eh? I'll explain later.' She touched his shoulder when she passed him to go to the sink. 'It's just that he's only come to see Granny Flo.' She ran cold water into a cup before adding, 'And I don't think he's all that well.'

'He'd better not be bringing anything into this house.' Ethel narrowed her eyes at her daughter. 'We don't want any foreign germs in here. We have a shop to run that people depend on.' Her voice followed Winifred.

Horace had his head on Florence's lap and she was still stroking his hair. His voice was hushed when he next spoke. 'It was 'ell, Mrs Duffy, sheer 'ell. I didn't think I'd get out alive. A lot of me mates didn't.'

'Hush now, lad, you're safe now.'

'We were all so cold.' Then there seemed to be a smile in his voice. 'That balaclava you knitted for me were great. I wore it all the time, though I weren't supposed to.'

'I'm glad.'

'I wanted to tell you that. I thought you'd be at our house but Ma said you'd moved to a posher place…'

He lifted his head as Winifred held the cup to her grandmother's mouth.

'Sorry, Miss.' There was no mistaking the admiration. For the first time Winifred saw the young man for what he must have been before all the atrocities that the powers that be had inflicted on him.

'It's fine.' She smiled and offered the cup to him, watching when he gulped down what was left of the water. 'Granny came to live with us after my father died. She's better off here.' Flushing as she realised what she'd said. 'I mean…'

There was a long silence before he smiled and said, 'You're right.' He shifted on his knees, turned back to Florence. 'But really I wanted to thank you for all you've done for Ma and the kids. It wasn't easy when Da went and they moved to Wellyhole Yard. You were good with them.'

250

Florence moved her shoulders in a shrug. 'Aw, lad…'

'I mean it.' They stared at one another for a long moment before he placed his hand on the floor and pushed himself, unsteadily, into a standing position. 'I'd best be off.'

'Tell your mother I'll call over in a couple of days to see you all.'

'I will.' He bent and kissed her forehead, nodded to Winifred and tipped his hat, looking past her.

'Bye son,' Florence said.

Winifred hadn't seen Tom standing in the doorway between the kitchen and shop. Now he came towards Horace, an admiring smile creasing his face. They shook hands.

'Bye sir,' Tom said.

'Just 'Orace will do.'

'I'm Tom. I'm seven.'

'You're a good size for your age, Tom.'

The boy grinned. 'Thanks.' He stared at the empty sleeve. 'How did you—'

'Tom.' Winifred gave her son a warning look. 'Sorry, Horace.'

'It's okay.' He bobbed his head. 'I'll get off, then.' He looked shyly at Winifred. 'Miss.'

'Look after yourself, Horace. I'll bring Granny round to your house as soon as I can.'

She locked the door behind him and watched as he struggled through the snow. She couldn't stop the rush of despondency.

Chapter 64

The springs on the iron bedstead twanged as Winifred slid, shivering, out of bed the following morning, glad she'd kept her woollen socks on during the night. She picked up the clock from the cupboard at the side of her bed; it was only five.

Glancing over at Tom she saw he was still asleep, a small lump under the bedclothes, his breathing a soft snuffle.

Parting the thin curtains revealed the mosaic of frost on the window, sparkling in the flickering flame of the gas street lamp. She pressed her finger on the pane and peered through the small hole she'd made. Snowflakes fluttered in the darkness and snow banked up against the houses on the opposite side of the road.

There'd be no rush to open the shop. Even so, Winifred knew she wouldn't go back to bed; there was a pile of Tom's socks waiting to be darned and it would be good to sit in the kitchen on her own for once.

But when she crept downstairs Florence was already in the kitchen. Muffled in her coat over her dressing gown she was coaxing the fire into life with the large iron poker.

'Granny?' There was a spiral of steam coming from the spout of the kettle on the range; the old woman had obviously been up a while. 'Are you all right?'

'I'm fine, ducks.'

They spoke in whispers over their mugs of tea, not wanting to wake Ethel.

'I want to go to the yard, to see Horace and his mam. I thought he looked more poorly than he said.' Florence's mouth turned down. 'And his poor arm. How are they going to manage if he can't work? At least in the army he had his pay. Now he'll be thrown on the scrapheap. He'll be no good in the mines, or in any of the factories in Morrisfield.'

'I know. It's awful.' Winifred looked out of the window. The sky was still dark but the thick line of snow on the lavvy roof was a pale lemon, reflecting the light from the kitchen. 'Snow looks thick, Granny, and it's still coming down. It'll be hard walking.' Looking at the determination of Florence's face she felt a squeeze of anxiety but still joked, 'I'll have to give you a piggyback.'

'See how it is later, Winnie.' Muted footsteps passed the house. 'Not stopped that lot anyhow.'

Winifred went through to the shop to watch the miners, heads down, shoulders hunched against the cold, a sudden lurch when

252

the clogs of one at the back of the group slipped on the packed snow.

'No.' She went back into the kitchen. 'But we can't go out in this; it looks treacherous.'

'We'll see.'

Winifred smiled at her grandmother, shaking her head. 'If I'm as strong as you when I'm your age, I'll be very grateful.'

'Good Northern stock, ducks. You will be.' Florence laughed. 'Now, if you'll fetch my clothes down I'll put them on the range to warm up and I'll get dressed here, before she comes down.' Florence rubbed her hands together. 'And then I'll make some porridge to warm us up before we tackle those streets.'

But by late morning Winifred's grandmother was back in bed.

Chapter 65

'It's still snowing.' Winifred had been standing by the kitchen window for some time. The top of the yard wall and the steps up to the lavvy, were inches thick. Tom was gathering snow into a heap to make snowman. He turned to look at her, laughing and waving. She lifted her hand and laughed in return. 'Tom's having fun out there.' But he was the only one as far as she could see; they'd be stuck indoors with her mother and, to make things worse, there'd been no-one in the shop all morning. 'I really don't think we should go out.' When she glanced back at Florence she was shocked to see her struggling for breath, her cheeks bright red. 'Granny?'

Her grandmother held out her arm. 'I don't feel too good, Winnie.' Florence's voice was husky. 'I think I'll go for a lie down.'

'That's all right, I've got you.' Winifred moved quickly to help her to stand. She could feel the heat coming from her grandmother's body and, when she put her hand to her forehead, it was dry and hot. Hiding her worry, she kept her voice light. 'I think you're starting with a bit of a cold. Let's get you back to bed and under those covers.'

'I've got such a bloomin' headache.' Florence was trembling. It took Winifred all her strength to support her up the stairs.

'I'll get an aspirin and the hot water bottle.'

Helping Florence to undress, Winifred frowned; now her grandmother's skin looked a peculiar colour. She looked at the window and then back to the old woman. Perhaps it was with the snow blocking out some of the light?

But when she came back with the tablet and stone bottle she was alarmed to see her grandmother's skin was blue. Fear travelled through her whole body.

'Here we are. Open your mouth, take this.' Winifred popped the aspirin into her grandmother's mouth and held the glass to her lips.

'I can't… I can't swallow it.' There was panic in Florence's eyes. She pushed the tablet out with her tongue. 'Throat hurts.'

'Okay, I'll get some honey instead, that should help.' The old woman grabbed her wrist. 'Don't be frightened, Granny.' Winifred pushed the stone hot water bottle into the bed, her heart pounding with agitation; trying not to show it. 'I'll be back in a minute.'

Downstairs Winifred grabbed her coat and ran into the shop. 'We need to send for the doctor for Granny.'

'What for?' Ethel frowned. 'What's wrong with her this time?'

'Well, can't you hear? Just listen.' The sound of harsh prolonged coughing came from upstairs. 'And she looks dreadful.' Winifred pulled open the door and a wedge of snow fell in.

'Now look what you've done. You can clean that…'

Winifred didn't wait to hear her mother's words. Slipping and sliding, ankle deep in the smooth snow, she ran, dragging the cold air into her lungs. Outside the doctor's surgery on Morrisfield Road she stopped to catch her breath.

The waiting room was full of people. A fug of antiseptic and lavender furniture polish was mixed with a variety of human odours. The hushed, resigned group followed her progress across the room to the reception alcove.

'Can I help you?' The doctor's wife smiled at Winifred.

'Oh, Mrs Kirby, it's Granny, Florence Duffy.' Winifred blurted the words louder than she meant to. 'I think–I think she has the influenza.'

She heard the intake of breath behind her. Saw the wary flicker in the eyes of the woman she faced.

'That's the second I've heard today,' someone whispered.

And then the deeper gruff tones of a man. 'Young Horace from the yard died this morning, an' all.'

Winifred spun round. 'Horace? Horace Corbett?'

'Aye, that's right.' The man tucked his scarf higher around his neck, even though he was scarlet and sweating in the heat of the room. 'Poor lad got all through the war in one piece...'

'Well, not quite.' A woman at his side corrected him.

'But he's dead? I only saw him yesterday. How did he die?' Winifred asked the question but didn't want to hear the answer.

There was an uncomfortable silence.

'The influenza,' the man muttered.

'Oh dear god.' Winifred clutched the edge of the counter of the alcove, her legs suddenly weak. 'I need to go. Mrs Kirby, please ask the doctor...'

'I will.'

Winifred pulled the door closed behind her and stood on the step, her hand to her throat.

The man's voice followed her. 'Much good the doctor will be.'

Florence died within twenty-four hours. Even as she grieved, Winifred acknowledged it was a relief. Her grandmother's pain through the prolonged bouts of coughing was unbearable to watch. With each attack frothy blood covered her mouth and nose choking her and splattering onto the bedclothes. The light seemed to hurt her eyes so Winifred sat in the darkness throughout the night placing cold compresses on the old woman's forehead that gave no relief. The room stank of blood, urine and sweat. The only sounds were the gasping breaths and the coughing. When Winifred tried to hold her hand Florence flinched as though the touch gave her pain.

When dawn had finally arrived it was still snowing and the snow that had settled on the windowsill was halfway up the panes, cutting out most of the light in the bedroom. Startled from a restless sleep in the chair Winifred sat up, rubbing at the tightness of dried tears on her face. The silence in the house wasn't strange at first but there was a stillness in the room that frightened her.

'Granny?' She stretched forward, her hand hovering over Florence's shoulder. Standing, she moved closer. Her grandmother looked younger in death than she had in life. Except for the darkness of the blood around her mouth her skin was pale and smooth. 'Oh, Granny.' Winifred touched the old woman's forehead with the back of her hand. Cool, but not cold. Not yet.

'Mam?' Her son's voice revealed his anxiety.

'Don't come in, Tom. Go downstairs.'

'Mam? I don't feel well.'

Winifred dragged her eyes away from her grandmother's body, unable, at first to take in what her son had said.

'Tom?' She moved swiftly towards him and touched his forehead. His skin was dry but he was burning up. Lifting his chin with her forefinger she studied him, her heart thumping. Blue shadows under his eyes made them appear larger, more hollowed than usual.

'Bed,' she said.

'Great Granny…?'

'She's asleep.' Winifred didn't know what else to say. 'Now, let's get you snuggled down in bed.'

Whenever Winifred looked back to the following week the days merged into a blur of tears and desperation. Everything that her

256

grandmother had gone through in a day took seven with her son. Slowly but surely his temperature rose despite the compresses to his forehead and the times she wiped his whole body with cold cloths. She held him through the paroxysms of coughing, her own body jerking with the convulsions.

With the door of their bedroom closed, she didn't even notice when the undertaker took her gran away. The few times she left Tom, either to go to the lavvy or to fetch more cold water, she and her mother didn't speak. But there was always a bowl of soup or a mug of tea waiting for her. The same bowl, the same mug. Ethel didn't go near the bedroom. Winifred knew she was terrified of catching the influenza. But at least she was trying to be kind, something Winifred hadn't seen before, and she was grateful. Sometimes, with a nod of thanks, she took it upstairs with her, other times she couldn't face it. She became thin and drawn, her own throat dry and sore. The fear of losing her son curdled in her stomach. It was a new fear, one she'd never expected and she wasn't prepared for it. She found herself praying, saying the same thing over and over again in her mind; please God, please God. To someone, something, she hadn't acknowledged in years.

Sometimes she heard the shop doorbell, the murmur of voices, the muffled clogs and boots of the miners, but that was a different world. The one she existed in was a small room filled with sickness and despair. Blood and sweat and phlegm.

Until the morning she woke, lying next to her son. He wasn't breathing. She held back her own breath and, balancing on one elbow she stared at his pale face, the pain of her loss spread from her gut to her throat. Touching his cheek with her forefinger he was cool. She didn't move, didn't want to leave him, didn't want him to leave her. Not like this.

And then Tom's chest moved, so slightly she almost missed it. His eyelids flickered, his cracked lips opened. She could see the tip of his tongue.

Her mouth stretched wide open. She didn't recognise the guttural sound of relief as hers.

Days later she discovered that Ethel had arranged her gran's funeral on a shoe-string and in haste. She'd told no-one when it was. She didn't even go herself. Her grandmother had been put in the ground without a soul to mourn her. It was Ethel's final revenge. A revenge that set Winifred's hatred for her mother in stone.

A week later, Ethel had put the sign in the window. ROOM TO LET.

Chapter 66

April 1919

The train pulled slowly out of the station. Bill settled back against the carriage seat and stared through the smeared window, watching the crowds waving daft little flags and hugging the soldiers who were on the platform. He couldn't hear the cheering now the doors were shut, but he saw the open mouths, the smiles of greetings.

No bloody right, he thought. They have no bloody idea what we've been through. Leave the poor buggers alone to get home.

Where would he go? He'd no idea. When he was stuck in the transit camp in France, waiting to get on a ship, he'd thought he would go back to see his stepmother. If she was still alive. But it never got further than a thought. It was over eight years since he'd seen her and his stepsister; he'd nowt in common with them then and he doubted he'd be welcome now – even if they were the nearest he'd got to family.

The gloom of the station and the tall brick walls that enclosed the railway lines gave way to industrial buildings and large stone woollen mills silhouetted against a grey sky, black smoke belching out of the chimneys. For a moment, Bill, regretted not getting off in Manchester. Surely there'd be work there?

Too late now.

He loosened his tie and twisted his neck from side to side; glad to be free of the restriction. Wincing, he rubbed his shoulder where the sniper's bullet had hit him. The bastard medic at the Dispersal Centre had refused to give him a certificate for free treatment; said the wound was healed. Bill wished he'd given in to the sudden urge to thump him; to thump anyone with the anger that brooded inside him.

His demob suit under his fingers was thin and coarse. Pretty poor quality he thought, fingering the material; he should have taken the clothing allowance, he'd have done better having fifty-two shillings and sixpence so he could have bought his own stuff.

The two blokes opposite him were still in uniform, muffled up in their greatcoats, helmets balanced on top of their kitbags between them. Stupid beggars had signed on again from the looks of it.

'You one of the Bantam lot?'

The question took Bill by surprise. He sat up, straightened his back, irritated. 'Yeah. What's it to you?' He narrowed his eyes, weighing up the tall thin soldier who'd spoken.

'Nothing. Just that I fought alongside some of you chaps towards the end; bloody fierce little devils and all. Can't fault your bravery.'

'Having guts doesn't depend on the size a bloke is, you know.' Bill clenched his jaw, cracked his knuckles one by one.

'I didn't say it did.'

'An' what good did it do in the end, eh? It's all a bloody mess. Them in charge didn't give a damn what happened to us. Still don't. We've done our bit and now they can't wait to get rid of us. And what with, eh? What with?' Bill pulled a small book from his jacket inside pocket. 'A Demob Ration Book to take to a Food Office for an Emergency Card. Beg for food, that's what we're expected to do.'

'Everyone has to have a ration book.' The other man spoke for the first time. 'And didn't you get half a year's pay as well, to tide you over until you get work?'

Bill snorted. 'Oh, aye, and two medals.' He pointed to the pawn ticket pinned next to one medal. 'And I'll be hocking this one as soon as I can. And I've a certificate to show what I've done in the army.' He sneered. 'Where d'yer think I'll get a job killing people and blowing 'em to smithereens? Cos that's all I've done these last four years. That and marched around in soddin' circles 'til whichever officer we'd got decided we'd gone far enough up our own arses.' He flung himself back against the seat, coughing and thumping his chest.

When he couldn't stand their silence anymore he asked, 'So, where're you off then?'

'What now?'

'Yeah.'

'Back home. My father has a sheep farm up on the moors beyond Ashford, so I'm going there. Just for a month.'

'You mean yer lived on a farm? Yer didn't need to join up, yer do know that, don't yer? It was a reserved occupation, yer daft bugger.' Something he'd found out too bloody late; he would have stuck it out with Moira if he'd thought it through. If he hadn't lied at the recruitment office and said he was unemployed with no home, he'd have had it easy.

The man shrugged. 'We didn't know what it was going to be like, did we?'

'But you've signed on again? Yer mad, man.'

'It'll be different now.'

'Huh! What was it them in Government promised us? "A land fit for heroes?" Well, it was a bloody lie. I've no time for 'em.' Bill spat on the floor of the carriage and turned to look through the window. He rocked with the soothing motion of the train. They were passing a town; rows of terraced houses and the occasional glimpse of people, trams, horses and carts, diminutive by the distance from the railway tracks. Further away on the skyline, the pit wheels and headgear of a colliery. He watched it all without really seeing.

'Anyhow, you haven't told me where you're going?' The soldier reached over to rest his hand on his helmet that wobbled precariously as the train rolled on the tracks. 'Where your home is?'

Home? Where would he go now? Bill didn't answer, he had no idea.

There was a time when he'd thought he'd have a home; a home, a wife. Perhaps even kids. They'd found a house to rent, him and Annie. Set the date for the wedding even. Sweet Annie Heap; so tiny, so pretty. His.

The first time they'd made love was after a picnic on the banks of the River Colne on a hot summer's day. Looking up to the sky, his arms folded under his head, he'd listened to the splashing of the water as she paddled and sang.

'Shall we marry now?' Annie looked at him as he dried her feet, anxiety clouding her eyes.

Bill stroked her white, slim calf. So smooth, he thought, letting his fingers trail up to her thigh.

She stopped him. 'Bill?'

'Is that what you want, love? For us to marry?'

She nodded. 'I don't want to bring shame to Da. So, yes, please.'

Bill rolled towards her, pulling her to him. He held her face between his palms and kissed her. 'If that's what you want, that's what we'll do.'

'Soon?'

'Soon.'

'You'll ask Da?'

'I will.' Bill jumped to his feet. 'Put your stockings and shoes on and we'll go and ask him now.'

'Spit it out, son.' Bob grinned.

He knows. Bill struggled to keep the embarrassment under control. 'You must know by now, Bob, that I think a lot of your daughter…'

'I should hope so; you've been courting her a while.' Bob chuckled. 'Look, lad, I know you're both so young but I'll put you out of your misery. Our Annie's told me, and I'm under strict instructions to tell you…' He stopped before clapping Bill on the back. 'To tell you yes, of course you can marry my girl.'

The date was set for two months' time. It was the happiest time of Bill's life but it lasted just a few sweet weeks. The cough that had plagued Annie for months became worse and she became lethargic and reluctant to leave the house. Sometimes, too tired to even talk, she just lay on the sofa in the front room with Bill holding her hand. As the weeks went by she grew worse. The date for their wedding came and went.

'We'll wait until you're better, love.' Bill stroked her forehead. 'We've got the rest of our lives to get wed.'

But, calling in one morning after a night shift he was met at the door by her father.

'She's worse, Bill. The doctor's been and said she's to have no visitors. It's bad.' His eyes were bloodshot and his mouth trembled. 'She's sweating and coughing up such phlegm. It's bad,' he repeated, closing the door without another word.

Bill stumbled home. Unable to sleep he left the house and climbed the steep path up to the moors, fighting against the wind that took his breath away and threatened to blow him over. Once he stood and, head back, screamed obscenities into the bleak grey sky before stumbling on over the tangled dead heather and dips of cracked peat. It was almost dark before he clambered over the last stone wall and back onto the path. In the distance he could see the lights in the windows of the cottage on Greens Tenement and felt sick with terror for Annie.

There were no lights on in the kitchen when Bill opened the back door. His stepmother was sitting in the rocking chair by a small fire. She spoke without looking at him. 'Message from one of the lads from the mine. That Heap girl died this afternoon.'

Staring through the window of the train; seeing nothing, Bill wondered if Annie had been his one chance of having a decent life. A home. The brooding anger burst from him and he spat on the floor.

'Hey-up, that's my bloody boot you filthy bastard.' The soldier opposite half-rose off the seat.

Bill lunged at him, fists clenched.

Chapter 67

1920

Willing to face a rough and dangerous task? Want to earn ten shillings a day to save your country? Winston Churchill, British Secretary of State for War, appeals to you. We need temporary Constables to assist the Royal Irish Constabulary against the illegal uprising. Three months training given before being sent to Ireland.

Bill studied the notice outside the town hall in Bradlow, his lower lip held between his teeth. Constables, he thought. Bobbies then. That's what it means. He grinned. Might be interesting to be on the right side of the law for once. No more ducking and diving, which was all he'd been doing for the last few months. Right, no harm in going along to see what's what, he thought, heaving his kit bag onto his shoulder. He was sick to death of dossing around anyhow, cadging the odd job here and there, living hand to mouth. Ten bob a day was three pound ten a week. It was a damn sight more than he had in his pocket.

And who did that lot in Ireland think they bloody were? Why did they always think they were so sodding special?

Sitting on his bed and polishing the metal buckle of his belt he looked around the church hall, watching the twenty men laughing and talking as they settled into the new place. There was a tense, excited buzz in the air. It was almost like the days in Manchester just before they were sent to France. Almost. Although it hadn't taken as long for them all to get to this out-station in the back of beyond.

They hadn't asked him much at the interview. They took no notice of his constant cough or acknowledge his explanation that the damp weather had given him a bit of a cold. But they must have known from his records that he'd been gassed. In fact he could tell they were desperate, glad to have him. Which was a change. The only bit he'd hated was being in the boat across the Irish Sea; too much like the time he was sent off to France. Too many shitty memories.

And then the training at that place, Phoenix Park, had been a bloody joke. The bloke from the RIC hadn't a clue how to handle men, especially the kind of blokes they'd recruited; a rough bunch. But it appeared that's what them in charge wanted. Most of the men he'd been living with over the last four months were ex-soldiers full of resentment against authority, and sour for the way they'd been treated after the war. They needed to be watched, he'd worked that out way back.

But Bill had got the measure of most of them, knew who to trust and who to avoid.

There was none of the easy friendship he'd found with Boardman and Riley, though. Bill screwed up his face. Why had that crossed his mind? He tried to shut out the thought, it always led to thinking about what happened to them. The nightmares were bad enough, he couldn't think about the way they copped it in the daytime as well.

The man on the next bed was reading a newspaper.

'Owt we should know about?' Bill nodded at the paper.

'Same old, same old.' Adam Brown had arrived at Limerick Junction among a crowd of other recruits on their way to Dublin on the same day as Bill. 'Bastards need a good lesson. Ambushed and killed two policemen in Cork. Middle of the day.' He raised his top lip into a sneer. 'And nobody saw, of course.'

'As usual.' Bloody Irish. Bill sniffed. 'I'm ready for some grub, I don't know about you?'

The smell of liver and onions, coming from the small kitchen area, filled the whole building. There was a clatter of knives and forks as one man dropped the pile of cutlery on to the long wooden table, followed by a cheer from someone at a bed further along the room.

'I'll wait until I see what it looks like first. Last night's effort was shite.' Adam Brown scowled. 'If it's as bad as that he'll get it shoved up his jacksie.'

'No, it's Simms in charge tonight. He's not a bad cook.'

The other man just grunted. Bill gave his belt a final rub and stood up to thread it through the loops of his dark green RIC tunic. That was another bloody cock-up; not enough uniforms. So RIC tunics, belts and caps, khaki army trousers. Bill gave the trousers a quick brush. Nowt matched but at least he'd make damn sure he was smart.

Tommy Simms, a short, thin man, appeared at the door of the kitchen, struggling to carry a large saucepan and a metal spoon.

'Grub's up, lads.' There was a mad rush for the table and he backed up to the kitchen doorway to avoid being knocked over. 'Whoa, you daft buggers, tha's worse 'n kids.' He struck out wildly with the spoon, balancing the saucepan in one hand before running forward, almost out of control and banging it onto the table.

Watching, Bill laughed. Simms was fiery, and his Birmingham accent grew thicker the madder he got. Which was often. The man had been in the middle of a scrap at the docks in Cork when Bill had first seen him after stepping off that damn ferry.

But later, lying on his bed, idly thinking about that, Bill knew the meal breaks, the training, the cleaning and pressing the daft uniform, was only passing the time. He was restless and ready for some action. Backing up the RIC in this place in the middle of nowhere was a job; they were being paid to suppress an armed rebellion of some militant Irish against the British Government. It was different from being at war with the Huns and being told what to do by some idiot junior officer who'd only just left his mam. Here, they were their own bosses.

Bill sucked on his teeth turned his head on the pillow to study the poster pinned to the wall above the door. He'd seen it many times since he'd signed on.

If a police barracks is burned or if the barracks already occupied is not suitable, then the best house in the locality is to be commandeered, the occupants thrown into the gutter. Let them die there – the more the merrier. Should the order ("Hands Up") not be immediately obeyed, shoot and shoot with effect. If the persons approaching (a patrol) carry their hands in their pockets, or are in any way suspicious-looking, shoot them down. You may make mistakes occasionally and innocent persons may be shot, but that cannot be helped, and you are bound to get the right parties some time. The more you shoot, the better I will like you, and I assure you no policeman will get into trouble for shooting any man.

RIC Divisional Commissioner for Munster,
Lt. Col. Smyth, June 1920

Well, that said it all. Bill cracked his knuckles one by one. Can't argue with that. They were being given full rein to do what they wanted. For the first time since he'd left France, Bill recognised that he had a purpose. He'd show the Irish bastards who was boss.

Chapter 68

July 1921

As far as Bill was concerned it was a routine patrol; just like they'd been doing for the last twelve months on the streets of Killaire. Mostly boring, sometimes spiced with a bit of excitement.

He and his six mates swaggered down the middle of Manor Street, pointing their rifles towards anyone who dared to catch their eyes, shouting at the kids, the 'dirty tykes' playing on the pavements, watching with satisfaction as women, arms crossed and chatting on doorsteps, melted back into the houses.

There were usually eight of them sent out together, but Ronnie Clayton had disappeared. The rumour was he'd scarpered back to the mainland, hadn't the stomach for the fight against the rebels. Never had. Secretly, Bill had a bit of sympathy for him, though he hardly acknowledged it, let alone told any of the men at the barracks. In the ten months he'd been in Dublin he'd seen things just as bad as he'd seen at the front in Arras.

A stone came from nowhere and hit him on the shoulder. He swung around with a curse but couldn't see anybody. He fired a couple of rounds in the general direction. The other men laughed, followed suit; the shots echoing in the now empty street.

Bill rubbed his shoulder where the stone had caught him. Bloody Irish were worse than animals. Leave them to rot in this stinking pit, he thought; there was nowt here he'd want, so why Lloyd George was so bothered he didn't know. Stupid bloody Government, it wasn't them in Parliament risking their necks for ten bob a day. Happen Ronnie Clayton had the right idea after all.

They stopped in front of the general store.

'You going in for the fags, Howarth?' It was more of a statement rather than a question. They took it in turns each day to go into the shop and take what they wanted.

Bill nodded, noticing one of the windows was boarded up. The lazy bloody owner obviously hadn't bothered to replace the glass that Irish bastard had fallen through last Saturday. He moved towards the shop. There was still blood, a large dark stain, covering the step in the doorway, where they taught those scum a good lesson. Where, as they lay unconscious, Bill and four of his mates had shown the scum's girlfriends what a good fucking was.

It had been a bloody good way to round off the last patrol of the night.

They'd intended to swing by their usual pub, McCarthy's, to sort the buggers out there. But, passing Guthrie's, they'd heard quiet music, voices singing low.

'"And will Ireland then be free?" says the Sean Bhean Bhocht..."' Hang on.' Brown frowned, thrusting his arms across the other men. Stopping them in their tracks. 'Listen.'

'"Yes old Ireland will be free from the centre to the sea, And hurrah for liberty," says the Sean Bhean Bhocht.'

'Bastards.' Brown glared towards the door of the pub and then at each of the men. He grinned. 'They need a good lesson.' He hit one clenched fist against the palm of his other hand. 'Let's give it to them.'

But when they crashed through the doors the singing had stopped. Four men were in the centre of the smoke filled room playing snooker. In one corner a couple of old men sat in chairs by the fire, flames blazing high despite the warmth of the summer's evening. A few others leaned against the bar, pints in hand, feet on the brass rail. The pub owner was wiping glasses.

'Don't stop on our account.' One of the soldiers deliberately knocked against the snooker table as they pushed their way towards the bar.

'We don't want any trouble gents,' the barman murmured, reaching for pint glasses from the hooks above him. 'Drinks on the house?'

'Keep 'em coming and we'll think about it.' Bill shoved two men aside, propping his rifle against the front of the bar. When he looked around the ones who'd been playing snooker had disappeared.

It was a good night. Free ale in Guthrie's pub. Two girls.

Bill told himself the girls had been up for it, coming out of the store and stepping over the bloodstain. He threw the packets of cigarettes to each of the other six men, pushing away the memory of the look of terror on the first girl's face, only remembering the defiance on the face of other one. And he chose only to recall the globule of saliva that landed on his cheek as he grabbed her. The red rage in him, fuelled by the beer, was the same he'd carried all through the war. Sometimes it had been the only thing that kept him going.

But it wasn't enough now. He was sick to the back teeth with Ireland, of having to watch his back whenever they went out on the streets, of the hatred from the bastards who lived in the poky houses, watching from behind the net curtains. Of the dirty way they fought. It was nowt like the war where you knew where the enemy was. Here they appeared from nowhere and buggered off just as quick.

The first drops of rain were slow and heavy, spreading splodges of dark grey on the pavements, settling then soaking into his jacket, drumming onto his cap. Even the bloody rain was different in this god-forsaken place, Bill thought, swiping his hand across his wet face.

The shot came from nowhere. The group of soldiers circled, backs to one another; rifles pointed first one way, then another.

'Where the fuck did that come from?' Bill could feel Tommy Simms's thin shoulders shake as they pressed closer.

He gritted his teeth. 'How the fuck should I know.'

'Take cover.' The new sergeant, Bill couldn't even remember his name, bellowed the order. 'Make for the church.'

The rain suddenly increased, pelting pebble-like onto the road and stinging Bill's face. His rifle was slippery in his hands and he felt the sick fear of everything being out of control. Barely able to see, he scrambled over the piles of rubble, slid on wet stone inside the bombed out church, making for some sort of safety.

He crouched against one of the walls of the old church cursing his luck and rubbing his shoulder. There was a wheezing in his chest; his cough was bothering him again. And the scar of his old wound throbbed, took him back to the other times when fear turned his guts to water. He'd got himself into another bloody hole with this lot. He thought about the words of his sergeant; a bluff red-faced Cockney, puffed up with his own importance.

'Remember the words of Lt. Col. Smyth,' he'd shouted, strutting along the front of the bedraggled line of volunteers from the mainland. 'I'll remind you of them now. You make these bastards pay for what they've done. If you see any of them with a gun, if you see them talking in groups, if you see someone walking towards you and you don't like the look of them, you shoot the bastards. And if they argue, you shoot them. We show them who's the boss; who's in charge.'

Well, Bill shifted uncomfortably, squinting into the rain and trying to find a drier place, he was damned sure him and his mates around him weren't in bloody charge right at this sodding minute. Those bastards on the roof had well and truly got them cornered. His ears rang from the echo around the ruins of the rifle shots that pinned them down like scared rabbits.

They got Tommy Simms. He tried not to look at the remains next to him, but he could smell the warm blood and piss. Half of Tommy's head was missing. Blood frothed on the rough stone

270

behind him, the pinkish slime of brain shining wet in the rain. Slivers of bloodied flesh and white shards of bone were splattered on the sleeve of Bill's jacket. He gritted his teeth against the rush of bile and swallowed, shuffling forward, squatting, anxious to get away from the corpse. When he glanced back it was as though the eye that remained in what was left of Tommy's skull was staring right at him.

He heard the scrape of wood above him as a window opened. Swathes of starlings rose above the ruins, chattering, spiralling against the grey bank of cloud. Bill flattened himself against the wall, squinting along the length of his raised rifle. The sky was momentarily blocked out by a shape and he fired upwards as it hurtled towards him. He collapsed under the weight of the body. The air taken from his lungs momentarily stilled him.

Cursing and crying, he fought to free himself. He threw the corpse off him. Pressing his boots on the ground he grabbed on to gritty stones for leverage and scooted backwards. The corpse was naked, the face battered beyond recognition. But he knew the tattoos on both arms, the image of Jesus on the cross, the word, "Mother". Slowly, unwilling, he let his eyes move along the twisted limbs, the fingers were splayed, bloodied. There were no nails. He slid his gaze over the shattered kneecaps to the feet. There were no nails on any of the toes. But it was the other mass of blood his gaze returned to. He closed his eyes but against the lids still saw where Ronnie Clayton's cock had been sliced off. He looked back at the head and saw what he hadn't seen before. The lad's penis was stuffed into his mouth.

Bill gave in to the lurching in his stomach.

On the Front he'd seen some bloody awful things; men, his friends, blown to pieces, the blood staining the slush of dirt, arms and legs scattered. Crows feasting on corpses. But nothing as vile as this, nothing where men had so tortured other human beings. He vomited again.

Pushing against the wall, he forced himself upright; he couldn't stop the trembling that moved every part of his body.

'Get down, fucking idiot.' His sergeant had hold of his leg, dragging him backwards. He kicked out. Heard the curse. Didn't care. All he needed was to get away. From the gaze of Tommy, from the horrible sight in front of him, from the bits of flesh stuck to the shoulders of his jacket. Frantic, he batted at the gore but it stuck to the fibres. Ripping at the buttons he tore the jacket off him.

Heedless of the angry shouts of his sergeant and the other men in his unit, ignoring the bullets that screamed around him, hitting the ground, Bill walked on. Let 'em all get on with it. 'I'm out of this shit hole, once and for all,' he muttered, hardly knowing he'd spoken aloud. 'This is not my fuckin' war.'

All this just because they'd killed two of the scum who'd tried to jump them outside Guthrie's. All because they'd had it off with two Irish tarts.

Chapter 69

August 1921

Bill's show of bravado dwindled rapidly once he realised he was a sitting target for snipers, or anyone who hated the Black and Tans. Which was most, if not all, of the Irish.

That first day and night he skirted hamlets and farms, feeling nothing but the desperate need to get away from Killaire, and to get rid of the rest of his uniform. With each passing hour his thoughts became more incoherent. Crouching behind hedges, squirming across fields on his belly, his one consuming urge was to escape; his one growing and overwhelming emotion was fear.

As dawn approached with the sporadic calls of birds, and the darkness became bleached with subtle blurred lines of light, the ground became wet and yielding under Bill's knees and elbows.

272

When he stood he saw a wide expanse of a glinting river in front of him. Collapsing, he worked his fingers into the earth and pulled at the grass. Hot tears mingled with snot. He didn't know what he was doing, what he should do.

He slept. At first into oblivion, but then came the images; of blood, torn limbs, bodies grotesquely angled in death, the sounds of bayonets slicing into flesh, the screams of terrified girls struggling as grinning men held them down, repeatedly raping them.

When he awoke he didn't know where he was. He sat bolt upright, his eyes still closed. Trying to get onto his knees he fell over, shaking, blood pounding in his ears. When he finally opened his eyes he looked along his body. Under the slime of mud he could see the black and tan of his clothes. Agitated, he tugged at the buttons of his shirt, rolled on the ground pulling it off his shoulders, from his arms. Dragging at his braces, he fumbled at the waistband of his trousers. A flashing image of the night he'd unbuttoned them and forced himself into the two girls brought a loud sob from deep within his throat. Wriggling backwards he tore at his trousers, kicked off his boots, until he lay panting in only his vest and long johns.

When he next came around it was night time again and he was shivering. Uncurling himself from, he stretched his limbs.

Something had woken him.

Trying to hold his breath, he heard the rustle of grass and murmur of men's voices within inches of him. Fear weakened him and he realised he'd wet himself; but the humiliation didn't hit him until whoever it was had moved away. Holding both arms over his eyes he lay still waiting for the shouts that would mean they had found his uniform. But the voices faded away.

Eventually, he scrambled to his knees and felt around for the shirt and trousers. Grubbing a hole in the ground, he stuffed them into it.

He was shivering uncontrollably by the time the next night had crowded in over him. He had to move on, but needed clothes. His long johns were still damp, and there was no way he could carry on without at least trousers and a shirt.

Following the line of the river he scuttled through scrubland, rushes and stunted trees until he came to a small stone bridge. Peering over the wall he saw a row of run-down cottages a couple of hundred yards away. A line of clothes dangled motionless from a washing line in one of the gardens. There was a dull light in one of the upstairs windows, but downstairs was in darkness.

The gate grated under his hand when he opened it and he stood still, every nerve tingling. Almost dizzy with fear he made himself move towards the washing, grabbing whatever he could get hold of. One wooden peg flew off and hit him in the eye as he yanked at a pair of trousers but he didn't stop until the line was empty.

He ran, his eye stinging and half-closed, the bundle of clothes held tightly to him, and kept on running until he was out into the countryside again. Hiding in a ditch, huddled under the undergrowth and squatting in mud, he began to cry.

In the years that followed Bill couldn't remember much of what he'd done in the following few weeks. The nights were filled with scenes of dismembered bloody limbs, of huge rats gnawing at his face as he lay beneath bodies laid out for miles in the trenches. Boardman and Riley appeared constantly shouting and screaming; blaming him for their deaths. John Duffy walked alongside them as they approached.

Always Bill awoke sweating and trembling. The days were a mindless stumbling along lanes and footpaths. Sometimes, later in the day, he found himself staring up at the same wooden signpost on the same lane he'd started from that morning.

Once, tramping along a path he looked up and saw a large flock of geese crossing the sky as it blended into bright, crisp daylight. And then, from somewhere he heard the wail of a siren. He couldn't see where it came from, or what it was but it shocked him into stillness. Sitting down on the grass he rubbed his hands over his ears, and held them there for a moment, staring down at the battered boots he'd stolen from a farmyard somewhere. It was as though hearing the noise had suddenly brought him out of the confusion he'd existed in for so long.

Brought back to him the distant memory of the day his father died.

Wilfred had given Bill a beating that morning for not getting up when first called, and had promised another when he returned home after his shift. He'd said he was getting Bill used to an early rise because the following day would be his thirteenth birthday; the day he was to follow his father down the mine as a putter. It didn't bother Bill; he'd always known that pushing the small wagons along the metal plates through the workings to the passages where the horses could be hitched up to them was to be his lot in life.

Bill remembered hearing the thump and rush of running feet on the cobbles outside his house at the same time he heard the warning siren from the mine. He'd run with the crowd before even knowing what was happening; seeing the strain on the faces and the hearing of the sobs and cries of the women and children around him, knowing that life in the village had changed forever.

'What's 'appened?' Bill caught the arm of a woman.

'They say there's been a flood.' Her eyes were wild. 'My three lads are down there. What am I going to do? I have two more bairns to bring up. Their da's already gone; killed in that explosion last year.' She grabbed his sleeve before dropping to her knees.

Pulled down with her Bill looked around for somebody to help the woman but there was no-one. They might as well not be there for all the notice paid to them.

He dragged her to her feet. 'C'mon. Unless we get to the gates we'll never know who's safe and who's still down there.'

The management had closed the gates. The cries of despair

soon changed to shouts of anger in an effort to discover what had happened. When a grey-faced man in a suit approached the crowd the silence was instant. He held up his hand to quiet them, an unnecessary gesture, before he spoke.

'From what we can gather there was break through to an old abandoned mine that was flooded. We know some of the men are safe…' He waited for the cries of relief to abate. 'But we don't know how many yet.'

Then a huddle of men, bowed, silent and trailing a thin stream of black water behind them, appeared, walking towards the gates.

Bill's knuckles grated together as the woman's gripped his hand. And then she screamed. 'Eddie!' She looked at Bill and laughed; a high-pitched noise. 'That's Eddie, my eldest.' Then turning she shouted, 'Where's your brothers?'

As the young man came closer Bill saw the white tracks cutting through the black of coal dust on his face.

'Gone, Ma. They're gone.' He shook his head, bewildered. 'There was so much water—water and thick mud. One minute we were working together and then all this water came flooding through and they were gone.'

She fainted. The manager unbolted the gates and the crowd surged around her, pouring into the yard before milling around in sudden confusion. The man's blank gaze fastened on Bill in a blink of recognition. 'Your da was with 'em.' He nodded, his voice trailing away. 'He's gone too…'

Bill thought his feet would never move from the spot he stood in. Then he turned, jumped over the lifeless form of the woman and ran for home, shocked by sense of release and freedom that coursed through him.

He tumbled through the doorway of the house.

'Didn't you hear the siren?' He held his side against the pain of the stitch.

'I did.' Marion didn't lift her head from staring into the small fire in the grate. 'I reckon someone would tell me sooner or later what's happened.' Now she did look at him, her eyes narrowed. 'And here you are.' She slowly moved her head up and down. 'Here you are. You're going to tell me he's gone, aren't you?'

Bill nodded, a succession of small bobs of the head. 'Yeah. The mine—'

'I don't want to know. All I want *you* to know is that you'd better make sure you're ready to take his place as wage earner in this house.'

It had taken months to recover some of the men's bodies. But they never found Wilfred Howarth's.

It took Bill months to realize his stepmother had received a pay-out from the mine owners for the loss of her husband. Angry, because he'd tipped up all his wages in the belief he was keeping a roof over their heads, each time he got promotion or was shifted to a better-paid job underground, Bill kept the difference in the money.

He knew he was only tolerated for what he could give to his stepmother and stepsister. They'd done nowt for him.

'Never did,' he muttered now. Wiping them from his mind with a grunt of satisfaction he looked around, forcing himself to think. Christ he was in a right fix.

His stomach rumbled. When had he last eaten? Finding food from somewhere was the first thing to do.

Then somehow he had to get to Limerick and then on to Kingstown to stow away on the freight ferry to Liverpool. He didn't know how he'd manage it, but that was what he had to do to get back on the mainland. And he had to do it under his own steam; there was no way he dare hitch any lifts, not with his accent. He'd got himself into a pile of shit. Somehow he had to dig himself out of it.

Pushing himself to his feet, he set off.

PART FOUR

Chapter 70

January 1922

The snow was dirty and mushy underfoot when Bill stepped off the tram in Lydcroft. He wasn't sure what he would do but having landed a job in Stalyholme mine as a chargeman tunneller he needed to find lodgings. After he'd had the interview with the son of the owner he'd wondered if he was mad coming back to Lydford. Now he was convinced.

But it had been a miserable six months since the day he'd walked away from that bloody mess in Killaire.

During the last month as he'd made his way to Kingstown he'd thought back to his early years, trying to work out how he'd got himself to this point.

Initially, Annie Heap was in his mind a lot of the time. The old agony he'd felt when she'd died returned in great waves of sorrow, sometimes even halted his footsteps. Sometimes he dreamt of the day he tramped the moors, the day he lost her. A week later, a heart attack took Bob, her father; the man who'd become his friend, perhaps even the man who would have become the father figure Bill had missed out on. He convinced himself for a while that, if she'd lived, his marriage to Annie would have been perfect. But he knew himself too well and admitted that, with his temper, it likely wouldn't have lasted.

And, as the days went by and he huddled frozen and seasick in the depths of the freight ferry on its way to Liverpool, the misty outline of Annie's face was replaced by the clearer one of Winifred

Duffy. The brown eyes of his first girlfriend – he was fairly certain they were brown – faded to be replaced by the clear dark blue eyes of the girl from Lydcroft.

Once on the mainland Bill felt he could breathe at last. In shoes he'd stolen from one of the crew of the freight ferry, he left Liverpool to make his way further north. He didn't know where else to go.

Still, it didn't stop his apprehension; the misgivings that he was making a bad mistake. But he needed to see Winifred Duffy again. Thoughts of her mingled with all the bad memories. He had to know whether the stirrings of his body at those times would be the same when he actually stood in front of her.

Sometimes he persuaded himself that nothing would have changed in Lydcroft; she would still live at the shop, still be the girl he wanted her to be, the same gentle, decent girl he'd first believed her to be. No woman since had got under his skin like she had. Yeah, he knew she'd be older but so was he. She couldn't have changed that much; she hadn't seen the things he had, women had much easier lives, every bugger knew that.

Other times, his old feelings of jealousy and doubts reared up a lot; she might have married the Irish bastard, might not even live in Lydcroft. But the urge to know grew stronger each day he tramped the roads.

He had to see her. Had to be sure.

He'd be mad to go back. Mad to go back into the mines.

But, as though of their own accord, his footsteps took him closer to Morrisfield. And then to Lydcroft. To Winifred.

And at long last he was standing outside the shop, looking up at the sign above the window. Faded now but still there. Duffy's. And in the window a sign. ROOM TO LET.

Bill hesitated, his insides churning, his bladder bursting. He badly needed a pee. Spinning on his heels he ran along Mine Road and found some shrubs to relieve himself in.

The wooden headframe of the mine was a stark outline against the purpling sky of dusk. He'd be there next week; a good job with decent pay. Security. And he'd found himself some digs; a room in one of the miners houses on Mine Road. A bit of a muck tip but he'd thought it would do for the time being. He hadn't had a good sleep in the weeks. But with the job and a bed to sleep in he'd believed his luck was turning.

Now this. 'Room to let,' he murmured. He couldn't, could he? Did he dare? Did he want to?

He stood outside the shop for five more minutes before gathering all his courage and going inside.

He rubbed his feet on the mat at the shop doorway, wiping off the grey slush of the road. The bell tinkled again when he closed the door and waited.

'We're closed.' The words came from somewhere beyond the shop.

Bill coughed. 'I know,' he called, aware that he was standing on the same spot as he had when he had thrown the box that killed Winifred Duffy's father. Shaking with cold and weariness he blinked rapidly; a nervous twitch. What the hell was he doing?

He almost turned to run from the shop; would Winifred remember him? But how could she? She'd hardly noticed he existed even when she shopped at Bertie Butterworth's fish shop. Why would she recognise him now? This was the moment he'd anticipated for months. He'd got this far, he couldn't chicken out now.

When the woman came through to the shop it was the mother. Bill swallowed his disappointment. And relief.

She hadn't worn well, he noted, when she finally appeared from the back of the shop, fussing over the buttons of her coat. She was fat, her face raddled and red. The navy felt hat she wore was jammed low on her head, but not enough to hide the thin red line across her forehead or the net drooping down over one ear.

But if she was still running the shop then Winifred could be around as well. He needed to know. He hadn't thought beyond that, but it had become an obsession. Why or what he'd do when he found out, Bill didn't know. It was more important than ever that he got lodgings here. He forced a smile onto his face.

'I said we're closed.' The woman didn't hide her irritation, eyeing him with suspicion. 'I was just going to lock up.'

'I've come about the room.' He gestured towards the window. 'It says there's a room to let?' He touched the peak of his flat cap, kept his voice low, respectful. Even though he had a room to go to this was the one he wanted. 'I wondered if it was still available.'

'Do you have a job?'

He watched her weighing him up from the old cap, down over the black overcoat he'd acquired from a coat stand in one of the pubs he'd been in, past his trousers, now frayed at the hems, and to his shoes. He was conscious of his appearance and stiffened. He wouldn't let the old bag make him feel worse than he did.

He took his time. 'Yeah,' he said, not trying to keep the pride from his voice. 'I've just been taken on as Chargeman Tunneller at the pit. Stalyholme mine,' he added.

'Hmm.' She sniffed. 'We had to let the last lodger go when he lost his job. And the one before him. I'm not a charity.' He waited as she stared at him again for a minute. 'Well, perhaps we'll have better luck with you. You'd better come through, I suppose,' she said at last. Standing back she lifted the flap of the counter so he could pass through to the small hall beyond the door at the back of the shop. He waited there for her, clasping his rucksack to his chest.

'Up there. Up there.' She flapped her hand towards the narrow stairs. 'First on the right. Only small, looks over the back yard but what can you expect for four shillings a week. You will be paying up front.' It was more a statement than a question.

He nodded. He was actually going to take it. He had to be mad.

As he looked around for somewhere to put his bag, he caught a glimpse of a small figure hovering just inside a room beyond the hallway, a lad dressed on oversized jumper and trousers, his fringe almost covering his eyes.

'Eh up.' Bill grinned at him.

The boy stepped back without a word.

Bill shrugged and followed the woman who'd obviously decided not to wait for him.

'I'm Mrs Duffy.' She spoke without turning her head. 'Rent includes breakfast. If you want an evening meal it's a shilling a week extra and you have it in your room.' She stood back, holding herself close to the door to let him pass.

Bill let his gaze sweep around the room, nodding slightly. He'd been in worse: the dark furniture, a wardrobe and a bedside table, too big for the room, thin curtains, a rag rug on the wooden floor by the bed. The bed was a small iron one with a thin mattress. but it was enough for him. It'd do. And it would mean he would see Winifred sometime, surely? 'Very nice,' he said, 'I'll take it.'

Ethel Duffy raised her eyebrows as though there'd been no doubt. 'Right,' she said, 'I'll get Win… I'll get the bed made up. You can wait in the kitchen until the room's ready. I'd appreciate the rent when it is.'

Bill hadn't missed her slip of the tongue; she almost said Winifred. So she was still here. But on her own or with a husband? By, he was playing a dangerous game. But there was no going back.

Chapter 71

March 1922

Coughing harshly, Bill jerked awake at the sudden sound, his hair plastered to his scalp with sweat; the nightmare still in his head.

Wiping his hand over his face he breathed loudly to still the quivering of his heartbeat, and stared up at the ceiling over his bed.

He'd been stuck on the snarl of barbed wire again, the explosions and crack of rifles pounded in his head. There was a chill inside him, cold that had nothing to do with his surroundings; the sun beating down on his head had no heat. Looking down he saw the splinters of bones, the blood seeping onto frozen ground where his foot should have been. He joined in with the screams around him, whirling his arms around to break free. No Man's Land. The land around him was pockmarked with craters and littered with bloody and torn limbs. The stench filled his nostrils, filled his lungs. He clamped his mouth shut but still it seeped through his whole body. A large crow landed next to him. He tried to kick out at it but his leg swung, useless from side to side. Snot mixed with tears of pain as the bird strutted around him, pecking at his flesh. When he struggled, the wire bit deep through his tattered uniform into his chest; stabbed pain.

He saw his image wither; grow old as he hung on the wire. Nobody could do anything for him.

But then he was scrambling around in the wire entanglements, up to his knees in mud, the strands of barbed wire clinging to his legs and his hands torn and bleeding through the struggle to drag them off. A shell screamed overhead and landed some yards away from him. He saw Reilly's decaying body. Then others, flying through the air, disintegrating, and landing all around him. He started to scream. And couldn't stop. Pushing his fingers in his ears, he strove to stop hearing his own agony but it was no good; the cry drilled through his head.

Bill's eyes became used to the darkness. He moved his head on the pillow, wet with his sweat, pushed himself into a sitting position to ease the sudden urge to cough, to clear the phlegm, and stared at the square of the window. A second later he flinched as it lit with flash of blazing light. He waited, aware of every twitch of muscle, every lift of his chest with each stuttering breath before the low growl of thunder finally hit a crescendo and subsided.

In the strange waiting silence that followed he heard someone rattling a poker in the fire grate downstairs.

He hadn't meant to go to sleep but over the last few weeks he'd found out there was little else to do on a Sunday afternoon after a session in the pub, after a pie and a pint.

The day was almost over and he was on early shift in the morning. He swung himself off the bed, shaking his head to rid himself of the memories the nightmare brought him time and time again. His vest was soaked with sweat, so he yanked it off and crumpling it into a ball wiped it over his face and armpits. The bedroom was freezing and the shaking was deep inside his body. Feeling the sheet on the bed he touched chilly dampness. There was no way he was getting back on that yet.

The sudden rattle of heavy rain on his window made him jump, brought back the images. He needed to get out of this room, but there was no way he was going back to the pub in that weather. With no idea of the time he wondered who was in the kitchen. Then he remembered that every Sunday evening since he'd rented the room the old woman went to visit a neighbour. Putting on his thickest jumper and carefully combing his hair in the small mirror over the dressing table, he convinced himself that it wasn't as late as he thought and stealthily opened the door. Across the landing *her* door was slightly open and he could see the boy in his bed. Oblivious to the storm outside.

He waited at the top of the stairs, listening for any talking. Nothing.

The nervousness inside him wasn't the same he'd had just before they went over the top in the war. Nor was it anything like the tension he'd felt in Ireland. Right at this moment he knew that this was his chance to impress Winifred; to get her to like him enough to let him keep her company tonight.

He took the stairs one at a time, sliding his hand palm downwards on the wall.

Winifred was just as he remembered her all those years ago, well perhaps not quite; thinner, a few lines around her mouth – a mouth that looked as if it hadn't been stretched into a smile for a long time. But still a good-looking woman; still the woman he'd tried so hard to get to notice him in the past. Except just before he left Lydcroft. Just after he'd killed… He stopped that thought.

Even with a kid she was still a good catch. Yeah, even with the boy. His stomach tightened; it had been a shock to find out he was hers, and he'd soon worked out that he was probably the by-blow of the Irish sod he'd seen her with. But he could put up with that; the lad couldn't help who his father was any more than he'd been responsible for his own drunken bully of a father. He actually seemed a nice kid. Quiet. 'Appen too quiet. Bill had seen the way the old woman looked at the lad sometimes, heard the sharpness of her words to him.

Chapter 72

Despite the thunderstorm Ethel had gone next door as she always did on Sunday evening. No doubt to have a moan about her and Tom, Winifred thought.

Her mother's parting shot had been to grumble about the lodger. 'Well at least this weather will wash down the yard. I'm sick of him upstairs; every time he comes back from the mine he leaves mucky footprints all over the place. He needs telling to take off his boots–clogs, whatever he wears, at the gate. I'm not breaking my back to clean up his mess.' She'd glared at Winifred. 'If business was better, if we hadn't lost so much custom down the years, we wouldn't ever have needed to rent out that room.' She'd slammed the door on her last words.

Winifred knew the last was a direct dig at her having had Tom out of wedlock, bringing shame on Ethel. Even after all the years her mother couldn't resist. She sometimes wondered what Ethel would grumble about if she and Tom weren't there. But there was no chance of that; they were tied to the place, bound into this life of bitterness, of scorn from the women who came into the shop; who still sometimes refused to be served by her.

The calm that filled Winifred the moment Ethel closed the back gate gave way to the old anger. But it was an anger she was unable to truly aim at her mother. In all honesty, she reflected, it was as much at herself for falling in love, for trusting Conal.

Leaning her head forward, she put her hands on the mantelpiece, breathing deeply to regain the calm she forced into herself every day, pushing the wayward thoughts back behind the door in her mind and closing it firmly.

The slight movement of the last tread on the stairs made her turn towards the door. The flames of the fire momentarily flickered yellow in the draught caused by the swish of her skirt.

Neither of them spoke at first, neither made eye contact. Winifred waited to see what he wanted. He'd been around for about a month but, if he wasn't working at the mine, the lodger was usually out. She supposed he went drinking in the Wagon and Horses but there was never the smell of alcohol in his room when she went to change the sheets and clean.

When he didn't speak she said, 'Can I help you?'

'Mind if I come in?' he said. 'It's a bit parky up in my room. This weather doesn't help.'

His request was a surprise; neither of the other lodgers had ever asked to come down into the kitchen once they'd made their way to their own room.

She stared at Bill, not sure what to say. With her mother out and Tom in bed it would be the first time she'd been on her own in a room with a man since Conal. She struggled to block the name, his image, out. But when the lodger spoke again she immediately compared the harsh Lancashire accent with the soft burr of Conal's Irish tones.

'Miss? Mind if I grab a bit of warmth?' He stepped into the kitchen. He wasn't much taller than her, she hadn't realised that, the few glimpses she'd had of him over the last weeks.

What should she do? He was right; his room must be icy cold. Her mother didn't allow him to have a fire up there. And what harm could it do? 'Not at all,' she said, speaking more decisively than she felt. 'This weather is dreadful, isn't it?' She waved her hand towards the chair at the far side of the fireplace but he chose to sit on Tom's buffet near her. Too near, she thought, trying to move away without him noticing.

But, 'It's okay that I sit here?' he said, taking a quick breath, as if realising his mistake.

When she looked at him she saw he seemed as uneasy as her. It made her feel a little more confident.

'I was just going to make a drink,' she said, not answering him. What could she say? I don't want you so close to me? How could she say that? She smiled at him. 'Would you like a cup of tea?'

'A brew would be very welcome. Thanks.'

She was quite self-conscious waiting for the kettle to boil and arranging the cups and saucers and milk jug and sugar bowl on a tray. But when she turned to carry it to the table he wasn't watching her; he was staring into the fire, his eyes half closed, legs spread, his hands on his stocky thighs.

He jumped up when he saw what she was doing. 'Let me…'

'No, I'm fine, thanks.' She put the tray down. 'I'll let it brew a while.' She stood, uncertain whether to stay by the table or go back to her chair. 'Do sit down, you look quite tired.' Was that too personal a thing to say?

He didn't seem to notice. And when he sat down again he went to the chair she'd indicated when he first came downstairs. Perhaps he'd noticed her dismay before.

'I'd just like to sit by the fire for a bit, if that's okay?'

'That's fine.' Winifred studied him. His thick dark hair was carefully arranged into two waves at the front above his broad forehead. His face was ruddy; a scatter of tiny blue scars marked him out as a miner. And although his lips were full they were stretched back into folds of skin at the edges as though he was a man used to holding in words. Or temper, she added to herself. She'd thought she'd remembered him from somewhere the first day she'd seen him. 'Are you from these parts,' she asked eventually, pouring the tea. 'Have you worked at Stalyholme before?'

'No, I'm from away.' He took the cup from her and settled back in the chair. 'Thanks for this.'

'You're welcome. I think there's some cake.' Winifred looked back to the cupboard. 'Would you—'

'No, honest, this is enough.' He rubbed his hands over the tops of his thighs. The material of his trousers made a low rasping sound under his short, stubby fingers. His nails were ragged with a thin line of black under them, she noticed. 'This is grand.'

Outside the rain continued. Winifred allowed herself to relax, pleased when he seemed to be as content as she was to sit in easy silence watching the flames of the fire rise and fall with the small gusts of wind that blew down the chimney.

Bill couldn't believe his luck. After all these years, after everything that had happened, he was sitting here like this. Every now and then he sneaked a look at her. The rest of the time he gazed into the fire, content just to be near her.

Chapter 73

Winifred looked forward to Sunday evenings. Too often in the past, once her mother had left, she'd let her thoughts drift back to Conal.

Being aware that Bill was waiting on the stairs, ready to make an appearance as soon as the gate closed, gave her no time to brood. And she was thankful for that.

But she knew the time would come when he would ask the one question she dreaded. It was inevitable. She'd thought long and hard about the answer she would give. There was no point in lying. And although an easy companionship was developing between them there was no indication that he was in any way attracted to her as a woman. It suited her, she often told herself, her throat constricting when Conal's face came into her mind; she had no interest in any man anymore. So it didn't matter one way or another. It surprised her how she'd grown such a thick skin since Tom was born, since Granny had gone; other people's opinion mattered little to her.

Even so the question took her by surprise when he asked it a few weeks later.

Leaning forward on the chair Bill held his hands out towards the fire, his profile revealing nothing when he said, 'Tom's father… He's not around any more?'

Turning her head Winifred saw the edges of his looming shadow on the far wall wavering, yet he sat so still, waiting for her to answer.

He'd lodged with them since January and there were enough who came into the shop with their spite and gossip. He's bound to have heard something. Why pretend he hasn't?

'Why do you ask?' she said.

It was his turn to look discomfited. 'Just making talk, like.'

Winifred looked down at the cup she was holding and then up at Bill. 'We're on our own, my son and me.' She fixed him with an even stare and drew in a long breath, steadying herself for what she was going to say. 'His father was the brother of a friend of mine. Irish. He was Irish.' She drained the cup she'd been holding, still looking at him over the rim. The tea was cold. 'We weren't married.' There, she'd said it. She put the cup down onto the hearth and straightened the folds of her brown skirt. 'I don't know where he is.'

He didn't speak. Winifred searched for a reaction in his face but there was nothing; only a tiny twitch at the side of his mouth. She cleared her throat. 'He didn't even know I was... I was having Tom, when he went away.'

She hadn't needed to tell him any of that. The only person she'd confided in was her grandmother. But increasingly over the years Winifred had become isolated, distanced from everyone. She'd had no friends since Honora left, and it was a relief to have someone to confide in. Even this man. Over time she'd learned that he kept himself to himself. She was sure he wouldn't resurrect any gossip about her.

The silence lengthened against the spit and crackles of the flames as he leant forward and dropped pieces of coal on top of the fire. When he sat back he rubbed his chin with his forefinger and thumb and looked at her. His eyes were kind, she thought.

'I was...we were, on a march. I'd joined the Suffragettes...' He said nothing and she made a deprecating sweep of her hand, seeing herself as he must see her. A drab, quiet woman; nothing of her past self to show. 'I know what you're thinking...'

'No.' Bill held out his hands, fingers spread. 'It's not my place to judge.'

'I'd started to believe we could get the vote. And some did didn't they – later?' She still couldn't tell what he was thinking. But, for the first time in years, she felt the excitement, the strength of belief in the injustice. 'But it shouldn't be about how old a woman is or what property she owns. All women should have the vote...' The words trailed off, her voice quavered. She gave a breathy laugh. 'Sorry.'

'No.' He leaned so far forward his knees were almost touching her. 'No, you're right.'

The astonishment must have shown on her face but she couldn't help it. She'd misjudged this man; taken for granted that his rough exterior meant he believed that women had one place in life – or perhaps two. She shocked herself by the last thought.

'An' all men should be equal, an' all.' He nodded earnestly.

'You think so? You vote?'

His ruddy cheeks grew redder. He moved back, pressed both palms together, rubbed them. The movement made a scratching sound. He shrugged. 'Well, no. Until now I hadn't settled anywhere. Had nowhere to live, not proper like. Not since the war.'

'I suppose it's been like that for a lot of men.' To cover the self-conscious discomfort that was suddenly between them Winifred took both cups over to the sink and rinsed them.

'I suppose.'

'Anyway, the day I lost Tom's father there was a violent end to the protest. The police attacked us. We were separated. I never saw him again.'

She'd barely finished speaking when she heard the back gate open. Moving swiftly she said, 'I need to go up, see if Tom's all right.'

'Aye. Me an' all.'

When the back door opened neither of them were in the kitchen.

In her bedroom the old pain rose from Winifred's stomach to her throat. She tried to muffle the sobs by burying her face in the hard pillow.

In his own room, Bill owned up to himself that he loved the woman he could hear crying in the next room. 'Hook, line and sinker,' he muttered. And with no competition from the Irish bastard he'd try to make her love him. She was the one woman who'd keep him on the straight and narrow, he was sure of that.

Chapter 74

Their Sunday evenings became a ritual both Bill and Winifred enjoyed. As soon as the back gate latch clicked behind Ethel, as soon Winifred heard him coughing, his tread on the stairs, she made the tea.

Sometimes, Tom hadn't gone to bed and she would see the way his eyes shone as he showed Bill the illustrations of King Arthur and his Knights, reading passages from the book to him, and she'd smile at the way the man shook his head in amazement at her son's enthusiasm and they'd all laugh, softly in case they were heard next door. Winifred was filled with a contentment she hadn't experienced for a long time. It was as though they lived in a different world for those few hours, complicit in a secret only they shared.

At first she was worried that Tom would resent Bill. But, in fact, it was the opposite, almost a welcome recognition of another male in his life; someone to share a grimace with, a rolling of the eyes when Ethel complained about the mess he made with his books of stamps or the jigsaws on the table.

Winifred guessed Bill couldn't read very well. But if Tom knew it he didn't say. It was enough for him to show the man the different countries on the map he kept with his stamp book, to read out the names.

And Bill was clever in his own way, she knew that. Often he and Tom would stand at the back door while Bill would point out the North Star or the Seven Sisters and talk about the time his grandfather had taught him the wonders of the night sky until Winifred, seeing the way her son's shoulders drooped in tiredness, would usher him upstairs.

And, somehow, even though she'd not said anything to him, Tom seemed to know not to mention the times they shared when his grandmother was out if the house.

Only once did Bill mention Tom's father again. Winifred

thought he seemed genuinely concerned. 'Tell me what happened that day he left.' His voice was gentle.

She wouldn't look at him. 'We got separated. I've often thought about what might have happened. He could have been arrested, sent back to Ireland.' She stopped, remembering the fear. It was as though the air had been taken from her lungs. She put a hand to her chest. After a moment she spoke again. 'It was very violent. I think he may have been killed.'

She turned quickly to see his reaction. He met her gaze.

'Anyway, I never saw him again.' The words were blunt.

He lowered his head. 'I'm sorry.'

'I have Tom. Whatever anyone says, I'm thankful for that.'

Bill smiled. Held her hand. 'He's a good lad.'

Winifred was glad he understood.

She savoured those few precious moments with him before her mother returned, refusing to think about the future.

Chapter 75

She'd known that he had something on his mind as soon as he came down the stairs.

'Your mother doesn't like your Tom,' he said. It was a statement rather than a question.

'What makes you say that?'

'She only talks to the lad to tell him off.'

Winifred sat opposite him. He hadn't sat in his usual place but at the kitchen table, his elbows firmly planted, his hands under his chin, watching her brewing the tea.

He'd been to the public baths; she could smell the chlorine in his damp hair, meticulously arranged, as usual, in the two waves. Unusually, he was dressed in his best shirt and trousers, although without a collar and tie.

Glancing at him she saw the way a nerve twitched under one

eye. He was holding his lower lip between his teeth. The smoke from his cigarette curled from his cupped hand.

To her enquiring look he said, 'Sorry, just needed a fag.'

'I'll open the back door so she can't smell it when she gets back.' His face relaxed at her casual tone.

'Tom's a good lad, does as he's told,' he said. 'I'd be proud of him if he was mine.'

Gratified, Winifred smiled. 'He is. Sometimes I wish Dad was still with us; he'd have loved Tom, done things with him and taken him walks on Errox Hill like he did with me when I was a child. We used to talk about anything and everything; things I'd done in school, books I'd read. Even when I was twelve and left school to work in the shop he'd make time for those walks with me.'

Bill had gone pale. When he next spoke she thought it obvious why; she'd brought back bad memories for him.

'My father didn't give a damn about me. Sorry for the language.' Bill spoke in a matter of fact way. 'And I hardly ever went to school.' He took a long drag on his cigarette. 'The day after he was killed, I went down the mines.'

'Didn't you go to school when your father was alive?'

'Not really. I was a sickly kid and me mam kept me home a lot. I think she liked me being there when he wasn't.' Bill nodded his thanks when Winifred put his cup of tea in front of him. 'We laughed a lot when we were on our own.

'I hated him,' he said abruptly. 'Friday nights he'd go to the pub with his wages. I'd lie in bed waiting for him to come home. When I heard him coming up the ginnel, I could tell how drunk he was from the sound of his clogs on the cobbles. If he was all over the place...' Bill threaded his fingers and rubbed his palms together; making a soft scratching sound. 'You know, clogs clattering and scraping...'

'I know.'

'Well then it wouldn't be so bad; he'd fall asleep downstairs. It was different if he was singing...'

He put his cup down and sat back in the chair, his eyes hidden from her. When he looked up they glistened with unshed tears.

'I knew then me mam was for it – in a way I didn't understand. Not then anyway…'

Winifred could feel the heat rise on her cheeks; it wasn't proper for him to speak in this way. Yet she didn't stop him; she knew he had to talk about it.

'I'd hear him throw his clogs on the floor; often he'd fall against the wardrobe or the tallboy. I'd hear him laughing and cursing.' Bill stopped, pinched his nose. 'And then all this noise, like struggling, and Mam crying as though she was in pain.

'I wanted to go in and kill him.' He sat very still for a few moments. 'But once, after a night when that had happened again, there were nothing like that for a long time. Instead they fought; a lot of fights. The worst one he beat her so badly that she couldn't get out of bed. We even had to have the doctor. Every time he'd make a note in a little black book of what we owed…' Bill made a writing gesture.

'One night Mam started screaming so loud the neighbours all came in. I was taken to sleep at someone's house. I was told in the morning she'd had a boy.' Bill closed his eyes and pinched his nose again. 'But he was born dead. Would have been my little brother.' He sniffed. 'I would have made a good older brother, I think.' He stood to throw his cigarette end into the fire and stayed there. 'Mam died a couple of days later.

'I don't know where all that came from, Win. You get me telling you stuff I've told no-one else in my life.' He paused, running his fingers through his hair, ruining the carefully arranged waves. 'Anyway, there's summat I want to say.'

'Oh?' Winifred was glad she was sitting down; all at once she knew what had been on his mind earlier. He was leaving. Her hand shook, the tea in her cup slopped over onto the tablecloth and she watched the stain spread dark on the green material.

'Will you marry me?' His voice was low.

The shock made her dizzy. She clutched the corner of the table so hard the edge hurt her palm. She closed her eyes, rocking back and forth on the chair.

'Win?' His fingers were warm, the skin hard, calloused, on the side of her neck.

She was glad he was touching her but she kept her eyes closed until everything stopped spinning. 'I'm all right.' She opened her eyes. The room was bright, everything was in sharp detail. She stared around the kitchen, the room that had held her prisoner for so many years. She wanted to remember every detail, every second of this moment. 'I'm all right,' she repeated turning, at last, to face him. 'Yes,' she said, 'I will. I will marry you.'

He would take her away from the life she thought was her punishment. He would take her away from a mother who despised her. He would make her respectable.

Chapter 76

Winifred's trust in him humbled Bill. Her belief in everything he said made him careful in what he did say. There was so much that could easily change how she felt about him. So much. The worst time was the day she told him about the way she'd found her father dead on the floor of the shop.

'I heard my mother shouting.' Winifred twisted the damp handkerchief between her fingers, the tears spilling down her face. 'He was just lying there, Bill, He must have been there for hours and I didn't know…'

'Don't think about it, love.' Bill put his arms around her.

'I can't help it. I think about it all the time. Please let me tell you.' There was pleading in her eyes. 'You've said that you have nightmares about the war. So I'll know what to expect…' Her cheeks flushed. 'I'll know what to expect at night when we're married. This is my nightmare that wakes me, makes me cry…'

'Okay.' He hugged her, but there was an unwelcome tightness in his throat. The guilt that flooded through him was something he'd had to live with. He'd stopped telling himself it was an accident; he'd faced up to the fact that, in his anger and desperation he went to the shop to steal and, although he hadn't meant to kill John Duffy, he had thrown the box in anger.

But there was still that vague sense of relief lurking beneath his thoughts; how different his life would be now if the man hadn't died.

Winifred pulled back and looked at him. He knew he'd been silent for too long. 'I don't know what to say, love.' He stroked her hair away from her forehead and looked into her eyes. 'It must have been awful for you.'

'It was. He was a lovely man, Bill. You would have loved him as I did. Not once in his life did he harm anyone.' Her eyes hardened. 'Unlike the thief that killed him. I wish whoever he is was standing here now, in front of us. He deserves to be punished. God forgive me, but even after all this time I'm still hoping that one day the police will find him and he'll be hanged. Granny was never the same after she he died; he was her only son. If he'd been alive I think she would have fought harder when she got the influenza. I believe the murderer killed her in the end as well.'

That night Bill slept badly and almost missed hearing the knocker-upper's whistle outside his window the following morning. After his shift, instead of going back to the house he went to the Wagon and Horses and washed pint after pint of ale down his throat to swill away the memory Win's words had conjured up. It was late when he let himself in by the back door and staggered up the stairs to his bedroom

The following morning one look in the scrap of mirror hung on the wall above the jug and basin told him all he needed to know. The dark pouches of flesh under his eyes, the red criss-cross of veins in the whites, the hammering of blood in his skull, pulled him up short. Had he seen her when he got back from the pub? What had he said? Had he given himself away? Told her the truth?

But, after a day-shift underground that seemed to last forever and a walk back to his digs when his footsteps on the cobbles hurt his whole body, he stepped into the kitchen to see Winifred smile at him

The relief loosened the tension. With a quick glance to make sure her mother wasn't there he took her in his arms and spun her around, leaving black smudges of coal dust on her clothes and hands as she held onto him, laughing.

She was so soft, so light in his arms. In that moment he promised himself that he wouldn't be so stupid in future, that it would be the last time he'd get so drunk. All the awful things he'd done were in the past; the actions of a different bloke.

He would be a better man. He would try to stop swearing as much because she didn't like it. He would work hard to give her everything she wanted. He would be a good husband. He would be a good father to the lad.

He pushed away the faint unwelcome underlying resentment of Tom. Because, always, when he looked at the boy, he saw the Irish bastard. Conal…bloody…O'Reilly.

Chapter 77

'I want to sell the shop, Mother.' Winifred paced the floor of the kitchen. 'I'm getting married to Bill and then I'm leaving Lydcroft. I want us to move right away and start a new life.' She stood still, clasped her hands at her waist and gazed at her mother. There, it was said.

Ethel slowly continued to wrap the small brown loaves in tissue paper and line them up on the tray to carry into the shop. 'Married eh? And to the lodger.' She didn't look up. 'And what about me? What am I supposed to do?'

'You may either buy us out—'

'Us?'

'Bill and me—'

'Oh, it's "Bill and me" now is it?'

'What's mine will be his as well when we're married. We'll share everything.'

'And have you?' The words were flung over Ethel's shoulders as she carried the bread into the shop. 'Have you told him about your wildness? About that one's...' she lifted her eyes upwards. 'Your son's father? The man who couldn't wait to run off as soon as he had his way with you.'

Anger crept up in Winifred. 'I have. He knows.' She followed her mother into the shop; she didn't want her son overhearing them. 'But that's nothing to do with you. I'm just telling you I want to sell up.'

'And if I don't agree?' Ethel transferred the loaves onto the shelf. 'There's not much you can do about it.'

'I think there is.' This was what Winifred had expected from her mother and she was ready. 'The shop is two thirds mine since Granny left me her share, so I have the greater say. And I'd have thought you'd be glad to sell. You've said yourself that the takings in this place have been down for years. You've even said you knew why. Now,' she pursed her lips, 'what was it? Ah, yes, it's because of me; because I shamed you, because I'm a fallen woman. You have a slut living under your roof.' The anger turned into cold contempt. 'But it wasn't that, was it Mother? The takings were down because you've been helping yourself to them for years. Did you really think I didn't know?'

'You...' Ethel swept the tray from the counter, her face contorted with rage. She lunged towards Winifred, her hand raised to slap her.

Winifred caught hold of her arm, held it until her mother shook her off.

'I took what's mine by rights.' Ethel spoke through gritted

teeth. 'You shamed me with your shenanigans and the takings did drop when the brat arrived. I hate you, madam. You're the cause of all I've had to put up with for years. All the sniggering, the gossip. Go – sell this place.' She waved her hands wildly in the air. 'I want you gone just as much as you want to go. Go! People might then begin to forget I have a slut for a daughter.'

'Better than them knowing I have a thief for a mother, do you think?' It was an instinctive response; there would be no way she could prove it and anyway who would care about something like that happening between members of the same family? And her mother knew that.

'I took what's mine. And, anyway, who would believe anything you said? No-one around here.' Ethel lifted her top lip in a sneer but Winifred didn't miss the apprehension in her eyes.

'Mud sticks, Mother. Isn't that what you've said in the past?'

Winifred closed her eyes, she wouldn't cry. She didn't, but her whole body shook so much she needed to hold onto the door handle of the store cupboard. Without seeing her mother go she sensed the woman was no longer standing in front of her.

'Well, that's that then,' she whispered, listening to the floorboards in Ethel's room above creaking. An overwhelming feeling of release flooded through her. 'It's done. She's been told.' She drew in long breaths, steadying herself. Now she should talk to Bill; he should know what she planned to do.

Chapter 78

'So you're willing to take her on? I wonder why...'

Bill heard the sarcasm in Winifred's mother's voice and frowned. What was she getting at? He crossed, uncrossed his arms, jammed his fists into his trouser pockets.

'And the lad?'

The swift sharp question took him by surprise. 'Of course. We

301

all make mistakes. I've loved Win since I first saw her.' He wouldn't have dreamt of leaving the kid with this old cow even if he'd thought Win would agree. But why was the old bat being so sarky?

'She says you have no intention of staying here after you're married.' Ethel watched him. 'You both want to move to away.'

Well, that was a turn up for the books. He'd thought he'd be set up here; house and job. He blinked rapidly, waiting for her to carry on. How did Winifred think he could afford for them to move? It had taken him long enough to find the job at Stalyholme.

But in a quick turnaround he wondered if she was right. Getting away from Lydcroft with all the memories and guilt might stop some of the nightmares. And he'd got a bit of brass put by that'd tide them over for a week or two.

Ethel moved around the kitchen, running her hand across the oilcloth on the table, re-setting the glass vase more into the centre of the cream crocheted mat on the sideboard, pushing at the drawers, adjusting the level of the country scene painting on the wall.

As though settling something in her mind.

Bill shifted his weight from one foot to the other, clenched his fingers. He couldn't make her out at all.

Someone came into the shop. He heard the soft tones of Winifred's welcome, the silence that answered her. She had the patience of a saint; he'd give the miserable bastards a mouthful if he'd been her. How she put up with the sanctimonious shit he didn't know. It'd be different when they were wed, he'd make sure of that, no problem.

Ethel had done a full circle of the room by the time she stood in front of him again.

He met her thoughtful gaze. 'You've summat to say?' he tilted his head to one side, challenging her.

'You obviously know this place mostly belongs to my daughter.'

Her voice had a hard edge to it. 'You'll know that in his will her father left his half of the shop to her and his mother. In turn she left her share to Winifred.' She spat out the name. 'So it will be sold. And you'll profit from that.' Ethel narrowed her eyes, studied him. 'After all, why else would you want to tie yourself down with such as her?' Ethel's nostrils flared again. 'You'll be well and truly set up when you marry her, won't you? You've landed right on your feet.'

Bloody hell. Bill struggled to keep the shock off his face. Yeah, one day, when this old cow had dropped off her perch, he'd thought the shop would be Winifred's. And it could be a decent little earner. He'd even planned for some time in the future when he could give up working in the mine and take over in the shop. That's why the idea that Winifred would want to move away had baffled him at first. But why the hell hadn't she told him she owned most of the place? Why hide it?

Ethel didn't see the turmoil in him; she was looking around. 'All this is mine by rights. I've slaved in this shop for years. But apparently, according to the solicitor, I have no rights. She can sell the shop and house from under my feet because she owns most of it. She's kicking me out.'

By God, she's well and truly browned off, he thought. Bill hid the grin behind his hand and coughed. The niggle of resentment stirring in him, because Winifred hadn't told him, vied with the excited realisation that her money would be his once they were wed. That's how it went, wasn't it? What's hers would then be his. Isn't that what the old bitch meant when she said he'd be set up?

He cleared his throat and smiled. 'Well you'd better pack your bags then, missus. No point in 'anging around.'

'Yes, you'd like that, wouldn't you?' Ethel glared at him. 'Well I'm not leaving until I get what I'm owed. I've watched you and I know your type and what you're after. I know you're not the man you pretend to be. You knew she had this place behind her from the start; you played it clever.

303

'My daughter thinks she's got the better of me, but she'll get her comeuppance.' She pointed her finger at him. 'Married to the likes of you, she'll get her comeuppance.'

Chapter 79

'All done, then.' Bill grinned at Winifred, running his fingers around his collar. There was a sheen of sweat across his forehead.

They stood blinking in the strong sunlight. Winifred's eyes hurt. After the gloom of the Registry Office with the brown paintwork and grimy walls, the brightness made the steps and walls of the small courtyard flicker.

Beyond the gates the High Street was quiet. Wednesday was half day closing for most of the shops in Morrisfield. When her eyes had adjusted, Winifred looked beyond the gates. There were few people around: a woman pushing a bike, her long purple skirt sweeping the floor, a shiny black motor carriage, with four people, sitting upright on the seats, chugged by, a couple, the man pushing a perambulator, the baby peeping out from under a parasol. Winifred watched them all with detachment thinking back to the night before.

She'd not slept well. The familiar rhythmic march of the miners passing the house roused her. Through the open window drifted a faint smell of cigarettes and muttered voices. For once, Bill wouldn't be joining them.

The room was already warm and perspiration ran between her breasts. Her eyelids were thick and heavy. If she didn't force them to stay open they would close; a screen to replay all the images that had haunted her all night. Images of everyone she'd lost: Conal, Honora, her father. Granny.

Granny. How any times had she cried for her grandmother? Especially about missing the hasty funeral her mother had arranged without telling anyone. Horace's mother had told her how angry the people in Wellyhole Yard had been when they found out. Too late.

Winifred lifted her head off the pillow and looked across the room. Tom was still asleep, arms and legs flung out at angles to his body. His pyjamas were now too small for him. Already his limbs were thickening with muscle, the skin showing a covering of hair. Next would be his jawline. She looked away. He was growing up. He was going to be tall like his father.

Stop it.

She rolled onto her back and crossed her arms over her chest, holding on to her shoulders. The curtains, moving in the slight breeze, let the sunlight in where they met, made a pattern on the ceiling.

Stop it. These were words she used often to prevent the memories, to bring herself back to reality. Bill was going to be Tom's father from now on and he would be a good father. He was a hard worker, a good man. He'd be a good father and a good husband.

And she'd be a good wife.

'Well, that's that then,' Bill repeated, still tugging at his collar.

'Take your tie off if you want.' Winifred smiled at him. 'Though it's a shame; you look so grand. Grand enough for any woman to marry.' From the moment he'd stepped into the kitchen two hours ago she'd thought how smart he'd looked in his three-piece suit and collar and tie. Even now, his face shining with sweat, his tie askew, he looked handsome.

'You think?' Bill smirked.

'I do.' Winifred pulled at the long sleeve of her cream dress and touched the oval amethyst brooch, surrounded by pearls that Granny had given her. The fleeting sadness passed and she straightened her shoulders, looking around, now hoping someone would see them; knowing they made an attractive couple.

On the pavement outside the gates of the Registry Office an

elegant woman, parasol held high above a large feathered hat, passed by.

'Hey, missus,' Bill called out. 'Fancy marrying me?' He held out his arms and spun around on one foot in a full circle. 'Well, you can't, cos I'm already wed to the most beautiful woman in the world.'

'Shush.' Winifred giggled.

The woman ignored them.

Bill tucked Winifred's arm through his.

'Come on, Mrs H,' he said, 'Time to move on. We'll celebrate with a swift 'alf at the Wagon and 'Orses. Then we'll pick up your – our – Tom from school, get out of this fancy clobber and get on with our new life.'

She squeezed his arm, grateful that he'd acknowledged her son as his. She'd made the right choice. It was going to be all right.

Chapter 80

The first night was a disappointment to Winifred. They'd moved Tom's things into Bill's room after he'd gone to school and before they set off for the Registry Office.

Winifred was conscious that her son wouldn't understand why he had to go in there, and that her mother was in the next room. But Bill had insisted that it was right that, on their wedding night, they should be in the same bed.

It was almost twelve o'clock before they finally went upstairs. Tom had been restless and Winifred had spent all evening trying to get him settled.

'I wish I could have watched you being married, Mam.' Tom's eyes were swollen from crying. Winifred knew it just wasn't the wedding; her son was frightened his whole world was changing and he was bewildered by that.

'I didn't want you to miss school, sweetheart. You needed to pick up your school report from the head teacher to take to your new school. It's exciting to start somewhere new.'

He turned his face away from her. When he spoke his voice was barely audible. 'I know. I'm trying to be excited, Mam. Honest I am.'

The guilt bit deep in Winifred. 'I promise you, you will make friends and have fun. Bill…' she stopped. 'Do you want to carry on calling him Bill? Or would you like to start calling him Dad?'

Tom moved onto his back and looked at her, his eyes so serious she thought she might cry.

'I think you should ask him what he thinks,' she said, smiling. Tom flung back the covers. Laughing Winifred caught hold of him. 'Whoa. Not tonight, sweetheart, tomorrow is soon enough.'

He wrapped his arms around her neck. 'I do love you, Mam. And it's all right. I'll be all right.'

'We'll all be all right, son.' She unwound his arms and pushed him gently back on the mattress. 'Now, sleep. It's very late.' She kissed him on the forehead. 'Night, night, sleep tight.'

'Mind the bed bugs don't bite,' he responded, his voice already drowsy.

When Winifred pulled the door to she heard him mumbling and stopped to listen.

'Dad. Dad. Dad.' He was practising saying the name.

Lying straight in the bed, her arms by her sides she watched Bill hang his suit jacket on the door of the wardrobe next to her dress. Somehow it felt unseemly to her as the sleeve draped across the bodice but she said nothing, her thoughts on her son, asleep in Bill's old room.

'He's just not used to being in a bedroom on his own,' she explained.

Bill had his back to her so she couldn't see his expression but thought she heard a stifled sigh.

He snapped his braces off his shoulders and turned to face her, unbuttoning his trousers. 'Well, the sooner he gets used to it the better, love.' He let the trousers slide down his legs and stepped out of them.

Winifred averted her eyes. 'Will you turn the light off?' she murmured. A quick thought passed through her mind that he looked vaguely ridiculous in his long grey socks and his shirt lap trailing down at the back to his knees, almost hiding his flannel drawers. And then the mattress dipped and he was in bed with her, one arm flung across her waist 'No, I want to see you, lass.' He nuzzled her neck; she could smell the beer and cigarettes on his breath.

Still in his shirt, Bill rolled on top of her and lifted her nightdress. He'd taken off his drawers; she felt his bare skin on her thighs. Sliding his hand along her body he cupped her breast. A moment later he arched above her and spreading her legs with his knee, pushed himself into her. With no preparation the intrusion was painful. Winifred gasped.

'Come on, Win, let yourself go.' Bill stopped moving and, taking his weight on one elbow, rolled his palm over her nipple and for a second she responded.

With a grunt of satisfaction Bill let go of her breast, rose on his knees and used both hands to lift her buttocks towards him.

It was over in a few short moments. When Bill collapsed, Conal's face was imprinted against Winifred's closed eyelids and, in that instant she knew she would carry his image in her head each time she had to endure what had just happened.

Bill cursed himself; all the years he'd waited for this night and he'd rushed her. He hadn't meant to. But the sight of her on the bed, the nightgown outlining the slenderness of her figure, her lovely hair spread on the pillow as she gazed at him, had been too much.

He'd felt her react to his touch but by then it was too late. As soon as he'd entered her it was all over. Humiliated he'd rolled onto his side, facing away from her.

Next time, he promised himself, next time he'd take it more slowly; make it better for her.

Chapter 81

'What d'you think?'

Bill and Winifred stood in the doorway looking along the hall of the house. Winifred could hear Tom pounding from room to room above her.

'Can't be worse than the last two,' she said.

It was the fourth house they'd looked at and Winifred's feet ached. She sat on the last but one tread of the stairs and took off her shoes. Rubbing her foot she asked, 'How much is it?'

Bill studied the piece of paper he'd got from the estate agent's office. 'It says bids around a hundred and ninety nine pounds,' he said. 'Houses are a bit dearer this side of the Pennines.'

'It's where I want to be.' She didn't add well away from Mother; he would know what she meant. 'Ashford seems a decent place.'

'And it's handy for work; nearer than the last house.'

'Lucky they needed a Tunneller there.'

'Aye.' He gave a short laugh. 'Not a Chargeman so bit of a drop in pay to what I was before at Stalyholme. Still, money's decent enough; as long as the unions keep pushing the owners to keep it like that.'

'You'll be fine.' Winifred smiled up at him. 'And you're in the union, you'll make sure you get a fair deal.'

He nodded. 'Fresh start.'

'Fresh start. All right, let's have a look around.' Putting on her shoes Winifred pushed open the first door and walked to the centre of the front room. It was empty except for the maroon paisley carpet and some threadbare velvet curtains of an indistinct colour. They'd have to go for a start, she thought, taking off her hat and pinning back a few strands of hair.

'Can we afford it?' she said again.

'What do you think?' There was a strange expression on his face.

Winifred waited. Was this the right time to tell him she could buy the house twice over when the shop was sold? She hadn't yet told him that she owned two thirds of the shop. She didn't know what was stopping her but if there ever was to be a right time, surely this was it. She didn't speak.

'I 'ave the money,' Bill said at last.

Had he really managed to save so much money in the short time he'd worked at Stalyholme mine?

'It'll take every penny but I 'ave it.' He didn't take his eyes off her.

Challenging?

He knows, Winifred realised all at once, he knows about the shop. There was only one way he would know; her mother must have told him. But why. She gave a mental shrug. Why didn't matter.

'When the shop is sold I'll have some money,' she said, finally.

He grinned, showing no surprise. In fact he was almost triumphant. 'Yeah?' was all he said.

'Yes.' Winifred returned his smile, pleased she could make him happy yet still a little uneasy. Why hadn't he told her he knew she owned part of the shop? Why hadn't she told him?

He slung his arm over her shoulder. 'Come an' look at the kitchen.'

'Mam, come upstairs.' Tom shouted. 'I've chosen my room and—'

'And you'll go where you're put, young un.'

Winifred shot a look at Bill, noticed the irritation. It was the first note of discord that day. Her husband had laughed at Tom's excitement on the train, tolerated him charging in and out of the carriage.

'Sorry, love,' he said. 'Just a bit knackered from all this traipsing around.'

310

She stroked his cheek. 'He's just as excited as me to be looking for a new home.' Even so she lifted her head. 'Tom, come downstairs. There's plenty of time to decide who's going where.'

When Tom appeared behind them his shoulders were slumped and he kept his head lowered, a definite sign he was upset. 'I was only looking around,' he whispered, holding on to her coat sleeve.

'I know, love. Don't worry. Dad's not really cross.' Winifred nudged Bill. 'Come on, then, let's see the rest of this house.'

Bill flung open the next door and peered inside 'Looks like the kitchen.'

There was a sideboard and table and chairs pushed against the back wall.

'Do you think the furniture is part of the deal?' she asked.

Bill lifted his shoulders. 'Dunno.' He went through to a small scullery and struggled with the lock and spoon-shaped latch of the back door.

The long clothes rack, hung from the ceiling above the range, swayed gently in the draught when Bill at last flung the door open. 'There's a good size yard to 'ang out the washing.'

'I should have told you I would have money from the shop sale. I'm sorry.' Winifred placed her hand on the surface of the square wooden table. 'Bill?'

'S'okay, I knew.' There was a false flippancy in the way he said it.

'Why didn't you tell me?'

'Why didn't you?' He gestured towards the yard. 'The lavvy's there.'

She was positive he'd pointed that out to embarrass her into silence.

Ignoring him, Winifred followed him into the scullery. She could picture herself doing the washing at the large stone sink. She ran her hand over the cream metal top of the mangle, touched the handle, the smooth rubber rollers. It was new.

'Well? What do you think?' Thumbs tucked under his braces

Bill looked pleased with himself. As though he'd won an argument. Winifred couldn't help the thought.

'It's all lovely, Bill. I just don't understand how you, we, could have afforded it.'

His face darkened. 'Never mind about that.'

'But I do.'

'I told you, I 'ad savings.'

'Yes but… you haven't borrowed money as well, have you, love?' Winifred tried to say it as casually as she could. 'We could have waited. I do have the money to come eventually.'

'Well, I didn't know that at the time, did I?'

Even though they'd only known one another for a short while she had measure enough of her husband to know she'd best not question him any more for the time being.

But she would find out, she wouldn't rest until she had. The one thing her father had drummed into her all her life was that she mustn't get into debt. She hoped she wasn't beginning married life already owing money. She'd be glad when the shop sold.

Chapter 82

'So it's done then.'

Ignoring the sullenness in her mother's voice, Winifred waited until the solicitor ushered the new owner of the shop out of his office. 'Mr Patton was pleased to have the business,' she said. 'I'm sure he and he family will love living at the shop.'

'So he should. He paid only a pittance for it.'

'He paid a fair price.' Winifred kept her tone mild. All she wanted was to get away from Ethel.

The solicitor came back into the office rubbing his hands together. 'I think that went well, ladies.' He kept his eyes firmly fixed on Ethel. 'Just a few more details to arrange.' Winifred hated the way he bent over the two of them far too close. She was relieved when he moved to his side of the desk, the smell of sweat hung around him. 'I'll need your forwarding address. Need to have a few things typed up, you know.' He paused, looked at them.

Her mother spoke first. 'That won't be necessary. I'll call in, in a few days to pick up whatever is necessary.'

So she was as reluctant as me to say where she will move to. Winifred nodded. 'And so will I.'

Her mother sniffed and stood, holding her handbag at her waist. 'I'll bid you good day, Mister Winterbottom.' She left without a glance in Winifred's direction.

Bill was waiting in the outer reception room of the solicitor's.

'Yer mother looked none too chuffed.' He grinned. 'Everything went okay?'

'Everything went all right.' She confirmed, holding out her hand to him. 'We need to go to the bank, and then I need to call in somewhere before we catch the train to be in time for when Tom gets home from school.'

On the pavement outside the solicitor's tall brick building Winifred drew in a long low breath. For the first time in her life she was free.

Chapter 83

It didn't take much to persuade Bill to wait in the Wagon and Horses while she went to visit Bertha on Wellyhole Street. It being warm for October Winifred expected to see her sitting outside the house but, although the door was open, there was no sign of anyone.

She lifted the knocker and let it drop. 'Bertha? It's Winifred Duffy.' The woman wouldn't know her married name. 'Bertha?'

'Winifred?' Her voice sounded weak. 'Oh, yes. Do come in, child.'

The hall was so dark it took a while for Winifred's eyes to adjust when she entered the kitchen. It was a shock to see how much her gran's friend had aged. Seeing her sitting on an old wooden chair Winifred could tell how much thinner she was than before. And her hair was now completely white. She pulled out a chair from the table and moved closer to the old woman, taking hold of her hand. There were dark smudges beneath Bertha's eyes, the lids swollen.

'We've just sold the shop and I thought I should call. I need to say I'm sorry I haven't been before, Bertha. I feel so bad about that.' Winifred was ashamed to think that in the last three years she'd never given the residents of Wellyhole Yard another thought.

'I've always felt rotten about not going to your gran's funeral.'

'Mother arranged it while I was looking after Tom, my son. He caught the influenza as well.'

'But he got better. I was glad to hear that.'

Unlike Horace. Winifred found herself feeling guilty even about that; even as she felt the great wave of gratitude.

'I knew nothing about Granny's funeral until it was too late.'

'None of us knew.' Bertha shook her head. 'A mean woman, your mam.'

'Yes. She didn't even go.'

'Mean,' Bertha repeated. The lines deepened at the corners of her mouth. 'The influenza claimed Tony as well. My youngest.' The tears came easily as she bent forwards as though in pain. 'I lost two sons.'

Only then did Winifred realise what was different; the house was silent. 'Oh Bertha…'

'I heard you were nursing your son at the time.' Bertha patted her hand. 'I wouldn't have expected you to be there. And my boys were buried together that day. They were company for one another.' She sighed. 'They say time heals, Winifred, but it doesn't. That influenza tore my family apart; we were never the same again. We were always such a crowd I used to think I'd never

314

get any peace. Now I have too much. But…' She moved Winifred's hand up and down in a gesture of determination. 'I do try to get out once a week to go to see them.' She smiled. 'You know, at the cemetery?'

Winifred nodded.

'We have a good talk. And I go to see your gran as well.'

'Do you?'

'I do. And, when my old knees let me, I get down on the ground and weed her grave.'

The self-reproach was overwhelming. 'There's still no headstone on Gran's grave.' Why had she let so much time pass without doing anything about that? The fact that she'd had little money to spare; that she'd only ever taken from the shop takings what she and Tom needed was no excuse. 'Would you like to go there now, Bertha? With me?'

Bill would be all right, especially as he had taken five shillings from the bank money she'd drawn out. Which she now recognised was a mistake; she'd have a job getting him home if he spent it all on ale.

'Oh, I would, Winifred, thank you.'

They walked slowly; Bertha muffled in a thick coat and woollen hat and scarf, limped on swollen feet.

'It's my arthritis,' she explained, leaning heavily on Winifred's linked arm.

'There was no rush. And we're here now.' Winifred pushed open the wooden gate into the cemetery. The chapel doors were closed and no-one was around.

Leaving Bertha at the grave of her sons she walked along the gravel path to the small mound where Granny lay. It was covered in grass and weeds. Sorrow caught in her chest and she inhaled steadily to control the tightness. Dropping to her knees she yanked at the roots and threw the plants to one side with such force that in a few minutes she was panting.

'Winifred.'

The touch on her back was too much. She twisted, seizing hold of Bertha's coat, the tears coming through great spluttering sobs.

'I should have made sure Gran had a headstone,' she gulped as her tears gradually lessened.

'It'll be fine, love.' The soft patting soothed.

She scrambled to her feet. 'It will, Bertha. I'll make it right.' Blowing her nose she managed a faint smile. 'I'm glad we came, I should have come a long time ago but I felt guilty that I couldn't give her a headstone.'

'She'd understand.'

'She would.' But that didn't help. 'And now I can do something about it.'

Linking arms they ambled back along the path to the chapel gate. Fastening the catch, Winifred stared over to the corner towards her grandmother's grave. I'll buy you a headstone, Granny, she promised under her breath.

She paused, glancing around at the familiar countryside. I shall only once come back to Lydcroft, she thought. And I shall never see Mother again.

Chapter 84

March 1923

Bill whimpered and, despite the cold night, kicked the covers off him. In her sleep Winifred clung on to the blankets, hoisting them up to her chin.

He was crouching in a trench covered in slime and mud, his arms over his head, protecting himself from the large yelping rats scurrying over him. But it wasn't the rats yelping, it was the youth that was tied to the lamppost and the men around him were laughing and jabbing him with bayonets. Men, not dressed in the usual British uniform, but in khaki and black. And they weren't in a field anymore but in a street where women and children were watching them in silence, standing before houses with the doors wide open like gaping mouths. And then he was the youth, feeling each cruel stab, each vicious cut as the men worked their way up his body with the steel blades. And the blood was running in his eyes and he couldn't see. But still he heard the screams. His screams. And somewhere, there was the dull thud of bombs. And the sharp crack of rifle shots.

'It's all right, love. I've got you.' Winifred held onto him as he struggled to free himself. 'Calm down, it's just a dream. You're safe now.'

'I can't find my brooch.' Winifred rummaged through the tin that she kept her mementoes in; Tom's birth certificate, her marriage certificate, a brass tiepin, watch chain and cufflinks of her father's, a lace handkerchief embroidered with the letter F that had been her grandmother's, a metal suffragette badge with the inscription "Votes for Women" in green lettering.

The small oval amethyst brooch, surrounded by pearls pinned to a velvet cushion that Florence had given her wasn't amongst them. 'Bill?' She emptied the tin onto the kitchen table and spread the contents out. The brooch was definitely missing. She tried to think when she'd last saw it. Not after they moved to Ashford she was certain. She'd worn it on her wedding day. She remembered that because her husband had admired it against the cream dress.

Bill was crouched in front of the fire. The air in the kitchen still held the sooty smell from the billow of smoke that had blown from the chimney. Outside the wind howled, plastering the rain against the window. After a bad night's sleep his chest was always worse and he was in a foul mood.

She knew he was worried about the trouble that seemed to be brewing between the owners of the mine and the miners. He'd ranted all the previous evening about Baldwin and the Tories, and how miners' wages were low after the strike in nineteen twenty-one. He kept telling her that, as the new union representative, it was up to him to keep talks going. But she often thought he was absolutely the wrong man for the job with his fiery temper. She put her hand to her stomach; with another mouth to feed she was fretting herself about the amount of housekeeping he allowed her. Let alone the amount he spent on beer.

Still, however much it irritated him, she needed to know where her brooch was.

'Bill, I can't find my brooch,' she said again. 'Any idea where it might be?'

He started a prolonged bout of coughing before spitting into the fireplace. The globule sizzled on the fender.

Winifred swallowed against the gagging that overwhelmed her each time he did that but said nothing; he wasn't to blame that his chest was weak. But it was his fault he refused to use the pieces of cloth she'd cut for him out of one of his old shirts instead of the revolting spitting.

She was wary of him today; when he was under the weather he was prone to explode with temper.

'Bill?'

'Shurrup, woman, for God's sake. Can't yer see I'm bad?'

Winifred compressed her lips, suspicion growing in her mind. Standing over him, her hands on her hips, she couldn't stop herself. 'You sold it, didn't you? Why?' The realization struck her. 'You sold it to buy this place?'

'And what if I did?'

'You said you'd saved the money from your wages.' Her mouth was suddenly dry. She tried to stay calm, twisting her wedding ring round and round her finger.

'On the pittance that old skinflint in Lydfield gave me. And after paying the bloody rent to your soddin' mother?'

'You should have told me.'

'And you should 'ave told me right from the start that you'd 'ave money from selling the bloody shop.' He thumped himself on the chest, making himself cough again. 'Keeping it secret.' He scowled. 'Why didn't yer tell me right from the off?'

'I don't know.' She did; she remembered how angry she'd become when her granny had told her that everything she'd owned had belonged her grandfather once they were married. The law had long since changed but she'd hated the idea that Bill would assume that what was hers, earned by her own hard work for years, had become his. And she didn't tell him she was worried that would be the only reason he would want to marry her. 'It was too soon then. I needed to know…' Humiliation vied with the urge to shout, to rage at him. 'That brooch was the only thing I had of Granny's.'

'Except for the shop.' He was mocking her.

'Which was nothing to do with you.' Winifred became reckless in her anger. She was shouting now, her face close to his. 'We will always need that money to live on. With your weak chest and that old leg injury of yours there will always be times you can't work. You had no right to steal my brooch. No right at all.'

She didn't see the blow coming, wasn't ready for it. The next thing she knew she was lying on the floor. When she sat up her head swam. She tasted blood. Her lips were split. And there was a large lump on the back of her head where she'd hit the floor.

Struggling to her feet and stumbling to the sink Winifred wet a teacloth. Thank goodness Tom wasn't in the house; the last thing she wanted was for her son to see what had happened. She dabbed at her mouth and examined the spreading stain on the cloth. The whole of her body quivered with shock. If Tom had seen and tried to defend her against Bill it would have been hopeless, however tall her son had become.

It was the first time Bill had hit her – it would be the last. The anger was slow to rise but when it did she savoured it. She had been frightened of him. She'd tell him that if he ever did it again she'd leave. She had been bullied by her mother. She wouldn't be bullied by any man.

319

When Bill did appear later that day and saw the state of Winifred's face he was contrite. Kneeling by her side he put his head on her lap. 'I'm that sorry, Win. And you with a babby inside you. I don't know what came over me.' When he looked up at her there were tears in his eyes. 'I'm that angry with meself, I could cut my right arm off. It'll never 'appen again, love, I promise.'

And I promise you I'll leave if it does, Winifred thought.

Chapter 85

July 1923

'Mrs Jagger?' Winifred banged on the wall of the kitchen. 'Mrs Jagger.'

'What is it?' The voice was thin, querulous.

'The pains have started. It's the baby.'

She'd felt the dull ache all night but said nothing to Bill, he said often enough that he didn't like to be bothered with 'women's troubles'.

So as soon as she heard the back gate close and the sound of his clogs fade away, she'd summoned her neighbour.

'Winnie?' The woman crashed open the gate, tying her wrap around pinny. Crossing the yard she yelled, 'Is it time?'

'Shush. Please.' Winifred held on to the doorframe. 'I don't want half the neighbourhood hearing.'

'What?' Mrs Jagger tucked her hair under her turban.

'Never mind.' Winifred turned back into the kitchen, holding on to the chairs around the table 'I think it is…' She gasped, the warmth of the fluid pouring from her shocked her into silence. She looked down at the puddle around her feet and then at her neighbour, feeling the swell of panic.

'Young Tom in school?' Hands on hips the older woman studied her.

'Yes.'

'Good. It'll be over before he gets back home.' She rolled up her sleeves. 'Everything ready?'

'I think so.'

'Kettle boiled?'

'No… I'll…'

'I'll sort it.' Mrs Jagger bustled over to the sink in the scullery. 'You get upstairs and strip off those wet underthings.'

Hauling on the bannister, Winifred dragged herself upstairs.

She heard her neighbour banging around in the kitchen and then the sloshing of water on the stairs. Even breathing against the rise of another contraction, Winifred couldn't help thinking it would take ages to dry the coco-matting on the treads.

'All ready?' Mrs Jagger set the steaming bowl of water on the tallboy, her breathing rasping in her throat. She coughed. 'Towels?'

'Oh. No. Sorry.' Winifred heaved herself upright.

'S'all right, I'll find them.'

'That drawer.' Winifred fell back. She turned her head sideways on the pillow watching as her neighbour deliberately opened each drawer of the tallboy. Obviously enjoying rooting around, she thought with an inward sigh. Still, there was no other choice but to have the woman there; she had the best reputation for delivering babies for miles around.

'Right, let's see.' Mrs Jagger dumped the towels on the bed and pushed Winifred's nightdress up around her waist, spreading her knees apart.

Winifred flinched as the bony fingers explored her. She saw the grimace on the old woman's face.

'Hmm, think you've a bit to go yet, love, you'll need to be patient. This one's in no hurry to get out into this wicked old world.'

The wave of pain circled Winifred's stomach, taking her by surprise. She clenched her muscles.

'You'll need to relax if you don't want this to go on forever,

321

Winnie. This isn't the first babby you've had. The lad must be twelve now but you must surely remember what to do.'

'I know,' Winifred panted as the spasm subsided.

Outside a horse and cart rattled on the cobbles.

'Milkman's late today.' Mrs Jagger shuffled over to the window and lifted one corner of the net curtain. 'Oh, no, it's the coalman, he's early and I haven't opened the grate. She squinted at Winifred. 'I won't be a tick. Stay there.'

Nauseous and desperate to move, Winifred waited until she heard the back door bang to before she eased herself to the edge of the bed and lowered her legs to the floor. The lino was already warm from the early-morning sun. Holding onto the black metal headboard she steadied herself before waddling to the window. The coalman was backing up to his cart to grasp the top of the first sack. His face and hands were already grimed in coal dust. Bowing his back he turned and spun around to pour the coal into the cellar under the pavement, while Mrs Jagger peered suspiciously at him, counting the bags.

The man's horse pawed at the road. Winifred heard the sharp clatter of his hooves as the cart shifted between the shafts, heard the man's impatient shout. 'Whoa!'

From the house opposite a woman appeared at the front door to scatter breadcrumbs. Sparrows, oblivious to her, fluttered down from the roof and darted about, pecking and squabbling. The woman wiped her hands on her apron, looked up and saw Winifred and waved.

She lifted her fingers in response, envying the freedom of Miss Cropper.

The next pain seemed to start in her thighs and rise up to ripple through her stomach. Winifred doubled over, holding the weight of it. She staggered back to the bed, all at once frightened of being on her own.

It felt a long time before she heard her neighbour slowly climbing the stairs.

Chapter 86

1924

The man that the undertaker employed had made a beautiful headstone. The black marble shone in the sunlight and the lettering was just right. Plain gold lettering spelled out her grandmother's name and inscription:

Florence Duffy
1839 – 1919
Always Loved.

Bill had been furious when the account from the undertaker had arrived and he'd discovered she'd spent twenty pounds on it. She'd stood up to him. After all, as she'd reminded him, if it wasn't partly for her granny they wouldn't have the house on Henshaw Street. She'd even dared to say it was her own money. Winifred smiled; it was ridiculous how satisfied she'd been standing up to Bill. And it was well worth the week of sulky silence from him.

'It's nice isn't it, Mam?' Tom jiggled baby Mary in his arms while Winifred placed the daffodils in the glass vase on the grave.

'It's lovely, Tom. Granny Florence would be pleased, I think.'

It had taken her six months before she was able to visit the grave to see the headstone. Bill always tried to make sure he knew where she was every minute of the day. But Winifred had overheard him talking to one of the neighbours who also worked at the mine and she knew that, after his shift, he was going to a union meeting. With a bit of luck they'd be home before he was.

Getting to her feet she stroked the top of the headstone. 'Sorry Gran. I don't know when I'll be able to come again. It's difficult.' She knew in her heart she wouldn't be back. 'Right, love.' She smiled at Tom. 'We'd better get a move on. I know you're tired and you've been such a good help to me today with the baby and everything.' It had been a long day and he'd been so patient. At thirteen he was taller than she was and a strong lad. She knew he felt protective of her. 'If we hurry we'll be able to get the tram into Morrisfield for the three o'clock train. We'll be home before Dad is, with a bit of luck. I should just have time to put his tea on. He need never know we've been out.'

She knew she shouldn't make Tom her accomplice in all the things she did without Bill knowing, but he was old beyond his years and she was aware he sensed the fear that sometimes quivered inside her. He didn't understand that there were days, weeks, when she was content; when Bill was relaxed, even kind; like the man she first knew. She was aware that Tom treated Bill with a silent disdain, but never spoke to her about it. It was in his eyes though, and she dreaded the day that her husband recognised the emotion that seeped from Tom when there were rows.

They hurried along Harrison Street, Winifred averting her eyes when they passed the shop.

At the tram stop she gave Mary to Tom and stretched out her arms. 'She's getting to be quite heavy.'

The shock rippled along her skin, her scalp. There was a loud humming in her ears. The man walking towards them was the image of Conal. An older Conal, there was some grey mingled in the thick blackness of his hair and he was sturdier than she remembered. But as he came closer she saw the same strong straight nose and determined chin.

'I knew I'd find ya one day.' There was elation in his dark eyes.

He reached out to touch her.

'No!' Even as she yearned to feel his fingers on hers the anger flared. She couldn't speak. She knew she was crying; she could feel the pain in her chest, the burning behind her eyes but she made no sound.

'Win?'

Ah, the sound of his voice, that endearing accent remembered from long ago. But the words hammered inside her head. 'Too

324

late. You're too late.' So many times over the years she had dreamt of this. The words were dragged up from her throat. 'You're too late.'

'Mam?' Tom had tucked Mary under his arm so he could catch hold of Winifred. 'Mam, what's the matter. Who's this man?'

Winifred wiped her face with the sleeve of her coat. 'Sorry, Tom.' She stepped away from Conal. 'This is… This is an old friend of mine,' she said, her tone dull with the despair that simmered under the words. 'I haven't seen him for a long time. It was a shock, that's all.' She took the baby from her son and held her close.

She watched Conal glance then stop to look again at Tom for the first time. He turned to Winifred. She saw the question.

'Yes,' she said, quietly.

Chapter 87

The tram trundled into view.

'And now I have to go.' The nausea rose up even as Winifred spoke. But she needed to be strong in front of the children. Every muscle in her body was clenched with determination. 'You shouldn't have come back.'

'Aw, no.' Conal stiffened, reached out to her. 'Ya can't be after leaving it like this.'

'I can, I have to. I can't…' Winifred threw the words at him, conscious of Tom's concern, of the baby crying.

'We need to talk.'

'No.' When the tram screeched to a halt at the kerb she ushered the children up the step.

'Win. Ya can't be—'

His last words were lost when the doors closed and the tram clanking on the overhead wires, set off.

Winifred collapsed into a seat by the window. Conal was

running alongside. Shouting. 'When can we talk?' he yelled. 'We need to talk.'

It was no use. The anguish in his eyes was too much. She knew she was asking for trouble but still she half-stood, both palms on the window. 'There's a park in Ashford. Skirm Park. By the lake. Monday morning,' she shouted, oblivious to the stares of the people around her, not caring. He was frowning; she was convinced he couldn't tell what she was saying. Oh, why had she said it was too late for them?

The tram gathered speed and soon Conal was left behind. The last Winifred saw of him he was standing staring after them, hands dropped by his side. She slumped onto the seat. The shock, draining from her, made her legs shake.

'Mam?' Tom gripped her hand.

Winifred forced a smile. 'What a surprise,' she said, brightly. 'An old friend from years ago.' It was the only thing she thought to say. 'But don't tell your dad about him, you know what he's like. I'll explain one day, Tom. I'll tell you who that man was. Is. One day.'

Chapter 88

It had taken a lot of coaxing and two bottles of stout to get Mrs Jagger to take Mary for the morning.

Winifred didn't know what to expect from Conal; she had been alternately sick with excitement and anticipation and frightened that Bill might discover what she was about to do. Unable to eat or sleep she'd passed the weekend in a daze of hope and despair.

Having left the baby with her neighbour she hurried to Skirm Park.

He was there already, standing by the edge of the lake watching the ducks, hands casually pushed into his trouser pockets, whistling. Winifred was glad she'd worn her best hat and gloves;

he looked so handsome and smart. When he saw her he walked to meet her and greeted her with a kiss on the cheek.

'No,' she peered around. 'People might see.'

'Aw, who cares?' he whispered. His breath on her skin made her heart leap.

She gave him a tremulous smile. 'Let's sit down over there.'

She perched on the edge of the bench looking towards the lake. The park was almost deserted, but not taking any chances that they might be seen, she sat as far away from Conal as she could and took out a piece of stale bread from a paper bag, breaking it up. The ducks scrambled up the banking and waddled towards her.

After a few moments she said, 'Tell me what happened. That day of the protest. Where did you go?' She spoke under her breath, conscious of a couple walking along the path nearby. 'Don't,' she warned when he shuffled along the seat towards her. She couldn't stand it if he came closer. 'You just disappeared.'

'Before we left I wrote a note. I said I would be back when I could.'

'I received no note.'

'And I wrote to the house on Gilpin Street for months. Honest to God, I was after thinking some of the lads there would get the letters to ya.'

'They'd gone when I went looking for you.' Winifred shook her head. 'Some horrible people were living there.' She flung a look towards him. 'I got nothing from you.'

'When I didn't hear anything from ya. I believed ya didn't want me.'

And didn't come to look for me. 'I didn't get your note,' she repeated. 'Nor any letters.'

He lifted his shoulders. 'Honest to God, I wrote.'

There was nothing she could say to that. 'So, tell me what happened.'

'I searched for ya when the police left that day. But then I found Honora. She was in a cruel way; she'd been beaten. I couldn't leave her. Sure, the only thing I could think to do was to take her home to Ireland. I was told the police were looking for both of us.' Conal rubbed the heels of his hands over his eyes.

And you didn't think to let me know? Winifred didn't voice her recriminations but they were there, unwanted. Insistent.

As though reading her mind Conal said, 'Some friends got us to Liverpool and we were smuggled onto a ferry. It took a mighty time to get to our village. In the end she still died. But I think she was at peace knowing she was back home.'

It seemed impossible that Honora, lovely, high-spirited Honora was dead. A deep sadness engulfed Winifred.

'After Honora died and I lost ya—'

'You hadn't,' Winifred interrupted.

He reached out and gave her hand a squeeze and her skin tingled with his touch. 'To be sure, *cailín*, I thought I had. I was wrecked for months. But then I thought if I'm going to be doing something with my life I should finish my training. And now I'm a doctor in Dublin.' He hesitated. 'I would have come looking for ya then but I got involved in the fight and I thought it wasn't fair…'

'The fight?' Winifred stared at him. 'You mean…?'

He nodded. 'After the Easter Uprising in sixteen. Oh, I wasn't part of that but I knew lads who were. And then all the executions. It was wrong. Wicked.'

She struggled to comprehend that all the years she'd hungered for him she'd been completely out of his mind. *I could have been with him. Tom and I could have been with him.*

'The British Government brought men over from the mainland to retaliate; ex-soldiers, criminals, so they were. The Black and Tans.' Anger tightened his mouth. 'Vicious thugs. Murderous bastards.'

'I read about some men being employed by the Government to quell some riots—' Winifred jumped when he cut in.

'Not riots.' He let go of her hand. 'Our fight for freedom; for ownership of Ireland. For Home Rule.'

He'd changed. She no longer knew him. Perhaps she never had. Perhaps the fight for the vote for women, his involvement with the Suffragettes was just a cause he joined in on because he disliked authority. No, she chided herself, it was more than that, it was because he believed in freedom for all; the right for everyone to live life as they were entitled to do. She couldn't think any less of him. She wouldn't.

'I'm trying to understand, Conal. I've tried to understand why you've been away for so long.' She frowned in a concentrated effort to grasp what had been more important than the love he'd promised her.

Conal leaned forward, clasping his hands between his knees. 'I'll tell ya something. Ya'll be after understanding then.' He breathed in, a great intake of air before he started. 'One time, round about June in nineteen-twenty, I was with a group of men. We were on our way to a *teach sábháilte*. A safe house, ya know? Where some of us met? Ya understand?'

'I think so.'

'I'd been told a couple of comrades were injured. Because I'm a doctor they'd sent for me, ya see?' She nodded. 'We were ambushed by the Black and Tans. They beat one comrade to an inch of his life. He was only eighteen.' His eyes were bleak as he glanced at her. 'All because he wouldn't say his name. His brother went after the one who was using his rifle butt and they shot him. By the time they were finished there was only me, one other and the boy alive. Why they let us live God only knows. They just walked away laughing.' He rubbed his hand over his face. Winifred waited. The horror of what he was saying made her scalp crawl. It was too terrible to even envisage. 'We took the boy to a nearby cottage. It wasn't a safe house, just an old couple that live there. They cleaned him up and I did what I could for him. He died anyway. Two days later I went back to the cottage with food. As a thanks, ya know?'

329

'Yes.'

'The cottage was razed to the ground. The old couple were cowering in a shed in the back garden. The Black and Tans had heard they'd helped us and went back to burn the place down. They'd even killed their dog.'

'Oh!' Winifred gripped her hands so tightly that her nails dug into her palms. She wanted him to stop, it was all so horrible. But his next words shocked her.

'The English are hated in Ireland.'

The balance between them shifted. For the first time in three days, Winifred recognized that she had misread Conal; that, perhaps, after all, he hadn't returned to claim her.

'So what about me, Conal?' The pain stunned her so much she choked the words out. 'I'm English.'

When he looked towards her his face was inscrutable. 'It's different, so it is,' was all he said.

'Why?'

'You're different.'

'I am. At least from those monsters, I am. But I'm still English. How could we ever be together?'

The silence between them was unbearable. Unable to sit still any longer she threw the last of the bread onto the grass. When the ducks scattered she stood and walked towards the lake. The water was still, pale in its reflection of the light grey sky. Weeds floated under the surface. She folded her arms, hugged herself, thinking the vagueness of them was the same with Conal; there was something just out of her sight under his words.

Turning quickly Winifred said, 'Was it a coincidence? Our meeting. You being in Lydcroft on Friday?'

'To be sure, partly it was,' he admitted, a glimmer of a smile crossed his face. 'I was looking for ya. I thought I'd start there. But ya weren't at the shop.'

'We sold it.' But I lived there for years after you'd gone; I would have been easy to find then. But why had he come now?

'Then I remembered ya once said where your grandmother lived and I went there.'

'Granny died.' She didn't bother to explain that her grandmother had moved in with her. Why was she feeling apprehensive all at once?

'Aw, I'm sorry, Win.'

It was the first time he'd said her name since they'd met earlier. Bill's name for her. The thought intruded, unwelcome, even through the guilt. Despite her husband's moods she knew he loved her. And she loved him. He didn't deserve what she'd been thinking; what she'd been willing to give up for this man.

Conal was still talking. 'But then I saw a family loading up a horse and cart so I asked them on the off chance.' He laughed. 'Lucky eh? The old woman said she was a friend of your gran's. Bertha Corbett?'

'Yes.'

'She gave me the address of where ya lived.'

Winifred persisted, even as she dreaded the answers he might give. 'So, why now, Conal?'

'Shall we walk?' He crooked his arm. 'Ya'll understand when I explain.'

She didn't want to slip her hand through it but found herself unable to resist even while the distrust lay heavy in her stomach. They strolled along the path away from the lake towards the far side of the park which was deserted.

'Last month, in Dublin, I met a friend, from the old days in Lydcroft. Denny Logan. Ya once gave him a message for me?' Conal squeezed her arm to him and smiled at her. 'He told me about Tom. My son.'

Up to that minute Winifred had forgotten the chance meeting with the man. 'I remember him; Sophie's boyfriend.'

'That's right. Poor Sophie.'

'When I was looking for you,' Winifred said. 'I told him.' The old panic returned so easily thinking of those early days when she

331

found out she was pregnant. 'I wanted you to know. To come back for me.'

'He'd only just returned to Ireland, so he had. He was arrested in London for robbing a bank in nineteen twelve. He'd been in prison for twelve years.'

'So you never knew about Tom.'

'I never knew. Tis why I'm here now. I'll... we'll make things right, *cailín*.'

Chapter 89

Bill knew there was something wrong. There'd been a different feel to the house over the last few days. When he'd got home from work on Friday morning Winifred was singing as he crossed the yard. It wasn't that he didn't like her being happy, in fact it made him feel bloody good, much like he used to when they were first courting. When he'd opened the back door she'd looked surprised even though it was his usual time home from night shift.

He'd hoped her happiness was because they seemed to be getting on better lately. He'd managed to keep his temper in check for months before that business with her gran's headstone. It was a soddin' lot of money but, as she pointed out, they wouldn't be at Henshaw Street if it wasn't for the old woman leaving Winifred the money. And he'd quite liked the way she stood up to him that day; bit like getting back the spirited woman he married.

He'd grinned at her when he closed the door and held out his arms. 'Are you all right, love?'

'I'm fine, husband dear,' she'd said. But she'd skipped out of his way when he'd suggested a kiss and a cuddle.

'What? The state you're in.' Winifred kissed him on the cheek. 'We'd both need to get in that if I let you come near me.' She pointed to the steaming bath on the linoleum.

'And that's such a bad idea?' Bill made another grab for her.

She avoided him again. 'I can hear Mary; she's awake. How about you have a wash-up and I'll get her down for breakfast.'

Bill was thoughtful as he soaped the rough towelling cloth and rubbed it over his arms and legs. 'Things are on the up,' he said to himself.

Even having to share her with Tom was really okay. He used to try to have a bit of a rough and tumble with the lad when he and Winifred were first married but it hadn't gone down well and it had caused rows. So Bill had stopped trying to toughen him up. But they still sometimes sat at the kitchen table with the stamp collection, or when Tom read one of his books to him. He just didn't seem to get the same admiration from the kid that he used to.

And he certainly didn't like that fact that Tom was now taller than him. But, to be fair, that wasn't the lad's fault

It would all work out, especially as the lad was getting older.

There had been that quarrel when Bill thought Tom should go part-time down the mine but Winifred had been adamant.

'He's going down no mine, Bill, and that's that,' she'd said, when Tom had turned thirteen. 'He's stopping on at school until he's fourteen.'

Ridiculous! Fourteen years old and still going to school in short pants. No point in arguing about it though; there were some things she wouldn't shift on, and her son's education was one of them. 'I want him to get a job in an office,' she said, over and over again. Well, if it brought money in eventually who was he to argue; it might mean Tom could help him with the all the Union and Labour party stuff more, instead of just reading it to him.

But still the worry wouldn't go away; there was definitely something going on. Sitting over his pint in The Crown on Saturday dinnertime he mulled over what it could be. It wasn't the same as when she hadn't been straight with him about the shop. Or when that business with the stupid brooch came out.

Supping his ale he cringed, remembering that time he'd hit her. When he was young and saw his father knocking seven bells out of his mother he swore he would never do the same. Yet what had he done the first time she'd crossed him?

Even after that she'd been the one comfort when he had one of his nightmares. She understood, she held him until the fear and horror went away. And he was grateful. He loved her. And yet still he couldn't control his temper. He should just walk out of the house; stay out until he calmed down. Why didn't he do that?

Why did she put up with it?

Bill placed his pint pot carefully down on the small round pub table. Perhaps that was what was wrong. Perhaps she wasn't going to. It was like she'd made some sort of decision to be happy in some way. What if she was going to leave him?

Chapter 90

'It's wrong. I'm married. I can't go to Ireland.' The thought of being a stranger in a strange land frightened her. Let alone taking the children as well.

He turned his head away from her. What was wrong with him? 'Conal?' Winifred pulled her hand from his arm and stood still in the middle of the path.

He carried on walking so she had to strain to hear him. 'I should have told ya right at the first.' He spun around. 'I'm married.'

'I don't believe you.' The denial opened up a chasm inside her; a deep, mournful sorrow that had lain dormant for many recent years. 'Then why are you here?'

She might as well not have spoken.

'We… My wife can't have children. We tried for years. Two years ago we were told we could never have children.'

She tensed. Was she supposed to feel sorry for him?

'It broke Branna's heart, ya know?' Winifred listened in silence, conscious of the sway of the grass on either side of the path, the fluttering of birds above in the budded trees, the odd rumble and whine of trams on Huddersfield Road.

'So, why are you here, Conal?' she said again. 'What is it you want?' What a fool she'd been; all that time grieving, wondering what had happened to him. Hoping he would come back for her.

Well he'd come back. But not for her. The slow throb of resentment and distrust turned into a wrenching anger and then to a sudden realization. 'You want Tom.' She wanted to hit him, to scream and shout and hit him. She was surprised to hear how calm her voice was. 'You've come to take him from me after all these years.'

'Branna and me, we've talked about it. She's willing to take him on.'

'Oh, is she?'

Her sarcasm was lost on him. 'He's my boy, my son.'

'He's mine. Only mine.'

'I've seen how ya live. The house—'

'What? You've spied on me?' And as though for the first time she saw him, his clothes well-tailored, good shoes. Obviously he had money. 'I don't live up to your so-called standards? You've done better? As a doctor then?'

'I have,' he said eagerly. 'I could give my – our – son a good life.'

Was it wrong not to give Tom a chance of a better life? It was then she thought back to what he'd said earlier. 'You've told me that the British… English people are hated. How could I let you take my son to a place where he would be hated?'

'He'd be seen as mine. No-one would know about…'

'About me.' The rage was instant. 'The English mother. You've thought of everything, haven't you?' And to think she'd been willing to give up her life here for this man. Suddenly she was frightened that she might have already lost her life, her marriage

335

anyway. Bill might have somehow found out what she was doing. She needed to be at home. 'I'm going now.'

'No.' He stood in front of her, preventing her from leaving. 'Please. Think about it, Win.'

She gave Conal's chest a small shove. 'I have.' All those years believing in something that had always been a falsehood. He didn't love her. 'The answer's no. How dare you even think you have the right?' She shrugged him off, stumbled along the path. She'd didn't look back.

Chapter 91

The trees, streets, houses, passed in a blur of tears. If anyone saw her, running with her skirts raised above her ankles, Winifred didn't see them. Holding her side, trying to catch her breath she slipped and staggered over the cobbles of the alleyway at the back of the terraced houses.

It was as if she was coming out of the shadows of the past into an unknown darker future.

Bill had been quiet all weekend, as though he was waiting for something to happen. When he did speak it was in an odd hesitant way. What if he's guessed what she'd done? What if he hadn't gone to work, if instead, he'd followed her to the park, seen her with…? She couldn't bring herself to say his name.

What if he'd packed her bags; was waiting to throw her out? Her and Tom. Somehow she knew he'd keep Mary with him. Oh God; she repeated the words over and over. Oh God. Please. Please.

She halted, her hands on her knees, pulling air into her lungs, forcing her heart to slow. Listening to the blood whooshing and pulsing behind her ears made her nauseous. This terror was nothing like anything she'd ever felt before.

And then she heard laughter. Dragging herself upright she

walked slowly forward. When she neared number twenty-seven she heard it again.

Pressing the latch down without a sound she pushed open the gate, peeping through the narrow gap into the yard.

Bill was there. He was tossing Mary into the air. The baby was shrieking with laughter. Tom was sitting on the stone windowsill of the kitchen, squinting into the sun as he watched. He was laughing as well.

They hadn't noticed her. She studied her son; he had a look of her father in him when he was happy. She remembered one of her dad's many mottos: "One chance you get at this life. Make sure you do what's best for you."

Had she taken Tom's chance away from him; giving him no choice? Whether she'd made the right decision or not it was one she would have to live with. Right or wrong he didn't ever need to know who his real father was. Conal was a stranger living in an unfamiliar land. She knew her son; he'd be more scared of the unknown than he'd ever be of Bill.

They noticed her at the same time. The only two men in her life.

'Mam.' Tom jumped down and came to hug her as she closed the gate.

'Winifred.' Bill caught Mary one last time and, cuddling her, grinned at his wife. Was there a note of relief in his voice? 'You're home, lass.'

'What? Did you think I'd run off with the tally man?' she said, smiling.

They all laughed.

She walked towards Bill. As she passed him to go into the house she touched his hand. 'I'm home.'

ABOUT HONNO

Honno Welsh Women's Press was set up in 1986 by a group of women who felt strongly that women in Wales needed wider opportunities to see their writing in print and to become involved in the publishing process. Our aim is to develop the writing talents of women in Wales, give them new and exciting opportunities to see their work published and often to give them their first 'break' as a writer. Honno is registered as a community co-operative. Any profit that Honno makes is invested in the publishing programme. Women from Wales and around the world have expressed their support for Honno. Each supporter has a vote at the Annual General Meeting. For more information and to buy our publications, please write to Honno at the address below, or visit our website: www.honno.co.uk

Honno, 14 Creative Units, Aberystwyth Arts Centre
Aberystwyth, Ceredigion SY23 3GL

Honno Friends

We are very grateful for the support of the Honno Friends: Jane Aaron, Annette Ecuyere, Audrey Jones, Gwyneth Tyson Roberts, Beryl Roberts, Jenny Sabine.

For more information on how you can become a Honno Friend, see: http://www.honno.co.uk/friends.php